PATRICIA –
Great Meeting
you!

THE CROWN LORD

I HOPE you enjoy the book!

:)

PATRICIA –

Great Meeting
You!

I HOPE You Like Book!
G.G.

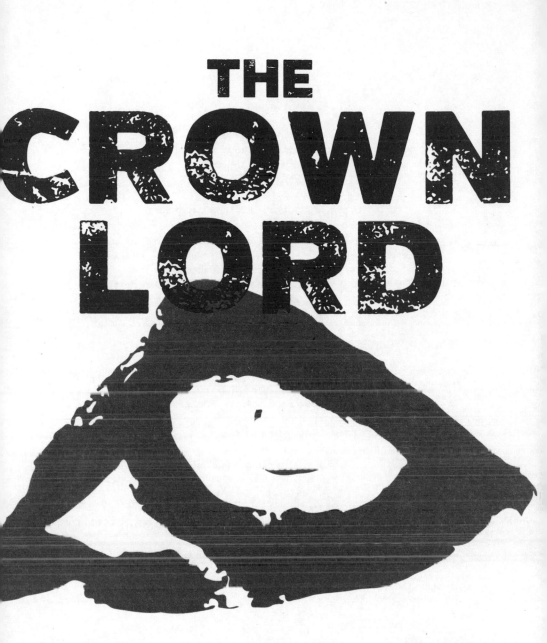

THE CROWN LORD

WILLIAM SIRLS

THIS IS A GENUINE VIREO BOOK

Vireo | Rare Bird
453 South Spring Street, Suite 302
Los Angeles, CA 90013
rarebirdbooks.com

Set in Dante
Printed in the United States

HARDCOVER ISBN: 9781947856462
PAPERBACK ISBN: 9781947856783

10 9 8 7 6 5 4 3 2 1

Publisher's Cataloging-in-Publication data
Names: Sirls, William, 1964–, author.
Title: The Crown Lord / William Sirls.
Description: A Genuine Vireo Book | New York, NY; Los Angeles, CA:
Rare Bird Books, 2018.
Identifiers: ISBN 9781947856462
Subjects: LCSH Race relations—Fiction. | Drug addiction—Fiction. | African
Americans—Fiction. | Family—Fiction. | Alternative histories (Fiction) |
Bildungsromans. | BISAC FICTION / General
Classification: LCC PS3619.I753 C76 2018 | DDC 813.6—dc23

For Eric

Prologue

Georgie Winthrop followed his five-year-old sister along the shoreline and pretended to be watching after her. Father always said to walk right behind her, that way she wouldn't wander off into the waves and disappear, leaving Georgie an only child at the age of fourteen.

Georgie didn't like being referred to as a child but longed for the days when he was the only one because Emily was truly a problem—an unplanned wedge between Georgie and the occasional affection of his father. But it wouldn't be much longer.

> *Emily falling out of her bedroom window.*
> *Emily happening upon Father's loaded pistol.*
> *Emily unexplainably dying in her sleep.*

Though there were endless possibilities, Emily wouldn't be wandering off into the waves anytime soon. Big Jonah would never allow anything to happen to her. He was six and a half feet tall and whenever they left the house, he was never more than a few steps away, keeping a careful eye not just on Emily but on both of his master's children.

There was a slight breeze and the dying waves covered Georgie's feet with cool salt water as he and his sister walked across the wet sand. They were there to gather the tiniest of seashells for the necklaces Mother liked to make—the ones she would give to the townsfolk that couldn't afford any of what Father called "real" jewelry. Father was convinced the craft was the only thing that kept Mother busy, and he frequently reminded her that she led a life void of responsibility.

Though it was Mother that inherited the plantation, she never dared talk back to Father, even when he threatened to sell off all the house slaves, Big Jonah included, and render her completely helpless.

The whole town knew they had more slaves than anyone in the county. They also knew the ones that worked indoors were there specifically to serve Father. In fact, Georgie once overheard Mr. Bellamy say, *"George Winthrop has so many negroes in that house, two bits says he keeps one handy just to help him change his mind."*

Mr. Bellamy had tears in his eyes and begged Georgie to never repeat what he had overheard. It was pathetic to see a grown man cry, and Georgie could only imagine what the man did when he closed the doors to his small haberdashery, less than two months after Father decided to start his own—right across the street from Mr. Bellamy's.

Georgie shook the burlap satchel he carried. It would normally be full of shells by now, but the three of them had spent the better part of the last hour watching the ships. There were more than twenty of them spread out down the coastline, all grayish in color, and huge. Huge enough that Georgie guessed the one closest to him had to be easily three times the size of those he had seen earlier that summer when he and his fellow cadets from Elm Hill Academy visited the Portsmouth Naval Shipyard up in Maine.

"Look how sparkly it is," Emily said, the breeze tossing her blonde curls back and forth across her small shoulders.

She was talking about the sun and how it glistened off the silver cannons that stuck out from one of the ships' sides. There were so many of them, one about every forty or fifty feet for the entire length of the ship. At least Georgie thought they were cannons. If they were, he'd never seen them that color, nor that long, and he couldn't fathom them all firing at once and the destruction they would certainly bring.

"Georgie," Emily yelled through the wind. "Look!"

He ignored her because he'd noticed something else about the Navy's newest ships. Though they were clearly more advanced, they were missing something, something very important, and he was baffled that he hadn't caught it earlier.

"They don't have masts," Georgie said, not sure who he was talking to. "I don't get it."

"Georgie!" Emily shouted again.

He glanced over at her and then looked where she was pointing.

Men were heading toward them.

They were about a hundred paces away and coming from the edge of the forest where the shoreline bent back into Carlson Cove. Behind them, Georgie could see the top of one of the ships sticking up well above the tree line.

He counted thirty-two men in two perfectly straight lines of sixteen. Though Georgie excelled in War Theory at Elm Hill, anyone could tell they were military. All looked to be carrying rifles and moving in formation, yet Georgie didn't recognize them as Navy.

Big Jonah stepped out in front of Emily and held his hand up behind him, signifying Georgie and Emily to be still. Georgie studied the size of that enormous hand and could only imagine Big Jonah's productivity in the tobacco fields, doing what he was meant to do, instead of babysitting. What a waste of a truly valuable asset.

As the men came closer, Georgie noticed that their rifles were each equipped with bayonets and that the men all wore matching black coats, pants, shoes, hats—

And faces.

The men were all black as well.

But something was different about them.

They didn't move like normal slaves did. They didn't seem sad and defeated.

All had their chins up and were looking straight forward as they held their weapons out in front of their chests. Their left feet all hit the sand at the same time and then their right feet followed, reminding Georgie of a big machine with identical parts, moving with an unstoppable confidence and sense of purpose he'd never seen in people before—not even white people.

Big Jonah craned his neck forward and shook his head, as if he couldn't believe what he was seeing. The men were coming faster and fanned out into four lines of eight and then eight lines of four.

"Nwọn ti wá," Big Jonah said.

Georgie was shocked. Big Jonah would be the last of their two hundred slaves that would even dare to break one of Father's biggest rules, which was to speak in English only.

"Who are those people?" Emily asked.

"I don't know," Georgie said.

Whoever they were, they were now running. And though it scared Georgie, it also made him thankful that Big Jonah had never touched a single leaf of tobacco.

"Maybe they want some shells," Emily said.

Left, right, left, right. They kept coming until they were no more than twenty feet away.

One of the men shouted something, and they all stopped at once. Big Jonah began walking toward them. Three men fell out of formation and surrounded him, one in front of him and one on each of his sides, not as if they intended to harm him, but to protect him.

"*Nwọn ti wá!*" Big Jonah shouted, his back to Georgie. His fists were raised over his head, and he was jumping up and down as if a prayer had been answered. He finally dropped to his knees and cradled his face in his hands.

Georgie knew what would happen if Father heard Big Jonah speak another language just once, let alone twice. Georgie glanced up the hill and wondered how much longer Father would be in meetings. Though it was well over a quarter mile away, Georgie could still see the entire east end of their plantation. The rear of the mansion was darkened by a shadow cast from one of three pearl-white clouds that hovered over the grounds. To the left of the mansion was the guesthouse and to the far right a dozen of Father's prize horses pranced around the stables. Father was hosting the governor along with a dozen statesmen, and the second they were through, Georgie would certainly inform him of Big Jonah's transgressions.

Big Jonah raised his head and looked back over his shoulder at Georgie and Emily, tears streaming down his shiny black cheeks before he wiped them away with the back of his hand.

"Don't cry, Big Jonah," Emily said, standing in the waves, which now covered her small calves. She dropped her shell satchel in the water and ran to comfort him. Before she reached him, another soldier left formation and positioned himself between Emily and Big Jonah, bringing Emily to a quick halt.

"I just want to give him a hug," Emily said. "Can I do that?"

The soldier said nothing. He was a large man, close to Big Jonah's size with broad shoulders and muscular arms. Thick veins stuck out on both sides of his neck as he looked down at Emily.

Big Jonah stood and walked out in front of the soldier. He leaned over and picked up Emily, who wrapped her arms around his head and hugged him tightly.

Big Jonah closed his eyes and smiled. When he opened them back up, he was staring right at Georgie.

"*Nwọn ti wá,*" he said yet again.

"I'm telling Father," Georgie said. "And I look forward to you getting the lash."

Big Jonah only nodded, then put Emily down. And then he took his shirt off and turned in a complete circle, making sure everyone could see the crisscrossed scars that covered his back.

"Young Georgie," Big Jonah said, pointing up toward the plantation. "Your father is finished."

Georgie laughed and looked up the hill.

At least fifty soldiers, all dressed in black, were now spread out around the mansion, guesthouse, and stables. Another hundred were marching up the hill.

"You will all pay!" Georgie screamed. "My father is George Winthrop!"

The soldier that had stepped in front of Emily had been staring at Big Jonah's back. He whispered something to Big Jonah, who then nodded.

"Your father is finished," Big Jonah repeated. "And so are you."

The soldier walked quickly and Georgie cocked back his fist, instinctively assuming the fighting stance he had learned at the academy.

He was ready.

The soldier clenched his teeth and those veins that bulged from the sides of his dark black neck began to pulse as he pulled something out from behind his back and then over his shoulder.

It was a sword.

"Help me, Big Jonah!" Georgie cried as the man raised the sword and gripped it with both hands.

"Nwọn ti wá!" Big Jonah shouted.

"Why do you keep saying that?" Georgie yelled, his heart pounding like an icy mallet at the insides of his chest. "What does that mean?"

Georgie knew Big Jonah's translation would be the last three words he would ever hear.

"They have come."

WILLIE

Up North. The Crown.

The Unwinnable Case.

Modern Day

It was a week after Willie's seventeenth birthday when the whole thing started.

His father had finally caved and given him what he wanted. The new car was a great gift and all, but for Dad to fly him up to Detroit to see the outside of the courthouse was beyond anything he'd ever expected.

They were in a white stretch limo and the driver was an older black man who reminded Willie of his grandfather, the one on his mother's side. He had to be in his late sixties and hadn't said a single word the entire time they were in the car. A real pro.

"Keep all the windows rolled up and locked," Dad said, leaning toward the driver. "I don't want them seeing Willie."

The driver nodded, and Willie laughed.

"What are they going to do to me?" Willie said.

The driver shook his head and then looked in the mirror. Willie knew the guy was hoping he hadn't gotten busted making a "this kid has no idea what he is talking about" face. Willie quickly locked eyes with him, making his own face that hopefully reminded the driver which one of them had a father who was the richest lawyer in the country and which one of them drove around all day kissing ass while wearing a stupid little hat.

The driver looked away and then slowly turned on to Commerce Boulevard, revealing skyscrapers to the left and hollow clouds of sewer steam that hung over the limo from both sides of the street. A light drizzle slowed traffic and made the tinted windows even harder to see through.

"What's that noise?" Willie asked.

"It's them," Dad said.

"Really?" A tiny shiver danced off the side of Willie's neck, and he sat up straight in anticipation of seeing *them*—members of the black supremacist group known as The Crown.

Willie leaned forward and looked between the intermittent sweeps of the windshield wipers. Past the older buildings and to the right, he caught the very tops of the enormous pillars down near the end of the street. He could already see the rest of it in his mind, as he had on the internet and television hundreds of times over the previous five months. He imagined the beautiful steps that led up to those pillars and the words that were carved so neatly near the top of the limestone building.

Court House and Custom House.

"Not sure why I waited so long to get you up here," Dad said, patting Willie's leg.

"Me either. I've only been asking you for three months to bring me."

Dad put his hand back on Willie's leg and gave it a little squeeze. Willie studied the *TDG* on his father's custom, gold cuff links and wondered why Dad hadn't come up with something a little more original than just his initials.

"I figured we were long overdue for you to learn just how fortunate you are to be black and to be a Southerner," Dad said.

"Give me a break."

Give you a break?

"Yeah," Willie said. "I know I'm fortunate to be black, but slavery ended like fifty years ago. Whites need to get over the whole thing and get their shit together."

"What am I going to have to do to get you to quit cursing?" Dad said, jotting a couple quick notes onto a legal pad before stuffing it into a briefcase that was so packed it could barely close. "But before you answer that question, I want you to tell me what *you* think whites should do to improve their circumstances."

"You mean get their shit together?"

"Should we turn around and take you straight back to the airport?"

"There's a lot they could do to improve their situation," Willie said.

"A lot?" Dad said. "That means you know several things they can do. Why don't you share one idea with me then—*just one*—so I can pass it on to them while we are up here."

"Okay," Willie said. "Tell them to all get on a bus and head south where things are different. Where whites at least have a chance."

"Easier said than done," Dad replied. "But I want you to explain what you mean by *different*."

"You know what I mean. It's like slavery never ended up here."

Dad nodded as if he agreed. But he should because he was the black lawyer that was defending a white man by the name of Donald Bondy that murdered—hang on, stop the press before Dad has a stroke—*allegedly* murdered a black man in a trial with a black judge and an all-black jury. The whole world knew there wasn't another lawyer in the country who would take the case due to the risks of it being *different* up in Detroit. Sure, defending the pinkie back home would have been one thing (as in, a hell of a lot less risky), but the farther north you went, it really did seem like slavery never ended and Michigan is seven hundred long miles north of Georgia.

They were less than a block from the courthouse. Beyond the roped-off sidewalks on both sides of the street, dozens of news crews from all over the country were waiting for things to heat up on the day when closing arguments would be made. Even with the window up, Willie could still hear The Crown from the courthouse, shouting the same word in consecutive shots of three that seemed to shake the entire block.

Ju-stice! Ju-stice! Ju-stice!

"Pull the car over," Dad said. "I'll let myself out and walk from here."

"How long do you want me to park in front of the courthouse?" the driver asked.

"Just long enough for Willie to watch me walk right through them," Dad answered.

"Just yell *boo* and I'll bet those hooded farmers scatter like scared rats," Willie said.

Dad patted Willie on the cheek and then looked back at the driver. He held his thumb and index finger about five inches apart. "When you reach the courthouse, go ahead and crack the window about this much so Willie can get a better look."

"Yes sir," the driver said.

"The Crown is early today," Dad said. He opened his door and the noise rushed in and passed through Willie like a gust of cold breeze.

Dad stepped out, flipped up the collar on his overcoat, and blew a puff of warm air into his dry black hands. Despite being early summer, it was cool and the rain made it feel colder.

"Can you hear them, Willie?" Dad shouted.

"I'm not deaf!" Willie yelled, knowing there was more to Dad's question than appeared.

"When you see them," Dad said, glancing down the street, "I want you to remember something."

"What's that?"

Dad leaned back into the car. "It's darker than you. But there is a light inside of you. A light that only you can find. If you find it, turn it on and you will lead others out of the darkness without even trying."

"What's darker than me?"

His father just winked at him and then stepped back and slammed the door. The car was still a block or so from the courthouse and Dad hadn't made it twenty feet before he was surrounded by cameras and microphones that followed him down the sidewalk.

The driver glanced back at Willie and then slowly drove forward. They passed Dad, who kept walking, and Willie edged closer to the window, finding it hard to swallow as the courthouse finally came into sight. As instructed, the driver lowered the tinted window about five or six inches, giving Willie a better view.

Gooseflesh tapped at the side of Willie's face and then another wave of it seemed to grab his neck.

"This isn't like back home," he told the driver as his throat went dry.

The driver didn't hear Willie. Willie wasn't even sure if he heard himself.

He struggled to catch his breath. The Crown was the real reason he begged Dad to bring him up here, but he had no idea what he was asking for. Seeing them in person was unlike any other time he had seen them before.

Not on the internet.

Not in any newspaper.

Not anywhere.

Media coverage of other cases involving a black victim and a soon-to-be-found guilty white defendant always included a quick clip of the courthouse exterior and a few brave pinkies squaring off against twice as many Crown.

But not in Detroit.

The Crown was organized. And there were so many of them. Both sides of the courthouse steps, and the steps themselves, were filled with hundreds—maybe a thousand—of them, all decked out in their shiny purple robes and pointed hoods, pumping their black fists in unison and calling for the accused's head. And there wasn't a white person in sight. Come to think of it, Willie hadn't seen a single pinkie on the way there, either. Not even the token white hooker or homeless person. Willie had no doubt, regardless of the verdict in the trial, Donald Bondy was a dead man.

The Crown's cry for justice had become a pulse, almost deafening, and Dad was walking right toward it, less than sixty feet from the first step that led up to the courthouse.

"How is my dad going to get past them?" Willie said, suddenly afraid for his father.

The driver didn't have a chance to answer before someone shouted, "Hear! Hear!" through a megaphone, and it was like someone hit the mute button on the world's sound system. Everything and everyone became quiet, as if they knew that making any sound whatsoever would be dealt with immediately.

The cameras and reporters quit following Dad, and as he approached the steps, every member of The Crown that was there, *all of them*, turned to face him.

Willie's jaw hung for a second when he realized the only noise he could hear were Dad's shoes hitting the concrete.

And then it was like the parting of a purple sea as they made way for him, creating a lane in the middle of them that went all the way up the hundred or so steps, right to the front door of the courthouse.

"You go, Dad," Willie whispered.

Dad was all by himself and it seemed like the only other movement within a mile were the heads of every Crown member, only a few feet from him on both sides, following Dad like smart security cameras as he went up each step.

When Dad made it to the top, Willie looked at the upper facing of the courthouse and all the old, Greek architecture that dominated public design back when pinkies ran the country. At the very top were gold-painted floral leaf moldings that surrounded little statues of fluttering and naked angels. He knew they were looking down over his father and were also offering comfort to those in need of something. He could see that one word, the same word, centered, almost balancing itself above a pair of columns that seemed to hold the whole building up. He had heard The Crown chant it hundreds of times in the last few minutes as he and his father drove up the street. But Dad had quieted them, and seeing the word etched into the building made Willie's heart skip a beat.

Justice.

A pair of armed guards opened the doors for Dad and then shut them in the faces of The Crown and the rest of the world.

The door hadn't been closed for more than five seconds when Willie noticed that not a single member of The Crown was moving. They were all perfectly still, seemingly frozen as they faced that door.

All except for one. A fat one.

He was halfway up the steps on the left side, right in the middle of the mob. He held his fist straight up in the air, and as the rest of them stayed fixed on the door, he turned and aimed that fist toward the street.

And then a short index finger sprung out from that fist and slowly waggled back and forth as if saying *naughty naughty.*

Willie slid back on the seat and clenched at his pant legs, never so sure of anything in his life.

He is looking at me.

And then he thought about how Dad had walked right through them. And how the window being rolled down only five inches was perfect.

Willie moved back over to the window and then stuck his arm out of the gap as far as he could. He thought for a second about waggling his own index finger back at the fat one, but he had a better idea.

He let a finger spring from his own fist.

He laughed and then waggled the finger, waving it slowly back and forth.

It was his middle one.

◆◆◆

THEY WERE EARLY FOR their flight back to Atlanta.

Willie and his father sat at Green's Diner, inside the Detroit airport. Neither of them had touched their food—Willie because the number of pills he had taken that morning wasn't nearly enough—and Dad because his wheels were still turning over his previous day in court.

"How long do you think it will take the jury to decide?" Willie asked, glancing over at one of the security checkpoints. Droves of black businessmen, most of them wearing pricey dark suits, rushed past the guards and headed to their gates. It made him regret not bringing more painkillers with him. The guards weren't checking anyone.

Dad finally tapped some pepper on his eggs and picked up the saltshaker. He paused and stared at it for a second, like the two shouldn't go together, before sprinkling a little on the eggs as well.

"The longer it takes them, the better," Dad answered. "And when they do, it'll be the last time I come up here for a while. Maybe forever. Still feeling safe at the house without me?"

"I was going to ask whether *you* felt safe."

"Don't worry about me, Willie." Dad straightened his neck as if he was surprised Willie cared about his well-being.

Dad was born in Michigan and had ties to just about every black leader here, which made his taking this case even more mind-boggling. Just a few days earlier,

Willie had watched a hot little ebony-skinned reporter on the news call Dad's defense of Donald Bondy "the most blatant demonstration of career and political suicide" she'd ever witnessed.

"Even after being here, I still don't get it," Willie said. "Why'd you take the case, let alone do it for free? I've thought about it, and it makes no sense."

Dad took a bite of his bacon and frowned, making him look more like a guy in his fifties than his forties. It wasn't the only time Willie had asked the question, and Dad looked more disappointed in him each time.

"It took me too long to understand, Willie," Dad said. "But I pray that you will know the answer one day."

"Me too." Willie hadn't prayed in years but it felt like the right thing to say. "But I still don't get it. Defending a pinkie pro bono back home is one thing, but—"

"I don't ever want to hear you say that word again."

"They call each other that all the time."

Willie used the word quite a bit as well. It didn't bother him because somewhere along the way he learned he could get away with it. That's as long as he didn't say it to a white person's face.

"Just because some of them call each other that doesn't make it right."

"Euro-American," Willie said, thinking the "P" word flowed smoother and was more popular in the real world.

"That's better," Dad said, pointing back at the same security checkpoint Willie watched earlier. Two little pinkie boys, maybe three and five years old, were bawling their eyes out as their mother was practically strip-searched by security in front of the whole airport.

"You still haven't given me a good answer," Willie said. "Defending a *Euro-American* up here in Michigan is flat-out stupid. You can't win either way. If he's guilty, the whites will blame you for not getting him off and even worse—"

"The man is white, Willie. And the law says that regardless of what color he is, he deserves a defense. And you were right when you said things are different up here. Just look at the judge, the jury, and the fifteen hundred visitors that were assembled outside the courthouse."

"There were fifteen hundred?"

"Maybe more," Dad said. "Regardless, the fact that I'm black can only help my client."

"But in the one-in-a-million chance you *do* win, The Crown will blame you for getting him off. And fifteen hundred of those racist morons are more than enough to be dangerous."

"There are two reasons you don't have to worry about that." Dad's tone was unusually nonchalant, practically indifferent.

"What are they?"

Dad paused and it seemed like he didn't want to say it, as if he were ashamed.

"One…as much as I hate to admit it, you have a family member that's more than just a little familiar with The Crown. In fact, he went about as high up the ranks as you can go."

Willie couldn't believe his ears. He had a relative that owned a purple robe! He thought it was a little pathetic, but after seeing a trillion of them at the courthouse, a small part of him thought it was actually kind of cool.

"Who?" Willie asked.

"Don't worry about that."

Willie thought about the fat finger-waggler and the irrational paranoia that led Willie to believe the guy was looking at him. Then he thought about the waggler's fourteen hundred and ninety-nine buddies that were parked around him. "How the hell did those haters get so big?"

Dad seemed to consider it and held up his hands before letting them drop to the tabletop. "Hate isn't contagious. But ignorance is."

"Pretty deep, Dad."

"Always a smart aleck."

"You said there were two reasons I don't have to worry about The Crown if you win. Other than having a family member 'more than just a little familiar with them,' what's the other one?"

Dad reached over and put his hand on top of Willie's. Even though the whole touchy-feely, public-affection thing would normally have him yanking his hand away, this time he didn't.

Then Dad gave him a fatherly wink and shook his head.

"The second reason is I won't win."

WILLIE

Dr. Cheever. Car Wash Pinkies.

Pool Time.

"It's darker than you."

Though it had been a couple days since his father had said it, Willie still didn't have the faintest idea what Dad had been trying to get across. It's not that Willie didn't pick up on things—he did, and quickly. It's just that whenever Tyrone Dwayne Gibbons used his courtroom voice, Willie knew it wasn't his place to ask for an explanation. It was more of a cue not to be a smartass, shut up, and then think about what his father had said until he was sure what it meant.

Regardless, Willie couldn't get those words out of his head as he and Dad sat across the desk from the family therapist, the esteemed Dr. Jazmin Cheever, the local shrink that all the rich people denied they went to. Cheever was in her midforties, a large woman with a bad complexion and teeth that were too perfect to be real. She was also black and a Southerner, and she and Willie had spent a great deal of time in his sessions talking about the benefits of both, undoubtedly subject matter that was inspired by his father.

Dad had already made up his mind that Willie was clean. Otherwise there was no way Dad would leave him at the house while he was in Michigan three days a week handling the trial. Dad usually flew home every Wednesday night, and after several thousand dollars of individual sessions for both Willie and Dad, Cheever figured it was best for the three of them to confer and "shake the trees to study the fruits of their labor."

On that particular day, it didn't take Willie long to see that what the good doctor really wanted to do was stab him in the back and declare his blame for the world's problems. It really sucked, because up until about a minute and a half into that meeting, Willie had really liked Cheever, and truth be told, he didn't like many people. He had become comfortable enough with Cheever that he finally reached the point where he could tell her anything, a hundred times more than he could ever tell his father. He guessed it was mostly because he'd really bought into the whole "this is just between you and me and nothing leaves my office" crap she had fed him up until now.

"Willie isn't exactly the emotional type," Cheever blurted. "He uses humor excessively to mask his inability to share his feelings. He's afraid to get attached to anyone and needs to open up and let those closest to him get a little closer."

In previous weeks, Willie and Cheever had discussed his feelings to the point where he actually *felt* a few things, but right then, he mostly felt like finding one of those little airplane vomit bags he'd seen tucked in the seatback on the flight home and loading it with puke. Cheever had already let him know that his lack of emotion didn't mean he doesn't have feelings. What it meant was that he wasn't all that good at showing them, and it was true, but the whole hiding-behind-humor thing was news to him.

"I think he seems to be opening up a little more," Dad said, glancing over at Willie and then back at Cheever.

"Oh, really?" Cheever asked.

To Cheever's credit, Willie didn't have the faintest idea what Dad was talking about, either. If he had made any progress at all, it certainly hadn't come in the form of expressing his emotions.

"Some parents manage their kids," Cheever added, pulling a piece of lint off her sleeve with those plump little fingers before plopping her hands down on that pot-ass-belly of hers. In fact, he'd never noticed how fat she really was until just then.

"Of course," Dad said

Cheever held up her hands matter-of-factly and then ran an index finger across the side of her left cheek. The cheek that was so acne-scarred, it looked like somebody had beat her face with a track shoe. Then she dropped what she thought was the therapeutic bomb: "And some kids manage their parents."

Dad crossed his arms and bit his bottom lip. He looked to mull it over before saying, "So you're suggesting Willie runs my life instead of the other way around?"

No, Dad. When she said that some kids manage their parents she meant that you play on a little league team and I'm the fucking coach.

Cheever looked right at Willie when she answered. "Willie is the textbook entitled teen that exemplifies an entitled generation. But to answer your question, that is exactly what I'm saying. Willie runs your life instead of the other way around."

"For example?" Dad asked, redeeming himself. Willie was with him on that one and wanted to know what the hell Cheever meant.

"Addicts can't survive on their own," Cheever said. "I'm not talking about enabling. I'm talking about you being manipulated while being addicted to his addiction."

"Addicted to his addiction?" Dad said, his head teetering toward his left shoulder. "Please explain."

"I believe that you give yourself some type of psychological reward for having a son that's an addict. Whether it's sympathy from others or something else, you need it, and you are addicted to that reward."

"But Willie has been clean for two years now."

Dad had no clue. Willie was buzzing pretty good right now and knew every trick in the book on passing drug tests. He was what many call a functional addict— which, as far as Willie was concerned, was the person you thought was high when he wasn't high. Regardless, he'd been on painkillers for close to three years now, ever since the accident...

"Abstinence and recovery are two different things," Cheever said. "But that's not what we are talking about. I normally wouldn't say this with a patient present, but you are being manipulated by your seventeen-year-old son, whose emotional unavailability is a valid concern, perhaps even dangerous."

"He always seemed like a good kid," Willie said, imitating the bewildered neighbor—the one that's always standing behind yellow police tape at a murder scene on the news, shaking his head in disbelief.

"Enough," Dad said.

"That's what she means," Willie said. "Am I right, *Jazmin*?"

"And there he is with another example of humor masking feelings," Cheever added, mimicking the voice he used. She leaned forward and lowered her fat chin almost to the desktop before whispering, "I'm not talking about being dangerous to others. I'm talking about being dangerous to yourself. And when we are in my office, you will call me Dr. Cheever."

Willie glanced out the window at the little statue of the white boy holding a lantern on the edge of Cheever's porch. Though he'd never do it, he wondered how long it would take him to go get it and chuck it at her black head. Hopefully she would consider that progress.

"I'm not dangerous to myself," Willie said. "This is absurd."

"I'm afraid I have to agree with Willie," Dad said. "He's too much of a fan of himself to do himself any harm."

It felt good that his father wasn't buying into Cheever's crap either. He and Dad gave each other looks that seemed to ask what the hell they were paying the bitch for. Then Dad said in a small voice, "But about the not showing his emotions thing. I don't know about the whole gamut, but I haven't seen him cry since he was a baby."

Willie couldn't say that was total bunk. The last time he'd cried was a pretty lousy time in his life. It was way back when he was in fourth grade when it became just him and Dad. He pushed the thought away and then glanced back out at the little statue. It looked smaller...lighter.

"We still have a lot of work to do here," Cheever said, standing and signaling the end of the session. "I've told you both in private that this isn't a drug problem as much as it is a reality problem. Let's just continue to be honest, blunt if necessary, and I'm confident we'll move toward some positive changes."

"Okay, but I still don't understand how I'm being manipulated," Dad said, standing and reaching to shake Cheever's hand. "But I'll pray that I do and will also pray that Willie opens up."

Cheever shook Dad's hand and then pointed out the window with her other hand at the $125,000 car Dad had bought him.

"Pray for Willie?" Cheever said, shaking her head. "Mr. Gibbons, Willie doesn't need God."

Dad looked puzzled for a few seconds, then held open his hands. "Why not?"

Cheever leaned forward and smiled, showing off those fake-ass teeth of hers. "Because he has you."

♦♦♦

ON THE WAY BACK from Cheever's office, Willie stopped by the drive-thru car wash to give his birthday gift a good once-over. He waited in line behind three other cars, freaking out about his tires lining up on that little track at the entrance to the wash. He could drive with the best of them, but the people waiting in line behind him made him nervous as hell. He'd been up there a hundred times on his bicycle, but only three times with his car, and on each of those trips, he'd missed the track horribly, setting off the alarm that let the whole town know he'd screwed up. Then the idiots behind him would start having their own aneurysms: honking their horns and yelling until the pinkies that worked there had to stop the wash and back him up to get him resituated. Embarrassing as fuck.

He took a deep breath as yet another car in front of him entered the wash and aligned perfectly on the tracks. Next to the car was Evan Keller, his pill guy. Evan was one of those Nordic pinkies with *white*-white skin that actually turned pink when he spent too much time in the sun. He had shoulder-length greasy blond hair and always wore the same black ball cap with a white capital *E* on the front. Willie had met Evan about three years earlier when Evan worked on the crew that tended their lawn at home. Even though he was a drug dealer whose legitimate job was two-handing a foamy brush and scrubbing tires, Evan was pretty sharp for a white dude and though Willie would never admit it, he always liked him.

As Willie sat there, three other car-wash pinkies came out from the far side of a pickup truck in front of him. Unlike Evan, who was so skinny you'd think he had cancer, the other guys were all big dudes and in good shape, not one of them wearing socks and each wearing pants that were straight floods—easily three inches above the ankles, worn just like all pinkies like to wear them. Willie guessed they were all former athletes that probably weren't good enough to play in college, which left them perfect candidates for the military, the drug trade, or in more honest jobs like working at car washes.

Willie avoided the other side of the bridge where most pinkies lived. Evan was the only white guy he ever really communicated with and that was always on his way to the car wash, normally on his cell phone and riding his bike to get a baggie of painkillers from him. Willie would normally call him up and when Evan saw his bicycle coming up the road, Evan would drop the baggie of pills in a garbage can near the self-serve vacuum, and when Willie picked it out, he'd drop an empty soda can with cash in it right back in the garbage.

"How can I help you today?" Evan asked, checking out the new car. Willie rolled the window a little farther down. Evan was sweating and had a funny smell to him, which reminded Willie of a wet dog.

"Hey, dipshit," Willie muttered. "I'll take the ten-dollar wash."

Evan was smart enough to reach into the car instead of Willie reaching out. He dropped the baggie on Willie's lap and took the money. Eighteen hundred (folded perfectly in half) for the drugs, and eleven bucks for the wash. He quickly pocketed the eighteen hundred without anyone possibly seeing and then walked over to the register, put the ten bucks in, and dropped the extra dollar in the tip bucket.

Evan came back to the car and ran his hand across that sweaty forehead of his before tapping his knuckles on the roof.

"This car is too damn sweet to run through a wash like this," he said. "I've told you before to get this hand-washed. It's gonna get scratched up if you keep coming here."

"I didn't pay for it," Willie said.

"Your daddy hook you up with this ride?"

"What do you think, dumbass?"

Evan was the only white guy on earth that Willie would ever talk to this way. He guessed part of Evan deserved it, though, because whenever he was around other pinkies, Evan acted a lot different, a lot whiter, and when they were in groups, they always scared the living fuck out of Willie.

"Keep running that mouth of yours and shit's gonna happen someday," Evan said, giving a dismissive look, followed by a little smile that told Willie that though he was a little serious he was also just playing with him. "Show some respect, cuz you got no idea how good you got it."

"I'm not washing cars, so I must have it good." Willie lifted the baggie a few inches off his lap. "And I ain't selling this shit, either."

"You ain't got four kids, either," Evan said, rapping his knuckles back on the roof of the car. "And I wasn't just talking about you, Willie. I was talking about *all* of you."

"That sounds a little racist, Evan," Willie said with a grin. "Maybe one day my people will get our very own entertainment channel like the one *your* people have, The White Entertainment Network."

"You already do," he said.

"Which one is that?"

"All the other channels except TWEN," Evan said.

Willie pondered it for a second and realized that Evan was more than just a little right.

"Touché," Willie said.

"Speaking of television," Evan said, "I see your daddy on TV about every day. It's a pretty noble thing he is doing, defending that Bondy guy up in Michigan."

"I think what he's doing is crazy." Willie pointed at Evan's coworkers. "Speaking of crazy, you are nuts for not carrying a gun, particularly with them around and all the cash you carry."

"Guns scare me," Evan said.

"How many times have you been robbed, dumbass?" Willie asked. "Isn't it like three? An ounce of prevention is worth a pound of cure."

"Never had a gun and you will never see me with one. They are nothing but trouble."

"Don't worry," Willie said. "If you ever get a gun and find yourself in trouble, I'm guessing my father would defend you."

"Maybe," Evan said. "You should be proud of him."

"I am," Willie said. "In fact, I was just up in Detroit with him. Saw over a thousand Crown on the courthouse steps. They told me to tell you hello."

"That ain't funny, man. To hell with them."

"Whatever," Willie said, followed by a short laugh.

Evan took a few steps back, reeling his index fingers and guiding Willie slowly into the wash as the other pinkies began spraying the passenger's side of the car. Willie rolled his window up and his heart felt like it was trip hammering right before he felt the bump of his front left tire as it went over the edge of the track.

Fuck.

That pain-in-the-ass alarm went off and he could see the beginning of a smile form at the edge of Evan's mouth.

He knew Evan's pinkie ass made him miss.

"Go back a few feet and let's try again!" Evan shouted, pointing behind the car to the entrance.

Willie put the car in reverse and, before he took his foot off the brake, rolled the window down just enough to give Evan an above-average look at his middle finger.

Evan's smile widened, and he tapped on the window. "I told you shit was gonna happen."

◆◆◆

WILLIE SLEPT THE NEXT day until almost noon.

When he finally got up, he'd jumped in the shallow end of the pool and had been chilling with his arms and legs hanging over the edge of an oversized red inner tube for close to an hour before Dad walked out of the house.

"Your lunch is ready," he said. "DeeDee made us a nice salad."

DeeDee was the live-in maid. She was white, in her fifties, but looked a lot older. She always talked about how washing your hair only once a week was a valuable beauty tip. She had no idea how greasy it looked and Willie had told her at least a thousand times that she needed an oil change, but she never got the joke.

The house had twenty-three rooms in it and they rarely saw DeeDee unless some type of cooking or cleaning was in process. She stayed in one of the bedrooms on the second floor and had been with them even before Willie's mom and sister died. She was dumber than a bag of dog shit, too stupid to steal, and her three primary gifts included speaking only when spoken to, being able to make the best peach pie in the history of man, and an extrasensory ability to walk into a room immediately after Willie silently farted.

DeeDee knew Willie still took pills but was too afraid to tell his father. She had once told him she "understood things" when it came to his addiction and then explained the reason she never drank anymore was because she had already taken enough alcohol for one lifetime. Willie usually ignored her when she babbled about that stuff. Besides, he really didn't care if she was a wino because she was really good at her job, which was doing whatever he asked her to do. In fact, she obeyed him more than she did his father and Willie knew it was because he scared the shit out of her. Maybe it had something to do with that emotional unavailability Cheever blabbered about.

"I'm not hungry," Willie said. "I think I'm going to pass on Deedee's salad."

"What do I pay DeeDee for?" Dad asked. "And when you get out of the pool, dare I ask you to straighten up your room a bit?"

"*That's* what you pay DeeDee for," Willie said, smiling and using his arms as oars to paddle away from Dad. "I have her do it."

"What would you do without us?"

"Most likely wither up and die."

Dad stepped closer to the edge of the water and crossed his arms. He never went in the pool. In fact, Willie had never seen him with his shirt off. "Have you been in the safe?"

Dad was a perpetual candidate for the cover of *Rhetorical Question Magazine*.

"Yeah," Willie said. Some form of honesty was always the best policy. Of course, he had been in the safe. Dad had given him the new combination as a reward for his impeccable abstinence. Oops.

"Why?"

Willie lifted his midsection out of the water and above the inner tube before tapping on his swimsuit.

"I needed a new pair of trunks and some socks."

Willie needed new swimwear like he needed eye cancer. Or like he needed Dad asking him about the safe. Besides, Dad usually kept at least thirty or forty grand in there and never knew the balance or what Willie took out, so it was really no big deal.

"Okay," Dad said, apparently believing Willie, which was a surprise. Then Dad stood and nodded before saying, "Just remember the money is in the safe for emergencies."

"I know," Willie said, justifying his pill withdrawals as bona fide 911 material. He took a deep breath, leaned back on the inner tube, and closed his eyes. Then he smiled and took a good ten- to-fifteen-second piss in the pool, knowing there was no way Dad would know about that either.

"Why don't you come in the house and let's spend some time together before I head back up north?" Dad said.

"Maybe later. Can you have DeeDee bring me a couple towels?"

"Maybe you should get off your backside and get them yourself," Dad answered. What Dad had in courtroom authority rarely—actually never—translated into parental sternness. Willie pretended to close his eyes (the old close them, but not all the way trick) and waited Dad out. Dad finally gave up and shook his head before walking back in the house. Willie opened his eyes all the way and wondered for a second if maybe some of that garbage Dr. Cheever fed them about Dad being manipulated was starting to sink in.

Three minutes later, DeeDee came out with a pair of towels tucked under her arm. Willie stretched his arms out behind his head and closed his eyes again. This time all the way.

Life was good.

And with a fresh supply of pills and his father going back up north to Michigan, it was about to get a whole lot better.

JOSEPH

Thankful.

Nineteen-year-old Joseph Springsted knelt in the grass at the side of Mr. Reggie's old farmhouse and then cranked the cast-iron handle of the rusty pump. It took a few seconds, but the cold water finally started spilling out over his head, cooling his neck and upper back. It sure felt good.

It had been a cool and rainy week, but now it was close to ninety, too darn hot for June in southeast Michigan. But it didn't matter too much, because his workday had ended and he could smell the ham and beans Mama was cooking at their little place behind Mr. Reggie's. He couldn't wait to get some.

Joseph stood and picked up the hedge clippers and figured he'd best walk out front to the gravel road to get a different view of the shrubs to make sure they were nice and straight. Mr. Reggie never complained about the way they looked, and Joseph was thankful, but he wanted to be extra sure because Mr. Reggie was always so kind to him and Mama for letting them stay on his property.

He walked to the road, turned around, and then smiled as the breeze cooled the water on his neck. He admired his work. The shrubs all appeared straight and the flowers that surrounded them were prettier than ever. He looked at all the land that surrounded Mr. Reggie's house and thought about how nice it would be if there were more houses around where he could fix shrubs and plant flowers. It's what he loved to do.

Then he glanced over at the rosebushes at the edge of house. Mr. Reggie said he didn't mind if he did it once in a while, as long as things still looked good, so he decided to go clip one of the roses and take it to Mama.

He knew she'd appreciate it, and just the thought of it made him smile.

WILLIE

The Verdict.

A Call from Uncle Reggie.

After exiting the pool and leaving the towels on the patio, Willie decided to head up to the third-floor den for a few hours to sit in the special recliner Dad bought him that was designed specifically for video games. He was playing *Gunrunner3*, a first-person shooter where the object was to terminate pinkie terrorists trying to overthrow the European and Canadian Colonies. Though he only had the game a few weeks, Willie was already rated in the top one hundred players in the world—not bad considering the case had a little sticker on it that read *9 Million Copies Sold*.

Willie peppered the side of a van with machine-gun fire and then tossed a grenade through the open passenger-side window. The driver, a wide-eyed French-speaking pinkie, quickly bolted from the vehicle just in time to get shot in the back of the head and then warmed up by Willie's flamethrower.

Willie paused the game and laughed, wondering if maybe there was a shred of truth to Dr. Cheever's belief that he had an unhealthy obsession with guns and things getting blown up. She'd noticed it in one of their initial sessions and had brought it up one other time, but at the end of the day, her concern was straight hogwash because the truth was that Willie had never come into contact with a gun or any type of explosive whatsoever. Regardless, Willie was confident Cheever would think (because Willie was possibly "dangerous") it was better for him to take out his pent-up aggression shooting digital pinkies in a video game than to do something crazy in real life like run over a bunch of white employees at a car wash or pipe bomb his therapist's vehicle.

The pills Willie had taken were starting to kick in nicely.

He kept the game on pause and thought about ringing DeeDee's pink ass to run him up a bowl of that salad when Dad walked by, holding his cell phone to his ear. Dad had his game face on and Willie knew he was talking about the trial.

Dad stepped into the library, which was adjacent to the den, and closed the door. Willie took off his headphones, stood, and then hustled over to put his ear against the wall so he could hone in on the conversation. He couldn't hear squat, so he went back and sat in the gaming chair.

Less than a minute later, the library door opened and Dad peeked his head in the den.

"I'm flying back to Detroit."

"Holy shit," Willie said. "We just got back."

"I have to be back in court and watch your language," Dad said.

"Sorry."

"Do you want to go with me?" Dad asked. "We've been communicating well lately and I was sort of hoping we could spend some time together to keep it up."

"Really?" Willie said, not sure if he was more surprised he was invited to go or that Dad thought they had been communicating well. Either way, the thought of having Deedee and the house to himself for a few days sounded best. "If you don't mind, I think I'm going to just stay home and chill out."

"I understand," Dad said, clearly disappointed.

"No, you don't," Willie said, because Dad didn't understand. He never did.

"I guess you are right."

"I'll go to Detroit with you next time," Willie said, as if dangling a shiny carrot over his father's head.

"There won't be a next time."

"Fine," Willie said. "Be that way if you want."

"I have no choice."

"Why is that?" Willie asked, anxious to hear why going to Detroit was now or never.

Dad stared at him for a good twenty seconds before he answered.

"Because the verdict is in."

♦♦♦

GUILTY.

Shocker.

Willie had heard it on the radio the next day around dinnertime. An hour later, he turned the television on and the verdict was still interrupting practically every program on every channel, even The White Entertainment Network. Willie couldn't understand why it was such a big deal. After all, if anyone in the world was surprised that the jury found Donald Bondy guilty, it was either their first day on the planet or they were recovering from some sort of closed head injury.

Willie checked his phone a couple times over the next few hours and was a little surprised he still hadn't heard from his father, so he tried calling him right before going to bed.

Dad didn't answer.

The following morning, Willie arrived at Dr. Cheever's office around quarter after nine for his nine o'clock appointment. He was looking forward to laying into that pig for tossing him under the bus in front of his father. Her door was open and she was facing the other way, watching coverage of events still happening outside the courthouse up in Detroit. Now that they had the verdict they wanted, there wasn't a Crown member in sight and all that was on the screen were a handful of protesting pinkies getting power washed by two muscle-bound cops holding a fire hose. One of the pinkies was a skinny little woman that couldn't have weighed more than ninety pounds (soaking wet), who kept getting knocked down but kept getting back up. Looked like Donald Bondy had a few followers that weren't smart enough to realize that sharing their thoughts on his conviction probably wasn't their best play unless they were looking for a free bath followed by what would certainly be a trip to jail.

Cheever poked at the air a couple times with the remote, and a flabby black meat curtain jiggled from the back of her arm. When the television finally went off, she turned to face Willie and crossed her arms as he sat in the chair in front of her desk.

"Real nice body language," Willie said. "Cold. Closed. Defensive. What kind of message are you trying to send to a dangerous teen who is seeking professional guidance?"

"How do you feel about that?" she asked, nodding back at the TV.

Willie wasn't sure if the session had started or if she really gave a shit. Fuck her but he still wanted to know.

"Feel about what?" he asked.

"The verdict."

"If I answer, how long will it take you to call my father in and tell him about that too?"

"I'm just trying to help, Willie. Can you believe that?"

"I believed you when you said our chats were confidential. My dad says trust is something that is given until it needs to be earned back."

"I see," she said.

"The trial is over. You think my dad is going to pay you to keep babysitting me now that he doesn't have to go back to Detroit every week?"

Cheever smiled and Willie mimicked it. She also didn't answer, which pissed him off more, so he tried the guilt card—the one that always worked for him. With Dad, anyhow.

"I really liked you until yesterday," he said.

"Oh please. You may be the most intelligent person I've ever met. Brilliant and capable of things beyond what most people dream of. And the only thing important to you is swimming endlessly in a sea of entitlement, occasionally diving down low to avoid the lifeboats that come along to prevent you from drowning."

"Wow," he said, pulling out his phone. "You care if I make a call?"

She nodded. "Suit yourself."

"Need to call an engraver so we can put that one on a plaque."

"Humor masking feelings."

He held the phone out toward her. "Better call Dad and tell him then."

Cheever leaned forward and gave him a look that was easy to read. *I see right through you, you little shit.*

Willie put his elbow on the desk, rested his chin on his hand, and then smiled.

"Let's go back to your question," Cheever said. "The one about your father paying me to watch you. But I want you to answer it. Do you think you need a babysitter?"

"Addicts can't survive on their own," he answered. "You said it. More pearls."

"Glad to see you were paying attention." Cheever leaned her head toward her left shoulder. When she did it, two rolls of fat hugged each other, forming what looked like a little black butt that had been glued between her neck and shoulder.

"I hear everything you say," Willie said.

"But you don't listen," she said. When she straightened up, the butt shoulder unfolded and morphed back into what was just her fat neck.

"Not true. I listen more than you do."

"But you know you are smarter than me," she said. "And it makes no sense to you to get help from someone beneath you. In your case, that's everyone, including your father. You think you have all the answers and if you don't, you believe you will figure it out. You ignore the experience of others and the only one allowed to analyze Willie Gibbons is Willie Gibbons."

Cheever was good. Really good. But he'd never let her know it.

"Whatever," he said. "Maybe you should just tell me what's really wrong with me."

"I've told you."

"Yeah, yeah, yeah. My inability to deal with loss. That as good as you can do?"

"What do you think is wrong with you?"

Willie had no clue. And he didn't like that he couldn't fire back with something that, at the very least, resembled a smart-ass answer. Preferably one that had teeth...poisonous fangs that would attach said answer to the side of Cheever's fat head.

"Cat got your tongue?" Cheever asked.

"Nope."

"Maybe you won't let me help you. I mean, after all, who can help you, Willie? Is there anybody you will listen to?"

Willie paused, making direct eye contact with her. He had read the monologue from one of his father's guest lectures at some east coast law school. Dad spoke about how to intimidate someone in the courtroom and how important it is when you make eye contact with someone to never be the one to look away first. Cheever finally turned her head toward the window and Willie smiled victoriously before answering.

"I don't see the benefit of listening to someone like you," Willie said. "Now that the trust has been broken."

"Fair enough," she said. "But I would like to learn from you, then. Can I ask you just a couple more questions?"

"Thrill me," he said.

"What do you stand for?"

He knew what she meant but didn't have a specific answer. Again.

"Lots of things," he said.

Cheever resumed eye contact when she said, "Well, it should be easy to name just one then, shouldn't it?"

He shrugged. It kind of reminded him of Dad asking him to come up with just one thing whites could do to improve their lives.

"You are afraid of something," Cheever added. "And it's up to you whether you want to keep coming here. But I think you need to uncover that fear. Bring it out in the open, conquer it, and then be free of whatever it is that prevents you from getting close to anyone."

"Let's do that," he said dismissively as they maintained eye contact.

"Why do you act like you don't care about anything or anyone?"

"Who said I was acting?"

Willie's cell phone rang. He didn't recognize the area code so he ignored it.

"What's wrong with caring about someone other than yourself?" Cheever said. "It's risky, isn't it?"

"Risky?" Willie said with a dismissive laugh. "Now you are babbling."

"It's risky because things can happen. Things you can't control."

Willie's phone rang again. It was the same person, clearly looking for someone else, so he answered it to prevent his phone from ringing all fucking day.

"Wrong number," Willie said.

"Hello?" It was a throaty voice with a Northern accent that sounded like it belonged to a smoker.

"You've got the wrong number," Willie blurted.

"Is this Willie Gibbons?"

"Yes," Willie said. "Who the hell is this?"

"This is your uncle Reggie."

It was a man he'd never met and a voice he'd never heard, but Willie could remember the face from photos his father had shown him years ago. It was similar to Dad's, but the head was long and round, like a watermelon. And his uncle's face did an amazing job of suggesting he'd been shortchanged at the intellect store. Willie was still eye-locked with Cheever and wondered for a fleeting moment if maybe she had read about Dad's lecture as well.

"Hello, Uncle Reggie," Willie said.

"There's news regarding your father."

"I already know. I think the whole world does."

There was a pause and then a bit of static.

"I don't think you understand," Uncle Reggie said.

Of course, he understood. Willie understood everything because he and his shrink had concluded he was the world's smartest person.

"He lost the case," Willie said. "I understand."

"No, Willie," Uncle Reggie said, followed by another pause, one that was considerably awkward.

"What is it then?"

Another thread of static and then a couple of clicks. Willie thought they were disconnected for a second before his uncle said it.

"Son, your father is dead."

WILLIE

I-75 to Uncle Reggie's.

Badass Cop. Curb-Painting Pinkies.

Willie hadn't been in his father's room in probably three years. He just sat on the edge of Dad's bed, holding the framed family photo they had taken when Willie and his twin sister were around four or five. Mom, Dad, Desiree, and even young Willie were all smiling. Willie closed his eyes and thought about how Cheever could be right. The part about his emotional unavailability.

Why am I not crying?

He really tried to—wanted to—but for Willie, trying to cry was like drilling at a well that had long run dry. He took a deep breath and decided to look at the other pictures. The ones on the wall of his father with the governor, the president, and then another of Dad holding up a trophy for winning the club championship in golf over at the country club the previous summer.

You really should be crying. Dad is dead.

After losing his mother and sister, the news of his father's death was like flicking a lighter across a third-degree burn. He wondered if the nerves were gone and shook his head, assuming that people can only handle so much, and when they hit their limit, something happens between their ears that is meant to protect them. And whatever that was, on top of the seven pills he had just taken, it really was helping him, *protecting* him, from what he should be feeling.

Now it's just me.

A thick finger of doubt tapped at his gut and he knew if he was going to make it, he finally needed to get his shit together. For real. And that meant the pills had to go.

Yeah. Easy to say after you just took some.

Willie went back down the hall to his bedroom and grabbed his baggie of pills. He made his way into the bathroom to give them the old flusharoo, the first step in quitting. He opened the baggie, held it in his palm over the toilet, and stared at the contents, wondering how many he had taken in his life and what they had done to him.

He tilted his hand to the side and watched the pills slide toward the opening of the baggie. Two of them fell out and he quickly caught them with his other hand. He put them in his mouth and then put the baggie back in his pocket.

I'll quit later. Real soon.

Willie returned to his father's room and took another look at the family portrait. Then he stared at his cell phone and Uncle Reggie's phone number. He realized he'd typed in *Uncle Redgie* for his contact information and then fixed the spelling. He exhaled in a loud puff and as a small amount of stress left his body, he could feel a dark shadow forming in the back corner of his mind. It was cold, numbing, and it seemed to be growing…spreading throughout his body, making him more afraid. Of what, he didn't know, but he had a good guess.

He didn't have any real friends. All he ever wanted was to be left alone, because being alone was one of the few things he really enjoyed. When he was by himself, he didn't have to explain the way he felt or why he took pills to feel a different way. But now it was just him and as he sat there, he could feel that thick finger of doubt becoming fingers, then a fist—one that pounded at his gut—reminding him that he finally got what he wished for. And for the first time in his life he understood the difference between lonely and alone.

I'm alone. And Cheever said addicts can't survive on their own.

Willie tapped the word Connect on his phone to call his only living relative.

Uncle Reggie answered it on the second ring and sounded like he was either tired or drunk.

"Hello."

"What happened to him?"

There was a pause before Uncle Reggie said, "We'll have to let the police sort that out. But I reckon you will find out soon, because it didn't happen in Detroit, it happened right here in Woodruff. Either way, I think this is a conversation we should have face-to-face, son."

Using the word *reckon* in that Northern drawl didn't make Willie feel any better about Uncle Reggie's smarts, but he was the only person in the world that had the information Willie needed.

"What now?" Willie asked.

"We'll take it slow. Your father left me instructions in the event anything happened to him. I think it's best that you come up here for a bit."

"Why don't you come here?"

"It's what your father wanted. I reckon it's best we do what he asked. And for starters, he wanted his funeral up here."

Willie *reckoned* his uncle was out of his fucking mind. "Away from my mother and sister? You are nuts. There is no way he would want that."

There was a pause. "I'm not here to argue with you, son. You should probably get up here as soon as possible. I'll make arrangements for a flight."

"I'm not going anywhere," Willie said. "He is my father and he is coming down here. If you try to stop that from happening, I'll shove a lawyer so far up your ass you won't walk for a year. You know what my father did for a living. His partners are the best and I'm not fucking around here. You understand me?"

Another pause.

"You must be talking about Mr. Barnes and Mr. Kilmer?"

"Damn straight," Willie said.

"Spoke with them this morning," Uncle Reggie said. "If anything happened to your daddy, he wanted me to call them as well so they could help me understand everything I need to do. Never been a trustee before and this is a lot of money to divvy up."

"*What?*"

"Not quite sure how to do all this, so when the time comes, they are going to help us get through this. Nice fellas, those two."

"Divvy up the money with *who?*"

"We can go over that and the rest of the paperwork with those lawyers when the time comes," his uncle said. "But for now, let's get you on an airplane and put your daddy to rest."

"I'll drive," Willie said. Despite airport security only checking pinkies, it would be just his luck to get busted with pills if he tried to fly. And with the latest barrage of news, quitting pills was suddenly the furthest thing from his mind.

"Suit yourself," his uncle said. "Give you some thinking time."

"You think one of those Bondy protesters killed Dad because Bondy was found guilty?"

"Like I said, the police can sort through all that."

Willie looked at the clock and then back at the family portrait with all the smiles. He was mostly looking at Dad's and thinking about how he'd declined Dad's invitation to go up to Detroit and how he'd love for him to be able to ask Willie just one more time.

And then he couldn't stop some of the last words he'd heard his father say from dancing around inside of his head.

There won't be a next time.

"You still there?" his uncle asked.

"Yeah," Willie said. "Somebody is going to pay for this."

"Nothing would make me happier," Uncle Reggie said. "But we are just going to have to be patient and let the process run its course."

"Okay," Willie said, wanting justice served and served *now*.

"How long 'til you get up here, you think?" Uncle Reggie asked.

Fucking pinkies, Willie thought. *Snowflake ghost pinkie fucks.*

He wanted them all dead.

"You still there?" his uncle said again.

"Yeah...I'll be there in a couple days."

◆ ◆ ◆

DESPITE ALL THE MEDIA coverage of his father's murder, Willie didn't hear a peep about the cause of death, though most speculated that it was exactly what Willie thought, or as what one newscaster called "a result of the white community."

Cheever had phoned Willie a few times before he had gone to bed, but he didn't feel like answering. He was pretty sure she may have even come to the house because he faintly remembered someone knocking, but he was too pill-trashed to get out of the den.

The following morning, he got off to an early start and left the house by noon. He took eight grand out of the safe and dumped a third of it when he stopped by the car wash to get a mega-supply of painkillers from Evan. Willie didn't have any idea how long he'd be up north, two weeks he guessed, but if he ran short on supply and push came to shove, he figured he could always wave enough hundreds over Evan's head to get Evan in his car and Michigan-bound with some more pills. At least enough to get him through the summer until he came back to Georgia to start his senior year in the fall.

Fuck. You are only seventeen. Are they even going to let you come back and live by yourself?

Willie wasn't sure how many times that question ran through his mind during his eight-hour drive to the Kentucky-Ohio border. But what he was certain of was how many times Cheever had called him. Nine. Just one shy of Willie pulling the car over and blocking her number.

By eleven o'clock, he was bushed. He exited off I-75 in some small town named Hanemann about sixty miles west of Columbus, to get some gas and find a place to spend the night.

Columbus. Fucking really?

Columbus supposedly discovered what was called the New World. Though Willie was confident that the people that already lived in the New World didn't think it was all that new, Columbus still ended up having a city named after him. Then whites came over and had black slaves, naming even more cities after people and places from Europe. Then the gold-rich Emandi came over in the mid-1800s, kicked a ton of white ass, made whites slaves, and then went to Europe and kicked even more ass for some additional no-cost white labor.

Then why, to this day, isn't there a single city named after any person, place, or thing from Africa?

The pat answer in school was always some bullshit about how city names had origins from other countries that we ultimately conquered and how the names served as reminders of our global dominance.

Who gives a fuck? Shut up. You are tired and need to go to sleep.

Willie pulled into a place called The Slate Motel where you can "Rest for Less" and parked the car.

In less than a minute, it was clear that the guy behind the counter, a portly black dude with a cheap suit on, wasn't going to rent Willie a room because he was a minor. Willie offered him an extra hundred bucks and the guy told him he couldn't do it because he'd lose his job if anyone found out. Willie asked him if losing his job at that dump would actually be a bad thing and the guy behind the counter informed him he'd also lose his job if he kicked Willie's ass, so Willie left and decided to just take a little nap at a rest area a little farther up I-75.

When he woke up eight hours later, he was getting his ear gnawed on by a mosquito that had made its way through a tiny opening in the passenger-side window. He was a little less than three hours from Michigan and decided to leave an anonymous voicemail with the Slate Motel's corporate office to file a complaint against the manager. Then he went online via his phone and made up a tasty little review about the motel's rude employees, the filthy state of the rooms, and their horrific bedbug problem.

Despite an unusual amount of freeway construction through the rest of Ohio, it was relatively smooth sailing. Thirty miles north of the Michigan border, Willie took the exit for Woodruff, the town where his father had been born and where Uncle Reggie still lived at the house they grew up in.

Woodruff was a throwback, old-school, blue-collar, rural, black community that upheld a strict adherence to Northern values. And as Willie drove down Main Street that Sunday afternoon, all he could see on the sidewalks were smiling black faces out in front of one-hundred-year-old brick buildings that were most likely built by white slaves.

And speaking of pinkies, Dad had told Willie on more than one occasion about another part of the town's culture. The part about how unless a white person worked at someone's home or offered janitorial or low-wage services to one of the businesses there, Woodruff probably wasn't the best place to be, as it had long been known as the national hub for The Crown.

Willie turned off the air conditioner, rolled the windows down, and as he continued up Main Street, he could feel the occasional stares that all seemed to ask the same thing: *Where did this young kid get the money to drive such a nice car?*

He spotted an ice cream shop and parked in front, giving the locals all the car gawking they needed. Inside, a smoking-hot black girl, maybe a year younger than him, was behind the counter, handing change back to a man that had two little boys with him that were carbon copies of each other.

"Twins?" Willie asked.

"They are," the man said, peeking over the edge of his glasses. He looked like the prototypical black accountant or the man next door. He was clean-cut, probably in his early thirties, and struck Willie as someone that went to church twice a week and never cursed.

"How old are they?" Willie asked. He really didn't care but couldn't think of anything else to say.

"They will be five next week," the man said, smiling proudly, almost too proudly…like a television father, the perfect type whose wife irons his underwear.

"That's great," Willie said.

"It is indeed," the man said, guiding the boys toward the door. The one closest to Willie already had what looked to be strawberry ice cream melting from the bottom of his cone on to his little black hand.

"See you later, Mr. Bellows," Hot Black Girl said.

"Have a nice day," TV Dad said kindly, nodding at both Willie and Hot Black Girl.

Willie smiled and shook his head. "I'd bet a dollar that guy is an accountant."

"You'd be out a dollar," the girl said. "He teaches fifth grade."

"I was way off," Willie said. "Seems like a nice guy."

"The nicest," she said. "All the kids love him."

After grabbing a double scoop of chocolate in a paper cup, Willie leaned against the counter and asked her for a pen and paper. She smiled at him and slid both toward him.

"Even if I lost that dollar, I'd probably survive," he said, pointing over his shoulder without looking. "See that car out there?"

She nodded, and Willie smiled as he wrote down his number. He slid it back across the counter top and she picked it up.

"I'm going to be in town for a little bit," he said. "Let me know when you want a ride and I'll do my best to make it happen."

She glanced down at the piece of paper and smiled yet again. Then she crumpled it up and pitched it in the waste can behind her.

"Please accept my apology," Willie said. "I didn't mean to be so bold."

She seemed surprised and smiled a third time, this one genuine. "Apology accepted."

"Thank you," he said. "I didn't have the faintest idea you were a lesbian."

He walked outside and sat at a small wooden table between the storefront and the edge of Main. To his left and maybe thirty feet away, two pinkies were kneeling at the edge of the street. They were painting address numbers on the curb and they both looked at him at the same time. Willie figured they were brother and sister, both with dark brown hair and light-colored eyes, attractive for pinkies. The man was maybe around twenty-five and the girl about Willie's age, and when she gave Willie a second look, her brother tapped her on the side of the face and pointed back at the curb in a get-back-to-work sort of way.

Across the street, a chunky black police officer with a handful of helium balloons was stepping out the front door of a place called Brown's, which looked like a dime store that also served as a pharmacy. Despite being overweight, the cop was clearly a badass. He was wearing sunglasses, a tan police uniform with matching hat, and jet-black leather boots—flawlessly spit-shined—that came up to his knees. He knelt and began to pass a balloon to each of the five or six black kids that surrounded him. About fifty feet to their right was a little white girl, wearing a dress that looked like it was made of blue cheesecloth. She was maybe four or five years old and was straying from her mother, who was being chastised by a black man that was most certainly her boss.

"I couldn't leave her by herself," the woman cried, watching her daughter as the little girl began walking faster toward the balloons. "Please. I need this job. We won't be able to eat."

Her boss just shook his head and went back inside.

The woman's shoulders sagged, and she looked to her left. Her daughter was only a few steps from Badass Cop, so she quickly darted toward her and scooped up the little girl as if she were approaching an alligator breeding pond.

They sure got them trained up here.

Badass Cop finished passing out the balloons and then stood. He crossed his arms and stared at the white woman who scurried back down the sidewalk with the little girl in her arms. Once she was around the corner, the cop's stare shifted over to Willie's car. He patted one of the black kids on the head and then started walking across the street without checking for oncoming traffic. With each step Badass Cop took, it became more difficult for Willie to breathe. The man slowed when he reached Willie's car, perusing through the back window and then the driver-side window before turning to face Willie.

"This yours?" he asked in a bass voice, one reserved for those that meant business. He had a little puff in his cheek that had to be chewing tobacco and when he grinned, it was confirmed as a few specs of it were on his front teeth, which were capped in gold.

"Yeah," Willie said, not seeing any signs that would have prevented him from parking there.

"What's she do?" Badass Cop asked, spitting tobacco on the street. "About a hundred and fifty?"

"Wouldn't know," Willie said. "Illegal to drive that fast."

"Good answer." The cop smiled and his fat cheeks puffed before the smile faded. "You are the Gibbons boy, aren't you?"

Willie nodded.

"Shame about your father."

Willie nodded again.

Badass Cop came up on the sidewalk and when he held out his hand, Willie stood. The cop had to weigh an easy two eighty, and though they were about the same height, Badass Cop's fingers were short and fat, reminding Willie of black sausages.

"Demetrius Green," Badass Cop said.

Willie could feel the power in Cop Green's handshake. The tight grip hurt Willie's hand as he muttered, "Willie Gibbons."

"I'm sure I'll be seeing you over the next week or so as we get things sorted out," Cop Green said. "We are doing our best and will keep you and your uncle informed."

"Okay," Willie said. "Thanks."

"Going out to Reggie's?"

"Yeah." Willie didn't have the faintest idea what else to say, because something about the *badass* in Cop Green had Willie awed.

Cop Green pointed one of his sausage fingers up Main Street. The finger damn near looked like it had been cut in half, but it was all there, a dirty nail at the end.

"Pretty simple to get to his place," the cop said. "Main ends about four miles that way at Cossit Creek. That's his road. Hang a right and there's only two places out there. One on the right side and one on the left. First house you come to will be on the left. You'll see a dog, that's Mack. He'll be sitting all by himself on the side of the house, chained to an empty silo. You'll see a couple hundred pigeons on top of that silo all standing on a few tons of pigeon shit. Anyhow, that property is the widow Vee's place. If you see the ugliest creature you ever laid eyes on, that's not Mack—that's her. All you have to do from there is go another mile down the road and Reggie's place is on the opposite side. Can't miss it."

"Thank you, sir," Willie said, not sure if he called him *sir* because he truly was a badass or because he was a cop and Willie had enough pills in the car to get him charged as an adult with the intent to distribute.

Cop Green stared at him for a long second, nodded, and then spit a silver dollar-sized wad of moist tobacco on the sidewalk.

"Hey," he yelled to the curb-painting pinkies. "Come here!"

They popped to their feet, dropped their paintbrushes like hot potatoes, and ran up next to Cop Green.

"Yes, sir?" the male pinkie said. He was missing a few teeth up top to the right side, but Willie paid most of his attention to the girl. She wasn't just good-looking for a pinkie, she was hot.

Cop Green pointed at the wad of tobacco. On second glance, it looked like something a poodle had punched out its ass after eating a bowl of chili.

"I'm going across the street for lunch," Cop Green said. "Go finish the curb you are working on, but when I come back, that tobacco better be cleaned up."

"Yes, sir," Bad-Tooth Pinkie answered.

"Yes, sir," Hot Pinkie Girl echoed, and unlike the stuck up asexual ice cream bitch, she gave Willie a quick smile and a raised eyebrow that had *come get me* written all over it. Or so he thought.

"See you, Willie," Cop Green said. Then he walked back out in the street, not looking left or right as if a car were coming from either direction, its driver already knew it was best to fucking yield, or else.

Willie killed the rest of his ice cream and then got busted by Hot Pinkie checking out her ass. It was a little too flat for his liking, but other than her hair being too straight, he couldn't find another thing wrong with her.

He got back in the car and as he pulled out on Main, he looked back at her and knew it was just a matter of time before he had her.

MAGGIE

Cute Black Boy. Rich Black Boy.

Asking for Trouble.

"Did you see that black boy staring at me?" Maggie Carpenter said, kneeling beside her big brother in front of the curb. "He must be rich."

"They are all rich," Alan said, using the serious voice that normally led into a lecture designed to keep her safe. He picked the thinnest of the four paint brushes out of a plastic bowl, dabbed it in the can of black paint, and then finished tidying up the edges of the 2 that would soon be the 529 on the curb in front of Keyshawn's Barber Shop. "And you were staring right back at him, not to mention you were doing it in front of Sheriff Green. Why are you always looking for trouble?"

"I'm not looking for trouble," Maggie said. She really couldn't care less who was rich and who wasn't. She knew she'd never have any money, nor would she end up with someone that did, but it kind of felt nice knowing she'd sparked the interest of the black boy. She glanced over her shoulder at his fancy car as it made its way up Main Street. Then she dipped her finger into the can of black paint and ran it across her milk-white arm, knowing how different the town would look if the rest of her were that color.

"Do that again and you will buy the next can of paint from your half of the pay," Alan said, handing her a cloth. "We spent good money on this stuff and can't be wasting it."

"It's just a little." She wiped it off her arm. "And because you are overreacting, you have to clean up Sheriff Green's spit this time."

"This time?" Alan laughed.

"Yeah."

Sheriff Green had made a point of spitting around them every day they were in town, followed by an order to make sure it was gone by the time he came back. She and Alan played rock-paper-scissors to see who would clean it up. So far, Alan had won six times and she'd won two.

But he cleaned it up every time.

WILLIE

Halfie Son. Pinkie Mama.

Willie headed down Main Street until it turned into a dirt road with only a junkyard and an abandoned miniature golf course (Javeon's Wonder World—Where Children Under 5 Play Free) separating the downtown area from the sprawling spread of dairy land where a woman named Vee, a dog named Mack, and Uncle Reggie lived.

All he could see to his right and left were fields and a few pockets of trees that hugged the road on both sides until he finally reached a "T" where Main Street (or whatever the fuck it was called at this point) dead-ended into another dirt road. An old wooden sign with bullet holes was nailed to a post that had freshly painted black letters that read Cossit Creek Road. Apparently, replacing the sign altogether wasn't in the town's budget and Willie laughed, wondering if maybe they paid Hot Pinkie Girl and Bad Tooth Pinkie fifty cents to paint over the old letters to spruce things up a bit.

He followed Cop Green's directions and hung a right. Though he was only going fifteen miles per hour, he could hear the gravel bumping under his new ride and getting it dirty as hell until the first house on the left came into view. It was a single story made of wood, about a trillion years old, and it had a roof that looked like it was about ready to cave in. There were no cars in the dirt driveway and about thirty yards to the side of the house, just like Cop Green said, was a dog chained to a pigeon-shit-covered silo in the middle of the field. The dog just sat in a pile of dust, staring at Willie and looking abused and mangy with exposed ribs that suggested it hadn't eaten in a while.

Uncle Reggie's place was much bigger and a lot older than the first house, probably even older than the downtown area. It was a traditional farmhouse, and it had one of those little lookout towers that formed a square on the roof above the second floor. Despite its age, the house seemed to be well-kept and Willie noticed that the shrubs were perfectly manicured, maybe even better than their shrubs at the house in Georgia. In addition, tons of flowers surrounded an old wooden porch that wrapped around the whole house.

Willie pulled into the gravel driveway and drove past the house before stopping next to a freshly painted red barn. It was one of those old barns with warped sides and despite the new paint job, had clearly been there forever.

No other cars were around, but Willie still parked next to the barn. When he got out, it felt about ten degrees cooler than it had downtown. He guessed it was around eighty and the difference was the breeze, one that came from behind him, carrying the sound of a crow and a smell that hinted of cow shit. He did a quick three-sixty, wanting to know where the cows were, because the only thing he could see past a hundred yards of wavy knee-high grass were dirt fields.

He double-checked the address and wondered where the hell his uncle Reggie was. He walked up on the porch and rapped his knuckles on the back door a couple times. Nobody answered so he pressed his face up against one of the back windows to see inside the house. An old-fashioned sitting room was all he could make out and he saw no signs of movement anywhere, so he went back and tried turning the doorknob. He was struck by a sickening thought that Uncle Reggie was maybe at some funeral home, picking out a casket for Dad.

Dad's dead. He really is gone…and you still haven't cried.

Willie caught his breath and looked around the rest of the property, not having the faintest idea what it was that Uncle Reggie "farmed." Then he saw a little plume of smoke running away from the back side of the barn.

He went to check it out and found a little hut back there. It reminded him of a playhouse with no more than one or two rooms in it. It was made of wood painted the same color as the barn and had black shingles that needed to be replaced. Willie was surprised he hadn't seen the place from the road, but what was even more surprising was that, unlike the barn, the hut looked no more than twenty years old.

He walked past the hut and stood downwind. The scent of the smoke quickly trumped the cow shit smell, and it was obvious that his uncle was using the shack as a little cooking area to make jerky or some other disgusting Northern food. The closer Willie got, the more it stunk like boiling meat. He knocked, noticing two enormous crates of apples on each side of the door.

"Coming, sir," a woman said, sounding dopey and a little white. He shook his head, realizing he'd probably just knocked on the door of some low-rent tenant Uncle Reggie had. But that made no sense because the place was too small for anyone to live in.

The door pushed open and a tall pinkie woman in her mid-thirties with shoulder-length brown hair was standing there. She startled the shit out of him, and he took a few steps back.

"You must be Mr. Willie," she said, stepping in front of the door and drawing it closed. She was about his height, close to six feet, and though she wasn't as pretty as the curb painter, she was attractive, with high cheekbones and clear skin that was shiny and clean. "Mr. Reggie said you'd be coming."

Willie didn't say anything. He just looked down at all the apples. Of course. Pinkies loved their apples. Then he looked back at her and wondered what she was doing on his uncle's property.

"Son," she called behind her. "Let's get Mr. Willie's things for him."

Holy shit, there's two of them in there.

A teenage pinkie about Willie's age stepped into the shadow of the doorway. He had his jeans pulled up like all pinkies do and they were filthy, with bread-plate-sized holes in the knees and dark oily stains that ran down the sides of both legs. Willie looked up at the kid and wondered what in the hell the two of them ate to make them so tall. Pinkie Kid was maybe around six five, clearly getting at least part of his height from his mother. He also had a beefy neck, muscular arms, and looked like he could bench-press Willie's car.

"We don't go in the house when Mr. Reggie ain't here," Pinkie Mama said "But he told me it was okay if you got here before he came back to get your things situated upstairs."

Pinkie Kid stepped outside into the sunlight. On second glance, his pants weren't filthy, just badly stained. On third glance, the kid wasn't straight pinkie either. He was a hash brown, a halfie, and it was clear somebody had taken their sex life across the race line with Pinkie Mama.

Halfies weren't all that unusual down south, mostly in the ghettos, but anyone that knew anything about the North knew the rules were different up here—unwritten rules that said a black man getting some recreation with a pinkie woman was good fun while a pinkie man violating a black woman was on the no-no list that could potentially lead to a visit from a Crown-sponsored dip mob.

Dipping was originally used on runaway pinkies, and when slavery ended, The Crown thought it was only appropriate to continue the practice when needed.

Willie remembered reading about dipping in seventh-grade history class. It's a pretty simple process, yet it's some serious shit. That is, if you are white.

What you do is tie a pinkie's hands behind his back and then tie his ankles together. Then you hang him upside down and dip him headfirst in and out of the water until he squirms and shakes. Then you dip him longer and longer...until he doesn't squirm, doesn't shake, and then finally agrees not to live any longer.

Halfie Son stepped closer and Willie immediately thought of those photos he'd seen of Uncle Reggie. It couldn't be more obvious that his uncle had been playing around with Pinkie Mama, because other than being six inches taller and a lot lighter skinned, the resemblance between Halfie Son and Uncle Reggie was tough to ignore.

Just as the door to the little shack started to swing shut, Willie stole a quick look inside and could see a pair of cots that straddled the stove where the food was cooking.

Holy shit. They both live in there.

Willie couldn't imagine getting a good night's sleep with Northern pinkies living so close. But then again, if they were stupid enough to live there, they were probably too stupid to be dangerous. And then he felt a little safer yet, remembering his father telling him he had a family member that was "more than just a little familiar with The Crown."

You go, Uncle Reggie.

What a piece of work he must be. The poor hick farmer apparently wasn't all that keen to the fact that slavery had really ended.

Willie couldn't wait to meet him, knowing these three were the sure thing for some laughs.

WILLIE

Racist Uncle. Things That Go Boom.

Dusty Bones.

Pinkie Mama was strong as hell.

Willie had no idea how long he was going to be staying, so he'd stuffed his suitcase with his gaming system. When he tried to get the suitcase out of his bedroom the previous day, he'd had to drag it by the lift handle before it almost took him down the stairs with it, not to mention the stroke he practically had trying to lift it into the car. It was obviously too heavy for most people to reasonably handle, so he didn't think too much of it.

Until they were out in Uncle Reggie's driveway.

Pinkie Mama jerked the suitcase up and out of the trunk like it was nothing and then passed it to Halfie Son who carried it like it was his lunch pail.

They went back up on the porch and Pinkie Mama unlocked the front door before insisting that Willie go in first, and he did. The greeting area of the old farmhouse smelled like someone unloaded on the place with lemon furniture polish and oil soap. On top of the dark wooden floor was outdated furniture, probably worth a fortune at most antique stores. The old-school phone where you had to put your finger in the number and turn it clockwise, coupled with the rabbit ears on top of the television, made it clear that his uncle wasn't up on technology, but the house itself was spotless and in perfect order. Willie suspected it was Pinkie Mama's work and assumed she wasn't on quite the same pay scale as DeeDee was back in Atlanta.

Pinkie Mama and Halfie Son took their shoes off and Willie knelt to take his off as well.

"You are allowed to keep yours on," Pinkie Mama said.

"Why can't you wear yours?" Willie asked.

Dumb question, genius. Maybe your uncle being in The Crown while these two live outside in a wooden shit shack is a clue.

Neither of them answered and Halfie Son pointed at the staircase, suggesting Willie go up before him. The kid hadn't said a word since they'd met and Willie decided to relabel him Mute Halfie Son. But again, there was an above-average chance the kid had been well schooled in Northern pinkie etiquette, which gave priority status to speaking only when spoken to.

Willie slipped his hand into the front left pocket of his jeans and held his breath until he could feel the baggie of pills. He needed some as soon as possible, but it would have to wait until Pinkies One and Two were out of sight.

Willie led the way upstairs. When they reached the large hardwood landing, three doors stood open. To the right was a decent-sized guest bedroom, followed by the master bedroom (maybe one-tenth the size of his dad's bedroom back home), a small sitting room, and then a fourth door that was closed that most likely led to stairs that went up to that lookout perch he noticed on his drive up. Willie's gut told him that about a century earlier, somebody sat up there to keep an eye out on the field pinkies that didn't work in the lumber mills.

They went into the guest bedroom and Pinkie Mama pulled a dustrag out of her pocket and hustled to the edge of the window to wipe a couple specks of dust off the sill as if somebody had taken a dump on it. He figured whoever trained that woman should be given a gold star.

"Do you mind seeing us to the door?" the woman asked.

"Why?" Willie said.

"We don't like to come in or leave the house by ourselves. Mr. Reggie says it don't look good."

Willie assumed the reason why it didn't look good fell under the same umbrella as the shoe thing. He nodded, walked out of the bedroom, and led them down the stairs to the front door. When they reached the porch, an older gray car, one of those ancient, gas-guzzling, boat-like sedans, was pulling up the driveway. The car stopped and Uncle Reggie leaned out the open window and muttered in that Northern accent of his, "Nancy. Joseph. Come give me a little help now."

Willie had just hit the name lottery and figured it would be prudent to use their real names instead of the pet ones he'd been using.

By the time he and the un-emancipated reached the car, Uncle Reggie was standing and threw his arm around Willie's shoulder to pull him in for a buddy hug.

"Hey there, Willie," he said. "I'm your uncle Reggie."

His uncle was around six one, about Dad's height, but much thicker. He smelled like whiskey and pipe smoke and had dark shit all up under his fingernails—clearly a man that worked with his hands. The whites of his eyes were an unhealthy yellow against his black skin, and his left eye seemed as if it were pinched halfway closed. The same side of his face appeared frozen and drooped when he talked, and Willie suspected that somewhere along the line, his uncle had shaken hands with Mr. Mini-Stroke.

"Nice to meet you, Uncle Reggie," Willie said, not sure if what he was saying was the truth or not. At the end of the day, it didn't really matter.

"It's about time we saw each other," his uncle said. "Shame it took so long."

"Yeah, kind of tough getting together, living so far away from each other."

Actually, it's because you are a hick racist and my dad probably didn't want me around you...

His uncle smiled, and it looked more like a sneer. Despite the accent and tilted face, his voice sounded kind and sincere, nothing like one you would associate with a guy whose favorite color was shiny purple.

Uncle Reggie walked around the back of the car and popped the trunk. There were six brown paper bags of groceries. Nancy took one in each hand and Joseph grabbed two in each of his and they headed toward the house.

His uncle leaned farther into the trunk and pulled two wooden boxes toward him. Each had the word DYNAMITE stamped in bold black letters.

Wow. Real dynamite.

Behind the boxes was a rifle that had scratches all over the stock, but the shiny barrel had been kept clean, making the trunk smell like gun oil.

"This is Varmint Killer." His uncle tapped on the stock of the rifle. "Coyotes, gophers, and other pests know better than to cause problems around your uncle Reggie."

"Cool," Willie said, finding it a little odd the gun wasn't in a case. He was still a little baffled at how friendly his uncle sounded. But again, when you wore a robe with a pointy hood and had guns and explosives in your trunk, you didn't need a mean voice to terrorize white people.

"Ever shoot a gun?"

"Yeah," Willie said. It wasn't a total lie. *Gunrunner3* had a pistol and he was one of the best.

"Think you can handle one of these?" Uncle Reggie pointed at one of the boxes of dynamite.

"Sure," Willie said. When he lifted it, he was pretty sure one of his balls took refuge halfway into his stomach, but after a few seconds it dropped back into place.

Uncle Reggie balanced the other box on his knee while he closed the trunk and Joseph ran out of the house and snatched it away. About halfway to the barn, the box Willie was carrying was getting heavy and it was hard to breathe.

"Let me take that," Uncle Reggie said. So much for the theory that he had suffered a stroke. Both arms were extended as if he wanted to take the box.

"I'm all right," Willie said. He wasn't going to let his uncle's first impression of him be that of a spoiled rich kid weakling, so he kept walking and changed the conversation.

"Where's my father?"

"Medical examiner."

Willie still couldn't understand why he didn't feel sad…why he couldn't feel anything. It had to be the pills that had been short-circuiting his feelings for so long.

"I want to see him."

"Once they get him over to the funeral parlor," Uncle Reggie said. "He didn't want a big shindig. He just wanted a few of us there." His uncle pointed toward a field past the barn. "We are going to have us a little family ceremony and then he wanted his ashes scattered back there. We spent a fair amount of time out there when we were boys."

"Don't I have any say in that?"

"No," he said.

"No?"

"Like I said, I'll show you the paperwork when the time comes. But that paperwork also has some instructions involving you, at least until your eighteenth birthday."

"I obviously have to go back to Georgia."

"In time," Uncle Reggie said. "Your daddy and I didn't always agree on things, but I gave him my word if anything happened to him, I'd do my best to see that his wishes were met."

"What didn't you guys agree on?" Willie asked.

"Different things," Uncle Reggie said. "Brothers don't always think alike."

No shit.

They went inside the old barn and Willie and Joseph put the boxes of dynamite on top of a bunch of other boxes that all looked exactly the same. It seemed like Uncle Reggie was planning on blowing up the world. Willie glanced around and despite the feeling that it could collapse at any second, the barn was spotless, and other than an old tractor and pickup that sat side by side, all the place seemed to be used for was storage.

The three of them went back outside and Willie did another three-sixty, wondering again what all that land was being used for.

"What do you farm, Uncle Reggie?"

"I don't farm anything," he said. "I'm in the landscaping and tree-removal business."

Willie figured a compliment was in order. "Explains why those shrubs and flowers look so good out front."

Uncle Reggie put his hand on Joseph's shoulder and winked with his good eye. "It's all Joseph's work. He's a natural at it. I've been in business since I was twelve and he's tenfold the best I've ever seen."

"The dynamite," Willie said, glancing at the boxes. "Now I get it. It's for tree stumps."

"You're smarter than a tree full of owls," his uncle quipped. "Your daddy said you were a quick one. Said the lowest grade you got since third grade was an A."

"Had an A minus in seventh-grade gym, but pretty close," Willie said.

"Ever seen dynamite go off?"

"No, but I'd like to." Willie was reminded of Dr. Cheever's theory that he had an unhealthy obsession with guns and things getting blown up. Maybe she was right.

"Doubt if we'll be setting anything off tonight, but I'll see that Joseph teaches you how to rig up a stump. Me and him are going to check out a job after dinner if you'd like to come along. If it helps keep your mind off things."

"Sure," Willie said, glancing at Joseph. Good thing he was good at landscaping and blowing shit up with dynamite, because he was never going to make it as a motivational speaker. Willie became motivated to reach in his pill baggie and then stopped, deciding it would be best to wait a bit before getting some additional help to "take his mind off things."

Nancy appeared out of nowhere, and Willie wondered if there was a secret pinkie trap door somewhere in the yard. One that had a ladder that led down to a railroad that was *really* underground or some other top-secret pinkie meeting place from days gone by—days when they'd go off unseen to escape or hide out to cast spells on evil black masters. Willie laughed and both Uncle Reggie and Joseph gave him a look like he was crazy.

Maybe I am crazy…

Nancy walked toward them, holding a couple of bright green apples. She offered Willie one, which he declined, and then gave Joseph one who immediately went to work on it, biting into it like it was the last one that would ever be. Willie couldn't keep his mind out of his basket of pinkie jokes—many of which involved pinkies and their apples. Willie looked at the size of Joseph's arms and paused, imagining what would happen if he did tell a pinkie joke. Regardless, there was no way he would because he wouldn't want to have to explain it three times...

"Get the truck ready before dinner," Uncle Reggie said.

Joseph just kept gnawing on the apple and nodded his head. Willie was curious if maybe he or Nancy knew the pinkie that killed Dad.

Willie took another long look at Joseph and the kid shied away. It wouldn't have bothered Willie if Joseph knew the murderer. But what did bother him was that Joseph still had his mother and Willie didn't. It wasn't fair. Then he thought about his mother and sister lying side by side in holes back in Georgia, nothing but dusty bones in dresses.

Why didn't Dad want to be buried with them?

JOSEPH

The Nice Car. The Big Highway.

A Promise to Mama.

"That sure is a nice car Mr. Willie drives, isn't it, Mama?" Joseph said, peeking out the small window on the side of his and Mama's home. "I don't know what it costs, but I'd like to save up some money and get something like that for me to drive you around in one day."

"Don't you worry about that," Mama said, walking up next to him and putting her arm around his waist. She pulled him closer and leaned her head against his side. "You want to make Mama happy?"

"Yes, Mama." Nothing was more important to him than making Mama happy, and even though he knew what she was going to say, he always let her say it again.

"You just worry about getting you out of Woodruff one day. Car or no car, you get out on that big highway and go south. Go south where people like us are treated better. Leave your mama behind. Get up and go do Joseph. And when you get to doing you, regardless of how long it takes, *then* you come back and get your mama."

"I'll do that," Joseph said, looking at Mama's old dress. He'd buy her a new dress too. Then he glanced back at the fancy car. "Mr. Willie's father died. He must have been real important."

"Must be true," Mama said. "Somebody had to pay for that fancy car."

"Mr. Reggie also said they were going to spread his ashes right here on the farm," Joseph said. Then he looked at the fancy car and at the license plate. "But if the license plate says he is from Georgia, why are they doing that here?"

"Mama's not sure, baby. He probably wanted to be put to rest near his brother."

"I didn't even know Mr. Reggie had a brother. He never talked about him. Why didn't we ever meet him?"

"Because Georgia is far, far away."

"Georgia is down that freeway you always tell me about, isn't it?" Joseph said, remembering it from a map at school. *Interstate 75.* "It's one of the places you might want me to go, isn't it?"

"Nothing would make Mama happier than to wake up one day and know you are there. That you got up to go do Joseph."

"I will," he said with a smile. "And then I will come back and get you, Mama. I promise."

WILLIE

House Rules. The Reverend Jackson Kettle.

Chuckles the Clown.

Willie sat at the kitchen table with Uncle Reggie and Joseph as Nancy carried over three bowls of whatever it was she had been cooking in the pinkie hut. He wasn't prepared to classify it as pinkie food just yet, because at first glance it looked more like just plain Northern food—black-eyed peas with ham in some sort of funky broth. It didn't really matter to Willie because he was hungry enough to eat the north end of a southbound skunk as he tried to remember the race rules and the inconsistencies of how things worked around here:

Nancy and Joseph weren't allowed to come in the house unless Uncle Reggie was there.

Nancy and Joseph had to take their shoes off, but Willie and his uncle Reggie didn't.

Despite those two rules, Uncle Reggie still let a pinkie and her son, *their* son, sit at the table and eat with him.

What the fuck?

"Can you get me a refill, please?" Uncle Reggie said, holding up his empty glass to Nancy.

Willie snickered.

"What's so funny?" Uncle Reggie asked, smiling as well.

"My bad," Willie said. "Was just thinking of something that happened to me a couple weeks ago." Not true. He was actually surprised that his racist uncle used the word "please" when dishing out orders to Nancy. It wasn't like Nancy was going to say *no* or *get off your black ass and get it yourself, Reggie,* or *I'm cutting you off next time you come out to the barn to play the old in and out.*

Nancy took the glass (shocker) and filled it to the top with some cheap, reddish-looking whiskey as Joseph and Willie continued taking turns catching each other staring at one another.

Nancy sat down and Uncle Reggie barked off some bunk to the Lord about being thankful for the food and the opportunity to come together as family and friends. And then he thanked God for all their other blessings and then asked for comfort as they dealt with the loss of Willie's father. Willie couldn't think of anything to be thankful for other than his irritability level dropping from about a ten to a three thanks to the four happy pills he swallowed before he came down to dinner. At the record pace he was going, his two-week supply was going to be more like a one-week supply. Tops.

"You gonna go to summer school?" Uncle Reggie asked, looking at Joseph.

"No," Joseph answered.

Holy shit. Mute Halfie Son, aka Joseph, actually had a voice. It was high and innocent like it belonged to an eleven-year-old instead of a guy built like a linebacker.

"I've decided I'm just not good at it," Joseph said. "I'm not even going to try to go back and start tenth grade in the fall. Wasting my time, I believe."

"You can still do whatever you want," Nancy said. "You just forget about that dumb school anyhow. Not a single child that's gone there ever made it out of Woodruff anyhow. And you know that's all I want for you."

"Tenth grade?" Willie said, looking at the kid in disbelief. He wasn't sure if he was more surprised that Nancy was telling Joseph to leave the plantation right in front of Master Reggie or that Joseph was only supposed to be going into the tenth grade. "How old are you?"

"Nineteen," Joseph said.

Nineteen. He is two years older than me and he hasn't made it out of ninth grade.

The whole summer school thing should have tipped things off that Joseph had the IQ of a houseplant, but now there was no doubt the other pinkie kids weren't peeking at Joseph's paper during test time.

And then another light went on. This one in reference to his uncle telling Joseph he could teach Willie how to use the dynamite.

How far am I going to be from peabrain when he is showing me how to use explosives? Willie made a mental note to be on full alert because it was just a matter of time before one of those sticks of dynamite changed Joseph's name to *Lefty*.

Willie was tired and asked to be excused. Then he went to his room and fell into dreamless sleep until Uncle Reggie came to get him to go check out that job with him and Joseph.

◆◆◆

"I'VE ASKED REVEREND KETTLE to say a few words at your father's service," Uncle Reggie said as they pulled out of the driveway in the old pickup Willie had seen in the barn. The windshield had a pair of spiderweb cracks in it and the leather dashboard was peppered with an army of smoke stains, and though he said the truck was Joseph's, it clearly belonged to Uncle Reggie because it smelled like a combination of stale tobacco and a shower fart.

"Who is Reverend Kettle?" Willie asked as they chugged down the road. His eyes were glued to the mirror on the passenger-side door. The truck had made a quarter-mile rooster tail of dust that had powdered up off Cossit Creek Road, but what he was really looking at was Joseph, who was trying to sit in the bed of the truck. The half-pink idiot had already been pinballed twice from rail to rail as Uncle Reggie's drunk ass hit every crater in the road, and the poor kid had to be using all his strength to prevent from getting ejected over the side.

"Kettle is a good man and I think you will like him," Uncle Reggie said, covering his mouth with his open hand for a couple productive coughs. He studied his hand and then wiped some lung pudding on his dirty jeans, causing Willie to lean closer to the passenger-side door in a state of disgust. "It's his house we are going to. Putting in a deck and needs a handful of trees removed. We are going to do some landscaping around the deck as well."

"What about the people from Georgia?" Willie asked dreamily.

"Whatcha mean?"

Willie thought about the other attorneys and people from his father's office, then DeeDee, and even Dr. Cheever, who hadn't called him in over three hours. Apparently, she was getting hip to the concept that her last fifty voicemails probably weren't going to inspire him to call her back any more than the first.

"Aren't any of them going to be here for the funeral?" Willie asked. "You know, let them pay their last respects and all?"

"Your daddy said family only."

"I'm his only family," Willie said, realizing what he had said. "And you."

"It's what he wanted."

They passed the other house on Cossit Creek, the one with the dog, and Willie noticed old Mack was still chained in that field. Damn thing looked like a statue. Like he hadn't moved an inch since the first time Willie saw him.

"Those people ever let that dog off that chain?"

"Never seen him off it," Uncle Reggie said. "Mrs. Vee is crazier than an outhouse rat and, Lord forgive me for saying, the ugliest woman I've ever seen. Scare the stink off poop. Husband capped himself years back and darn near every time I drive by here I think about shooting that dog to put him out of his misery too."

Willie wondered if maybe people that drove by his uncle's place thought the same thing about Nancy and Joseph. He also thought it was a bit ironic that his Crown member uncle was taking him to a minister's place. Yet another chapter to the crazy-ass rules Uncle Reggie lived by.

"You go to this minister's church?" Willie asked as they passed the T that connected Cossit Creek to Main Street. Then he wondered if maybe Cop Green was down there making sure the pinkies were cleaning up the latest spitball he left for them.

"Every Sunday," he said. "You go to church?"

"No," Willie said.

"Why not?"

"My father went every week. Told me I didn't have to go. That it should be my decision, not his."

"Why don't you go then?" Uncle Reggie asked.

Willie shrugged. He wasn't sure why he didn't go to church, and even less sure if the answer he was about to give would fly or not. His right leg quivered, most likely an involuntary result of losing lung function from that stinky-ass purple smoke coming from Uncle Reggie's pipe.

"I think church is boring," he said. "When I go, I spend half the time staring at the bulletin, counting how many songs are left until the service is over. Plus, as I see it, God hasn't been all that good to me."

"Life been that tough, eh?" his uncle said with a laugh.

It was good to see being a smartass ran in the family.

"I mean, look at me," Willie said. "I'm seventeen and orphaned."

"I understand. When the smoke clears with your daddy's passing, I'd encourage you to try to stay focused on the things you do have, instead of the other way around. Good-looking boy, great head on your shoulders, and when you get your share…you'll have more money than you could ever spend."

"My share?" Willie asked, imagining a pair of sticky hands reaching into his father's till. "I remember you saying the money is being divvied up. Who else is getting some?"

"Your daddy made provisions that I need to make sure are seen to," Uncle Reggie said. "And as I mentioned, I'll show you the paperwork when the time comes, and I know you'll probably make better sense of all that jargon than I will."

"I'd like to see it," Willie said. "But other than what's happening with the money, can I ask who I am going to live with when I go back to Georgia?"

"We will deal with that—"

"Let me guess…when the time comes?"

"Smart boy." His uncle tapped him on the leg. "But back to talking about God. You're welcome to join me Sunday up on the hill. Reverend Kettle delivers a tremendous message. I think he'll keep your attention off that bulletin."

"Sure," Willie said, still finding it hard to believe Crown members went to church. But considering Uncle Reggie's house didn't have cable or a spare television upstairs, he couldn't play video games online, so his only other option was pretty much to stare out the window and watch all that cow-shit-smelling, knee-high grass bend in wind.

They made a right turn at the next T, onto yet another dirt road. About a half mile up, another farmhouse came into view, one similar to Uncle Reggie's, and considering it was the only one in sight, Willie guessed it belonged to the minister.

They pulled into a long gravel driveway and the first thing he noticed was that the house, like Uncle Reggie's, was surrounded by nothing more than grass and rolling hills. Uncle Reggie turned the truck off and Joseph popped out of the back and stood tall and quiet, as if he were waiting for orders. Willie had known the kid for six hours now and still wasn't sure whether he needed Uncle Reggie's permission to talk.

A bald man, maybe in his seventies, came out the front door. Though he was quite thin, he'd clearly been drinking that special Woodruff water that made people tall, because even from a distance, he looked to be an easy six-four, maybe even as tall as Joseph. His head was shiny and clean, and Willie knew if you put an "8" on his bald black head, the first thing you'd want to do is line up next to him with your custom cue stick, call your last pocket, and give it a crisp poke.

He was also a fast walker and he came toward them the way a former military guy would with those long legs working overtime, deliberately covering a lot of ground with each step as if they had the cure for baldness waiting for him in the bed of the truck.

"Hello, Brother Reggie," Kettle said, reaching through the open driver-side window to shake Uncle Reggie's hand. His fingers were long like black railroad spikes and when Kettle smiled, you could see square teeth that were surprisingly white with a neat little gap between the front two. Willie couldn't explain why, but there was something about Kettle's voice that made Willie instantly like him.

Kettle glanced over to Willie and that voice softened.

"And you must be Willie," he said, leaning farther into the car and extending his arm across Uncle Reggie's chest. "I'm Jackson Kettle." Willie's hand disappeared into the minister's hand when they shook. His fingers were the longest in the history of man, literally like fucking cattails.

Kettle didn't give him any of that "your father is in a better place" crap Willie expected to hear from a minister. Something in Kettle's eyes told Willie the minister was sorry about what happened to Dad, truly sorry, making the man even more likeable yet.

Kettle walked to the back of the truck where Joseph stood, and Willie looked again in the passenger-side mirror.

"Joseph!" Kettle said, looking at him eye to eye. "How are you?"

"I'm good, Reverend Kettle," Joseph said, shyly. Willie still couldn't get over that tiny voice of his.

"I appreciate you lads helping me out," Kettle said. "Come on and let's get the truck pulled around back."

Kettle and Joseph walked in front of the truck and Uncle Reggie pulled up and around the back of the house. Kettle had a pretty uneventful backyard. The token barn to go with the farmhouse, no garage, and no barn-matching-pinkie-slave-hut like Uncle Reggie had. Willie immediately noticed that there were yellow lines spray-painted near the far back corner of the house and red stakes around a dozen or so old trees, which Willie guessed were elms. When Kettle turned the other way, Uncle Reggie pulled a leather flask out from under his seat, took a quick swig, and then they got out. It was clear that the booze and smoking had done more than just freeze up the left side of his uncle's face. It had also somehow convinced him that Kettle or anybody else within fifteen feet couldn't smell booze on his breath.

"Those trees had been full of health almost as long as the house has been here," Kettle said. "Even before my granddad built the place." He shook his head in disgust. "Climbed every one of them as a kid. I'm going to hate to see them go. Fell out of two before I was ten and darn near killed myself. Got lucky though." He winked at Willie. "I'm fortunate the falls didn't stunt my growth."

Willie found himself smiling. Kettle wasn't just likeable, but also funny, not exactly the stereotypical Northern black hick minister you'd expect him to be.

Uncle Reggie walked up next to the tree closest to the house, burped, and then pointed at the windows.

"We're gonna have to tarp up the whole back of the house, Jackson," he said. "If not, you're going to need a window company out here after the dynamite goes off."

"Whatever you say, Reggie," the minister said. "When do you think you can start?"

"Pretty busy for a while," Uncle Reggie said. "If you ain't in too much of a hurry, I'll come out and trim 'em down next week and then let Joseph and Willie come back sometime over the next few weeks or so to handle the rest. May be a little earlier."

And Willie? The next few weeks?

Looked like Willie had been nominated to have his first day of employment, but anyone that thought he was going to be sticking around once his pills were gone was out of touch with reality.

"I understand." Reverend Kettle sounded a touch disappointed. "I know you are busy."

"Busy is good though," Uncle Reggie said, turning to Joseph. "Before I forget, we need to go clean things up over at Devil's—" Uncle Reggie coughed, as if he caught himself saying something he shouldn't have. Whatever it was, Kettle seemed to be on to it and crossed his arms in what looked like disapproval. His uncle walked up to Joseph and whispered, "Devil's Drop."

Didn't sound like a place a minister would be too fond of, but Willie really didn't care. He didn't owe Uncle Reggie any favors in terms of joining his workforce and was going to stick to the Michigan agenda he had planned out before he left Georgia:

Funeral.

Figure out who killed Dad.

Somehow deal with it.

Make sure justice would be served.

Look at that legal paperwork to find out when the money comes.

Go back home.

In the meantime, it looked like kiddy-voice Joseph could read his mind. He had a little smile on his face and apparently thought the whole thing was funny.

Uncle Reggie and Reverend Kettle surrounded the first tree and Willie seized the opportunity to walk up next to Joseph. Willie swore the kid knew he had it coming.

"What's so funny, dipshit?" Willie whispered.

Joseph's smile widened and then it faded. "Why are you calling me that?"

The thought of Joseph tearing Willie's head off and punting it over Kettle's house ran through his mind. "I'm just kidding with you. Lighten up."

"Didn't sound like you were kidding. I thought Southerners were supposed to be good folk."

"That's a stereotype. Besides, I really am kidding."

"What's a stereotype?"

"Is this your first day on the planet?" Willie said.

"You kinda looked surprised when Mr. Gibbons said you'd be helping me out," Joseph said. "Sorry. I just thought the face you made looked a little funny. I meant no harm."

"I believe you," Willie said. "Chill out. I thought it was funny too."

Willie knew Joseph was sorry. What he really wanted was for Joseph to pulverize him, right there in front of his uncle and the minister. Because the last time he got in a big white kid's face and did something he shouldn't have, the kid didn't retaliate, and it cost Willie everything.

But Joseph had learned the same thing all pinkies did, particularly the Northern ones, and that was to never lay a hand on a black person. Ever.

Kettle touched one of the trees and then pointed at the fungus that had been eating away at it. "Unbelievable. I sat here forever and watched this ugliness grow and never did anything about it. What's wrong with me?"

"Some things are out of our control," Uncle Reggie said.

"And some things aren't." Kettle gave Uncle Reggie a come-to-the-confessional look that Willie's gut said was a poke at his uncle being in The Crown. "We always wanted to put a deck out here and now we've finally got a good reason."

"There *theeey* are!" a woman shouted. It was a voice that stretched out words. A high-pitched, melodramatic one that belonged to a person that would quickly annoy you. Willie felt like a prophet because when he turned around he knew he'd already called it.

It was Kettle's wife, and Willie almost had to look away when he saw her. If they were going to make a movie and have auditions about Northern belle wannabees, nobody else would show up because she was a lock for the part. She was wearing a yellow dress and a ridiculous matching bonnet that looked like someone folded a pancake over her black head. She weighed an easy three bills but had the strangest body he had ever seen. Her upper body was that of a thin woman, but her lower body started with what had to be a half acre of ass. She wasn't built like a *belle*, but rather a *bell*.

He could smell her perfume from thirty feet away and she had about an inch of makeup on her face, reminding him of a television show he watched as a boy— *Chuckles the Clown*. The fact that the reverend married this woman, or that anyone would, was proof that there is a God.

She walked right past Joseph like he was invisible and was holding her arms open in that corny come-give-me-a-hug country club kind of way.

"You must be Willie," she said.

That makes it official, Willie thought. *Everybody in Podunk knows who I am.*

She was all somber-like, as if Willie were ready to off himself over his father's death. She put her arms around his shoulders and hugged him without letting go, and he felt like his head had been dipped in a perfume bottle.

"Your Uncle Reggie told me you were coming," she said. "I'm Shanice Kettle, but you can call me Auntie Shanice."

Auntie? If she thought he was going to call her that, she needed to be in rehab more than he did.

"Hi," Willie said, unable to say what he really wanted to. Had his father been there, he would have said something rude and then let Dad make an excuse for him.

"Shanice," Reverend Kettle said in an apologetic tone. "You aren't the boy's aunt so he's not going to call you Auntie. Come on now."

Every time the minister opened his mouth, Willie liked him more, and his not-so-better half gave Kettle a look that suggested she'd married beneath her.

"Well, I can at least hang on to this hug then," she said, spinning Willie around. Joseph gave him a sympathetic look and Willie appreciated it. She pulled her head back and Willie could see a little white booger shooting in and out of her nose as she breathed. "For heaven's sake, Jackson. Just look at him. He is in mourning and if it comforts him, he can call me Auntie if he wants."

Had Willie been in mourning, the head rush from the perfume she was wearing would have snapped him out of it. He buddy-tapped her shoulder in that I-really-don't-want-to-be-hugging-you sort of way or how a wrestler would tap the mat saying he'd had enough

"Your father's in a better place," she said, nailing the classic one-liner for the grieving Willie expected from her husband. "Are you okay?"

It sounded like she really didn't give a shit, and Willie couldn't resist the opportunity to test it.

"I think I'm going to hang myself," he whispered loud enough for her to hear, but as he figured, she wasn't paying attention. She let go of him, walked past Joseph again like he was the plague, then held out her hand for Uncle Reggie to kiss as if she were the fucking Queen of Africa.

Uncle Reggie paused, then held out his hand to shake hers. It ended up being one of those handshakes that wasn't a handshake, but more of a meeting of fingertips. She looked at Uncle Reggie like he was a peasant, then turned back to Willie.

"If you need anything at all, you just tell me," she said, waddling over, then pulling him in for another hug. "Were you in town earlier today? I think I saw you."

"Yeah," Willie said.

"What a nice car you have!" She gave the minister a we-should-have-a-car-like-that look and then said, "I saw you talking to Sheriff Green."

Sheriff?

Turned out Cop Green was the boss. Willie knew he was a badass.

"I really like the sheriff," Willie said, turning to Joseph.

Joseph shied away like a dog that had messed the floor. And then Willie thought about how that white woman snatched up her baby girl when she got too close to the sheriff, and how the curb-painting pinkies were ordered to clean up his spit.

And when Joseph looked back at Willie, something in Joseph's eyes reminded Willie of that sad day that had cost him everything. It reminded him of a pinkie he used to know named Lucas.

Willie excused himself over to the truck, reached in his baggie of pills, and took care of business.

When he came back, Shanice Kettle gave him one more hug and went into the house.

Uncle Reggie pointed toward the sky that looked like it was split in two. To the south, fluffy white clouds sat in the air like torn pieces of cotton. To the north, dark clouds rode a cool wind in their direction.

A storm was coming.

MAGGIE

Rainy Days. Potato Soup.

Something Better.

Maggie dumped the bucket of rainwater out the door of their hut and then put it back under the fist-sized hole in the wooden ceiling. She wasn't sure how many times she and Alan had tried to fix the hole over the last year, but it looked like they were finally going to have to spend money they didn't have for a new sheet of plywood.

"I'll bet that black boy that was looking at me today doesn't have a hole in his ceiling," she said. She knelt next to the pot of potato soup Alan had just brought in. Potato soup was what the community had every third day and it wasn't anywhere near as good as the fish or venison they had on the other days. She dipped her bowl in the pot and then sat next to her brother.

"So, you think that just because he was driving the most expensive car we ever seen that he doesn't have any holes in the ceiling where he lives?" Alan said, sitting Indian style while two-handing his bowl of soup. "You're pretty smart."

Maggie rolled her eyes and ducked as thunder boomed outside. "He must be the happiest boy in the world. Can you imagine all the things he must have?"

"About all I can do," Alan said. "I'm twenty-three years old and never seen a car like that. Georgia license plates too. I wonder what brings him to Woodruff."

"I wonder what keeps us in Woodruff." She adjusted the third do-rag she'd put on her head in the previous hour—the latest *dry* one. "What's stopping us from leaving? I've been eating potato soup for seventeen years and have no idea why."

"It's better than eating nothing."

"Barely," she said. "But seriously. What is stopping us from getting out of here?"

"Here we go again," Alan said. "Every time you see someone that has something you don't, you want to leave. You start spouting that same stuff that Joseph talks about. The stuff his mother tells him. How about appreciating what we do have?"

"Oh yeah," she said. "I'm thankful. I mean, after all, this soup and this box we live in would be so hard to find somewhere else."

"How about our friends here on The Row?"

The rain picked up and the bucket was already half full again. Maggie stood, grabbed it, and then pushed open the door. Out in the muddy road, the Johnston kids were laughing and playing in a puddle as the wind made the rain come down sideways. She looked to her left, then to her right, at all the huts in the community. There were probably two hundred of them on both sides of Cossit Creek Road, creating The Row that separated the rest of Woodruff from Devil's Drop. She closed the door without dumping the bucket and wondered if her, her brother, or any of their friends that lived there were capable of something better.

"Think things really are different in the South?" Maggie asked. "Think whites get a fairer shake down there?"

"Don't know," Alan said. "I doubt it. How would Joseph's mother know? She's never been there. Maybe it's stuff Reggie Gibbons is telling her. I mean... why would things be any different? People are people and the same rights we supposedly have here are the same they have there. And there are just as many blacks as there are whites down there. If it were true, and things were better, we'd all be gone, wouldn't we?"

"I don't know," she said. "I just want a better life."

"Nothing wrong with that." Alan wiped his mouth with a small hand towel. "But we don't have it all that bad. Be thankful."

"But nothing is going to get better if we don't get off our backsides and make it happen. I'll bet the whites in Georgia don't live right next to where The Crown has their meetings."

"Come on, now," Alan said. "You know I want what's best for us. Don't be like this."

"I don't want to spend the rest of my life in Woodruff."

"What are you going to do?"

Maggie opened the door back up and dumped the bucket.

"I don't know. But the first chance I get, I will be gone. You can be sure of that."

JOSEPH

Reading to Mama.

Minding Own Business.

Joseph closed the Bible and glanced out the tiny window toward Mr. Reggie's house. There was a light on upstairs and he could see Mr. Willie sitting on the bed in the guest bedroom. It looked like he was just staring at the floor.

"Thank you for reading to me," Mama said.

"You are welcome, Mama," he said, thankful he could read to her. "Mr. Willie is just sitting up there looking at the floor. You think he is okay?"

"You don't worry yourself with that boy. And don't be watching people unless they know you are watching. It's not polite."

"I'm sorry, Mama. I was just wondering."

"He is Mr. Reggie's family, so just be courteous and mind your own business."

"He cursed at me today," Joseph said. "I thought you said Southerners were nicer to white folks."

"Look at me," Mama said, walking right up behind him. He turned around and she put her hand on his shoulder and looked up at him. "You don't concern yourself with the things that boy does. Things come to him. People like us have to go to things, and he don't care about the difference."

"If you say so, Mama," Joseph said. And when he turned to look back up at the window, Mr. Willie was standing at it, looking right at him.

WILLIE

Being Nice. The Woodruff City Building.

Perception. A Reminder.

The next morning, Willie went downstairs and joined Uncle Reggie, who was sitting outside on the porch in an old wicker chair. His uncle clenched his pipe between his teeth and then glanced at his watch before giving Willie a little wink. "Good afternoon, Prince Willie."

He appreciated his uncle's sarcasm.

"Sorry I slept in so late," Willie said. "I guess I'm just not myself right now, Uncle Reggie."

He nodded as if he understood, and Willie laughed inside. If this guy thought sleeping in until eight was late, he would have thought Willie was comatose back home.

"Heat yourself up some of the egg casserole Nancy made and then we will head out to start getting some closure on what happened to your daddy. Are you sure you want to go see him? You don't want to wait until the funeral parlor gets ahold of him and makes him a little more presentable?"

The laughter inside Willie died.

"I'm not hungry," he said. "Let's go now."

Uncle Reggie flipped his wrist over for another glance at his watch and then nodded. "I'll call the sheriff and tell him we are on our way. Reverend Kettle wanted to meet us there for support as well."

Willie held out his cell phone for Uncle Reggie to use and he looked at it like it was an equation from Calculus 5. Uncle Reggie just shook his head and they went inside where Willie waited as his uncle used the old phone. Uncle Reggie was yelling into the mouthpiece as if he'd been taught the farther away the person is, the louder he had to speak. A few minutes later, they got into Uncle Reggie's car, and as they were backing out, Willie saw Joseph step out of the little hut to wave goodbye.

Uncle Reggie waved back, and right before they were out of the driveway, he put his foot on the brake and nudged Willie with his elbow. "He's waving goodbye to you, too, or are you too hoity-toity for that boy?"

"Wow," Willie said, leaning away from Uncle Slave Owner. "Seriously?"

"He's just trying to be nice to you, Willie."

Willie laughed and waved. "There ya go. I'm being nice back. Feel better?"

Uncle Reggie smiled. "A little bit. But you can do better."

Willie shook his head. "And you can't?"

Uncle Reggie shrugged. "I guess we can all do better."

♦♦♦

THE WOODRUFF CITY BUILDING was easily twice the size of any other building around and looked relatively new. It would have fit in better up in Detroit, made mostly of bricks and tinted windows. The street-level windows also had thick black bars on them, leading Willie to believe the jail must be beneath the building. All in all, the place had a hint of seriousness about it that said only those that worked there or had pending legal troubles should enter.

Inside, there was a cream-colored sign against a dark brick wall with black letters and thin arrows pointing in the direction of Sheriff's Station, Mayor's Office, Thirty-Third District Court, and City of Woodruff Medical Examiner.

They made it to the lobby of the medical examiner and Reverend Kettle was there waiting for them. A few minutes later, Sheriff Green walked in. He was wearing those sunglasses and boots, and he didn't say a word to anyone. He shook Willie's hand, then his uncle's, and then ignored Reverend Kettle. Willie guessed with it being a small town and all, the two had maybe had words about how the sheriff treated people. Willie's best guess was that somewhere along the line, Reverend Kettle probably suggested to the sheriff that we are all children of God and that we should treat each other with love and compassion. Then the sheriff most likely hocked a chewy ball of moist tobacco on the floor and invited the minister to go fuck himself.

Despite their apparent differences, Willie appreciated that the minister was there for comfort and the sheriff was there for justice. Willie was extra appreciative that he was feeling the added comfort of the five pills he had dropped before going downstairs that morning to meet his uncle on the porch.

"Sure he wants to know?" the sheriff asked, breaking his silence. One of his gold teeth was a bit shinier than the others.

"Yes," Uncle Reggie said.

Willie knew exactly what they were talking about.

"Tell me," Willie said.

"Cause of death is strangulation," Sheriff Green said bluntly.

Uncle Reggie put his arm around Willie and talked right into his face with that pipe-smoke breath of his. "I'm sorry, Willie."

Sheriff Green continued. "Your uncle told me what you thought might have happened to your daddy and it looks like you were right. Seems some white fella didn't think your daddy did a good enough job representing that Donald Bondy."

"But he was the only one who *tried*," Willie whispered, imagining a pair of white hands collared around his father's throat as Dad choked out the words to his killer: *Stop…please…I did my best…there isn't a white lawyer on the face of the earth that would touch this case…the fact that I'm black could only have helped him…*

"I know he tried," Uncle Reggie said. "But your father is being rewarded now, Willie. He really is in a better place."

Oh yeah, Willie thought. *A way better place. Instead of playing golf or making a guest appearance to chat at some law school, he's tits up in a cooler in the next room.*

"Amen," Reverend Kettle said. "He's in the best of places."

Willie couldn't quite explain it, but because Kettle said it, a little part of him believed that maybe Dad was somewhere better. Then he turned to Uncle Reggie and said, "I thought you didn't know what happened to him?"

"Found out this morning before you woke up," Uncle Reggie said, nodding at the sheriff to take over the conversation. "Figured it would be best for the sheriff to explain."

"We have a suspect in custody, but haven't made that public yet," Sheriff Green said. "And you can rest assured, if he is found guilty, he will be brought to justice."

It hadn't been that long since Willie heard The Crown chanting for *ju-stice* on the courthouse steps over in Detroit. They got what they wanted. The killer, Donald Bondy, was found guilty and he had a date coming with Mr. Gas Chamber. Now, Dad's killer was in custody and Willie took comfort knowing Uncle Reggie and his purple-robed friends would probably be looking for more justice still.

Sheriff Green pointed toward a door that led back to where Dad's body was. Part of the visit was for Uncle Reggie to formally identify the body, while the other part was so Willie could see Dad and begin what Uncle Reggie and Reverend Kettle mutually called the "healing process."

The sheriff opened the door and they walked in. Willie's throat closed and then it felt like fingers made of ice squeezed his heart.

It wasn't like a television show where the bereaved walked into a refrigerated room and then an employee slid the body out in some metal drawer. His father wasn't in some cooler.

He was lying right there on a table in the center of the room.

His arms were at his sides and he was covered with a blanket from his armpits to his feet, which stuck out from the end of the blanket and pointed straight at the ceiling. Though he had to be the most famous corpse in the history of Woodruff, they still had a white tag attached to the big toe on his right foot with *T. GIBBONS* typed in thick black letters. Dad looked like he was taking a nap, except his skin looked a little lighter and you could clearly see bruising or some sort of trauma to his neck. It seemed like it was only a few seconds earlier that Willie had been sitting in the den, playing video games, and Dad had told him he was going back to Detroit for the verdict.

But Dad was dead. Dead at forty-two.

He'd lived eight years longer than Willie's mother and thirty-four years longer than his sister. Willie still wanted to know why Dad wasn't being buried next to them, but it wasn't the time to ask. And then he looked back at his father and an unexplained emptiness hit him, making his buzz disappear. He needed more pills right then, and he knew they wouldn't be as good without Dad alive. Maybe they would never be as good. Dr. Cheever was right about something, but he couldn't put his finger on it. Then he tried to remember the last time he hugged his father. And as much as he wanted to right there, he couldn't, because somewhere inside of him a little voice was telling him that part of himself was dead on that table as well.

Addicts can't survive on their own.

Those were the words he'd forgotten.

Fuck you, Dr. Cheever.

Willie took a deep breath and walked up to the table. Reverend Kettle joined him and quickly took Willie by the arm before covering Dad up completely with the blanket.

"Maybe you shouldn't see too much of him like this," Kettle said, looking at Willie. "Remember something good about him, not this."

Their eyes met, and he could see that Kettle was the real deal. Something about those eyes assured him he was looking out for Willie's best interest, unlike most people he knew, which pretty much covered the whole world.

"Okay," Willie said. Then he put his hand on his father's shoulder and the second he felt his cool skin, he wanted to see the killer.

"Show me the guy that did this," Willie said. "I want to talk to him."

"Ain't gonna happen," Uncle Reggie said.

"Right now," Willie said, looking over at the sheriff. "Is he here in the building?"

"Yes," the sheriff said, "but I'm afraid I can't allow that."

"Why not?"

"I don't think that would be good for you," Uncle Reggie said. "I reckon that fella may say something you wouldn't appreciate." Then his uncle's head tilted. "Or the other way around."

The sheriff's eyebrows lifted well above his sunglasses, and then a peculiar, slightly creepy smirk appeared. "I don't think our suspect will say much of anything to anyone, at least not around here. Maybe we should let Willie have a look. He's practically a grown man now and this is a special circumstance. Let's respect his wishes."

"He's not getting anywhere near that cell," Uncle Reggie said. He looked away, like he was afraid of challenging the sheriff. And then he seemed to regroup and that squinty left eye of his actually widened, waiting for the sheriff to respond.

"Relax, Reggie," Sheriff Green said. "The monitor. We can step over to the station and let him have a look at the suspect through the monitor. No sound. Just a quick look-see and that's it."

"I want to see him face-to-face," Willie said. "I said I want to talk to him."

"Ain't gonna happen," Uncle Reggie repeated. "But if the sheriff says it's all right, you can have a glance at him from the monitor. That's it and it ain't up for negotiating."

Willie nodded, and they headed toward the sheriff's station, which was just a short walk down a poorly lit cinderblock hallway, one that reminded Willie of a portal that connected underground bunkers, maybe like the one they captured Hitler in. Willie paused and shook his head, thinking about that nutjob. He could never figure Hitler out. In the 1940s, New America controlled 75 percent of Europe and before taking over Germany, they decided to step aside and let Hitler do his thing to the Jewish pinkies—to the tune of about six million times.

Once that business was taken care of, the German leader got a little too big for his own britches and got Heil-Mother-Fucking Hitlered right there in his own backyard. The first time Willie saw a photo of Hitler dead was in that same seventh-grade history class where he'd learned about dipping. Willie could remember the picture of his pink ass, creepy little mustache and all, right after they dipped him in front of his headquarters for the whole world to see, hanging by his feet in downtown Berlin.

When they made it over to the sheriff's station, the only other people present were a small woman that appeared to be responsible for dispatch and a pinkie janitor. They walked right past both of them and into Sheriff Green's office. His wall was loaded with all kinds of awards given by Woodruff, the county, and the state, but Willie was already looking at the monitor of the holding cell, and it was loaded with pinkies. Easily a dozen of them were jammed into the cell that was made for maybe five. One of them had killed Willie's father.

"Which one is it?" Willie asked.

Sheriff Green grabbed a little remote and toggled with a knob. The screen widened and blurred, and then came back into focus before zooming in on a pinkie that was crouching in the corner, right next to the toilet. His shirt was torn and blood-soaked, his lips were swollen, his nose looked to have been broken, and both eyes were on their way to shiners. His face was also truly pink, not white, and he'd clearly been crying. Willie's throat dried out again and his heart started pounding. And then he was thankful. Thankful not just for the man that was standing next to him, but also for the group of people he was associated with.

Uncle Reggie.

"Seen enough?" Uncle Reggie asked.

"When is his trial?" Willie asked. "I want to talk to that man."

"No date set for the trial," the sheriff answered. "And I don't think that man's attorney would think too kindly of us allowing you to talk to him."

"Pray for him, son," Kettle said. "I know it's tough, but pray for him and forgive him."

Willie looked at Kettle. He didn't like the minister's idea and even if he did, he knew it wouldn't make him feel any better.

"I hope they let him out on bail," Willie said.

"Why is that?" Kettle asked, sounding surprised.

"Things happen around here to pink pieces of shit like that, don't they?"

"Watch your language," Uncle Reggie said. "Your emotions get you a pass this time."

"Things happen like what?" Kettle asked.

Willie didn't answer. He just turned his head and stared at Kettle. Kettle's eyebrows were raised as if he were curious to hear Willie's answer. And then the minister's face settled and there was no doubt in Willie's mind that Kettle knew what he meant.

Sheriff Green did too. And as they left the room, the sheriff gave Willie a little wink, smiled, and then leaned closer so only Willie could hear.

"Come by Sunday afternoon around two," the sheriff whispered. "Let some dust settle between now and then and keep it between us. I'll be the only one here, and you can park down in the garage. And take it to the bank that when you get back up in here, you can say whatever you want to that pinkie bastard."

Willie didn't care if every pinkie in town had to pick up tobacco spit for the rest of their lives. He and Sheriff Green were on the same page and Willie wanted nothing more than to be there when the pinkie made bail, because he had a feeling Uncle Reggie and his fellow robe wearers would take care of business.

Crown style.

◆◆◆

"Joseph should be back anytime now," Uncle Reggie said as they walked across the front yard. "I'll let him take you out back and give you a test run with the dynamite. After that, I was thinking you two could go and do some weeding out around the stage at Devil's Drop. But I know it's been a tough morning, so we can hold off on that for a few days if you'd like."

"What is Devil's Drop?" Willie asked. "You mentioned it when we were at Kettle's house and then sort of muffled yourself."

"It's where The Crown does business."

"You want me and a half-white guy to go hang out where The Crown does business? Nice."

"You will be fine."

"What if some Crown member shows up?" Willie asked. "They will think I'm in cahoots with Joseph and I'm not a big fan of getting my ass kicked. If I see one of them, what do I do? Should I tell them I know you?"

"There is only one person other than us that will show up there in broad daylight and he will know you are working with me."

"Who is that?"

"Don't worry about that and I certainly understand if you aren't up to it."

Willie considered it. A close-up of The Crown's stomping grounds would be cool, particularly when all he'd been thinking about was them dealing with the pinkie fuck he had seen at the sheriff's station.

"I'll go," Willie said. "I'll help."

"Appreciate it," Uncle Reggie said. "Joseph and I normally knock it off in about an hour, but considering you never worked a day in your life, you won't be there any more than three or four hours."

"Very funny," Willie said. "If you'd like, I can change my mind about helping out."

"Your help is much appreciated. Now back to the dynamite. As you are aware, it is serious stuff. Be careful and pay close attention to Joseph."

"Dynamite is illegal in Georgia. Bunch of guys got in trouble over near the Alabama border not that long ago. I'm pretty sure they were charged as terrorists."

Terrorism was frowned upon. It hadn't been five years since half the Middle East was turned into a parking lot. Willie remembered watching the outcries on the news from all the pansy liberals looking out for the women and children over there. Their voices were never heard because the powers that be had determined that the women gave birth to the little ones, and the little ones eventually grew up to be terrorists. It had taken less than a half an hour for the air strikes to wipe out two countries. Millions died, but there hadn't been a terrorist attack or anything that has even resembled one since. The land ultimately became one of the best resorts in the world. In fact, Dad was going to take some time off once the Bondy case ended and the two of them were going to go over there for a long weekend.

"Dynamite is illegal here too," Uncle Reggie said. "But I've been using it at least once a week for thirty years and it ain't exactly the quietest stuff, so I reckon it ain't much of a secret."

"I'm guessing Sheriff Green lets you slide?" Willie asked. "He seems to be the final word on just about everything around here, eh?"

"Known each other since we were in diapers," Uncle Reggie said. "Plus, I ain't hurting anybody with the stuff, not to mention he and I along with your daddy did tree removal together when we were teenagers. He knows the stuff every bit as good as I do."

Willie could see the old pickup coming toward them down Cossit Creek, its engine in full labor, chugging louder and louder the closer it came. Joseph's dumb ass was behind the wheel and when he pulled in the driveway, he drove all the way back behind the house.

"How long have they lived here?" Willie asked, pointing at the little red shack Nancy and Joseph called home. He guessed the answer would be close, if not exact, to the number of years it had been since Uncle Reggie knocked up Nancy.

"Both of them been at the farm their whole lives," Uncle Reggie said.

"Even Nancy?" Willie stared at the tiny red house. "Nancy has to be in her mid-thirties. The little shack is that old?"

"No," Uncle Reggie said. "That was built for them about six months before Joseph was born. But Nancy, her parents, and their parents' parents lived here too. Worked here forever."

"Slaves?" Willie wondered how in the world Dad ended up being such a pacifist while his brother was still into the whole free-help thing.

"Yes, sir," Uncle Reggie said. "Her grandparents were slaves and her parents were as well when they were young. But other than the mill, jobs aren't exactly growing on trees around here for white folks and The Row people get first crack at the mill because they live so close to it."

"The Row people?"

"Low-income housing. It's not too far from McLouth Steel and Lumber. They can walk to work from where they live."

Lumber, Willie thought. Pinkie slaves in the south took over for the black slaves in cotton, but the Northern ones worked in the lumber industry.

"Anyhow," his uncle said. "Nancy's family sort of just stuck by to help out with things around here. Mostly corn and beans, but your granddaddy had enough of farming and went into the tree-removal business before he died and I took over. Either way, I thought Nancy was going to be the end of things, but when Joseph showed up, I sort of became obliged to take care of them."

What a stand-up guy.

Willie's father would have hooked Joseph and Nancy up with tickets to Freedomland, but not Uncle Reggie. In fact, if the tree-stump-removal business needed any more employees, he could just drag Nancy out for a little roll in the hay and presto, hash brown in the oven.

"Aren't you worried about them...I mean, for your safety?" Willie asked. "We have been pissing whites off for so long it seems like something is bound to happen. I mean, just look at my dad."

"Your daddy is a little different. He had a bigger audience. Mess with a few bees, nothing's gonna happen. Poke at a hive, you're likely to get stung."

"Dad wasn't poking at any hive," Willie said. "But you aren't afraid of them at all?"

"Afraid of Joseph and Nancy?" Uncle Reggie asked with a little chuckle. "Why would I be afraid of them?"

"I don't know," Willie said. "Joseph's a big dude. Seems harmless, but sometimes the nicest dog can bite. If he woke up on the wrong side of the bed, it may take a couple of pops in the kneecaps from Varmint Killer to slow him down."

"Truly harmless," Uncle Reggie said. "He ain't the sharpest knife in the drawer, but he's a good boy. Wouldn't hurt a fly. In fact, probably the nicest human being I know."

"Why don't you let them in the house when you aren't home?" Willie asked, surprised a Crown member referenced a pinkie as human. A lot of them even used Biblical references to suggest whites *weren't* human.

"Makes things easier," Uncle Reggie said with a little roll of the eyes, even the bad one. "I 'spect you already know things are a little more segregated up here than where you are from. Most don't take too kindly to whites up here and it wouldn't look good with them traipsing in and out of the house with me not here. Frankly, I don't care what they do, but perception can cause as many problems as the actions themselves, for both them and for me."

"I see." Willie really didn't see because what his uncle said didn't make any sense.

"But you are safe," Uncle Reggie added. "They ain't gonna hurt you."

"I ain't afraid of Joseph, I just wondered if you were."

"Sure about that?" Uncle Reggie asked with an accusatory smile. "You will like him once you get to know him. Maybe you ought to leave all those preconceived notions of yours checked at the door. *Your* perceptions, if you know what I mean."

"You fucking serious?" Willie asked. "Me?"

"We don't talk like that around here, Willie. Am I clear?"

"Sorry," Willie said. "It's just a bad habit I have."

"I understand." Uncle Reggie lit his pipe. His lips puckered (mostly the right side of them) a few times and smoke came out his nostrils.

Joseph came around the side of the house. He was shirtless and wearing a beat-up pair of coveralls that were way too short. He had on a pair of high-top sneakers that had to be ten years old, and even with the shoes, he looked like a textbook pinkie from the slave days, standing there with a vacant look on his face and waiting for orders.

"Want me to show him?" Joseph asked. "I got it hooked up already."

"Please," Uncle Reggie said, turning to Willie. "Just gonna let you hear the dynamite go off first so you can get used to it and then he can show you how to do the whole shebang when you go over to Kettle's place. Once again, assuming you are up to it, that is."

"I'm ready," Willie said.

He lied. He wasn't anywhere near ready. Because Joseph reminded Willie so much of that other pinkie boy. The one from so long ago.

Lucas.

It's when all of Willie's troubles started.

WILLIE

Earplugs. Twenty Questions.

Animals Gone Bad. Used to Did.

Joseph and Willie walked around the side of the house and headed toward the barn. Neither of them said a word and Willie made sure that he didn't walk too far in front of or behind Joseph. They stopped at the old pickup truck and Joseph grabbed a gallon-sized jar of nails out of the front seat. Willie then followed Joseph into the barn where he put the nails on a shelf and grabbed two tiny plastic bags of what Willie guessed were yellow earplugs. He handed Willie one and smiled.

"I don't always use these, but you may want to if you've never heard this stuff go off before. But remember, you always want to use them if you are pretty close to it."

"I've heard it go off before," Willie said. Pure bullshit.

"Okay."

Willie figured he could have told Joseph he held dynamite in his hand and watched it go off and the kid probably would have believed him.

"You like Georgia?" Joseph asked.

"It's okay," Willie said. "Been there before?" Dumb question.

"Never been anywhere," Joseph said. "You are up here for your daddy, right?"

"We playing twenty questions or something?"

"What's that?"

Willie wasn't sure if it was Joseph's first day on earth or if he'd never quite counted to twenty before. "It's a game."

"I'll play if you teach me," Joseph said.

Willie still couldn't match the kid's voice with his body. He sounded like he was in second grade. "Yes, I'm up here for my father," Willie said. "My father died."

"Sorry for your loss," Joseph said. "But I don't understand. If you're from Georgia, why are you up here then?"

It was clear that Joseph was paying closer attention to his and Uncle Reggie's conversation about Willie's father than he ever did to his teachers at school. Dad's death had to be fresh news to Joseph and he must be oblivious to the trial because there wasn't a satellite dish on top of the little red shack nor was there a newspaper in sight. And Uncle Reggie sure as hell wouldn't have talked about the trial, particularly with The Crown being there and all.

"My dad died up here," Willie said. "He was killed. He was Reggie's brother and my uncle is helping with his affairs."

Joseph nodded as they walked out of the barn.

"You never met my dad?" Willie asked. "He never came around here?"

"Not that I know of," Joseph said.

"And you never heard about a famous lawyer getting killed?"

"No," Joseph said.

They went behind the barn and then to a little clearing in the high grass. Joseph knelt and fiddled with some wire and then with what Willie guessed was a detonator box—the old-fashioned kind with the handle that you press on, just like the one in cartoons where the dumb-ass dog plots to kill the cat and ends up, in some fashion or another, blowing off his own balls instead.

"You like living here?" Willie asked. He wasn't quite sure why he asked it, but was even less sure of why he was talking to Joseph so much, or any pinkie, for that matter.

"I'm thankful to live here," Joseph said. "Mr. Reggie is good to me and Mama."

"It sounds like you are giving up on school, eh?" Willie asked.

"Yeah. I ain't too good at some stuff, so I was supposed to take two classes over so I could still graduate in a couple years. Ain't gonna do it."

"Football?" Willie said, without thinking. Again. The kid was the size of a tree and Willie guessed it was his only chance of ever leaving Uncle Reggie's backyard and the world of explosives. "You are a big dude. Did you play?"

"I used to did."

Of course. He *used to did*.

Willie still couldn't figure out why they let Joseph play with dynamite. Or how he made it into ninth grade. "Why don't you play anymore?"

"I broke Timmy Finnegan's leg while we were practicing. He was my friend and I didn't want to hurt anyone else, so I stopped playing. Plus, there is too much to be done around here."

"Don't you want to get out of here one day?"

"I'm gonna join up with a landscaping crew one day," he said, pointing back at the bushes and flowers that surrounded the house. "I like doing that and I think it's about the only thing I'm good at."

"You really did that?" Willie asked. There was no denying the kid was beyond good at it. The landscaping around the joint looked like it was done by twenty professionals. It was perfect.

"Yeah," he said. "Mama always tells me I should make like a crow. Just get up and leave. And that I should forget about her and forget about Mr. Reggie. And that I should go south and never look back. And once I get settled, I can come back and get her. She says I can do whatever I want."

Willie remembered her saying something like that at dinner, but Mama was full of shit. It would take an act of God or charity for this kid to ever make it off Uncle Reggie's farm. Even if he did, he wouldn't know the difference between north and south and would probably end up in the Upper Peninsula, working at a logging mill like his ancestors.

Not exactly like them. At least he'd be getting paid.

"Put your earplugs in," Joseph said.

"I don't like being told what to do."

"Sorry," he said. "From this close it's probably best that we put earplugs in."

"I guess if there is anything I'd like less than being told what to do, it would be not knowing I was being told what to do, so I'll put the earplugs in."

Joseph looked at him like he was speaking Chinese and just stood there and waited to see if Willie was going to say anything else before he could take his turn talking.

"See that stump?" Joseph asked, pointing a thick finger about thirty yards from them.

"Yeah," Willie said.

"Ready?"

"Yeah." Willie wasn't sure what he was supposed to be ready for.

"Say goodbye to the rot," Joseph said as he pushed down on the handle. The boom sent Willie to his knees.

"Holy shit!" Willie yelled, followed by a little laugh. "That was awesome!"

Joseph laughed at Willie and when Willie stood, he looked back at the stump and it was gone.

"You should have seen the look on your face," Joseph said, still laughing.

"Hey, Cuz," Willie said, tapping Joseph on his chest with his index finger. The *Cuz* was an inside joke that Joseph was too stupid to ever solve. "Not a huge fan of being laughed at either."

"Sorry, Mr. Willie," he said.

Willie caught himself smiling. The kid really was harmless, not a confrontational bone in his body.

"No biggie." Willie figured there was no harm in being nice back. "And will you quit calling me Mr. Willie? Save that master shit for my uncle."

"White people don't ever say *master* anymore," Joseph said. "It ain't funny."

"Sorry, man," Willie said, and he actually was.

Joseph just stared at him, and Willie thought about the occasional news blurbs he'd seen where lions maul their trainers or those DVDs for sale on late-night television—*Animals Gone Bad*—or something like that where harmless things like deer get cornered and end up ripping someone a second asshole.

Willie held his breath as he waited for Joseph to accept his apology. He hoped he hadn't really pissed the kid off because now Willie had a choice not to be mean. *Not like the Lucas thing...*

Uncle Reggie came around the corner carrying his rifle, good ole Varmint Killer.

"Mr. Reggie can shoot a gnat off an apple at fifty yards," Joseph said.

"Don't know about that," Uncle Reggie said with a little laugh that morphed into a productive cough. He cleared his throat and spit a nice wad of lung yogurt into the grass that would have made Sheriff Green envious. "I can maybe hit a gnat at forty yards, but we aren't gonna do no shooting today."

Willie crossed his arms. It would have been cool blowing shit up *and* shooting stuff on the same day.

Uncle Reggie handed Joseph the gun.

"Been a while since we cleaned it," he said. "Let's get her shined up real good. By the way, don't want you boys out to Devil's Drop today. Changed my mind. Wait a couple more days and then get her knocked off."

"Will do, Mr. Reggie," Joseph said, shrugging at Willie. Then he leaned in and whispered, "I don't have to call you it, but I still better call him *mister*."

Willie shook his head and wondered if Joseph would ever be able to do his own thing, something where he wouldn't have to call anybody *mister*. Maybe Nancy was on to something. Maybe Joseph could go down south and fix shrubs and make everything pristine at some Georgia mansion.

Willie could already see Joseph and the homeowner making small talk:

Wow, young man…great work. Where did you learn your trade? Your accent suggests you once lived in the North…

Yes, Joseph would say, proud that he didn't have to call the man *mister.* Then he would say, *You are right about the accent. I don't live in Michigan anymore… but I used to did.*

REGGIE

Piece of S - - t.

"You just keep a good eye on him," Demetrius said.

"I will," Reggie replied. What he really felt like saying was something along the lines of *"Quit telling me what to do,"* or *"Go get yourself killed stopping a bank robbery you piece of shit."* But he didn't like to curse, and saying something like that to a loose cannon like Sheriff Demetrius Green was just plain dumb.

"I know he is your nephew," Demetrius said. "But I can't tell if his diluted Southern thinking and our way of thinking are quite on the same page. Pretty sure he's one of us, but just watch him."

"He's a good boy," Reggie said. "Been through a lot. There is nothing to worry about."

"Don't know about that," Demetrius said. "I was watching the way he was looking at our suspect in that jail cell. There's something in Willie's eyes that is... well, let's just say I think he's different."

"Maybe you shouldn't have let him see the suspect."

"I wanted to see how he'd react."

"Okay."

"Just keep an eye on him."

"Will do," Reggie said.

"All that aside," Demetrius said, "I think the boy has potential to join us."

Demetrius didn't ever think anyone had the potential to join The Crown. Everybody knew he never recruited a single man because the process was beneath him. He left it up to everyone else to bring in new men.

"He ain't joining anything," Reggie said. "The least you can do is respect that."

"Just keep an eye on him," Demetrius said.

"Don't have to tell me four times. I'd appreciate you respecting that as well."

"Sure." Demetrius shook his head and then spit some tobacco into the dirt and gravel, a little too close to Reggie's feet. "Whatever you say, Reggie. Whatever you say."

WILLIE

The Row. Devil's Drop.

Love Your Neighbor.

It was the first time Willie had gone the other way down Cossit Creek Road, past his uncle Reggie's house, and farther away from Main Street. They were in his uncle's sedan and Willie wasn't sure what was bothering him more, his decision to go to church or the combo smell of booze and smoke that filled the car. The egg-sausage breakfast that Nancy made was tasty as hell but had Willie feeling a little gassy, so he was half tempted to press a retaliatory fart off to even the smell score.

He glanced at his watch. Unless church was at ten in another Woodruff, they had left way too early.

"Isn't church at ten?" he asked.

"Reckon I want to show you something before we get there."

"What?" Willie asked.

Uncle Reggie didn't answer and, despite not liking being ignored, Willie didn't make a big deal of it.

They drove for another mile and the rain from a couple days earlier made Cossit Creek seem like a different road without the rocks and dust flying everywhere. Willie also noticed the terrain becoming gradually hillier. With the hills came more empty fields, but unlike those back near Uncle Reggie's and the other side of Main Street, these fields were separated by clusters of trees that became progressively thicker until the fields disappeared and Cossit Creek Road was surrounded by nothing but forest.

They came to the top of a steep hill and three deer meandered out into the middle of the road. Uncle Reggie slowed and one of the does came to within a few feet of Willie's window. The other two frolicked into the woods and the doe just stared at him. Its nose was jet black and moist and its eyes were like shiny brown marbles. Willie reached his hand out the window to touch it. It took a step closer and snorted, scaring the crap out of Willie, who quickly pulled his arm back in the car.

Uncle Reggie laughed. "She ain't gonna bother you."

Willie laughed as well. The deer stepped back and then joined the other two in the woods. "Never been that close to one before."

"You'll get used to 'em around here. Darn things are everywhere in Woodruff."

Uncle Reggie tapped the brakes as they went down the hill and then shifted the gear on the old car until they made it back up to the top of the next hill. From that point, it took about three seconds for Willie to realize where all the pinkies in Woodruff lived. And what Uncle Reggie meant by *low-income housing*.

"This must be The Row," Willie said.

"Correct. You certainly aren't afraid to pay attention, are you?"

"Not bad for a kid diagnosed with ADHD."

"What's that?"

"Nothing," Willie said. The diagnosis was absurd. He didn't have any attention issues. He just didn't give a shit about what anyone had to say, not to mention it was a free shot at some supposedly amazing medication. He only took a few of the ADHD pills and didn't like how they made him feel. It messed up the effect of the stuff he already took, so he ended up giving them to Evan in exchange for some more pain pills.

Shanty after shanty lined both sides of the road. They reminded Willie of those things ice fisherman sit in on frozen lakes. They were maybe half the size of what Nancy and Joseph lived in and appeared to be made of plywood with some sort of black tarp covering the roofs. They were no more than ten feet apart, had no lawns, and the spaces that separated the dwellings from the road were littered with hundreds of muddy puddles, additional aftermath from the storm. Willie rolled his window up, realizing that he and his uncle were outnumbered by easily five hundred (far exceeding his two-to-one rule, which he'd already violated with Joseph and Nancy) and it was obvious Uncle Reggie knew what was going through his head.

"Relax," he said. "They aren't going to bother you either."

"Let me guess," Willie said, "I'll get used to them too because the dang things are everywhere?"

"Not everywhere in Woodruff," Uncle Reggie said. "Everywhere up here though."

"They all work at the mill?"

"Most of them," his uncle said. "Others do what they can to get by. Odd jobs around town or out at some of the farms. They pool their resources to keep the community going."

"Community?" Willie said. "This place is a shithole."

"Willie, I'd appreciate if you wouldn't talk like that. Is that asking too much?"

"Sorry," Willie said. He pointed, and he could see his uncle's eyes follow his finger. An older pinkie, maybe around sixty, was buttoning up his pants and walking out of the woods behind one of the shanties. "I wonder where he was."

Uncle Reggie smiled and tapped him on the leg. "Lord, forgive me for saying this, but I'm pretty sure he is coming from the shithole."

"Can you please watch your language?" Willie said.

"Well done," his uncle said.

Pinkies sat on wooden crates in front of the homes and stared. Most of them were fanning themselves from the early morning humidity and kids were everywhere.

First comes love, then maybe comes marriage, then comes pinklette in a baby carriage. Except nobody in The Row can afford a baby carriage.

"You sure we are safe here?" Willie asked.

"You really don't get it, do you?"

Willie considered the question and the possibility the ghetto people knew Uncle Reggie was in The Crown.

"I'm guessing they know who you are?"

"Almost all of them. But that doesn't matter. They aren't going to hurt anyone."

"Dad probably thought that too," Willie said. "That didn't turn out too well. And I have to tell you. I still don't understand why his funeral is so small and why he is being put to rest up here."

"I told you I'll show you the paperwork when the time comes."

"I just want to make sure justice is served and get the whole thing over with."

"Me and you both," his uncle said. "There is nothing that would make me happier."

Willie thought the way his uncle said *nothing* was a little odd but decided not to press the issue.

White children ran in and out between the huts, chasing each other until they noticed the two men in the big car. Even though the pinkies knew who he was, Uncle Reggie's ride felt like it served as some sort of pause button, causing most of the pinkies to temporarily freeze and stare until the car passed. A little pinkie boy, maybe two years old with snot running down his face and only wearing what looked like a burlap diaper, scurried back into the arms of his big-titted mother. The mother's hair was up in a bun and she was wearing what looked like a paper dress. When she picked the boy up and turned sideways, Willie guessed she was easily seven months into making another baby.

I wonder if she knows what causes that...

The Row made the ghettos back in Georgia look like paradise and Willie wondered what these people did when it got cold.

"How do they stay warm in the winter?" he asked. "Things get pretty vicious up here around December, don't they?"

"Ain't easy for them," Uncle Reggie said. "Gets well below zero and the community will usually lose a few little ones each year. State doesn't seem to be in much of a hurry to do anything about it. Particularly in these parts."

Two men were up on the roof of one of the shanties, trying to do some type of repair. Willie recognized one of them as the good-looking dude with the top teeth missing that had to pick up Sheriff Green's spit out in front of the ice cream shop. The other was a thirtysomething that looked like he hadn't eaten or bathed in a year.

In front of the next hut, two teenaged pinkie boys just stood there with their arms crossed. The smaller one, most likely the little brother, was wearing pants (certainly hand-me-downs) that were too big and pulled up so far you could lay him on his stomach and park the front tire of your bicycle between his ass cheeks. Regardless, the sight of them somehow made Willie nervous because there was more than a fair share of truth to the oldest white joke in the world—the joke that inspired his two-to-one rule.

What do you call a black man with two white men?

Victim.

Another fifty feet down the road, four women came out from between two other shanties. The three on the left each gave Willie a "what the fuck are you staring at" look as the one on the far right smiled. The smiler was Hot Pinkie Woman, the other member of the tobacco clean-up team. Willie smiled back and it didn't go away until he and Uncle Reggie made it all the way out of the ghetto.

They drove another quarter mile down the heavily wooded road before the distinct smell of sulfur began to fill the car. Willie wondered if perhaps Uncle Reggie snuck a whiskey fart out on him or perhaps even shit himself. It was flat-out brutal.

"I want to show you Devil's Drop," Uncle Reggie said. "I was second-guessing letting you go down there with Joseph to work, but the more I think about it, I figure it may even be good for you."

"Good for me?" Willie said, wondering who in the hell came up with the name Devil's Drop...no pun intended.

"Your daddy said you are a bit taken by The Crown," Uncle Reggie said.

Willie wasn't embarrassed to admit it. He wondered if his uncle could hook him up with some sort of temporary membership to see justice served on Dad's killer. *Perhaps a nice little dipping...*

Cossit Creek Road started heading back up yet another hill, higher than the one Pinkieland was on, and when they hit the top, Uncle Reggie pulled the car over to the side of the road, right next to a little opening in the trees.

His uncle got out of the car and reeled his index finger at Willie.

Willie opened the door and realized the smell wasn't coming from Uncle Reggie. It was everywhere outside—and the insane humidity immediately made it feel like the stink was sticking to him.

"What's that smell?" Willie asked.

"There are those that would say The Crown," Uncle Reggie said. Pretty honest statement for a card-carrying member. "But it's the sulfur in the water down where I'm about to show you."

Uncle Reggie waved him on and they walked across a couple pieces of plywood, reinforced with two-by-fours that had been stacked on top of each other, serving as a makeshift bridge across a narrow ditch. They walked into the woods, following a thin path, until they came to what was damn near the edge of a small cliff. Willie's fear of heights clicked on, making him want a handful or two of pills, and Uncle Reggie pointed down below them.

"Welcome to Devil's Drop."

Well beneath them, in a valley, was a clearing that had been cut out of the woods. It ran from left to right and was about the size of a football field, one with nothing but solid yellow grass, half dead from being trampled. The far side of the field was surrounded by cattails and swamp that ran away forever. The right side of the field ended at the base of the valley, and Willie could see what looked like a road or entrance that had been whittled down the hillside through the trees.

At the opposite side, or the very left end of the field, was a platform or stage. It backed up against the trees at the edge of the valley and was maybe fifty feet long. The deck or floor of the stage had to be easily fifteen feet high, built on top of old stone walls that looked like they'd been there forever. Missing stones created holes that littered the walls, making Willie wonder how the whole thing didn't collapse. Against the wall closest to them, he noticed a ladder that led up to the deck.

Across the deck, in the back corner, was a tiny wooden hut, about the size of Nancy and Joseph's place, with thick chains across its door. In front of it, at the very corner of the stage, what looked like gallows leaned over the edge of a dark and shadowy pond. The water looked cold and was littered with algae and lily pads, making Willie think of bluegill and frogs and…

Holy.

Fucking.

Shit.

That's for dipping.

A chill danced across Willie's back as he wondered how many pinkies had met their maker in that pond. He could only imagine the panic and terror they had felt as they tried and failed to take just one more breath, only to feel their lungs fill with that stinky-ass water.

Willie noticed a narrow stream that flitted from the far side of the pond into those never-ending cattails. Above the swamp, in the distance, he noticed the upper edge of smokestacks.

"What are those smokestacks for?" he asked.

"McLouth Steel and Lumber," Uncle Reggie said. "Been there about a hundred and something years. Some of the first white slaves were put to work there cutting trees that came in off the boats. They still do their thing there, but now they get paid a little for their efforts."

"I'm sure it's a *little* little," Willie said.

"Reckon that's true. Spooky as heck over around that factory. Kinda like you can still sense some of the unhappiness that had gone on there way back when. But again…it could also be from some of the stuff that blows over there from what's happened—*and still goes on*—right below us here."

Willie perused the open field that made Devil's Drop, still blown away by the whole thing. You'd never know it was where The Crown did their business. It'd be easier to believe a small fair had set up shop, ran for a long weekend, and then left.

Except for the cars and trucks that had clearly been burned. He wasn't sure how he'd missed them. There were maybe twenty of them lined up along the near edge of the field, burned beyond recognition.

"What's with all the car carcasses?" Willie asked. "I'm guessing The Crown wasn't roasting marshmallows."

"Dynamite," Uncle Reggie said. "Crown blew them up. A lot of noise and a lot of fire. A little extra entertainment for the one to two thousand that usually come to the meetings."

"Two thousand?" Willie said.

"Yes, sir," Uncle Reggie said. "From Toledo all the way up past Detroit, if you are in The Crown, you attend meetings here."

Willie couldn't take his eyes off the charred remains of the vehicles. "Who do the cars belong to? Some of the people that get dipped?"

"I'm not going to touch that question with a ten-foot pole," Uncle Reggie said. *That means yes. Holy fuck.*

"Sure are a lot of stones missing on those walls," Willie said, looking back at the stage. "Looks like it's about ready to come down."

"Been like that for fifty years. And probably will be for another fifty."

"What's that little shack up on the stage for?" Willie asked.

"Trio," Uncle Reggie said. "Three highest-ranking Crowns. They are The Crown brain trust and they gather in there before meetings start. And once everyone arrives, they come out and the show begins."

Willie had read about the Trio and had seen more than his fair share of photos on the internet. Each region of The Crown had three leaders. Instead of wearing shiny purple robes with black stitching, the Trio wore shiny black robes with purple stitching.

"When do they meet?" Willie asked.

Uncle Reggie laughed. "Meetings aren't exactly posted in the newspaper, son."

"The police just let them come out here and do their thing?"

"I'm not going to touch that question with a ten-foot pole either," Uncle Reggie said.

Willie guessed that maybe Uncle Reggie was hinting that some law enforcement wore purple robes as well, law enforcement like Sheriff Green, but getting into particulars was probably member taboo.

"If I find out when they meet, can I come sit up here and watch?" Willie asked.

Uncle Reggie shook his head as if a smart kid had just asked a stupid question. He pointed down into the opening.

"Not unless you want to go in that pond over there. Headfirst."

"I don't think so," Willie said.

"You know what dipping is?" Uncle Reggie asked.

Willie nodded.

Uncle Reggie put his hand on Willie's shoulder. "I reckon it's best that other than helping Joseph clean up down there, you stay clear of this place, okay?"

"Okay," Willie said. "But can you just take me down there real quick? I want to see it up close."

"You and Joseph will be straightening up down there soon enough."

Willie's eyes slowly followed that yellow grass from the very front of the stage all the way to the other end and the little man-made road that spilled out of the trees. "The mouth of that road over there. Am I correct in assuming that's how everyone comes and goes out of Devil's Drop?"

"You assumed correctly. Except most wouldn't call that the mouth."

"Where does it start? Cossit Creek is the only road out here, isn't it?"

"Yep," Uncle Reggie said. "We passed it. Ain't that hard to see. You prolly just weren't looking. Cuts straight down through the trees. You will see it when you and Joseph go down."

"I can't believe Joseph goes down there."

"I'm the only landscaper in Woodruff. Been keeping things straight down there for years. He works for me, everybody knows that, and I need all the business I can get."

"Still can't believe Joseph goes down there. It's crazy."

"Nobody gonna hurt that boy."

"Where is his pride? He wants to help *them*?"

"He is helping me."

Same thing.

"One more question," Willie said.

"What's that?"

"There's about a trillion acres of farmland around here. Why does The Crown meet so close to where all the whites are?"

Uncle Reggie pulled him close in a fatherly way that reminded Willie a bit of Dad. His uncle smiled with those yellow teeth and then the smile vanished.

"Because they can."

◆◆◆

FIRST CHURCH OF WOODRUFF was perched on the highest point in town at the absolute dead end of Cossit Creek Road, out in the middle of nowhere, overlooking Lake Erie to the east, thousands of acres of trees to the west, the Detroit skyline in the distant north, and the well-hidden valley to the south…that gathering place for purple-robed pinkie haters known as Devil's Drop.

Willie laughed to himself and wondered if there was a *Second* Church of Woodruff and if it was built specifically for whites.

Uncle Reggie said the church was as old as the town, and Willie wondered how many times the wooden exterior had been repainted to keep it looking so pristine. The steeple was tall, easily forty feet high and centered perfectly on the roof above the entrance. After they parked, Willie read the words that were spelled out in big block letters inside a glass-cased box on the lawn:

FIRST CHURCH OF WOODRUFF
REVEREND JACKSON KETTLE
"3 NAILS 1 CROSS 4 GIVEN"
SUNDAY SERVICES 8 AND 10 A.M.
AA MEETINGS M–F 7 A.M.

The first thing Willie did was study the program he had been given to see how much material was between the beginning and what would certainly be his favorite part of the service, the end. It didn't look too bad. A few songs, an offering, a couple readings—including one from Matthew—a message from Reverend Kettle, and then a baptism.

How many of the men here were in The Crown? Then Willie smiled, imagining his uncle going to the lectern to lead them in an opening prayer: *God is great. God is good. Now let's suit up and go scare the living shit out of some pinkies...*

He glanced around. A dozen stained-glass windows lined each side of the church and he guessed there had to be around forty or fifty rows of pews, all wooden with gray seat cushions and matching backrests. One main aisle, neatly carpeted in a darker gray, split the pews into two sides and led up to three steps and a landing that had a little area for the choir and then a standard lectern for Reverend Kettle.

Needless to say, only black people were there.

Shanice Kettle spotted them. She was dressed in another corny-ass bonnet that had Willie feeling a little embarrassed for her. She stood and waved them down, insisting that they sit with her in her regular spot up in the front row.

All the women were dressed well (though only one of them was wearing a dorky-ass bonnet) and literally all of the adult men were wearing suits.

The first fifteen minutes of the service was nothing but the choir. Willie thought about killing himself halfway through the fourth song, "Trust and Obey" because he was pretty sure he had agreed to come to church and not a fucking concert.

"Trust and Obey" finally ended (because there's no other way) and another song started as three men quickly passed around a few collection buckets. Willie just looked at it when it came by him, and he passed it to his uncle Reggie who plopped a little white envelope in it. Mrs. Kettle gave Willie the "why isn't the rich kid giving any money to God" look, so he pulled a roll of hundreds out of his front pocket, peeled a couple off the top, and dropped them in, only to get another look from Auntie Shanice that suggested he gave too much and that he should have given some to her so she could go down to the ugly hat store and add a bonnet to her collection.

After the offering, Reverend Kettle came out of a door, most likely an office near the back of the landing, and approached the lectern. You could have heard a pin drop and it was clear that Willie wasn't the only one that both liked and respected Kettle and the things he had to say.

Willie wasn't all that familiar with the Bible, but he still found it easy to relate to Kettle and though he didn't normally do the whole God thing, Kettle said something that caught his attention:

"And the second is like it," Kettle said, quoting something from Matthew. "You shall love your neighbor as yourself."

Kettle held the Bible up in one of those big hands and poked at it with the pointer finger from his other hand. Each poke became progressively louder. Kettle knew how to get people's attention and the fact that he clearly believed in what he was saying created some electricity in the room. Willie half expected the three people in wheelchairs to his left to get up and start dancing.

"The Bible tells us right here in Matthew that loving your neighbor isn't any less important than loving God!" Kettle shouted. "It's also not any more important. And maybe the Good Book is also telling us that you can't love God unless you love your neighbor and that your neighbor is *everyone*. Including that boss that didn't give you that promotion. That person that made fun of you growing up. That friend that betrayed you and even that spouse that cheated on you."

And those Crown members that are listening to you right now...

Willie was pretty sure that even though Nancy and Joseph lived right behind Uncle Reggie, most people at the church didn't consider them to be the type of neighbors Kettle was preaching about.

Kettle finished and then walked over to that bowl thing babies were baptized at. Willie glanced at his watch and then at the program. It was the grand finale.

A young couple, maybe in their mid-twenties, was called up to the bowl that held the holy water they were going to toss on the baby the woman was holding. Another couple followed—most likely the godparents. The woman took the little hat off the baby and its black forehead shone under the light as Kettle ran a wet finger across it, welcoming the child into the Christian faith.

Willie tried to remember who his godparents were and then he thought about all those little pinkie kids he had just seen, scurrying in and out from between all those little ghetto huts. The biggest difference between the life those kids would lead and the life of this baptized baby was determined by nothing more than a flip of a coin...a color lottery that either had you born into a privileged race or running around a hut all day, chomping on apples with piss in your pants until you were old enough to really know the difference between you and those with darker skin.

And then he wondered if the average white person that lived on The Row called the pinkie next door to them that special word. That endearing term that qualified someone to be loved by all Christians.

Neighbor.

And then there was Joseph. The kid who landed smack-dab in the middle of two colors. The halfie. The hash brown. The kid who arguably belonged nowhere.

It saddened Willie and made him think once again of that punch he threw at Lucas Adams back in third grade. The punch he didn't want to throw because he knew better.

It had been wrong.

WILLIE

Mr. Hideinduit.

Ten Means Two.

G et anywhere near these bars and you'll get another crack upside your head," Sheriff Green said. "In fact, don't even think about standing up. This young man here has asked to have ten minutes with you and he's going to have it."

The name of Dad's killer was Stanley Collins.

Collins was alone, moved to an isolated cell down the dark hallway from the main holding area Willie had first seen him in. He sat at the edge of a metal bunk that had no mattress, no sheets, no blanket, and no pillow. He had his head down and his hands over his ears. His shoelaces and belt had been removed and he'd also traded his blood-soaked shirt for more stylish gray prison garb with the number 1168 in white across the chest.

"You hear me?" Sheriff Green yelled, startling both Collins and Willie.

Collins finally nodded as if even looking at Sheriff Green was a bad idea.

"Be back in ten minutes," the sheriff said, patting Willie on the shoulder.

"Thanks," Willie said, seated in the hallway, right in front of the cell door.

"You got it," Sheriff Green said. "You have any problems with Mr. *Hideinduit* there, just shout."

"*Hideinduit?*"

Sheriff Green laughed and then disappeared down the hall.

Willie waited before saying anything to Collins. There were so many things running through his mind. So many answers he needed, so many questions he wanted to ask. And though he wanted to shout it, his first word came out as nothing more than a whisper.

"Why?"

Collins didn't move. He didn't even flinch.

"Why'd you do it?" Willie asked, this time louder. Loud enough for a tiny echo.

Collins slowly looked up and then faced Willie. Prisoner 1168 had clearly been beaten more. His eyes were nothing more than slits and his cheekbones were gone, hidden by yellowish-blue swelling. His nose looked like it had been broken again, this time in a different direction, and his blood-caked nostrils were now tilted up and out like a pig's.

"Hideinduit," Collins mumbled, lowering his hands from the sides of his face. It was clear he had also taken what Sheriff Green referred to as a "crack" to his left ear. It was blackish-blue and twice the size of his right one, standing out against the top of his milk-white jawline.

"I don't know what that means," Willie said. By the time "means" left his lips he'd figured it out, and he held up his hand before Collins could say it again. "I've got it now. You are telling me you didn't do it."

Collins nodded and then slowly glanced up at the camera in the back, left corner of the cell. And then he turned to Willie, shrugged, and spoke as if he wanted nobody else to hear. "Still don't know who it is they say I killed."

"The man was my father. He was the *black* lawyer defending Donald Bondy, a *white man*, up in Detroit."

"I don't know who Donald Bondy is either. I'm from Flat Rock and was just up here to see if I could get hired on at the mill. Was walking up the driveway of the plant and the next thing I know the police is pointing a gun at me and I got arrested."

"Only time they ain't lying is when their lips ain't moving," a voice crackled over an intercom from somewhere in the cell. It was Sheriff Green, and though Willie suspected they were being watched and listened to, he was surprised Sheriff Green let it be known.

"At least that Donald Bondy fella had a lawyer," Collins said quietly. "And I ain't saying nothing more."

"Damn right you aren't," Sheriff Green blurted. "Meeting is over."

Willie didn't care that the meeting was over because there was something about the way Collins spoke that poked at Willie's gut in a way he didn't like. And whatever it was, it was pointy, sharp, and injected little shots of certainty that immediately sickened Willie.

This isn't the man that killed Dad.

Willie heard a door open and then Sheriff Green appeared at the end of the hall. The sheriff walked toward them, and with each step, Collins cowered farther back into the corner of his bunk.

"Didn't know who you supposedly killed, eh?" Sheriff Green said, banging the cell bars with his flashlight. "Then why don't you tell us where you got this little keepsake from?"

When Sheriff Green opened his hand, the sickening feeling in Willie's stomach was immediately replaced with one that not only wanted Stanley Collins to die, but one that wanted him to first suffer in unimaginable ways.

Sheriff Green lowered his hand to give Willie a better look at the cuff link.

And the three initials on it.

TDG.

MAGGIE

Minnows. Walleye.

His Name Is Willie.

"When is Joseph supposed to be here?" Maggie asked as her and Alan walked behind their home. "I'm still going to ask him who that rich black boy is that was with Reggie Gibbons."

"You are asking for trouble," Alan said, unwrapping the tarp that they kept their fishing poles in. He grabbed four of them and inspected the reels. "You are white. He is black. You are dumb. He's probably smart."

"Ha-ha."

Maggie scooped a cupful of minnows out of the metal basin and dumped them into the bucket Alan was holding. "That should do it."

Alan glanced in the basin and ran a hand through his dark hair. "I think we are good on minnows for a while. But we are gonna need some hooks soon. Probably lost ten of them last week. Seems like we are getting snagged up more and more. We may have to switch spots if that keeps up."

"Maybe we should just work at the mill like everyone else," Maggie joked.

"Shush. We do way better fishing and painting. Plus, we get to fish."

Maggie laughed. She knew better. Fishing was everything to Alan and he was the best fisherman on The Row. Nobody pulled the walleye in like he did, usually bringing in thirty to forty of them every time he went out, with half the catch going to the community and the other half being sold for twenty cents a fish to a few of the restaurants in town. Didn't seem fair considering she heard that the restaurants would slap a pinch of coleslaw and a piece of bread next to the fish and sell it as a ten- to fifteen-dollar dinner. Still, she tried not to complain about it and Alan never did because she and her brother were two of the richest people on The Row.

"Hello, friends."

Maggie smiled. Joseph was holding his fishing pole (which had seen better days) in his right hand and a cottage cheese carton filled with night crawlers in his left. It probably took him a half an hour to walk here from where he lived because even though Reggie Gibbons supposedly gave Joseph the pickup truck, he wasn't allowed to drive it unless it was work-related.

"Joseph Springsted," Maggie said. "You are going to latch on to a big walleye or a carp one of these days and that old pole of yours is going to snap clean in half."

Joseph held the pole above his head and studied it with wide eyes. "Think so?"

"I know so."

"I hope you are wrong, Maggie," he said. "Don't know what I'd do about that. I couldn't replace it for a while."

Maggie didn't know what he'd do either. Joseph didn't live on The Row, but if he did, he certainly wouldn't be one of the richest. But he would definitely be the nicest. Everyone knew that.

"Hey, Joseph," Alan said. "We saw a boy downtown that Maggie has taken a liking to."

"Maggie likes all boys, doesn't she?" Joseph said.

Alan laughed and so did Maggie. Joseph didn't mean it the way it sounded.

"This boy is black," Alan said. "And that same boy drove by here twice today. To and from church with Reggie Gibbons."

"If he was with Mr. Reggie, you are talking about Mister—" He paused abruptly, like someone had reached into his mouth and grabbed his tongue. "You are talking about Willie."

"Willie is cute," Maggie said. "Is he staying at the house?"

"Yes. He is from Georgia. He is Mr. Reggie's nephew. You should see his car."

"Saw it," Alan said. "When he was talking to Sheriff Green downtown."

"Why was he talking to Sheriff Green?"

"Don't know," Alan said. "We were putting addresses on curbs."

"And cleaning up after Sheriff Green," Maggie said, "I'd give everything I have to see somebody put a boot up his ass."

"Hush!" Alan said. "You don't want to get in the habit of saying stuff like that."

"Who cares?" Maggie knew Joseph considered himself white, certainly more than he considered himself half-black. "I ain't gonna say it around any *black* people."

"Every once in a while, something stupid comes out of your mouth," Alan said. "Actually, something stupid comes out of your mouth daily, but saying stuff about Sheriff Green is always dangerous and you know that."

"Blah blah blah," Maggie said. "How late are we going to fish until? We have to paint close to twenty addresses tomorrow, and I need a good night's sleep."

"We will fish 'til dark," Alan said.

"Good." Maggie nudged Joseph. "That will give you plenty of time to tell me all about that Willie boy."

WILLIE

Retard. Bitter Mama.

Her Name is Maggie.

Fuck.

Willie was too tired to get up for breakfast, which happened to be at six sharp. But he was awake.

Thanks, Joseph. You retard.

He didn't see Joseph all of Sunday and only saw Nancy at dinner, but it didn't matter, because he knew how they spent their day. Well, almost. He assumed Nancy spent most of hers with her head up Uncle Reggie's ass, but he was positive what Joseph had done. The kid was downstairs, still talking about the fishing excursion. He was all excited about it and was laughing—make that squealing, in an obnoxiously high pitch—about how he, some guy named Alan, and some girl named Maggie caught sixty walleye and fifty perch. Yippee.

Regardless, it couldn't be clearer that Sundays were the big break from the other six days, which were all carbon copies of each other:

6:00 a.m.—They all eat the breakfast Nancy makes at the ass crack of dawn. Nancy cleans up.

7:00 a.m.—Joseph goes outside and fails to start the old pickup truck fifty times before it finally works. Joseph heads off to whatever landscaping assignment Uncle Reggie has him on. Willie takes some pills.

12:00 p.m.—Nancy makes lunch. Joseph comes home. They all eat. Joseph returns to work. Willie takes some pills. Nancy cleans up. Then Nancy cleans more things that don't need cleaning, like polishing the other polish on the coffee tables in the living room nobody ever uses.

6:00 p.m.—Nancy makes dinner. Joseph returns home. They all eat. Willie takes some more pills.

9:00 p.m.—They go to bed.

Wash. Rinse. Repeat.

Joseph finally shut up about fishing and Willie lay in bed all day, dozing off for a few different three-hour-plus spurts until around 5:45 p.m. But the sleep wasn't good. It was filled with dreams about his father, mother, sister, Joseph...and Lucas.

He was starving and could smell bread cooking. As a rule, pinkies were phenomenal cooks and Nancy was no exception. In fact, other than kissing Uncle Reggie's ass, it seemed to be what she did best.

Willie decided to go downstairs to join them for dinner, which sounded much more appetizing than thinking about Stanley Collins, Dad's upcoming funeral, or about blowing shit up at Kettle's house, even though the blowing stuff up was a close second.

"Good afternoon!" Uncle Reggie said, smartass sprinkled all over his tone of voice.

"Hi, Willie," Joseph said, nicely. Too nice. And Willie wasn't awake enough to be nice back. But he tried.

"Hey," Willie yawned out, studying the loaf of bread on a plate at the center of the table. He glanced at Nancy and there was something about the way she was looking at him that reminded him a little bit of Dr. Cheever. He had no doubt she wasn't a big fan of her son working his ass off all day while Willie sat on his.

He stared her down for a bit.

I'm higher up the food chain than you are. Now hush and make me some fresh bread... that loaf on the table has gotten a little too cold for my liking.

"Maybe Willie would want to go fishing some time," Joseph said.

Willie would rather kill himself than fish, and if Joseph was going to recap the fishing excursion again, Willie quickly decided he was going to go upstairs and take all his pills at once to put himself out of his misery.

"I think that would be a good idea," Uncle Reggie said. "You two spending some more time together."

"Can you cook up whatever we catch?" Willie asked, aimed at Nancy.

"Oh yeah," Joseph said. "Mama makes the best walleye there is."

Willie just smiled at Nancy and didn't feel the love coming back.

"Mr. Willie," she said. "Maybe I could teach you how to cook it. That way you can do it for yourself sometime."

"You never showed me," Joseph said.

"Maybe Mr. Willie wouldn't be in the mood to learn how to cook," Nancy said. "After all, tomorrow they are putting his daddy to rest."

Did she say that sincerely or was she being nasty...as in, your dad is dead so suck on that?

"I'm not really into fishing or cooking," Willie said. "Thanks, though."

"Too bad," Joseph said. "Maggie wanted you to come. I think she likes you. She said her and Alan met you when you were talking to Sheriff Green one day. She talked about you all day yesterday."

Shit. Stop the presses. Maggie is Hot Pinkie.

Uncle Reggie winked at Willie.

"I've never fished before," Willie said, preparing to set the bait, no pun intended. "I wouldn't know how to do it."

Joseph swallowed it. Hook. Line. And sinker.

"I can show you," he said.

Willie paused for theatrical purposes. "I guess I can give it a try then."

Uncle Reggie smiled and shook his head. "I better go with you guys, then. I have a great spot over near the mill."

"You are going to let all of us go there too?" Joseph said, all giddy. "To your secret spot?"

"Yeah," Uncle Reggie said, dismissively. He turned to Willie. "Nobody else ever goes back there. Nice and private and nobody will bother us."

That explained why Uncle Reggie wouldn't mind being seen in public, relaxing and fishing with pinkies. It's because nobody would see them.

"I'd like to join you if that's all right, Mr. Reggie," Nancy said.

"Of course," Uncle Reggie said, swiping at a hefty drift of dandruff that had formed on his right shoulder. "Pardon me. Darn stuff is getting so bad if I leaned over an aquarium, the fish would think it's feed time."

"I get it," Joseph said, followed by that high-pitched, squealing laugh. "Get it, Willie...get the joke?"

"Yeah," Willie said. "I get it."

WILLIE

Empty Justice. Mini-Funeral.

Adios, Cheever. Adios, Head.

The day of Dad's funeral was the first morning Willie had actually been downstairs before the breakfast table had been cleared. Joseph was already outside fiddling with the old truck and his uncle had gone somewhere. Willie and Nancy sat at the table for close to fifteen minutes, neither of them speaking.

"Where's Uncle Reggie?" Willie asked.

"Not sure," she said.

Willie held up his plate to Nancy, who quickly took it to the sink and started washing it by hand.

"Make sure you clean that real good," he said.

She didn't respond, which bothered him a little bit.

"Morning," Uncle Reggie said, coming through the front door. Willie hadn't heard him pull up and Uncle Reggie immediately sat at the table, crossed his arms, then cocked his head toward Nancy. "You're done in the house for the day, Nancy. I need you to excuse us."

Nancy wiped up around the sink, folded the cloth she was using, and placed it neatly over the water tap.

"Tell Joseph I don't want him to go anywhere today," Uncle Reggie said. "Am I clear?"

"Yes," Nancy said, heading to the door before putting her shoes on.

Uncle Reggie stood and went to the counter. He grabbed a cup out of the cupboard and poured himself a coffee and then pointed at the pot, asking Willie if he wanted a refill. Willie shook his head and Uncle Reggie walked to the kitchen window and stared outside.

"That white fella they were holding in jail hanged himself this morning."

Willie leaned back in his chair, not entirely satisfied, wondering how justice could be so bittersweet. He felt like his team had just won the world championship, but that he hadn't been allowed to play. In fact, he felt like he missed the bus ride to the fucking game.

"Apparently he was moved to his own cell and they found him dead a few hours ago," Uncle Reggie added. "Sheriff Green called and asked me to come down."

Of course, he did. And maybe the good sheriff called a couple other Crown members to come down to encourage Stanley Collins to put the noose around his own neck...

"Crazy that it happens the morning of Dad's funeral," Willie said. "What a coincidence."

Uncle Reggie gave him a dismissive look. "Now we can put your father to rest today and move forward."

Willie rolled his eyes, still unsatisfied.

"Uncle Reggie," he said. "If the man killed himself, why would Sheriff Green have you come down?"

"Your daddy was my brother. Maybe Sheriff Green wanted me to have a little closure as well."

"Or maybe he's in The Crown," Willie said. "Maybe that police reference you made at Devil's Drop was about him. Maybe he invited you because he wanted your help."

Uncle Reggie's eyebrows arched and his right eye squinted, matching his left, giving him a sincere look of disbelief in what he'd just heard.

"I'm going to act like you didn't say that."

"Sorry," Willie said.

After all, the cuff link was the smoking gun and Collins was clearly guilty, so he probably realized that considering his circumstances, Woodruff was the worst possible place in the world for him to be. And whether it came from a Crown dipping or the state's gas chamber, he knew he was dead.

That was it. He saw no way out, so he decided to hang himself.

Then Willie closed his eyes and took a deep breath.

He hanged himself without shoelaces, a belt, or a bedsheet to do it with...

♦♦♦

AT THE FUNERAL HOME, the room they had Dad's coffin in had been partitioned into a tiny square, unlike any funeral Willie had ever been to. When Uncle Reggie told Willie that Dad wanted family only at the funeral, he wasn't kidding. Dad knew thousands and thousands of people, and it felt weird when Reverend Kettle stood and walked up to a small podium next to Dad's coffin and started talking, because the only people there were Willie, Uncle Reggie, Reverend Kettle, and, of course, Dad.

Willie just stared at his father as Kettle spoke.

Dad looked much better than he did over at the morgue. Willie recognized the suit he was wearing. It was dark navy with white pinstripes you could barely see. The tie wasn't done in a tight Windsor the way Dad liked it, and there was no matching kerchief fluffed out of the breast pocket. Other than that, it pretty much just looked like a dead version of Dad.

I still haven't cried.

Willie hated the stale floral smell of funeral homes. As Kettle finished talking, Willie tried to not think about how the smell reminded him of his mother and sister.

"You come by the house and talk to me later," Kettle said.

Willie snapped out of his trance. He didn't even see Kettle walk away from the podium.

"Okay," Willie said. Though he barely knew the guy, if there was anyone that could make him feel better, it would be Kettle.

Willie stood and went to the coffin. The funeral director told him it would be the last time he ever saw his father.

He tried to think of something good to say. He couldn't.

He wished Dad was wearing cuff links.

So he leaned forward, fixed Dad's tie the way he liked it, then left.

◆◆◆

WILLIE SAT IN THE bedroom, staring at his phone. Dr. Cheever had called him twice while he was at the funeral and he figured it was time to call and put her out of her misery, or at least put her out of *his* misery.

Her answering machine came on and right as he was about to hang up, she picked up the phone.

"Willie?"

"No, it's Santa Claus."

"I've tried to contact you several times."

"Give up, please. You are being a pest. I just came from my father's funeral. He obviously won't be paying you anymore, so I'm only calling to tell you your services are no longer needed."

"Willie, I know you don't believe this, but I want what is best for you. You have been through a lot and—"

"I don't feel anything. Because you haven't helped me."

There was a pause and then she said what they both knew was the truth.

"It's because you are using, Willie. You mask your feelings not only with humor, but with painkillers. Please. When you come back home, let's get you into a good facility and get you cleaned up once and for all. We will get you a good sponsor, get you a good support group, and get you back on track."

"Yeah, yeah, yeah."

"I know where you are coming from, Willie. For what it's worth…I've been where you are."

"Your whole family isn't dead. You have no idea *where* I am."

"Pills, Willie. I'm talking about the pills. Please let me help you."

"I already told you that you can't make any more money off us. Give up."

"I will never give up on you, Willie," she said, her tone convincingly sympathetic. "And I don't want any money. Come down here and get the help you need. Let me be your sponsor. Please let me help you."

"I'm going to be up here for a while until my uncle settles my father's affairs. I really don't need any help, so please leave me alone. I have enough stress in my life without your phone calls every five minutes."

Willie hung up.

Cheever hadn't said a single word about his dad being gone.

Did Cheever just say she was on pills before? And that she wants to be my sponsor?

Yeah, right.

Willie laughed and then thought about his pill supply which was looking a bit lame. Just the thought of cutting back to make them last or even going a single day without them damn near gave him the runs. He had been up north for a little over a week and had gone through well over half of his supply, and though he didn't need anyone's permission to leave, he wondered when he would go home.

He opened his baggie of pills, put some in his mouth, and washed them down with the bottle of water he grabbed off the dresser. Between the pills and his visit later with Reverend Kettle, maybe he would feel better.

Or at least feel something.

♦♦♦

"SHANICE WON'T BE BACK for a couple hours," Kettle said, pointing one of those long-ass fingers at the couch in the living room. "Have a seat and I'll be right back with a couple lemonades for us."

"Thanks," Willie said, studying the back of Kettle's shiny head as he ducked into the kitchen.

"I'm sure it breaks your heart Shanice ain't here," the minister yelled, followed by a belly laugh that sounded more like a *hee-hee-hee*.

Willie could hear ice being tossed into a glass, then a *whoosh* pouring sound, then with a few long steps, the minister was handing him a lemonade.

"Thanks," Willie said again.

Kettle sat on the loveseat to Willie's right and placed his lemonade on a coaster on the table next to him. The minister shook his head and smiled. Then he laughed out a couple more *hee-hee*s before he said, "*Auntie Shanice*. What in the world is that woman thinking?"

Willie tried not to burst out laughing along with Kettle. It was the first real laugh he'd had in what felt like forever.

"What do you do for fun?" Kettle asked.

Willie shrugged. "I like to play video games."

"Lotta kids your age do," Kettle said. "Kinda funny to think that when I was your age, televisions were still a relatively new thing. Times sure change, don't they?"

"I guess," Willie said. "Makes you wonder what they will have in another twenty years."

"Amen," Kettle said. He leaned back on the loveseat and laced his fingers together on his lap. "You know, Willie, the reason I asked you to come over is to share a little story about something that happened to me when I was about half your age. I wanted to share it to let you know we have something in common. I haven't talked about it in years, but that doesn't mean I don't think about it every day. Would you like to hear me out?"

"Sure," Willie said. He took a sip of his lemonade and leaned back as well.

"My daddy was killed by a white man too."

"I'm sorry to hear that."

"Things happen, Willie. We don't always know why, but they do."

"What happened?"

"I didn't ask you over to tell you what happened, just that it did happen. But I will tell you if you'd like. But I have to warn you, the story isn't for the ears of babes."

"If you don't want to talk about it, I under—"

Kettle held up his hand for Willie to be quiet. The minister's head dipped and his eyes were aimed at the floor. On second glance, his eyes seemed to gloss over, as if the story he was about to tell had already began to play in his mind.

"It happened right here in Woodruff," Kettle said. "I was nine years old. A slave by the name of Joey Winters killed the mill owner he belonged to. Happened up at a mill in Port Huron, a place up past Detroit on another lake up there. Winters hightailed it out of there, hid, and must have jumped on a train or a boat to end up in Woodruff. It was the middle of winter, a cold and windy winter that put the average day about twenty-below with the wind chill. In those days, slaves that ran away in the winter weren't chased that long. Owners knew they'd come crawling back, willing to take a beating in exchange for warmth and something to eat. Either that, or the owners would find the runaway frozen stiff out in the woods somewhere when spring broke."

Kettle's head never moved. Nor did his eyes. Willie wanted him to blink, but he didn't. He just reached over with one of those long arms, grabbed his lemonade, and started talking again.

"So, all in all, they never made too much of a fuss about runaways in the winter. That is, unless the runaway was a murderer. There were bulletins all over the state with Winters' picture on it. I remembered seeing dozens of them posted downtown with specific instructions for anyone that saw Joseph Winters to shoot him on sight. I remember seeing his picture for the first time on one of those bulletins and thinking how well he was named. I mean it would be like you or me having the last name of *Black*. I mean that guy looked like *winter*, with skin as white as snow and hair the same color...I swear to you. Anyhow, I am the oldest of four kids, two boys and two girls. My daddy and I left my brother and sisters at the house with mother one night to run into town for some milk at the old market, which is now an ice cream shop down on Main."

"I've been there," Willie said.

Willie wasn't sure if Kettle heard him. The minister had gone back in time and was temporarily stuck there, so Willie decided to stay quiet.

"There was a lot of commotion going on that night. It was only a little past six o'clock, but it was winter and after dark. The town only had one police cruiser and the cherry light was going full bore along with four other cruisers from neighboring towns. They were a couple blocks past the market and had we shown up five minutes later, the store would have been closed. In fact, they were shutting the whole town down. About a half an hour earlier, old man Tate, the fella that ran the butcher shop, caught Joseph Winters hiding out in the back of his store. He said he got a shot off, thought he hit him, but that Winters got away, carrying a three-foot machete that Tate chopped meat with. Police told everybody that had a business downtown to lock up, go home and lock up again, so we headed back. When we got home, we parked in the barn, and when we were walking toward the back door, we noticed a zigzagged path of what looked like gunpowder sprinkled in the snow. It ran from the side of the barn all the way to the back door. Like I said, it was dark, pitch-black out, so my father knelt and pinched a little of it between his fingers, brought it up close to his eyes, and still couldn't tell what it was. When we went inside, Daddy turned the light on and we both looked at his fingers. Plain as day it wasn't gunpowder that he touched outside, it was blood. Daddy smelled trouble—Joseph Winters trouble—and was pretty quick on his feet so he had me crouch down behind the laundry basin to take cover until he could see what was going on."

Kettle paused and took a deep breath like he had just come up for air.

"I watched as he entered the kitchen and when he disappeared around the corner I could hear my mother gasp. *Don't hurt him,* she cried. *Please don't hurt him.* Like I said, I was only nine, and though my daddy was a minister as well, he was a big man and never hesitated to take a strap to one of our behinds for misbehaving, so I thought my mother, being the pacifist she was, was talking Daddy out of putting a beating on Joseph Winters for being an uninvited guest. I heard Daddy say something and then Joseph Winters said something, but I couldn't hear their words clear enough. Then there was a grunt and my mother screamed so loud I thought I heard glass break. I never heard a scream like that in my life. It was so high-pitched it made me shudder. It sounded like it came out of a movie and I'll tell you, it probably could have broken glass, but it was the police that broke the glass. Bullets came in the house at the exact same time my mother screamed. There had to be twenty shots or more. Right through the picture window in the living room. The front door sounded like it was kicked in. Men's voices, maybe four or five, filled the room. Two police officers, guns drawn, came through the kitchen and back to where I was hiding, but neither of them saw me. They went back to the living room and someone shouted, asking if anyone else was in the house, followed by the sound of at least two people running up the stairs, which happened to be right above where I was hiding."

Kettle finally looked away from the rug and took a sip of his lemonade. He put the glass back on the coaster and looked right at Willie as if he needed a break.

"We don't have to talk about this," Willie said. "If you don't want."

Kettle waited for a few seconds. "I'd like to finish if you don't mind."

Willie nodded.

The minister leaned forward and resumed his stare at the floor.

"After the men ran upstairs, it got really quiet for a few seconds," Kettle said. "And then a man yelled, *"I've got three children upstairs! They are all okay!"* I took that as meaning the coast was clear and left my hiding spot. I hit the entrance to the kitchen and when I turned to the right, I saw a police officer in the living room yelling toward the staircase, *"Keep them up there! Dear Lord...please keep them up there!"* I meandered into the living room and by the time anyone noticed me standing there, I got an eyeful."

Kettle shook his head as if trying to erase what was in his mind.

"My mother's arms hung straight down to her sides and she had her face buried in a policeman's shoulder as he held her. She wasn't crying. She was silent, too silent, hiding from what was on the floor. About four feet from her, Joseph Winter was lying on his side, surrounded by a pool of blood. It was hard to tell where he had been hit, a little bit of everywhere I guessed, but what I noticed was that he was still holding old man Tate's machete in his right hand. Two of the policeman rushed toward me, and before they got to me, I saw my father. He was about three feet to the left of Joseph Winters and was lying on his stomach in his own pool of blood that surrounded his shoulders. One of the officers snatched me up to back me out of the house, but before we made it to the kitchen, I saw it resting on the carpet about another three feet from my father's waist."

Kettle covered his face with his hands and shook his head again. It seemed liked it worked that time because when he opened his eyes, they were clearer, more present.

"What was resting on the carpet?" Willie asked. "Or do you not want to talk about it anymore?"

"Sure you want to know?"

"Only if you want to tell me."

Kettle bit lightly at his bottom lip and then looked straight at Willie.

"It was my father's head."

"Wow," Willie said. At least he thought he said it. If he did, he instantly regretted it.

Kettle pointed to Willie's left, toward the front window. "It was on the ground, right over there. Joseph Winters lopped Daddy's head off right in front of my mother."

Goose bumps riddled Willie's arms. He rubbed at them and did his best to think before talking. "I don't know what to say."

"You don't have to say anything," Kettle said. "Sorry about the gory details. In some way it helps me to talk about it. I forgot how young you are and I got a little carried away."

"That's all right."

"I appreciate it," Kettle said. "As I mentioned, I just wanted you to know that it did happen, that just like you, my father was killed by a white man. And more importantly, I want you to know that life goes on. People like us go on."

"Your dad was a minister like you, eh?"

"And a good one," Kettle said.

"I don't get it," Willie said.

"Get what?"

"Your dad is a minister and God lets that happen to him."

Kettle leaned over and put his hand on Willie's leg. "God didn't let that happen to my father. Joseph Winters let that happen to my father."

"Why didn't God stop it?"

"God wants us to follow him, Willie. We aren't robots following some program. We can do whatever we want when we want. It's called free will."

"What happened to your mom, brother, and sisters?"

"Brother was a doctor, one sister was a nurse, both dead around seventy. Youngest sister is a retired school teacher. Lives over in Gibraltar about two miles from here. She will be here for dinner on Tuesday."

"Your mom?"

Kettle's head tilted toward his right shoulder. "She never said a word again. Never quite mentally made it out of that night. Spent the next twenty-five years up at the psych ward in Northville. They tried every medication in the book, even tried electricity on her. She just couldn't come back to reality."

"Not sure I could blame her."

"Yeah," Kettle said. "She died up there when she was fifty-nine. My aunt and uncle moved in right after my father's death and finished raising us."

"Surprised they kept you in the same house. I mean the memories and all."

"Not everybody has resources to just up and leave when they want, particularly then."

"Glad you and the other kids turned out all right."

"We tried," Kettle said. "And had a lot of help from God along the way. We tried to not live in the past, to move on, because when you live in the past, you're pretty invisible in the present."

"It's just weird," Willie said. "Both of our dads helped people and ended up getting killed."

"Yessiree. My dad was a man of God and also a huge supporter of the abolition of slavery. He wanted whites to live as free as anybody. It's crazy how slavery ended not much longer after his death. But I agree, it certainly is ironic, that just like your daddy, my daddy was killed by people he was trying to help."

"Let me guess. I'm supposed to forgive the person that killed my dad?"

"Grown men don't like being told what to do, Willie. You do what you want."

Wow, was that refreshing. Willie never felt so comfortable around anyone in his life. He felt like he could tell Kettle anything. "I appreciate spending time with you."

Kettle smiled and said, "You too, Willie. God puts people in our lives for a reason."

The back door opened, the same one Kettle and his father came in the night Joseph Winter stopped by.

"I see that nice car out there! That means Willie must be here!"

It was Auntie Shanice and Willie guessed that Kettle knew he was looking for the escape hatch.

"I will see you to the door," he said. "I wasn't expecting her back so soon. Let's talk again over the next few days."

They stood, and Willie shook Kettle's enormous hand.

"Thanks again," Willie said, looking up at the tall minister. "It's good to hear someone that experienced the same thing I'm going through." His shoulders sagged. "I didn't mean that the way it sounded. What I meant to say was—"

"I know what you meant," Kettle said.

"Thanks," Willie said again.

Kettle was the coolest guy he ever met.

WILLIE

Apples. Butterflies.

Front Row Seat at Devil's Drop.

Willie made it through the night without any bad dreams about Mom, Dad, Lucas, or headless preachers. He also made it through breakfast without insulting Nancy and thought that maybe there was a chance these miracles were being provided as a reward for his spending time with a man of God.

Willie popped a few more pills than he should have to get him through the rest of the morning, and despite manual labor being involved, he was pretty excited about the idea of going to work at Devil's Drop with Joseph.

Still, he was well aware that there weren't enough pills in the world to make him comfortable enough to be a passenger in a car driven by Joseph, because Willie had sold himself on the fact that Joseph's lack of smarts could be a potential safety issue. So when Joseph started the old pickup, Willie felt the need to take charge, but in a nice way.

"You mind if I drive?" Willie asked. He sort of regretted not making it an order, but the more he got to know the kid, it was becoming practically impossible to mistreat him. He was just too damn nice.

"If that's what you want," Joseph answered. The way he said it led Willie to believe he could have asked him if he minded a kick in the balls and he would have answered the same way.

"It would be nice," Willie said. And it beat the hell out of worrying about Joseph driving and reading Stop, thinking it meant Go or thinking Yield meant Drive the Black Kid's Side of the Truck into a Tree.

Joseph got out and Willie sat in the driver's seat, noticing a brown paper bag that was on the dashboard. Joseph popped in the passenger's side and Willie put the truck in reverse. He damn near threw his shoulder out trying to turn the wheel on that old piece of shit, and he could tell Joseph knew he was struggling. Joseph reached over and yanked on the wheel before Willie had a chance to knock his hand away.

"This prolly doesn't turn like that fancy car of yours," Joseph said. "You sure you don't want me to drive?"

"I'm good, Joseph. Let me handle it."

"Okay," Joseph said submissively in that little kid voice.

Willie pulled out onto the road, and even though it took all hundred and sixty pounds of him, he managed to make a right turn without Joseph's assistance. Joseph reached into that brown paper bag and pulled out a couple apples and offered Willie one.

"No, thanks," Willie said. "We don't eat those things."

"What do you mean?" Joseph asked. Thankfully the kid didn't have the faintest idea what a stereotype was, nor did he catch Willie's involuntary racist statement.

"Nothing," Willie said.

"You mean just white folks like apples?"

Willie shrugged. Maybe Joseph was hip to at least part of what he said.

"Kind of like you not being good swimmers?" Joseph added, smiling.

Okay, so he did know what a stereotype was.

"I am a good swimmer," Willie said, lying through his teeth. "Great, in fact. We have a pool in my backyard and I'm in it all the time."

"Everybody knows black people can't swim," Joseph said.

"Everybody doesn't know that because it's not true," Willie said.

"And I know the jokes about white people and apples," he said. "I know what you mean and how black people don't like them."

"Whites just like them more," Willie said.

"Says who?" Joseph said. "And who cares? I'm eating it because I'm hungry and it tastes good."

The kid that hardly said a word the day they first met suddenly wouldn't shut up, but Willie guessed Joseph was at least a little bit right. He remembered trying an apple when he was younger and liking it, but that was way before he learned they were white people food. Sort of like taking a bite of wet dog food and liking it before reading the can. *Perception.* Though the apple he had eaten truly was tasty, the odds of anyone ever seeing him eat one again were up there with him working at a car wash or protesting a white man's conviction outside of a courthouse.

Then again, if someone had asked Willie if he'd be seen in Michigan, by himself, in public, in a car with a pinkie (or whatever the hell color Joseph was supposed to be), he would have laughed.

Neither of them said anything as they passed a couple of white dudes on the side of Cossit Creek Road. They were carrying a dead deer that's legs were tied to a branch. The deer had what looked like an arrow or gunshot wound in its side and Willie guessed there was going to be a feast up on The Row.

"Stop the truck," Joseph said.

"What for?"

"They gotta carry that deer all the way up the hill."

Willie figured he was safe with Joseph, so he stopped. Joseph looked out the window and told the men to throw the deer in the bed of the truck. They did, hopped in with it, and up the hill toward The Row they went.

Things felt different this time as they drove through the pinkie ghetto. All the whites didn't come to that screeching halt pose like they had when he and Uncle Reggie came through. Willie assumed it was because they were in the truck, not Uncle Reggie's car, which meant Joseph was on board. A couple of them stopped and waved at Joseph, who nodded and waved back. Willie wasn't afraid to admit it was good to see them wave, because it made him feel safer. Still, it was a little awkward because there were only two places to go down Cossit Creek once you passed The Row and one of them wasn't the church.

"Stop here," Joseph said.

Willie did, and the two pinkies jumped out, taking their kill with them.

"How did they kill that thing?" Willie asked. "It looked like it was shot with something, but they don't have any weapons on them."

"Can't tell you."

"Guns or bows hiding in the woods?"

"Not bows, but I can't tell you."

Joseph had no idea that he did just tell him, but it was no big deal. What was a big deal was that Hot Pinkie Maggie and her brother were walking right toward the passenger-side window.

"Hey, Joseph," Maggie said.

"Hey back," Joseph answered, hiking his thumb toward Willie. "Alan and Maggie, this is Mr. Reggie's nephew. This is Willie."

"Hello, Willie," Alan said. Willie looked at the gap in the right side of Alan's mouth, wondering what happened to the two teeth that used to be there. And then he looked at two other things when Maggie leaned into the car to shake his hand.

"I'm Maggie," she said. Her skin was soft, like those light green eyes of hers. And then those proverbial butterflies, just like the ones in corny romance novels, started to float around Willie's belly. At that moment, he didn't care if she was white, yellow, purple, or green. He wanted to know Maggie better.

"Hello, Maggie," he said. He tried to sound suave, but he didn't have to. Their eyes were locked. It was on.

"Willie is going fishing with us," Joseph said. "So is Mama and Mr. Reggie. Mr. Reggie is going to take us to his private spot."

Willie and Maggie just stared at each other. Willie didn't have the faintest idea what to say before Alan pulled Maggie away from the car.

"We are heading down to Devil's Drop to do some weedin'," Joseph said. "See you guys later."

Maggie and Alan both waved and Willie pulled out of The Row. About fifty yards before the place he and Uncle Reggie stopped the first time he was there, Joseph pointed at what looked like a small opening in the trees.

"Pull in there," Joseph said. "Then just keep driving until we hit the bottom."

Willie about blew out one of his balls trying to turn the wheel again, but finally made it on to the narrow path. The smell of sulfur surrounded them along with trees and a thicket so full you couldn't see a foot off the path. About a hundred yards later, they came out into the opening. Willie slowed the truck even more and had to catch his breath, thinking about some of the things that had probably happened here.

"Devil's Drop," Willie said. "It looks bigger from down here."

"You've seen this before?"

"My uncle showed me on our way to church Sunday." He pointed back up toward the road. "He showed me from somewhere up there. How long has this place been here?"

"Too long," Joseph said. "But don't tell anybody I said that."

Willie did a three-sixty, looking out all the windows, mostly up into the surrounding trees and hillside that ran around three quarters of the place. To their left were the scorched cars that had been blown up for The Crown's entertainment. To their right was nothing but swampland and cattails that led back to the mill and Lake Erie. About a hundred yards directly in front of them was the long wooden stage and the dipping post that hung directly over the black-watered pond. It all looked different than it did from up top.

"Go ahead and pull up to where the Trio goes," Joseph said. "You know what that means?"

"I do," Willie said. "The leaders. Any idea how they pick them?"

"Don't know and I don't want to talk about it if that's okay," Joseph said. "Can you just pull up next to the stage?"

Willie drove slowly, the place seeming to be getting bigger. He felt like he was driving through the center of a stadium and the trees that surrounded the place were watching him like a hundred thousand silent fans that all seemed to be thinking the same thing he was.

What in the hell are you doing here?

They reached the base of the stage and parked next to the front wall. Despite the huge gaps in the stones that exposed the area beneath the stage, Willie could see what Uncle Reggie meant when he said it would never collapse.

They got out of the truck and Joseph unloaded a push lawn mower and two Weedwackers. Willie had a hard time keeping his eyes off the dipping gallows that hung over the right edge of the stage, and then he pointed at the little wooden shack in the back-right corner and studied the thick chain across its door.

"That's where the Trio convenes before a meeting starts," Willie said.

It sounded like a question, but it was meant to be a statement.

"Yup," Joseph said.

"I can see why you probably don't want to talk about this place and why you don't want to be here," Willie said. "But can I ask you another question? And I would appreciate if you would answer because at the risk of sounding selfish, this one impacts me."

Joseph shook his head and bit on his bottom lip, making him look both a lot older and smarter. "You think you understand why I don't want to be here?"

"Yeah," Willie said. "There are some pretty bad things that happen to white people here and you are down here standing in the middle of it. I guess it's a little awkward."

Joseph leaned against the side of the truck and smiled. Not a "ha-ha, that was funny" smile, it was more of a "ha-ha, you are a fucking idiot" smile.

"This place doesn't scare me any more than any other place I'm ever at," Joseph said.

"Really?"

"You don't get it, do you?" he said. "The Crown can get any one of us any time they want, wherever we are at. And you know what?"

"What?"

"There's nothing anyone can do about it."

"Sorry," Willie said. "It must make you feel pretty shitty fixing this place up. I mean with all your friends back there, knowing exactly what you are doing... helping the enemy and all."

"They don't mind," Joseph said. "They know I'm helping out Mr. Reggie and they all know he is good to me and Mama."

But it's okay for him to be in The Crown? Fucking really?

Joseph fiddled with the lawn mower and Willie walked over to the left side of the stage and climbed up the fifteen-foot wooden ladder. Once up on the platform, he turned around and glanced at the empty field, imagining what it would be like to see it filled with hundreds, maybe thousands, of torch-wielding Crown, all calling for dominance and oppression of people...people like Joseph.

Joseph pulled on the cord and the lawn mower started right up. Willie walked over to the end of the stage and put his hand on the dipping gallows. He saw how it extended out over the pond and realized he'd already become used to the smell of sulfur that came from the algae-filled water below.

He walked back to the center of the stage and thought about every Trio photo or video he'd ever seen. They all looked the same. The three of them would stand at the podium that was made just for them. The Left Trio standing on the left side. The Right Trio, the one who did all the talking, standing on the right. And then, standing in the center on something that was normally six inches to a foot higher than the other two, was The Crown Lord. He never talked. He just nodded his head when he heard something he liked, and when he did, it brought down the house.

"Are you crazy?" Joseph shouted, turning off the lawn mower. "Please get down from there, Willie. Even regular Crown members aren't supposed to be up there."

"Holy shit," Willie said, heading to the ladder before slowing down. "Hang on... What are they going to do to me? I'm black."

"I'd get off there if I were you."

Willie laughed and then glanced again at the dipping gallows. At the very end of it was a relatively new-looking, freshly cut piece of white rope that was dangling down toward the water.

"They must have just used this thing," Willie said.

"I'm gonna say it again!" Joseph shouted. "I'd get off there if I were you."

JOSEPH

Crazy Willie. Shaken Up.

Joseph looked around to make sure nobody was watching as Willie climbed down off the stage. He was certain some of his friends from The Row had come into the trees to see what was happening with the black boy he had with him. Rarely did anyone do something down in Devil's Drop without it being watched by at least a few whites that were hiding somewhere in the hillside.

Joseph knew Willie was smart and wasn't surprised it took only one try to teach him how to use the weed trimmer. He also wasn't surprised that by the time they were through, Joseph had done almost all the work himself. Willie had spent most of the time fiddling with his phone and tinkering around the stage and the edge of the water.

"We need to clean up under the stage as well," Joseph said. "It's kind of spooky under there but we won't be there long."

He led Willie toward the ladder when Willie asked, "How do we get under there?"

"There is an opening around the back."

They walked through the wavy grass behind the stage until they reached the door-sized gap between the stones that made up the back wall. They both ducked and went underneath the stage, and despite being under there lots of times, Joseph hated it because it was so dark and musty.

"Now I see why they don't replace those missing stones in the walls," Willie said. "Even with the ventilation, it smells like ass down here."

"How do you know what that smells like?" Joseph asked.

Joseph couldn't make out what Willie said but thought he heard him say, "Your mom showed me" or something like that, but it didn't make sense.

"Holy shit!" Willie said. "I know they blow up cars but what the hell is all that for?"

He was looking at all the dynamite boxes stored under the stage.

"Mr. Reggie and I put those under here about a month ago," Joseph said. "They want to make Devil's Drop bigger and they are going to clear out some trees. Gonna use the dynamite and some big machinery from Detroit to get the job done."

"There has to be a hundred boxes here," Willie said. "How much bigger they going to make the place? Damn."

"There's exactly a hundred boxes there," Joseph said. "Good guess."

"I'm also guessing they don't have to worry about anybody stealing it," Willie said. "Get busted taking this shit out of here and you better be able to hold your breath for a long ass time."

"What do you mean?"

"Nothing."

"Let's get this Weedwacked and get out of here," Joseph said.

They were done in less than ten minutes and Willie did his share. When they made it back to the truck, Willie insisted again that he drive and insisted even more that they go into town and grab a couple sodas.

"I never had a soda," Joseph said as they drove back through The Row.

"How can you be nineteen years old and never have had a soda? I mean, it's not like we are talking caviar here."

"Don't know," Joseph said. "How can you be seventeen years old and never used a Weedwacker before?"

"Pretty simple." Willie slapped Joseph on the arm. "Because we pay people like you to do it."

"You mean white people?"

"Don't make me out to be a racist here," Willie said. "That's not what I meant when I said people like you."

"Are the people white that work on your lawn?"

"Well...yes, but I didn't mean it in a bad way."

"And they get paid money? Real money?"

"No, dumbshit. Fake money"

"What's fake money?"

"I'm messing with you, genius. They get paid in real money."

Right then and there, Joseph thought about getting on that big highway, going to where Willie lived, and doing what he loves to do and getting real money for it and then buying nice things for Mama. But he also knew he'd need real money to get there.

"Besides," Willie said. "Don't plan on me using a Weedwacker ever again."

"What if Mr. Reggie wants you to?"

"I don't have to do anything."

"What if he needs your help?"

"I hate when you and your mom try to make me feel like a piece of shit."

"Mama did that?" Joseph said. "Mama is never mean. And I'm not doing that, either. I just asked what you would do if he needed your help."

"I'd probably do it."

"Well if you ever do it again at Devil's Drop, don't go back up on the stage."

"They don't scare me, Joseph. They are just people like you and me."

"They ain't nothing like me."

"I mean they put their pants on one leg at a time like us. Maybe they don't pull them up quite as high as you do, but it doesn't matter. I can deal with them."

"It does matter," Joseph said. "Being up on that stage is just for Trio."

"Yeah, yeah," Willie said.

Neither of them said a word until they passed Mr. Reggie's house and reached Main Street.

"Okay," Willie said as they pulled into town. He parked the truck in front of the general store. "What kind of soda you want? There is a first for everything."

"I will have whatever kind you are having."

"Be right back."

As Willie went into the store, Joseph leaned back and closed his eyes, wondering why someone as smart as Willie thought he could "deal" with The Crown. What a dummy.

Willie got back in the truck and handed him a can. It was cool to the touch and Joseph held it against the side of his face before reading the word *Cola* on the side. He'd seen lots of empty cans of it near The Row from when the black teens would come up and dump trash in front of the houses there, but he had never drunk one.

"Cheers," Willie said, tapping his can against Joseph's. "Here's to your first soda."

Joseph cracked his open and the soda exploded all over his face. It was cold, but was sticky as it dripped down the front of his shirt and the sides of his neck.

Willie laughed so hard it sounded like he was going to pee his pants.

"Oldest trick in the book," he said. "Sorry, I had to do it. You shake up the can and then hand it to someone."

"Why did you do that?"

"Like I said, there is a first time for everything."

"That wasn't very nice," Joseph said. But he thought it was kind of funny.

"It's called a practical joke," Willie laughed. "Feel free to pay me back."

"Really?" It sounded like fun.

"Yeah. But you'll never get me. I'm too smart."

"We will see," Joseph said, looking at the spilled soda on his pants. Willie even had a little on his nice pants, not to mention some grass stains from Devil's Drop. He pointed at Willie's leg. "You keep getting your pretty clothes dirty like that, Maggie won't like you anymore."

"Did you just call my jeans *pretty*?"

"Yup."

"Not to mention I don't like white girls."

"You like Maggie." Joseph wiped cola off his face with the back of his hand. "I may not be smart, but I'm not dumb."

"I believe that," Willie said, tapping the side of Joseph's can.

"Really?"

"Yeah," Willie said. "But sit tight while I run in and get you another soda."

WILLIE

Sticky Ear. Secret Spot.

Diving Competition. Waggling Finger 2.0.

Willie slept in the next day until around nine thirty. Actually, he had set the alarm because they were going fishing at ten thirty. Even after he showered, he was still tired and he suspected it was because he hadn't taken enough pills. Regardless, he was getting low and until he got his hands on more, rationing had become his only choice.

But there was something else that was bothering him. *Still*. He wanted to know why he hadn't cried yet over his father's death. And though he wasn't much for admitting it, he thought that maybe Cheever was right about the pills and how they covered what he should be feeling. On the other hand, a big part of him still believed that there was a really good chance that all those feelings he was supposed to be experiencing were all used up years ago when his mother and sister died.

When Willie went downstairs, Nancy and Joseph were making peanut-butter-and-jelly sandwiches and stuffing them into one of those wooden lunch boxes that looked like it had been made in the previous century, the kind you would see next to the perfect couple as they sat on a red-and-white checkered blanket in the shade of a tree. Maybe fishing time was also picnic time, but the odds of him eating PB and J were right up there with him eating anything they hauled out of Lake Erie. In fact, the last time he ate fish, he had the chocolate squirts so bad it was like he had gone three days without pills.

"Good morning," he said.

"Morning, Willie," Joseph said.

Nancy didn't say anything. Shocker.

"I'm going to make you like me, Nancy," he said. "My guess is that you think things come too easy for me. And though you are probably right, I want you to know I worked side by side with your son trimming weeds and we got the job done. Together."

"Never said I didn't like you," she said, working on the sandwiches like it was the last day to do it. And then she stopped and slowly looked over at Willie. He waited for her to say something else and then she just nodded and smiled, letting him know there was something in what he had said that she appreciated.

He smiled back and nodded, almost as if he were acknowledging they were now somehow on the same team. "Where is Uncle Reggie?"

"Went into town," Joseph said. "Ready for fishing?"

"I guess so." He was certainly ready to see more of Maggie.

"You have your phone with you?" Joseph asked.

"Upstairs."

"Mr. Reggie wanted you to call him the second you got up," Joseph said. "Just use the phone in the sitting room."

"How am I supposed to call him? He doesn't have a cell phone."

Joseph handed him a piece of paper with a number on it. "He said to call him at this number."

Willie shrugged and walked into the living room. He picked the receiver up off the old phone, put it to his ear, and dialed the number. That irritating *this number is not in service* recording came on and he hung up the phone.

"This number is no good."

Joseph snorted and then squealed out one of his high-pitched laughs and put his hand over his mouth to muffle it. "I must have written it down wrong."

"What's so funny?"

"Nothing. You better get something to eat."

"I'm not hungry. What's so funny?"

"Nothing," Joseph said, wiping the phone off like it was supposed to be cleaned every time someone used it. "Let's leave then. We have to pick up Alan and Maggie and then meet Uncle Reggie on West Jefferson Road in a little bit."

◆◆◆

THEY PICKED UP ALAN and Maggie but didn't see much of them (they sat in the bed of the truck) until they pulled over behind Uncle Reggie's sedan on West Jefferson Road, a pothole-infested drag that ran along Lake Erie. About a quarter mile north of where they parked, Willie could see the smokestacks from the lumber mill hovering above the trees.

As they collected their gear (containers of worms, a bucket of minnows, fishing poles—three for Alan and one each for Joseph, Nancy, and Maggie) from the back of the old pickup, Willie couldn't help but notice the way Maggie was looking at him. It wasn't that "I think you are hot" look she normally gave him that drove him absolutely crazy. This was different, kind of like she spotted a booger in his nose. And then he got a strange look from Alan followed by another even more sympathetic look from Maggie. The latest being the kind the homecoming queen gives the fat kid as she passes him in the hallway at school…a week after she turned down his invitation to the prom.

Uncle Reggie was holding three fishing poles under one arm, a tackle box about the size of a lunch pail in one hand, and a bucket of minnows in the other. Willie felt obliged to ease his uncle's burden and took the bucket of minnows, which smelled awful. Then he noticed Uncle Reggie giving him a funny look, not unlike the one Maggie had given him.

"What in tarnation happened to your ear?"

"What?" Willie said. "Nothing."

"Left one's looking sickly to me, like you been shot at and missed and pooped at and hit. Let me see."

His uncle studied his ear. "What in the world is that? Looks like peanut butter."

Willie wiped at his ear and then smelled it. It was peanut butter. And then he could hear that high-pitched squeal. Joseph was buckled over, laughing so hard he almost fell down. He must have let Alan and Maggie in on whatever was so funny, because they were laughing too. Nancy just had that closed-mouth smile that said *I want to laugh too.*

"I got you!" Joseph said.

"How in the world did you get peanut butter on my ear?" Willie said. It was funny, but he couldn't laugh until he figured out how Joseph did it.

He had it on the phone when he asked you to call Uncle Reggie. That's why he cleaned it up so fast…

"The phone," Willie said, finally laughing. "Good one, Joseph."

"I wondered what that was," Maggie said, smiling—*gazing* at Willie once again…the way he liked.

Even though he didn't have the faintest idea what happened, Uncle Reggie joined in on the laughs as he led them down a wooded trail and up a hill until they came to a small hole in a fence. The part of the fence that had been cut away had a sign attached to it in faded black letters that read:

Woodruff Gas and Power

Trespassers Will Be Prosecuted to

the Fullest Extent of the Law

"This will take us to my private spot," Uncle Reggie said.

"Appreciate you bringing us here," Alan said.

"Yes," Maggie said. "Thank you."

"Quite welcome," Uncle Reggie said. "I don't fish much anymore, but I'd like this to remain my private spot after today. Hate to be that way, but it's special because nobody but me has ever fished from where I'm taking you."

Maggie nudged Willie's arm and whispered, "Or so he thinks."

Alan backhanded her on the arm and shook his head as they walked down yet another path toward a small opening next to the lake.

♦♦♦

THE SIX OF THEM sat where the woods met the lake. The spot was well hidden at the very end of the power plant's seawall and they all had their legs dangling over the edge, an easy thirty feet above the water, testing both Willie's fear of heights and drowning. Despite the bullshit he'd laid on Joseph, other than floating on a raft back home, his buoyancy had never really been tested and the stress had him feeling the need for a handful of extra pills, pills he couldn't take because he was running too low.

Willie leaned back and looked to his left at the grungy old coal plant and its matching red and white smoke stacks that damn near hit the clouds. Beyond it was McLouth Steel and Lumber, along with all the swampland that separated it from Devil's Drop.

Alan was sitting to his far left, followed by Nancy and Joseph. He was thankful Maggie sat in between him and Joseph and that Uncle Reggie was sitting to his right. They all had their lines cast into a little channel that fed out to Lake Erie, waiting for bites. There had to be three hundred boats of fisherman all stacked on top of each other out in the water and it practically looked like you could run over to Canada just by jumping from one boat to another.

Uncle Reggie promised Willie he'd catch a fish (and that he didn't have to eat it) because when the walleye were running, there was no better place to be than where they were at.

"If you get a bite, just pull back and keep reeling!" Joseph yelled. Fishing was clearly one of the highlights of the kid's life. Willie gave him a friendly smile.

"I'll do that!" he yelled back.

Willie guessed he could understand why pinkies were so into fishing: they ate what they caught. Fishing trips were equivalent to grocery shopping for them, even though the fish had to be all jacked up by whatever chemicals were sure to be spilling into the water from the plant and the mill.

"You sure we aren't eating fish tonight?" he whispered to his uncle.

"Ain't gonna happen," his uncle said, followed by a wink.

He was glad his uncle was sticking to his promise because unless it was the whitefish at the country club back home, he was more of a red meat guy and would put a dog turd in his mouth before he ate anything they caught. Well, almost.

"What do I do after I reel one in?" Willie whispered to Uncle Reggie.

"Joseph will take care of it," he said.

"I'll help too," Maggie said, overhearing him.

"I can handle it," Willie said.

"No, you can't," she said, giving him a nudge that seemed to grab Uncle Reggie's attention. "And it's okay that you don't know what to do. You don't have to have all the answers, Mr. Southern Boy."

Willie thought about what she said. Between that, the perfect smile she was giving him, and those green eyes, she was right. In fact, everything about her was right.

"I guess sometimes I like to have all the answers," Willie said.

"Just sometimes?" she asked. "Whatever."

Willie laughed. He was the rich black kid. She was the white girl from The Row. She was also from another state, which might as well have been another planet, but he felt that he somehow already knew her. But what really blew him away about her was the way she left him feeling *not* in charge.

"I'd like to hang out sometime," Willie whispered. He'd never been on a date before, partly because he didn't ask that many girls out and partly because those he did ask never said yes.

"Me, too," Maggie said, under her breath. "How we gonna do that?"

"Maybe we could go for a car ride or something. Head out to a town that's…" He paused to triple-check that Uncle Reggie couldn't hear. "A little less purple and black."

"That would be nice."

"How old are you?" Willie asked.

"Just turned seventeen. How old are you?"

"The same. So, I missed your birthday. What would you have wanted?"

"For you to surprise me."

"I'm full of surprises," Willie said, pointing over at Nancy.

Her pole was bent and she was smiling from ear to ear. Willie could see the muscles flex in her arms as she stood and started reeling.

"Keep him on there, Mama!" Joseph yelled, placing the handle of his rod into what looked like a spool that was attached to the corner of the seawall. He grabbed a net and leaned down and waited for her to pull the fish up about three feet from the top of the seawall before scooping it in. It was over a foot long and by the time it was on shore, Nancy's pole was in the shape of a comma.

"Beauty!" Uncle Reggie shouted.

Willie couldn't remember two people so excited about anything in his life. It was as if Joseph and Nancy had accidentally snagged a bag of cash.

"Big deal to them, eh?" Willie said to his uncle Reggie, low enough so Maggie couldn't hear.

"Yeah," Uncle Reggie said. "Just curious about something."

"What's that?"

"What's a big deal to you?"

"What do you mean?"

"What makes *you* tick, Willie?" he asked. "What do you care about?"

It kind of reminded him of Cheever asking what he stood for. But instead of saying "lots of things" like he did to her, Willie told the truth.

"Not really sure."

"I guess I get that way sometimes," Uncle Reggie said, reaching in his shirt and pulling out a little flask. Willie wondered how the hell he hid it in there. "But it seems like everything is a joke to you."

"I just try to not take things too seriously," Willie said. "What's wrong with that?"

"I don't mean to open a wound, but your daddy died and it's like water on a duck's back to you."

"I've been through it before, Uncle Reggie. And excuse me for saying, you don't seem all that busted up about his death yourself."

"Like I told you, we weren't all that close."

"Close enough to be counted in the will, it looks like."

"Think so, eh?"

"Let me guess, I will only end up with half."

"Good guess," he said.

"What? I was kidding."

"I'm not, and like I told you, it was your daddy's doing."

Willie couldn't imagine what his uncle would do with fifteen or twenty million. Maybe he'd throw a bonus room on top of Nancy and Joseph's place or buy a shiny gun rack to hang Varmint Killer on in the living room.

"Surprised you didn't make a joke about the money," Uncle Reggie said.

"A bunch of stuff just went through my head, but I don't think you'd find it all that funny."

"Think you'd be a different person if your daddy wasn't rich?" Uncle Reggie asked. "Would everything still be funny to you?"

The conversation had gotten too serious. "Don't know. And thinking about it is a waste of time."

"I used to be a little like that when I was your age," Uncle Reggie said. "Laughed at everything because it was better than facing any pain. Better yet, just acknowledging or admitting that there was pain."

Something about what his uncle said made Willie feel more human. Kind of how Maggie's telling him he didn't have to have all the answers made him feel.

"What do you mean by *pain*?" Willie asked.

Uncle Reggie took a swig off his flask and it was like the other four were a hundred miles away. "Things we have done to others or ourselves. Or not forgiving others for things that have happened to us. You know that feeling…the one you get when you know something is wrong but you aren't quite sure what it is?"

"That's my whole life."

"That's when we are doing something in our lives that we know we shouldn't be doing."

"That makes sense."

"Reverend Kettle said it two weeks ago at service," Uncle Reggie said, "and he was right. Whenever we feel like we are doing something wrong, there's a good chance that God is poking you with his finger, telling you so."

Willie wanted to tell Uncle Reggie about the talk he had with Kettle but decided to save it.

"What do you stand for, Uncle Reggie?"

He tapped Willie on the shoulder and gave him a look that suggested he was proud of him for asking a good question.

"Doing what's right," Uncle Reggie said. "Kind of like what Kettle preached to us about. You know…loving our neighbors?"

Drink a little more, Uncle Reggie. You are in The Crown, remember?

But Uncle Reggie sounded so convincing, like even he believed what he was saying.

"I think if we just focus on doing what's right," Uncle Reggie added, "good things have a tendency to come our way."

"What about those people?" Willie whispered, tilting his head toward the others. Alan was pulling in a walleye and Joseph was high-pitched squealing as if Alan had a bar of gold on the line. "When do good things come their way?"

"Those four?" he asked.

"White people in general," Willie said. "How are things ever going to get better for them?"

"Why do you care?"

"Not sure," Willie said. It was a good question, because he never cared before.

"I do my best for Nancy and Joseph," Uncle Reggie said. "I could easily have them living up on The Row."

"And be out of some free help."

"They will be out of the backyard sooner than you think," Uncle Reggie said. "But answer me. Why do you really care?"

"I've come to know Joseph and I like him," Willie said. "I don't think Nancy is a big fan of mine, but things are changing. Regardless, I'd like to see them do better."

"Like I said," Uncle Reggie whispered, followed by a little burp. "Things aren't what they seem. And before you know it, they will be doing much better."

"You going to take them down south or something?" Willie asked.

"Nope," he said.

Just then, the top half of Willie's fishing pole damn near bent in half. His heart felt like it leapt out of his chest, so he stood and started reeling.

"Get 'em, Willie!" Joseph shouted.

"Keep reeling!" Maggie said.

Willie jerked the rod back, and when he leaned forward, the next thing he knew he was waking up in a bed, looking at Uncle Reggie. The side of his face hurt like hell and it didn't take him long to realize where he was.

A hospital.

◆◆◆

"What am I doing here?" Willie asked.

Uncle Reggie grinned. "You decided to take a little swim. One of the diving judges gave you a "0" and the other four each gave you a "1." It wasn't all that pretty. I think you earned the "1" for originality. I guess you could call it a face smacker."

Perfect.

I told Maggie I was full of surprises...looks like I wasn't kidding.

Fuck.

Willie sat up and it felt like his head was going to split in two. "How did I get here?"

"Joseph dove in and got ya," Uncle Reggie said, hiking his thumb over his shoulder. Willie looked behind his uncle and could see Nancy and Maggie sitting in the corner behind the door with Joseph and Alan standing behind them. It looked like they were hiding. "Then an ambulance came and got you."

"An ambulance?" Willie asked. Not good. That most likely meant an emergency room visit and lots of tests that would quickly reveal some extra-curricular chemical activity in his blood.

"Yeah," Uncle Reggie said, with a sincere smile. "But it looks like you're gonna make it."

"I want to get out of here," Willie said. "Like right now."

"Not until they say so," Uncle Reggie said, leaning a little closer to whisper. "Don't be afraid to thank Joseph. I swim like a ton of bricks and the girls wouldn't have been strong enough to fish you out. Regardless, by the time Alan or the rest of us stood, Joseph was already in the water after you. Prolly saved your life."

"Thank you, Joseph," Willie said, lifting his head to peek around Uncle Reggie. "That's what you get for the peanut-butter trick."

Joseph nodded and a little grin etched his face. "I didn't go in there after you. I was just trying to save that beautiful fish on the end of your line. You just happened to be in the way when I was trying to get out of the water."

Willie scratched at the IV in his arm and took a deep breath. A nurse came in and tapped at a few buttons on some machine to his right.

"How are you feeling?" she asked.

"Ready to go," Willie said, admiring her smooth black arms and neck. She was pretty, but not Maggie-pretty.

"We'll get you out of here today," the nurse said. "But it'll probably still be a few more hours. You hungry?"

"I'm good," Willie said, not taking long to realize why he didn't want a pill. Whatever was in his IV seemed to be meeting his needs pretty well.

The nurse turned around and seemed a little startled that four whites were in the room. With the door half open, anyone coming in the room wouldn't notice them, and her body language suggested she wasn't all that happy about pinkies being in what was certainly an all-black hospital.

"I'm sorry," she said, "but we can only have immediate family members in the room at this time."

"Yes, ma'am," Alan said as Nancy and Maggie quickly stood.

"They are with me," Uncle Reggie said.

"We have procedures we have to follow," the nurse said.

"You do whatever you have to do," Uncle Reggie said. "They aren't going anywhere until I do."

"Very well," she said, replacing Willie's IV and tapping at a few more buttons before leaving. Willie guessed that she wasn't used to being talked to like that. His other guess was that she may have known what fraternity his uncle belonged to, as Woodruff was a small town.

The nurse must have run into Sheriff Green because he was in the second she was out. He was not in uniform but still wore the same mirrored sunglasses. His street clothes were baggier, which made him look less fat, and when he walked right up next to where Uncle Reggie was, Willie could see himself in the sunglasses. Uncle Reggie stood and shook the sheriff's hand and the sheriff just stared at Willie for a few seconds before talking.

"Dispatch told me somebody got an ambulance ride today," Sheriff Green said. "Thought I'd stop by and see how he was feeling."

Either that or he was stopping by to place Willie under arrest for all the painkillers that he had in his pocket.

Had. Holy shit.

Relax, dumbass. You were trying to save what's left and kept them back at Uncle Reggie's.

"I'm feeling pretty good, Sheriff," Willie said. "Thanks for asking."

"Doc says he is doing fine," Uncle Reggie added. "He fell off the seawall over near the lake. Had himself a pretty good drop. I think he was unconscious on his way down, but he hit the water face-first."

"How did you fish him out, Reggie?" the sheriff asked.

"Joseph there got him out," Uncle Reggie said, turning around and pointing at Joseph and the others.

"Didn't know they were here," the sheriff said.

When the sheriff turned around, Willie noticed all the white people in the room were wide-eyed, as if they had seen a ghost. Nancy was standing in front of Joseph, and Alan had Maggie by the arm.

Sheriff Green crossed his arms and just stared at them.

No one said a word and when Sheriff Green turned back toward the bed, Nancy pushed Joseph out the door with Alan following them, pulling Maggie behind him.

Sheriff Green cocked his head to the side and listened to them leave. A peculiar little smile showed those gold teeth and he shrugged. "They sure seem to be in a hurry to get somewhere."

"Nurse just left," Uncle Reggie said. "She wanted them out of here. You know how things can be with white folk being around here."

"That I do," the sheriff said, patting Willie's leg. He nodded, clearly understanding he was the reason they left, not the nurse. "Get better, young man."

"Thank you, Sheriff," Willie said.

"My pleasure son," he said.

And then the sheriff went to the door and turned around. He held up his right fist and his short index finger sprung out straight at the ceiling. And then he waggled it in that *naughty naughty* kind of way Willie remembered from the courthouse steps up in Detroit.

WILLIE

Syncopal Episode. Fourteen Farts. The Right Trio.

In Town with Joseph. Finally Got a Yes.

The next day at Uncle Reggie's, Willie perused the hospital report that his uncle had left on the nightstand next to his bed.

Seeing that Willie was unconscious, and *a minor*, they had obviously asked Uncle Reggie a few questions and it was clear that he had tipped the medical peeps off to the happenings in Willie's life that could have created his "syncopal episode," which he assumed was the medical term for the thing Maggie saw him do—which was *faint*.

How manly.

The report also suggested that "stress from life events" had led to Willie's passing out, the not-so-medical term he would be using to describe what happened in lieu of *fainting*, a word that made Willie feel like he had to be sitting down the next time he took a piss.

Willie had no doubt that stress from not having enough pills in his system played a larger role in his little swim than stress from life events. Regardless, he hadn't fooled everyone, and even though he couldn't read all the doctor's handwritten notes on the bottom of the report, he could see the words *opiate use* somewhat hidden in the middle of the scribble. Then he wondered if Uncle Reggie had seen it or even knew what an opiate was.

Or if Sheriff Green had seen the report...

Fuck.

"You awake?" It was Uncle Reggie from somewhere near the bottom of the steps.

"Yeah," Willie yelled. He glanced at his phone. It was only 8:00 a.m.

He heard Uncle Reggie hack off a couple productive coughs before an awkward creak in the wood let Willie know he was on the stairs. Willie counted fourteen farts and figured his uncle let one fly with each step before he reached the landing and peeked his head in the room.

"How ya feeling?" Uncle Reggie asked.

"Back to normal," Willie said. Whatever the hell *normal* meant.

"Normal as in you may want to take a ride over to Reverend Kettle's to put a hurtin' on trees with some dynamite?"

Willie wondered if a kid that had passed out from "stress" should be handling dynamite. It sounded like a risky proposition (not as risky as being the passenger in a car driven by Joseph), but he felt fine, and blowing some more shit up sounded fun.

"Give me a minute and I will be right down." Willie waited for his uncle to grill him about the hospital report.

He didn't.

Thank God.

That's if there were one.

◆◆◆

WHEN HE WENT OUTSIDE, Joseph was already sitting in the driver's seat of the pickup, so he tapped on the window and motioned for Joseph to move over, which he did. Willie popped in, turned the truck around, and then they were off, heading down Cossit Creek toward Kettle's place.

"I'm a good driver," Joseph said.

"Nothing against you. I just don't like being a passenger. It's a control thing."

"You are a passenger when Mr. Reggie drives," Joseph said.

"I don't mind if it's a relative driving," Willie said, realizing that Joseph fell under that umbrella somewhere in the cousin department.

"Sure you are okay to drive after yesterday?"

"Just peachy," Willie said, slowing the truck out in front of the Vee house to get a good look at old Mack the dog. Once again, the dog was in the exact same place, just sitting there like a lawn ornament in a dust pile out in the field, attached to that long chain, staring at them with defeated eyes. What a life. "I feel sorry for that dog all chained up out there."

"I hear you," Joseph said. "Can't run away and even if he could, where's he gonna go?"

"Anywhere but there," Willie said. "What could be worse?"

Joseph shrugged. "Dunno."

"Nothing would make me happier than to take him with me when I go back to Georgia."

"I'm sure he'd like that," Joseph said. "That'd make him the luckiest dog in the world."

"Why did you all jet out of the hospital room yesterday when Sheriff Green showed up?" It was a rhetorical question, but he wanted to get Joseph's take. "I saw him play hard-ass downtown with Alan and Maggie the first day I got here. What's he got against them? You four took off out of there like he was Satan."

"I best not say anything about Sheriff Green," Joseph said.

"It's okay. I won't tell anyone."

"Can I trust you like I trust Mr. Reggie?"

"Absolutely," Willie said. He didn't know if Joseph could or not, if anyone could, but Joseph seemed to believe him. "Why wouldn't you trust me?"

"Don't know. You Southerners I don't know anything about."

"C'mon," Willie said, getting ready to take one out of Dad's playbook. "Name something I've done to let you believe you can't trust me. I'm not asking for a list. Name just one."

"You are black."

"Wow," Willie said. "You aren't a racist so I'm going to insist that until I give you a reason not to trust me, that you tell me why you're so afraid of Sheriff Green."

Joseph paused.

"All pinkies in Woodruff are afraid of Sheriff Green," he said. "I mean *all* of them."

Willie had to muffle a laugh. Joseph saying *pinkies* seemed way out of character. "What...is Sheriff Green in The Crown or something?"

He already knew the answer, but Willie had no idea who knew what in Woodruff, and once again, he wanted Joseph's take.

"Are you crazy?" Joseph said. It wasn't the first time the kid had asked him that. "I definitely can't talk about that."

"For crying out loud, you can tell me about it," Willie said. "You can trust me, and I won't say anything. You saved my life yesterday. I owe you, man, and the last thing I'd do is betray you."

They kept driving toward Main Street and Joseph looked over his shoulder as if someone a mile away could possibly hear him. And then he whispered, "Yes, then. Everybody knows Sheriff Green is Crown. He ain't too shy about it, either. He even takes his hood off at the meetings sometimes. Seen it myself lots of times."

"What?" Willie said. He shook his head. "You've been to a Crown meeting?"

Joseph looked at Willie like his life was in Willie's hands and that he'd said something he shouldn't have.

"Hid in the trees for lots of meetings," Joseph said. "Sheriff Green is the Right Trio. Everyone knows that. He's not like the rest. You don't have any idea who is under all those hoods down there in Devil's Drop, particularly the Trio. Nobody ever takes their hoods off. But Sheriff Green don't care that people know what he does. I think he wants them to know. Wants them to be afraid."

"He's Trio?" Willie wondered why the sheriff wasn't wearing the black robe and hood The Crown leaders wore that day he saw him up in Detroit when he was waggling that fat little finger of his. He was wearing the standard purple robe like the other thousand-plus Crown there. "I was up here in Detroit a few weeks back and saw a whole bunch of them at a courthouse where my father was working. I didn't see any Trio there."

"Around here, Trio are only dressed as Trio at Devil's Drop," Joseph said as they turned left onto Main Street toward downtown. "They don't wear black hoods and robes at other places. Don't want to lose a leader. They think it's too easy for some crazy pinkie to show up at a gathering and start shooting at the three black hoods, so the Trio wear purple out in public to blend in."

"Makes sense," Willie said. "In a fucked-up way."

"Why do you swear like that?"

"Just a habit," Willie said. "You can swear if you want. Won't bother me."

"I don't want to."

Willie shook his head. "Let me get this straight. It's not okay for you to swear, but you can use the word *pinkie*?"

"Habit," Joseph said. "You can say it if you want, won't bother me."

"Not around white people," Willie said. "I'd get my ass kicked. But you can say it around whites and it's no biggie. Why?"

"Dunno," Joseph said, shrugging. "But what I do know is that I hate Sheriff Green and The Crown."

"I want to see a Crown meeting," Willie said. "How do you know when there's going to be one?"

"Sheriff Green and Devil's Drop," Joseph said. "Sometimes they do it three times in a week and then they won't have a meeting for a couple months. But—"

"But what?" Willie said. "And what about Sheriff Green?"

"As you know, I gotta bunch of friends that live right near it."

"Of course. The Row."

"Every night there's going to be a meeting, Sheriff Green goes out there the same morning."

"He probably drives by there a lot anyhow, doesn't he?"

"Yeah," Joseph said. "But on days where there is a meeting, he drives right down into Devil's Drop in broad daylight, right where we trimmed the weeds, hours before the meetings start, and parks next to the dipping gallows. He gets out, walks up on to the platform, and goes into that little shack the Trio meets in, stays for about half an hour, and then leaves until he comes back for the meeting at night."

"I can't believe he is so flagrant about it."

"What's that mean?"

"I'm just surprised he goes there by himself with hundreds of whites surrounding him. Seems like somebody would pick him off."

Joseph laughed. "What's a pink—what's a white person gonna do to Sheriff Green? Who is gonna stand up to him and get away with it?"

"And the whole Crown parades right by all your friends in The Row on the way to the meetings?"

"Yup. Only way to get there unless they want to cut through the woods or the swamps."

The Row. Willie wondered what went through their minds when all those cars came by. The Crown did their thing right in the faces of the ghetto people and there wasn't a damn thing the whites could do about it. Or at least that's what they thought. Perception really was a funny thing.

Joseph leaned back and exhaled loudly.

"Will you chill out?" Willie said. "Quit worrying. I won't say anything to anyone. Even my uncle Reggie."

"Mr. Reggie knows Sheriff Green is Crown," Joseph said. "Like I mentioned, everybody does. Other than that, I don't know anyone else that belongs."

Really? Not even your daddy, who lives in the big house in front of you?

Neither of them said a word until they made it into town to grab a few supplies from Woodruff Hardware. Willie found a parking spot on Main Street and pulled in. He glanced around the storefronts and thought again of how the town looked like something out of an old-fashioned movie set. As many pinkies as there were up north, he was baffled at how so few ever came into town. There were easily a hundred people walking around and the only whites he could see were Alan and Maggie, painting yet another curb about half a block away.

"Your mom ever leave Uncle Reggie's house and come down here?" Willie asked as they stood out in front of the truck. "She come out here?"

Joseph looked up and down the street. "What do you think?"

Willie pointed at Alan and Maggie. "What about them?"

"They make money here. They have to be here."

Minimum wage was around eight bucks an hour, but Willie had no doubt that was a number Alan and Maggie only dreamed of because Woodruff didn't seem to care.

"What does my uncle Reggie pay you?"

"We get to stay there, and we get to eat."

Go figure. "But your mom never leaves?"

"Church on Sundays," he said. "And fishing once in a while."

"You go to church? Willie asked.

"Yeah," he said.

"Kettle has got the whole town praisin' the Lord, doesn't he?"

"We don't go to that church."

"I know that," Willie said, wondering why churches, even in the South, never caught on to the whole end-of-segregation thing.

"I like Reverend Kettle," Joseph said. "But I know there are other people at his church that aren't too fond of white people."

"You ever think about talking to Kettle about those people?"

"You serious?"

"Yeah," Willie said. "Kettle has a lot in common with my father—he seems very sympathetic to everyone—to all his *neighbors*."

"Just me talkin' to him ain't gonna make no difference," Joseph said with a little laugh. "Why don't you put in a good word for us with Kettle when we go over there? See if he can make things better for whites around here."

"I'm not exactly a civil rights guy," Willie said. "My father could have talked with him until the cows came home, but I'll give it a try."

They were in and out of the hardware store in less than three minutes, minutes that had Joseph making eye contact with no one. He just stared at the floor, even while he signed for Uncle Reggie's account. God forbid his uncle ever let the kid carry, let alone ever see, cash. Willie also noticed a few odd looks he got, as if people were asking who the black guy was hanging out with the hash brown.

"Let's go say hi to Alan and Maggie," Willie said after leaving the store.

"Gotta be quick," Joseph said. "We can get in trouble."

"They won't say jack shit as long as I'm with you," Willie said. "Plus, I want to ask out Maggie, so when we get over there, step away with Alan so I can ask her in private."

"You really are crazy."

They walked down the street and Alan and Maggie both looked up from the curb.

"How is the diving champ?" Maggie asked.

"Like new," Willie said. "Sorry I ruined your fun."

"Hey, Alan," Joseph said. "Can you come here a second?"

Alan put his brush in a bowl and then stood and walked toward Joseph. Willie knelt and smiled at Maggie.

"I think we need to go for a car ride. Just you and me."

"Sounds fun."

"How about tonight?"

"I can't tell you why, but I definitely ain't going out tonight," Maggie said. "I can go Saturday."

"Saturday it is then."

"But still, how are you going to get me without everybody seeing?"

"I don't care who sees."

"I know you don't," she said, those light green eyes sending his heart into pitter-patter mode. "But I have to care. So whether you like it or not, we have to be secretive about it."

"Let me think about the best way to do it," Willie said. "Joseph and I will stop by The Row and we will figure it out."

"Okay."

"Get to work!" a woman yelled from inside the store. "No congregating out there. I don't pay you to chitchat."

Maggie started painting and the woman came out.

"It's my fault," Willie said. "I was inquiring about their painting services."

The woman crossed her arms and pointed at Alan and Willie. "What's their excuse?"

"No congregating, you two!" Willie yelled, struggling to keep a straight face.

"Something funny?" the woman said.

"Just you," Willie said.

"You could learn some manners," the woman said, arms crossed.

"As could you," Willie said. "I can talk to whoever I want out here and there's absolutely nothing you can do about it."

The woman shook her head in apparent disgust and went back inside.

Joseph lowered his head without saying a word and meandered over to where Willie was. They headed to the truck and Alan and Maggie quickly resumed painting.

"No congregating?" Joseph asked. "I almost laughed when you said that."

"You damn pinkies are always causing trouble," Willie said.

Joseph studied him for a second and smiled. "You are crazy, Willie."

They both laughed. and Willie said, "That's like the hundredth time you've said that to me."

"Hey," Joseph said. "You want to hear something weird? Only because we were just talking about it. Guess what Alan told me?"

"What?"

"The Crown's gathering tonight."

Willie glanced at his watch. "Sheriff Green went to Devil's Drop today?"

"Yes, sir," he said. "First thing this morning."

"No wonder Maggie said she couldn't go out tonight. We are going to that meeting."

"No way."

"Yes way."

"You really are crazy. No playing this time."

"Of course, I am," Willie said. "But again, isn't everybody a little crazy?"

WILLIE

Auntie Shitterpants. Religious.

God Doesn't See Black and White.

When they pulled on to Kettle's gravel driveway, the tall minister was out near the edge of the road, holding what looked to be a couple days of mail in one of those giant hands that reminded Willie of five bananas gone bad.

"Hello, men," he yelled with a smile and friendly wave. Willie's best guess was that Joseph wasn't used to being treated so respectfully. "Pull around the back. I'm going to do my best to stay out of the way and let you two do your thing. If you need anything at all, just let me or Shanice know."

Willie pulled the truck up the driveway and watched Kettle in the rearview as he walked toward the front of the house.

He drove around back and looked at what was left of the trees. Uncle Reggie had come out and had obviously chainsawed them down into a string of six-foot stumps, each with a pair of chiseled holes in its bottom. The upper parts of the trees were scattered around in messy heaps of leaves and branches, letting everyone know that "clean-up" wasn't part of Uncle Reggie's job description.

All the windows on the back corner of the house were covered with thick tarps and a mesh net dangled from the second floor all the way to the ground, covering the old porch and almost the entire back of the house.

They got out of the truck and Joseph grabbed two pairs of gloves from a metal box in the bed of the pickup. He handed Willie a big spool of yellow wire and then opened the only box of dynamite they had brought. He grabbed three sticks and a pail filled with what looked like clay. It took them close to a half an hour to fill the back of the truck with limbs and leaves, and then Willie watched as Joseph knelt and felt around in the hole that had been chiseled away in the first tree stump, the one closest to the house.

"This hole is called a mortise," Joseph said.

Joseph then pushed three sticks of dynamite in the hole along with a blasting cap. He attached it to the yellow wire and then packed the hole with the clay.

Kettle came out of the house. "Need anything?"

"No, sir," Joseph said. "You want to watch the first one go?"

"Sounds like fun," Kettle said.

The minister followed them as they pulled the spool of yellow wire back a couple hundred feet around the side of the barn to hook it to the box that had the handle thing you press down on.

"What's that box called?" Willie asked.

"Blasting machine, isn't it?" Kettle said in that half-statement-half-question tone people use when they aren't quite sure.

Joseph shrugged. "Sometimes Mr. Reggie calls it a plunger, but we usually just call it the detonator box."

Willie preferred to call it the kick-ass-cartoon-dynamite-pusher thing. Regardless of its name, it took Joseph less than a minute to hook up the wire.

"Sure we're safe back here?" Kettle asked. "Should I get Shanice out here or is she safe in the house?"

"Maybe it would be best if we told Mrs. Kettle it is going to be loud," Joseph said.

"She safe in the house?" Kettle asked again.

"Yes." Joseph walked to the back of the truck and grabbed three little baggies of earplugs. "Better put these in."

Kettle tore open the little plastic bag, removed the earplugs, and grinned. "If she's safe, let's set the first one off and see what Shanice does."

Willie smiled. He already liked Kettle, and the fact that he wanted to have a little fun with his uptight wife made Willie practically love him.

"You sure, Reverend Kettle?" Joseph asked.

Kettle patted Joseph on the shoulder, nodded, and the three of them crouched down.

"Say goodbye to the rot," Joseph said. "That's what Mr. Reggie always says."

So much for Joseph needing affirmation. He stood, leaned down on the plunger, and the shot was beyond startling. It wasn't a blast. It was a roar. It sounded ten times louder than the practice one they had done at Uncle Reggie's. Willie saw the upper half of the trunk rise above the smoke, an easy twenty-five feet in the air. It turned horizontal in midair and did a lifeless belly flop back through the smoke and into the yard. Willie could hear Shanice Kettle's shriek over the sounds of the dirt and shredded wood that rained to the ground around them.

"Wow," Kettle said. "I'm going to catch it good, and rightfully so. I've never heard any noise like that."

"Me neither," Willie said. "That was awesome."

"I wasn't talking about the dynamite," Kettle said. "I've heard *it* before. But I've never heard a noise like the one my wife just made come out of another human being." "Being" sounded like *bean* with that Northern accent of his.

They walked through the smoke and dust and before they made it to the hole in the ground where the tree once stood, Shanice Kettle's second scream was out and getting progressively louder as she got closer. And before you could say *Auntie Shitterpants*, she came tearing out the back door and under the tarp as if she were on fire. Willie had no idea that the first time he saw Mrs. Kettle, she was wearing a wig, and to say she looked like someone had taken an ugly stick to her head would have been a compliment.

"Good Lord above!" she screamed. Her lips looked like they never moved. It was like the words just springboarded off her tongue and straight out of the hole in that ugly burnt potato she called her head.

"Forgive me, Shanice," Kettle said, handing her his earplugs. "I gave these lads permission to let her rip. You may want to put these in and go sit near the front of the house before they do the next one. I'm guessing the rest of these ain't gonna be much quieter."

"Shame on you, Jackson, for putting a lady through that," she muttered. She looked at Willie and Joseph the way a dermatologist would a suspicious dark mole and then crossed her arms. "And shame on you boys too."

Willie felt sorry for Kettle and figured the only reason he stayed married to that train wreck he called his spouse was that divorce was frowned upon in religious circles.

"Now now, Shanice," Kettle said, putting his arm around her in a patronizing way. "I'll go in there with you and let these boys finish what they came to do. They are going to do a couple more today and then come back a few more times to do the others."

Mrs. Kettle stepped out from under his arm. "I'm going to go into town for a few hours then. Can you pull the car out for me?"

"Of course, honey," the reverend said.

"I'm assuming you will be done by the time I get back?"

"Yes, ma'am," Joseph said. "We are doing two more and should be cleaned up in probably two hours."

"Willie?" she said, as if Joseph's answer didn't cut the mustard.

"If he says so, Mrs. Kettle."

Willie and Joseph watched in silence as Kettle escorted his wife into the house. Willie turned to Joseph and smiled. "If you ever need a reason to not get married, there she goes right there."

"I'm just gonna keep my mouth shut on that one," Joseph said, leaning into the back of the old pickup for more dynamite.

Reverend Kettle came back outside.

"That went over real well," he said, sprinkled in sarcasm. He smiled and chuckled as he walked to the barn and slid open the door. They heard the car start and Kettle backed a white sedan out that was probably ten years old.

Shanice Kettle came out back. She looked like a fucking idiot. She had her wig on and it was partially covered with a blue bonnet that could have easily been mistaken for one of those oversized foam hats that crazed college kids wear at football games. She and her big ass made it to the car and by the way her head was moving, it appeared she was chastising the reverend as he got out of the car and she got in.

Kettle walked toward the front of the house and turned around. It looked like he was holding up his earplugs. "I'll put these in! Just knock on the back door when you boys are through!"

It took them a half an hour to blow up two more trees and another hour to create three piles that were nothing more than dirt and wood chips. They shoveled the piles into the back of the pickup, rinsed off their hands, arms, and faces with the hose beside the barn, and went under the tarps to knock on Kettle's back door. He opened it like he knew they were coming.

"Come on in and have some cold soda," he said. "How many did we get done?"

"Three," Willie said, realizing that he'd worked hard and actually enjoyed it.

"Three down," Kettle said, holding the door open for them. "Go and have a seat at the kitchen table."

"Sounds good," Willie said, following Kettle.

Joseph stayed put. "I probably shouldn't go in."

Joseph waited outside. Kettle smiled before opening his hand, exposing one of those jumbo palms, and held it out toward the kitchen in a welcoming way.

"Come on in and join us, Joseph," the minister said.

"Yes, sir, Reverend Kettle." Joseph walked quickly through the door and into the house like he was being timed.

Kettle pointed at the antique kitchen table. "Have a seat." He walked over to the refrigerator. Willie sat. Joseph didn't.

Kettle returned with three bottles of soda, one in his left hand and two in the right. He paused and smiled. "You can sit down, Joseph."

Joseph sat, and Kettle handed him a soda before he sat down himself. Willie noticed Joseph's brow furrow and he knew why.

"Don't worry," Willie said. "That one won't explode on you. The cans are the ones you got to look out for."

Joseph gave him a suspicious look and then glanced at Kettle. "Never had a soda in a bottle before."

Willie took a sip of his cola and grinned at Kettle. "I got Joseph with the old 'shake up the can right before it gets opened' trick. Got him good."

Willie thought about the soda going all over Joseph's jeans and how stained and messed up they were, even before the soda. And then he glanced at his own, which had taken their own beating from the day's work.

"How long you planning on being up here?" Kettle asked.

"Not sure." Willie was starting to feel a little irritable and he knew why. Not enough pills in his system, and until Uncle Reggie was ready to talk about splitting the money up, Willie was going to have to get Evan on his way up to Michigan with a new supply like pronto. "I'm thinking that being a minor and all kind of throws a wrench in things in terms of my living by myself back in Georgia. I still need to set aside some time with my uncle and go over the plans my father made."

"Your daddy was a smart man," Kettle said. "I hadn't talked to Tyrone in probably twenty years or so, not since he moved down south. But I'm sure things are laid out in a way that's best suited for you."

"I'm sure of it," Willie said. All except the part where Uncle Reggie gets fucking half.

"Hard to believe he is gone," Kettle said. "Truly is a shame."

"Yeah," Willie said. "Ain't a shame what happened to his killer though."

Kettle shook his head. "Taking his own life *is* a shame, Willie."

Willie laughed and looked at Joseph. "Excuse me for saying this, Joseph." Then he turned back at Kettle. "You don't think it was a Crown-sponsored suicide?"

"I'd prefer not to discuss that," Kettle said. "But your uncle tells me you enjoyed the church service you attended."

That was pure fiction, Uncle Reggie was just being nice, but Kettle was probably the most legitimate Willie had ever met when it came to the whole religion thing, so he played along.

"It was awesome. I liked the 'love your neighbor' part."

"Appreciate the kind words," Kettle said. "Coming to service Sunday?"

"Despite not being very religious," Willie said, "I'll be there." If it were anyone but Kettle he would have declined the offer.

"I'm not religious either," Kettle said. "Religion is a man-made word and a man-made thing designed to control people."

"I agree," Willie said.

"And how about you?" Kettle asked, tapping Joseph on the arm. "You a believer?"

"Yes, sir," Joseph said.

"Why don't you come too?" Kettle said.

"We were just talking about that," Willie said. "Literally right before we came here."

"I don't know, Reverend Kettle," Joseph said.

"Why not?" Kettle asked.

"I probably shouldn't say," Joseph said timidly.

"I'm guessing it's a black-and-white thing?" Kettle asked.

Joseph didn't say anything. He just took a swig of his soda and looked at the table.

"Please look at me," Kettle said, talking to Joseph, who faced him. "The Lord doesn't see black and white. Do you understand that?"

"I appreciate it, Reverend Kettle. But I don't think Mama would let me."

"I understand," Kettle said. "But if anyone ever bothers you anywhere, you just let me know. Okay?"

"I will," Joseph said.

Willie leaned back and realized he was listening to a conversation between the two nicest people he had ever met. Joseph was just plain old nice and Willie had never met anyone with Reverend Kettle's sincerity in helping others without asking anything in return.

Willie was looking forward to spending more time with Joseph and learning more about Kettle and the make-believe God the minister had so much faith in.

The God that didn't see black and white.

JOSEPH

Karma. Lucas.

Friends.

They were on their way back to Mr. Reggie's house and Joseph couldn't stop himself from asking a question about something the minister said.

"You really think Reverend Kettle would help me if somebody gave me a hard time?"

"Absolutely," Willie said.

"I like what he said about God not seeing black and white," Joseph said. "I know it's true, but then why aren't all black Christians nice to white Christians then?"

"Not sure," Willie said.

Joseph thought about Reverend Kettle standing up for him against a black person. And then he thought of something that was beyond his imagination. "Let's say Sheriff Green was mean to me...what could Reverend Kettle do about that?"

"Not sure again," Willie said, like he was thinking about something else.

"What's on your mind?"

"Thinking about my father," Willie said. "I'm still blown away that you never met him."

"Never did," Joseph said.

"Looks like my uncle wasn't kidding when he said he and my father fell out of touch. At least until near the end, when money matters were involved."

"At least you knew your father," Joseph said. "Be thankful. I never knew my daddy."

Willie looked at him and then shook his head in a way Joseph didn't understand. But again, Willie did a lot of things that Joseph didn't understand.

"To be honest with you," Willie said, "it also blows my mind to hear you say you never knew your daddy."

"Why?"

"Nothing," Willie said as he pulled the truck into Mr. Reggie's driveway and up to the side of the barn. He turned the truck off and faced Joseph. "At least you still have your mother. Mine is dead. And so is my sister."

"I'm sorry," Joseph said. "But I'm sure they are in a better place with your daddy."

"Sounds like something Shanice Kettle would say," Willie said. "But the truth is that my mom and sister are in holes in the ground back in Georgia and Dad is downtown at the funeral home getting ready to be turned into ashes."

"You know what I mean by better place, don't you?"

"Yeah," Willie said. "But I have a hard time buying into it."

"What do you think happens when someone dies?"

"Remember what it was like before you were born?"

Joseph mulled it over for a few seconds.

"Of course not."

"It's just like that," Willie said. Then he started talking faster and suddenly sounded angry. "When we die, the power switch goes off and the game ends. And the reason is that there is no God and there is no heaven. Only karma. In fact, if there is a God, he is karma, and karma takes care of business. And though we may never realize it, everything kind of comes out in the wash while we are here on earth."

"What do you mean? I don't get it."

"I mean we get what we deserve."

"No," Joseph said. "There is a place that's good. And if your parents and sister were believers they are at the same place that I will go when I die. Reverend Kettle is right. God doesn't see black and white. All believers will be together, and it won't matter what color your skin is."

"The last time any white person talked about the possibility of blacks and whites getting along in the same place…well, you know what happened to him, don't you?"

"They killed him," Joseph said.

"Why?"

"Because they are afraid."

Willie turned and looked at Joseph like he couldn't believe what he heard. And then his eyes widened as if a light had gone on inside of his head.

"You know what? You are very smart, and you are absolutely right."

Joseph smiled. The idea of someone thinking he was smart felt good inside. "Thank you, Willie."

"For what?"

"That was nice of you. Nobody ever called me smart before. I like it."

"Makes us even," Willie said. "Nobody ever called anything I've ever said *nice* before."

"You are nice, and friends say nice things to each other."

Willie smiled. "We are friends, aren't we? It's crazy."

"Why is it crazy?"

"Because I really don't have friends. I guess it's because of the whole karma thing."

"You said that God is karma." Joseph never heard that word until Willie said it earlier. "I'm assuming karma is a good thing then?"

Willie leaned back in his seat and it looked like he was staring straight through the windshield which was speckled with little dead bugs. "Karma is why I am who I am. It's why you are the only person to ever say I'm nice. It's why I take pills. It's why I'm a complete douchebag."

"You take pills?" Joseph said. "I take them too when I get headaches. Mr. Reggie gives them to Mama and she gives them to me."

Willie exhaled loudly and then covered his eyes with his hands. He waited a few seconds and then put his hands back on the wheel. "Ever hear that phrase 'the bigger they are, the harder they fall'?"

"Yeah," Joseph said.

"It's bullshit," Willie said. "The truth is, the bigger they are, the harder they hit you. Unless they are white and you are black."

Joseph laughed and then stopped because Willie wasn't laughing with him.

"I was in third grade when I punched Lucas Adams, the white kid that had stolen my twin sister's lunch pail."

"You went to school with pinkies?"

"Yeah," Willie said. He took a deep breath and exhaled loudly again before closing his eyes. "It was before my father made all his money. Before he settled a big case against an electric company. Some worker grabbed a live wire and got toasted. My father's cut of the settlement was like two million bucks and that pretty much springboarded him into being the super lawyer he became. But before that happened, me and my sister went to a public school."

"Wow," Joseph said. "I figured you went to school with one of those uniforms on. Wearing a tie and everything."

"I do now, but I didn't then. But back to Lucas taking my sister's lunch pail. I can still, to this day, hear my mother saying, *'No pinkie is going to get away with that. Give them an inch and they take a mile.'*"

"Your mother said that?"

"Yes," Willie said. "And what's weird is I never heard my mother say anything racist before. I mean ever. I have no idea why she would automatically think Lucas was the one that took it. It's like something inside of her was programmed to go off."

"What happened?"

Willie finally opened his eyes and Joseph immediately noticed he was talking slower.

"During recess, I had Big Luke follow me over to the corner of the playground, near the parking lot where my mother was watching from her car. She told me that morning that I had to confront him. I did, and Big Luke said he didn't take the lunch pail. My mother heard him and she yelled from the car that he was lying."

"What did you do then?"

"And then she yelled it again. *'He is lying!'* And then she said, *'Hit him! Hit him now!'* It was like she was a different person, repeating what someone else was telling her to say or following instructions from voices in her head. Voices that were telling her all the bad things she had ever heard about whites were true and now that it involved her child, something had to be done about it."

"What did you do?"

"Big Luke was easily a head taller than me, but I pulled back and hit him square in the nose. He just flinched and then a little stream of blood trailed out his left nostril, down the front of his white face, and then on to the shirt that was clearly a hand-me-down from one of his eight older brothers. Big Luke's eyes watered, and he just stared at me. I knew he could have easily kicked my ass halfway around the planet, but he knew the trouble that would bring from black people. I cried right there and really wanted to tell him I was sorry, that my mother made me do it… but that would bring another sort of trouble for me that was arguably much worse than the trouble Lucas would have gotten into had he chose to stomp on me."

"I get it," Joseph said. It sounded like maybe things down south in Georgia weren't that different after all.

"Anyhow…" Willie took his hands from the wheel and putting his palms flat on his legs. "I found out that same night that Luke didn't take the lunch pail. My sister confessed to my mother that she threw it away so she could get a new one. And it didn't seem to bother my mother in the least what happened to Lucas."

"Sounds like you're lucky Big Luke didn't swing back," Joseph said. "Lucky you got away with it."

"I didn't get away with it!" Willie yelled, smacking the dashboard. The knob on the end of the gearshift popped up and landed on the seat between them before rolling onto the floor. "And neither did my mother and sister!" Willie leaned back again. "Why did my mother make me blame a white kid?"

"Dunno," Joseph said, startled by the way Willie yelled.

"Why?" Willie asked again. "I mean, let's suppose Kettle is right and there is a God that doesn't see black or white. If he really exists, why don't the people that he supposedly created equally treat each other as equals? Why don't whites and blacks get along?"

"Because people don't like people that are different than they are?" Joseph said. It was a total guess, but his gut told him he not only answered Willie's question, but also the question he'd asked himself earlier about black Christians not being nice to white Christians.

"Exactly!" Willie said. "And it's not just blacks and whites, it's people of all colors."

"You are right."

"I was young," Willie continued, talking fast again, so fast Joseph could barely keep up. "Maybe I hadn't yet *learned* to not like white people or to treat them unkindly."

Joseph wasn't quite sure what Willie meant because for something to be learned, it had to be taught. "You think people learn to not like people?"

"They see how the people they love treat certain people and then they think it's what they should do. But not me. Though I was just a little kid, I knew that even though my mom told me to punch Lucas...I knew that I shouldn't do it... because hitting Lucas was...it was—"

"It was wrong."

"Yes!" Willie shouted, this time smacking his palm on the side of the wheel.

"It was God talking to you," Joseph whispered, tapping Willie on his leg. "Mama says we all have a little voice that tells us right from wrong and it's God."

"The reason I hit Lucas is because I was afraid of my mother. And like I said, Big Luke could have squashed me like a grape, but what I was really afraid of was what would happen if I *didn't* hit him."

"What do you mean?"

"I was afraid of the consequences."

"Afraid of not hitting him? Afraid of the consequences from doing what was right?"

Willie shook his head and laughed. It wasn't a *that's funny* laugh, it was a crazy person's laugh. "My father never heard about my sister lying about the lunch pail. My father never heard about my mother making me confront Luke. My father never heard about the punch I threw. But karma sure as fuck did."

"I still don't know what karma is."

"Karma is the thing that makes sure we don't get away with stuff."

"What happened?"

Willie gripped the steering wheel with both hands and Joseph could tell by the way his arms were shaking he was squeezing as hard as he could.

"The next day," Willie said. "I mean the *very next day* after I threw the punch...a man named Darnell Elliot tried committing suicide. He was driving over a hundred miles an hour and swerved intentionally into oncoming traffic. He hit the first car head on...my mother and sister were in it...and they were killed instantly."

"That's terrible," Joseph said.

"Yeah," Willie said, nodding. "That's the last time I ever cried."

"Why did that Elliot fella have to take them with him?" Joseph asked. "That's an outright shame if you ask me."

"He didn't," Willie said. "Darnell Elliot lived. And that accident and everything else that has happened in my life since is all my fault. Not just because I threw that punch, but because I knew throwing the punch was wrong and I still did it. God, Joseph, I've been waiting so long to say that, but I've always been afraid of what my dead mother would think and what other people would think."

"You were just a little kid. Your mama made you do it."

"It wasn't her fist that hit Lucas. It was mine. Like I said, I knew it was wrong and karma has been kicking my ass ever since. Even to the point that I tried to off myself about three years ago."

"What's that mean?"

"Kill myself."

"Oh." Joseph's throat felt dry and funny and he didn't know what to say.

"To this day, everyone thinks I was just trying to jump in the pool from the roof of the house. I landed on the umbrella of a table next to the pool and only broke my leg and some ribs. I was prescribed painkillers and the rest is history. I eat pills like they are fucking candy. I'm a hardcore addict. A lonely one. Now my father is dead and I'm all by myself and I'm wondering if it's true that addicts can't survive on their own."

"You are not by yourself."

"I'm sorry," Willie said. "I must sound like the biggest whining pussy of all time."

"You don't need to apologize. Friends are here for each other."

"You know something, Joseph?"

"What?"

"I've made more progress opening up to you in the last fifteen minutes than I have with Dr. Cheever in two years."

"Who is that?"

"Someone that tried to help me." Willie reached out of the driver-side window and adjusted the cracked mirror. "She's the one that said addicts can't survive on their own. I still don't know about that, but she was definitely right about something else. I've got more of a reality problem than a pill problem and that reality is why I keep taking pills."

"'Cause you hurt?"

"I hurt here," Willie said tapping on his own head. "But I can fix it. And I need to quit taking pills...soon."

"Just quit then."

"It's not that easy."

"Just stop putting them in your mouth."

"I'll need help. Medical help. And until I figure out where to get that help, I actually need to figure out how to get more pills."

"I'll help too," Joseph said. "Because like I said, you aren't by yourself. You got me and Mama and Mr. Reggie."

"Thank you," Willie said. "Maybe there is a God. And Kettle told me that he puts people in our lives for a reason. Either way, I'm glad I have you. I've never been so sincere in my life when I tell you I can't thank you enough for listening. And for being my friend."

Joseph never felt so good. He held out his hand and Willie shook it.

"You are welcome, Willie. You are welcome, my friend."

WILLIE

Evan. Reload.

Just get up here," Willie said. "I won't make it another couple of weeks. I don't have many left and there is no way I'm going to snoop around this town looking for a dealer."

"I ain't coming up there," Evan said. "It's too far and too *dark*."

"What will it cost you to lose a customer like me?" Willie asked, wondering if he sounded as desperate as he thought he did.

"Ain't worth risking my life over, man. Ain't gonna happen."

"Evan, I really need you here. If you are afraid, carry a gun. I've told you a million times you should carry one anyhow with all the cash you carry around."

"Hate guns. Never had one and never will. You know that."

"Blah blah blah," Willie said. "Can you mail them to me?"

"You are the stupidest smart black boy I know," Evan said. "Who knows how they check the mail nowadays? If they know what's in that package, they will follow it until you open it up and then put your black behind in the big house for a good long while."

"I guess you are right," Willie said, ready to drop the trump card. "Just tell me what I'd have to pay you for you to come up here. It's about a twelve-hour ride, tops. Everything has a price. C'mon man."

There was static on the line and Willie wondered for a second if they had been disconnected or if maybe someone was listening in on Evan's phone. For all he knew, every cop in Georgia could know he was a dealer.

"Three grand for the pills and three grand for the visit."

"Done," Willie said.

"Really?" Evan said. Then there was a little pause. "For that kind of money, I'm on my way."

"Okay," Willie said. "Thanks man."

"Thank *you*," Evan said. "And Willie. Why haven't you said anything stupid to me on this call?"

"What do you mean?"

"You know exactly what I mean?"

"Oh," Willie said. "Something derogatory or borderline racist?"

"Borderline?"

"Don't worry about it," Willie said. "Thanks again and see you soon."

REGGIE

Cherry Light. Recruit.

It Runs in the Family.

Reggie had already started to pull over to the side of Cossit Creek before Demetrius had the cherry light and flashers going full bore on his squad car. There was never another car within a mile, so why he always felt the need to make things look like an official stop every time he wanted to chat was something Reggie never understood. Regardless, he wouldn't be bringing it up or arguing with him about it because somewhere along the line, Demetrius had gotten a little too big for his britches and it wouldn't do much good.

Reggie took a swig off his flask and smiled as the sheriff exited his car. Despite all the yack he had to listen to from Demetrius over the years, Reggie took a bit of solace in knowing he would never get a DUI in Woodruff.

Reggie got out of the car and met him near the back bumper where the sheriff crossed his arms.

"Good thing you turned the lights on," Reggie said. "I probably would have never stopped. Next time maybe you can throw a chain across the road with spikes attached to it to take the tires out."

Demetrius pulled down his sunglasses just far enough to peek over the edge. "You look like hell, Reggie."

"Food poisoning or flu bug feels like it may be setting in."

"Too bad. Hope you feel better."

He knew Demetrius didn't give a hoot how he felt. The sheriff wanted something or he never would have come out to Cossit Creek, unless there was a meeting that night.

"So," Reggie said, taking another sip off his flask. "I know I wasn't speeding. Why'd you pull me over, officer?"

"Willie knows exactly who I am," Demetrius said. "He knows I'm Crown."

"I think the whole county knows exactly who you are, Demetrius. You don't exactly go out of your way to conceal your extracurricular activities."

Demetrius held up his index finger and moved it back and forth. "I went like that to him when we were up at the courthouse. Then I did it when we were at the hospital and I have this feeling he put the two together. That he remembered me."

"I'm guessing you did it on purpose, that you wanted him to know it was you."

Demetrius only shrugged. "He's a smart boy, and I asked you to keep an eye on him."

"I know," Reggie said. "You asked me four times. And I told you there is nothing to worry about, and I'm still telling you the same thing."

"What did he say about our little prisoner friend hanging himself?"

"What's he supposed to think?" Reggie asked

"Answer my question. What did he say?"

Reggie hit the flask again and wiped the corner of his mouth. "Didn't say much of anything."

"He don't suspect The Crown? I'm a little disappointed."

"He's just a kid and he ain't from around here," Reggie said. "Besides, I don't think he'd like all that goes on at Devil's Drop. In fact, I know he wouldn't."

"Of course he would," Demetrius said, spitting a big hunk of tobacco on to the dirt road. "It runs in the family."

WILLIE

Barf Bucket. Cool Uncle.

Thirsty Coyote. Anxious.

Willie spent most of the afternoon listening to Uncle Reggie barf his brains out of that watermelon head of his, so he figured he should pay him a visit in the "master" bedroom.

"I reckon it's food poisoning," Uncle Reggie said, lying in bed. He had a small oscillating fan perched on the nightstand aimed right at his big black head. Next to the nightstand was a white bucket that was clearly there as an emergency chunk catcher.

"You need anything else, Mr. Reggie?" Nancy asked, taking away an untouched bowl of soup.

"Unless you can think of a way for this body aching to go away, I think you can call it a day until suppertime," Uncle Reggie said.

"Anything I can do?" Willie asked as Nancy walked by him in the doorway.

Uncle Reggie waited to answer until Nancy was down the stairs.

"If I thought those pills of yours would help me," he said, "I'd take me a couple of those, but I think that's probably not all that wise to mix that with the drinking."

"Hospital told you?" Willie asked. Dumb question.

Uncle Reggie nodded. "That, and your daddy. He knew you never gave them up."

"Really?" Not a dumb question. He couldn't believe Dad suspected it, let alone knew. Fuck.

"Yes, sir," Uncle Reggie said.

"I appreciate you being so cool about it, Uncle Reggie."

"I understand getting attached to something. Been drinking since I was about eleven. It's taken its toll. I'm forty-four, but don't look a day over fifty-five. Been falling apart over the last five years. Every time I go take a tinkle, I'm still tinkling a good minute or so after I zip my britches back up."

"It's going to be hard for me to quit," Willie said. "And maybe even dangerous. And the thing that sucks is I'm almost out of the pills I brought with me."

"Your daddy knew you can't just go cold turkey," he said. "Said it could kill you. Said you need to detoxify or something like that. Prolly goes for me, too, but he also left a plan for that. He mapped out a couple nice medical places up in Detroit and a couple down Georgia way once we think you are ready to go for some rehabbing. You'll likely be gone close to a month when you do. I think twenty-eight days to be exact. We will have to wait and see which one of the places will be best."

"Who is we?"

"You and me," he said. "I'm your guardian until you turn eighteen."

"I'm guessing that's in the mystery paperwork I get to see when—"

"When the time comes and once again, it's up to me to determine when that time arrives."

"I wasn't really planning on spending the whole summer here," Willie said. "Dad's killer is dead, the funeral is over, now all I have to do is get the money thing figured out and have you appoint someone to stay with me when I head back. Why can't we do those things now?"

"Be patient. We've got another month and a half or so before you have to get back down there for school, so let's get this pill thing figured out first."

"Okay," Willie said, not ready to mention that Evan and the fresh supply were heading north.

"Why don't we just get you checked in somewhere up here then?"

"Whatever you think is best," Willie said. *Summer certainly turned out different than I'd planned.* "Care if I wait until my pills are gone though?"

"As much as I hate to see you put another one of those things in your mouth, with all that's been happening, I don't see anything wrong with that. Can I ask you something though?"

"Sure."

"Why take the darn things to begin with?"

Willie leaned against the wall next to the bedroom door. "Makes me feel better."

"Sounds like having a problem with your car engine and turning up the stereo so you can't hear the problem."

"Pretty close."

"Will you do me a favor then, Willie? It's the only thing I will ever ask of you."

"Okay," Willie said.

Uncle Reggie coughed. It sounded like it hurt.

"Don't end up like me," his uncle said. "Get those pills licked and don't let it do to you what the booze did to me."

"You can quit too, Uncle Reggie. Maybe we should check in together."

His uncle licked his lips and then glanced at the barf bucket like he was going to hurl.

"I'm about as excited for rehabbing as I'm guessing you are. Maybe you can test the waters of the rehab joint for me."

"I can do that," Willie said. He was dying to ask his uncle about The Crown meeting that night but knew it would be a mistake. "I think I may take a spin up to Detroit later this afternoon. Maybe do some sightseeing. Dad took me up there toward the end of the trial, but I didn't get much of a chance to see anything."

"You do that," Uncle Reggie said. "And park that car of yours in a safe place. As much as I hate to say it, there are white folk up there that are prone to permanently borrowing tires and other car parts, including the whole car."

Willie laughed and told his uncle he hoped he felt better.

"There's a coyote out in the field," Willie said, pointing out the window. It was drinking water out of a pond that was way past the back of the barn.

"Ain't seen one in a few weeks," Uncle Reggie said, not moving in the bed. "If I had Varmint Killer, I'd drop him in his tracks right through the window. Shoot 'em as a courtesy to other farmers in the area. Darn things breed like rabbits, then they start killing chickens and the like. Heck, I read something a while back that they aren't afraid of kids, either. Wouldn't be good if a few of them made off with somebody's little one."

Willie kept pointing at the coyote. "He is just sitting there, standing next to a pond out there."

"Gonna have to teach you how to shoot Varmint Killer for when I'm not around," Uncle Reggie said. "In fact, have Joseph take you out back soon and squeeze a few rounds off. Take a day off and get the hang of it. Next time that coyote shows his head, you put him down right where he stands."

"Sounds good to me," Willie said. "And Uncle Reggie?"

"Yes, sir?"

"Thanks again for being a cool uncle. I figured I'd be toast if you knew about me taking pills."

"No problem," Uncle Reggie said. He reached over to the nightstand and grabbed the empty glass that was there. "Now I was kind of hoping you could run downstairs and pour me a little glass of whiskey. I need to get myself some sleep or it's going to be a long evening."

"Will do," Willie said, anxious to watch his uncle and his friends doing their thing later that night.

Out at Devil's Drop.

WILLIE

Mosquitos. Bird's-eye View.

Chosen People. The Closet.

Are we going to get there any time this fucking month?" Willie asked. He'd have sworn he'd lost a pint of blood already. He'd been getting gnawed on by sparrow-sized mosquitos for over an hour and couldn't for the life of him understand what was taking so long to get to Devil's Drop.

They had walked all the way from Uncle Reggie's, taking a route that easily quadrupled the time it normally took to get there, but Joseph insisted the path through the woods was the safest way to go on the nights The Crown met, and that nobody had ever seen a black person on the path. Until now.

Joseph pointed away from the path at the thinnest part of the woods. They had finally made it close enough to The Row that they could see where most, if not all, of the ghetto people gathered on the nights The Crown got together. Both Joseph and Uncle Reggie made it clear that Crown members weren't all that shy about driving right through the ghetto on the way to the meetings, so the residents seemed to not only get out of their houses but well behind them and into the cover of the trees.

Willie speculated that the reason blacks never came down the path he was standing on was most likely because it would be the best and only place in Woodruff (maybe on the planet) for a white person (assuming he was brave or stupid enough) to try to whack a black person and get away with it. In fact, the way Willie figured, it wouldn't be all that hard to do:

Quick smash to the head with a rock.

Hide the body anywhere you want.

Watch the buzzards circle.

Then assume that the brush was so thick in the woods that Sheriff Green would never go out there looking for someone and that the evidence would soon be eaten by critters, making the case go cold.

"What if a Crown dude sees me out here the night of a meeting?" Willie asked. "This is a little different than Weedwacking for Uncle Reggie."

"Won't happen," Joseph said, pulling back at waist-high foliage that leaned over the edges of the path. "But if it does, you will be fine. Forget you're black?"

"No," Willie said, "and I also haven't forgotten that they may not like being spied on."

"You're black, dummy."

"I know, *dummy*. But you're not."

Joseph didn't respond, and Willie stayed right behind him as they made their way farther down the path. It was nearing dusk when they finally reached the edge of Devil's Drop. The place appeared different as they looked down on it, and as it got darker, it seemed more private and mysterious, as if someone were dimming the lights to shadow the sinister activities that were to follow. Willie took a deep breath and a fresh knot in his gut told him that being out in the woods that night was one thing and one thing only. A mistake.

"Right there," Joseph said, pointing at one of the trees in the thick brush to their left.

A makeshift ladder made of two-by-fours had been nailed to a thick elm. They walked to the base of the tree, and when Willie looked up, he could see the bottom of what looked like some type of half-assed tree fort about thirty feet above them.

"You are kidding me, right?" Willie asked. "I hate heights."

"We can see everything from up there."

Willie glanced back through the thicket and down at Devil's Drop. The only thing he could make out was the stage on the far side of the valley. A lazy fog had crept its way in from the lake and seemed to surround the base of the platform. Someone began lighting torches and Willie got his first look at the podium where the Trio would soon be standing and addressing The Crown. He looked back at Joseph and then his eyes followed the two-by-fours up the tree.

"What do you weigh?" Willie asked.

Joseph shrugged. "Don't know."

"I weigh a buck sixty. You got at least two twenty-five. That floor up there looks like it is made of plywood."

"It will hold us. Been four of us up there before."

It made Willie feel a little better, but the fact that Math 101 bullied Joseph out of school weighed on Willie's mind.

"Okay. If I die tonight, I'm never gonna talk to you again."

"Huh?" Joseph said.

"Nothing. Let's do it."

Joseph led the way, and about halfway up the tree, Willie's legs started to feel weak and rubbery, like they belonged to someone else. Naturally, when he told himself not to look down, he did anyhow, and was pretty sure he was going to shit himself. Fifteen feet was a hell of a lot higher than it looked from the ground and he still had that much more to go.

He wanted more pills.

Now.

He made it all the way to the last step and before he knew it, they were in the tree fort, lying on their bellies and elbows, perfectly hidden in the leaves and branches with about a three-foot clearing, practically a window, right in front of them, giving them an absolute perfect view of Devil's Drop—*all of it*. There were maybe a couple hundred Crown walking around the open field, but it was still early, and he knew more were coming—a lot more—and he wondered where they were.

It didn't take long to find out.

Willie looked down again. Less than ten feet straight ahead, but easily a hundred feet beneath them, he could see what he thought was the little road he and Joseph had taken the day they Weedwacked around the stage, the same road that cuts off of Cossit Creek and down through the trees. Droves of hooded Crown were on it, walking shoulder to shoulder in perfect silence, down into the valley that made Devil's Drop.

"Is that the path we took the truck down the day you got pissed at me for going up on the stage?"

"Shhh," Joseph whispered. "Voices carry. But yes, that's the same path. It's the only way you can get a vehicle down there."

"They can't hear us from up here," Willie said. And then that knot in his stomach tightened when he realized he could hear their footsteps and the *swish* of robes that brushed off the thicket on the edges of the path.

"Dumb rule that we don't get to wear purple yet," Willie heard. He knew it came from the path and to his left.

"You know it's because we ain't Crown yet," another voice said.

"Shut up back there!" a third one yelled, also from the left and farther up the path near Cossit Creek Road. Beyond them, Willie could see at least ten pairs of headlights lined up, most likely where the troops were getting dropped off.

"Who drops them off?" Willie whispered.

"Higher-ranking Crown," Joseph whispered. "Not high rank like the Trio, but more important than the other guys. They stand right up near the very front when the meetings start. There are eleven of them. They are the ones that drive those trucks and none of those trucks have license plates."

There were now so many of them coming down the path, Willie wasn't sure which three were doing the talking, but he had a good guess. In the middle of the pack and now about halfway down the hill, six men were wearing hoods and robes that weren't purple...and though it was getting darker and becoming even harder to see, he guessed they were wearing khaki.

"Hear them?" Willie whispered. "Why aren't those six wearing purple?"

"Shhh," Joseph said. "You heard what the one said. Because they ain't Crown yet. They are sponsored...but don't get purple till they get accepted."

"This hood smells like vomit," one of them said. Willie was almost positive it was the same one who filed the wardrobe complaint. The six trainees were now practically right beneath him and Joseph.

"Halt!" Willie heard. It came from in front of the new guys and one of The Crown held his arm straight up. The whole procession stopped and with his other arm, he pulled out what looked like a shotgun from under his robe. He turned around and faced the new dudes.

"Anything about being quiet you don't understand?" Shotgun Man yelled. "I know you were told by your sponsor and by me that you don't say a single word while you are here."

"It smells like someone puked in this hood."

Shotgun Man raised the gun and pointed it right in Barfmask's face, the end of the barrel only a few inches away from the left eyehole of his khaki hood.

"Take that hood and robe off and get the hell out of here."

"How am I supposed to get back?" Barfmask said. "I ain't walking through The Row."

Shotgun man pumped the gun, sending a shell into the chamber. Willie could hear him click the safety off. "You have ten seconds to leave or one of two things is gonna happen. I pull the trigger and you don't have a head to put under that hood or we will have us an impromptu dipping tonight. You understand me?"

Barfmask shed his wardrobe and dropped it on the ground in front of Shotgun Man. He couldn't have been a day over eighteen with round and innocent eyes and mega-white teeth. He was also *black* black, the kind of guy that made most black people look light-skinned. He turned and ran back up the hill toward Cossit Creek Road against a grain of purple and was knocked on his ass twice by Crown that didn't seem all that thrilled by the idea of his disrobing. Willie wondered what would be going through his mind when he hit The Row on his way back into town.

"If you can't listen, none of you gonna make it anyhow," Shotgun Man yelled. He raised his finger and pointed back down the road. "One of you grab that robe and hood, and let's go!"

They turned around and they all started to move again. Some were taller, shorter, but except for the now five new guys, they were all in purple with black hands sticking out the ends of their robes. From out in the opening, Willie could hear them start a chant, in all deep voices, almost as if someone were pulling back on the same note of an enormous bass guitar—*hum, hum, hum.*

Something about it reminded him of that day they were all at the courthouse, but this time it scared him because there is a huge difference between sitting in the back seat of a limo and hiding out in a treehouse like some type of half-assed peeping Tom.

Hum, hum, hum...

The pulse grew louder and seemed to take on a life of its own. A little voice in the back of Willie's mind made him wonder if maybe the sulfur smell that filled the air at Devil's Drop didn't come from the dipping pond and swamps that ran toward the lake—but rather from something else that was maybe rotting—like the souls of Crownsmen.

"Hear, hear!" a voice blared over a megaphone. Plain as Christmas it was Sheriff Green. He yelled it again, and in the middle of the second "hear," the entire platform became visible by what looked like a dozen simultaneously lit torches. In the dead center of the platform, behind the podium, stood three men. At Right Trio was Sheriff Green, who was holding the megaphone and not wearing his hood. In the middle was The Crown Lord, who was clearly standing on something behind the podium to elevate himself above Sheriff Green, and the Left Trio, who stood lower than him to his other side.

Sheriff Green raised his arm and glanced over at the Left Trio. The Crown Lord just stood there with his arms at his sides, but when the Left Trio raised his arm like Sheriff Green's, it seemed like every Crown member there lit a torch and held it as high above their heads as they could, lighting up Devil's Drop. And they were everywhere. Crown covered every blade of grass in the opening and Willie guessed there were more than a thousand of them.

"Salute!" Sheriff Green yelled. The word jumped out of the megaphone and as it echoed up the hillside, every Crown member, in unison, all leaned their torches toward the stage and cheered as if they'd each just been given a million dollars. The Crown Lord then raised his arm up above his head, and when he did, the place went dead silent. Spooky silent. So silent that you could have heard that proverbial pin drop—*in the grass*.

The Crown Lord waited a good thirty seconds, surveying the mob and nodding his head in approval. And then his right arm came down and shot straight out at the mob and when he did it, the place went absolutely apeshit. The roar was deafening and when Willie looked over at Joseph, Joseph said something, but Willie couldn't hear.

He leaned toward Joseph as the roar grew even louder and heard Joseph this time when he said, "Watch how quiet it gets again."

The Crown Lord pulled back his arm as quickly as it had gone up and it was like he hit a mute button. It became dead silent.

Sheriff Green left the other two at the podium, megaphone in hand, and when he did, the mob of torchbearers in the field broke into three groups—perhaps some sort of tribute to the Trio. They created what had to be rehearsed circles and walked around and around for two minutes before they broke off into twenty straight lines.

"Hear, hear!" the sheriff barked again. Even though Willie thought that one was getting a little old, everyone became quiet and still, exactly like they had on the courthouse steps before Dad walked past them.

"We are at war with the inferior races!" Sheriff Green yelled. The Left Trio and The Crown Lord just stood there, arms at their sides.

"And we are here to see that the war is won!"

The crowd didn't respond, as if they'd been trained when to be quiet and when to be loud.

"Every day is a battle against homosexuals, Jews, Arabs, and Mexicans, but we need to stay focused and disciplined on harnessing the growing cancer that breeds like rats in the underbelly of black society. The vermin. The lowest of the low. The whites. The pinkies. Let me hear you if you know what I mean, brothers!"

They erupted. Willie felt the noise shoot up and out of the valley until Sheriff Green popped off a quick "Hear, hear!" that immediately quieted them.

"And the daily battles will ultimately lead us to victory in the war…the war to keep the pinkie in its rightful place," the sheriff added. "Far beneath us…

God's chosen people...those of us that are called according to his purpose to see that this is done."

God's chosen people? And how in the hell could they call it a war? There was no competition. It wasn't a fair fight. It was a massacre.

Willie guessed that if Sheriff Green ever heard Reverend Kettle speak, he wasn't paying too much attention. At the very least, there was no doubt that Jews, Arabs, Mexicans, Pinkies, and anyone else that wasn't black didn't fall under the definition of "neighbor" in the sheriff's personal dictionary.

And then Willie glanced over at Joseph and realized the kid was none of those. And then he also realized that even if he was, it didn't matter, because the kid was the best friend Willie ever had. The only real friend he ever had.

"We better get out of here," Joseph said.

"We just got here. I want to listen to these nutjobs."

"You have to know rule number one when going to spy on a Crown meeting," Joseph said. "And it's the most important rule."

"What's that?"

"Don't stay too long."

◆◆◆

IT TOOK THEM CLOSE to two hours to get back. The entire path was like a horror movie—pitch-black with funky noises in the woods—and the only thing that had Willie not thinking about werewolves and other scary shit was the second wave of mosquitos that gnawed on them for the last half hour to where he and Joseph would surely look like fucking lepers in the morning.

When Willie made it home, he went upstairs and was a little surprised to see that Uncle Reggie had beat him back and was already in bed. He was sawing logs like it was the last day to snore and the poor guy had what was surely category-five sleep apnea. There were easily seven- to eight-second intervals between each of his grinding breaths and it wouldn't have surprised Willie if his uncle stopped breathing all together.

Willie walked over to the window, opened it a few inches, and hoped the little breeze that flitted in would help to get the puke smell out of the room.

Maybe I didn't go to the meeting...

On top of an antique dresser straight across from the foot of the bed, a tiny lamp had been left on. Willie turned it off and while walking back toward the door, he noticed the closet was open and how the moonlight cast a shine on something inside.

The snoring continued, so Willie crept closer to take a peek.

Holy shit.

There were two Crown robes on the right side of the closet. Right next to each other.

A shiny purple one with black stitches.

And a shiny black one with purple stitches.

Willie touched the black robe and could feel the hair on the back of his neck start to rise.

And then he remembered something else his father had said that day at the airport about that family member that was "more than just a little familiar" with The Crown.

"He went about as high up the ranks as you can go…"

Willie could feel the power pulsing off the robe and couldn't believe his uncle even had it in the house. He closed the closet door and stepped back, feeling like he'd locked up a demon.

He glanced over at the bed and as Uncle Reggie continued to snore, Willie couldn't stop himself from saying the word out loud.

"Trio."

WILLIE

Gray Powder. A Shooting.

Heather May.

"Morning," Willie said, surprised how awake he felt at nine thirty. "Feeling better?"

"Much better." Uncle Reggie was sitting at the kitchen table, holding a cup of coffee and looking back to normal. "Puked twice and had the squirts half the night but woke up about an hour ago feeling brand-new. Reckon it was one of those twenty-four-hour bugs or something. How you doing?"

"Doing good." Willie was looking out the back window at Joseph who was putting a box of dynamite in the back of the old pickup. "We going back to Kettle's today for some more dynamite action?"

"I don't want you boys going anywhere today," he said, standing. "Reverend Kettle called about forty-five minutes ago. Apparently, Sheriff Green shot and killed a man early this morning on Main Street. I guess there's a dozen news crews out there and half the town is on the sidewalks, rubbernecking what happened. Just stay around here and stay clear of downtown until the dust settles. Just take the day off. The stumps can wait."

"Okay," Willie said. Nothing wrong with taking the day off.

"Besides, we've got a little business of our own to take care of."

"Like what?" Willie asked, thinking so much for the day off.

Uncle Reggie stood and all he had on was a T-shirt and shorts. When he walked over to the window to look out at Joseph, half of his ass crack was hanging out the top of his boxers. Willie joined him and noticed Joseph lifting two bags of gray powder out of the front seat of the truck.

"Let me throw on some drawers and we can get this over with," Uncle Reggie said.

"Get what over with?" Willie asked.

"Be right back."

Uncle Reggie went upstairs and was back down within two minutes. They went outside and Uncle Reggie took the bags from Joseph and held one up.

"Take one of these and follow me," Uncle Reggie said.

Willie took one of the bags. Whatever the gray powder was, it was surprisingly light. He followed his uncle and couldn't get over the fact that Uncle Reggie wasn't just any card-carrying member of The Crown. The guy had one of the three platinum cards they gave out.

Fucking unbelievable.

They went past the barn and into the knee-high grass that ran all the way out to the woods that surrounded The Row and Devil's Drop. Dew that had collected near the bottom of the grass clung to Willie's bare ankles and the tiniest hint of cow shit was already riding the breeze on what was going to be another scorcher of a day.

"Where the cows at?" Willie asked.

"Ain't cows," Uncle Reggie said. "The smell is coming from a farm over in Lincoln Park. An old man named Lewis has a pig over there. Flabby-necked sow he calls Heather May. Even though it's over a mile away, if the wind is right and Heather May unloads, we're gonna smell it."

Willie laughed. "Must be some pretty powerful stuff."

"Oh yeah," Uncle Reggie said. "Took some shrubs out for him a couple years ago. Being that close to it, I swear the smell sticks to your lungs for a month."

They reached the little pond where Willie had seen the coyote from Uncle Reggie's bedroom. It was about the size of the pool at the country club back home. A family of ducks and a pair of geese noticed them but didn't seem to care.

"Kind of a random place for a pond," Willie said, "out here in the middle of nowhere. This man-made?"

"No," Uncle Reggie said, pointing at what looked like a foundation from a small dwelling that had been there a trillion years ago. "Great-Granddad's slaves lived in a building that was right there. They used to swim in the pond and clean their clothes in it. It's only about five feet deep in the middle. Your daddy and I used to come out here and play in the pond when we were kids."

"Probably nice on hot days," Willie said. "When it gets too warm back home, I like to hang out in the pool and float around."

"Ready to get this over with?" Uncle Reggie asked.

"Get what over with?"

"Why don't you go to the other side and sprinkle some in the water and around the bank and we will work our way toward each other."

Willie held up the bag. "Sprinkle this stuff?"

"Yes, sir," his uncle said.

Willie walked to the opposite side of the pond. He could see what he guessed were deer tracks and then paw prints, which must have belonged to the coyote. He opened the plastic bag and studied the contents. It looked like chunky gray sand. He yelled across the water to his uncle. "What's in the bags? Some type of coyote bait?"

Uncle Reggie looked at him and shook his head. "No." His uncle tipped his bag to the side. Some of the contents bounced off the ground and flitted away in smoky little puffs with the wind.

"What is it then?"

Uncle Reggie tapped on the side of the bag and a little more spilled out.

"It's your daddy."

WILLIE

The Dead Man

When dinner came, the only people that did any talking were Uncle Reggie and Nancy, and the only thing they talked about until the table was cleared was the shooting that had happened downtown that morning.

Uncle Reggie pointed at the clock on the wall and then at the living room.

"News comes on in five minutes," he said. "Let's get in there and see what they are saying about what happened."

Willie sat on the fancy couch and the other three looked at him like he had taken a dump on someone's sundae. Still, nobody said anything about it as Uncle Reggie turned the TV on and messed with the antennae until the rabbit ears were in just the right spot to turn the fuzz into a surprisingly clear screen, considering there was no cable. There was a close-up of an attractive reporter, Regina Evans WTCO 4NEWS@6, talking into a microphone inside a sectioned-off area on the side of Main Street. Behind her, locals stood behind borders created by that police tape Willie recognized from every crime scene on every police show ever seen on television.

Uncle Reggie turned the volume up and sat in the big chair next to the couch as Joseph and Nancy continued to stand.

Three black kids in their late teens were behind the cute reporter, waving their arms and making faces, cashing in on their fifteen minutes of fame, as she continued to talk:

"Once again…this morning…local police pulled a car over as part of a routine traffic stop right here on Main Street in downtown Woodruff. Eyewitnesses say that after approaching the assailant's vehicle and requesting identification…the officer was returning to his cruiser to run a standard check on the driver when the assailant emerged from the car…brandishing and then aiming what appeared to be a large caliber pistol at the officer."

A photo of Sheriff Green (one that made him look much thinner, younger, attractive, and a hell of a lot nicer) appeared in the top right corner of the screen as Regina Evans WTCO 4NEWS@6 continued to talk.

"Sheriff Demetrius Green immediately drew his service revolver and fired four times, striking the assailant in the neck, chest, and twice in the lower torso, killing him at the scene."

The screen went back to the studio where beautiful black anchors Jermaine Price and Kenyatta Jackson WTCO4NEWS@6 looked studiously at the camera before Jermaine asked:

"What do we know about the assailant? Seeing that he was willing to shoot a police officer, can we assume we are talking about someone that was already a person of interest to law enforcement? Someone that was possibly wanted?"

There was a pause, as if the sound were delayed, and then Regina nodded her head and spoke:

"Pending a further investigation…authorities are not releasing too many details at this time…but we have been told by a reputable source that a *significant* amount of narcotics was found inside the car."

Regina seemed to fade away when a picture of the man, clearly a photo from his driver's license, appeared in the top right corner of the screen. Willie quickly looked away and the first thing he saw was Joseph and Nancy. They both just stood there with their arms crossed, staring at the TV and the photo of the man that had been killed. Then Willie turned to his uncle Reggie, who shook his head and looked back at him.

"Drugs," Uncle Reggie said. "Bad news."

"Yeah," Willie said, dreamily.

Yes, the "assailant" had drugs in his car.

Yes, Sheriff Green had shot the "assailant" four times.

But there was no way the "assailant" was carrying a gun. He hated guns. Never owned one and never would.

Willie looked back at the television and at the face of the man on the driver's license. It was Evan.

WILLIE

The Scene of the Crime. Inertia.

Keepsake.

By morning, Willie had slept a total of maybe an hour. He had spent most of the night rolling around in the bed and watching his legs twitch uncontrollably, not sure if it was a result of withdrawals (restless leg syndrome) from not taking enough pills, or his nerves, knowing for certain that Sheriff Green hadn't just killed Evan, but murdered him.

He had also gone to the bathroom with the shits four or five times (another sign of withdrawals) during the night and with his pills almost gone and no replacements in sight, he didn't even want to think about what the days or weeks ahead held in store.

After another quiet breakfast, they loaded up the truck to go to Kettle's and Willie could feel his stomach turn as they pulled out of the driveway. They had to stop by the hardware for some more earplugs and he knew they would most likely be driving by the place where Sheriff Green had murdered Evan

Before they'd left, he'd caught a couple blurbs on the television that showed some whites protesting Evan's death around the country and even saw a few of them carrying signs that read *Whites Need Justice* and *White Lives Count*. Needless to say, there weren't any protests reported in Woodruff. In fact, by the time they made it downtown, it seemed like things were back to business as usual except for half the street near the hardware being quarantined by that yellow police tape. Right in the middle of it was the only remaining news crew and they were interviewing Sheriff Green. Apparently, he hadn't had enough attention over the previous twenty-four hours and Willie would have sworn the sheriff winked at him when he and Joseph drove by.

They had to park over a block from the hardware store and got out to start walking.

"Look," Joseph said, pointing at their shadows on the sidewalk. "We are the same color."

"And you don't look that much bigger than me," Willie said. "And nowhere near as ugly as you are in person."

"Funny," Joseph said.

"Hey, hash brown!"

Willie looked up. Two black guys were sitting on a picnic table, smoking cigarettes in the alley beside Burger World, the only fast-food restaurant in town. He wasn't sure which one made the comment, but everyone knew who the comment was directed at.

Both men wore name tags. "Tre" was skinny and about as black as you could be. "Daman" was light-skinned, and if he was the one yelling *hash brown*, he didn't have a lot of room to talk. Regardless, between his withdrawals and what happened to Evan, Willie wasn't in the mood for these two fucks.

"What's the problem?" Willie asked, walking toward the men.

Tre stood at the far side of the table. Joseph stayed back on the sidewalk.

"Your pet half-rican have a name?" Tre asked.

Willie just stared at him. Tre was about Willie's size, but looked older.

Willie turned to Joseph and reeled his index finger for him to come next to him. Joseph took a few steps, then stopped.

"Half-rican?" Willie said. "His name is actually Science Project." Willie nodded at Joseph and said, "Science Project...come over here and say hello to Tre and Damon. In case you forget who they are, or in case they forget, they have their names tagged on their shirts as reminders."

"Science project?" Tre said with a laugh. "What...you trying to see what happens when you mix an animal with a human?"

"That's not the project," Willie said.

"What is it then?" Tre asked.

"The project involves inertia," Willie said. "Know what that means? I'm guessing not because you are in your twenties and work as a fucking French-fry technician."

"Talking to me like that, for real?" Tre said. He stepped around the table and got in Willie's face. "Maybe you need to learn some respect."

"*For real,*" Willie said, mocking Tre while holding his ground. "My previous studies on inertia, though not fully tested, suggest that your head will not respond well if my friend here tries to put it through that brick wall behind you."

Tre smiled and when it quickly went away, Willie knew why. He had seen Joseph's shadow moving against the wall before he reached Willie's side.

Tre looked up at Joseph, stepped back, and then put his hands in his pockets. It reminded Willie of pistols going back into holsters.

Willie stepped right back up in Tre's face. "Are you volunteering as a test subject, or are you going to apologize for what you called him?"

Tre looked over at Damon and it seemed like he wasn't sure what to say. "Only because he's part black."

"Good one," Willie said. "Now I'm going to phrase this in a way you can understand it. You are an asshole and I want you to apologize right now."

Willie could see Tre's Adam's apple bob up and down.

"I'm sorry."

"Apology accepted," Willie said, patting Tre on his shoulder. "Now we are going to leave you two career men to yourselves. Enjoy your break."

Willie and Joseph made their way down toward the hardware store.

"Why don't you stick up for yourself when people like that give you shit?" Willie asked.

"Maybe I could do it in the South. But you don't seem to understand how it is here."

Willie thought about Evan and was never so sure of anything in his life. "Yes, I do. I *really* do."

"Up here I can't mess with people like those two guys."

"You could kick both their asses with one swing."

"They didn't do anything to me," Joseph said. "Words don't hurt me. Besides, I don't want to hurt anybody and I don't want to go to jail."

"They started it."

"That don't matter here. But would it really matter in the South?"

Willie waited before he spoke. "Things are definitely different in the North, Joseph. But there are idiots everywhere. Why don't you just get out of Woodruff?"

"And go where?"

"Anywhere is better than here," Willie said. "Literally anywhere. I mean it's not like there is a Devil's Drop or a Crown hub in every town. Everybody knows Woodruff isn't user-friendly for white people. Heck, even some people in the South know how shitty Woodruff is for whites."

"Really?"

"Yes," Willie said. "But regardless of where you end up, stand up for yourself. In fact, effective immediately, I want you to quit taking shit from people. Seriously."

"Okay," Joseph said.

"Except for him," Willie said, pointing at Sheriff Green, who was now coming out from under the police tape.

"What brings you two down here?" the sheriff asked, leaning against the side of his squad car.

"We are just here picking up some earplugs before heading over to Reverend Kettle's place," Willie said.

"Is that right?" Sheriff Green said. The bottom of his jaw made a circular motion, and then his mouth opened, making a soggy tobacco sound. "Stay there a second, Joseph. I want to have a word with Willie."

Willie left Joseph on the sidewalk and went to Sheriff Green.

"Looks like you had a little excitement yesterday," Willie said. "You are all over the news."

The sheriff nodded and pointed to the other side of the car.

"Dropped a man right over there," he said. "Chalk lines are still fresh. Had enough dope on him to fix up the whole town. Or at least someone with a big taste for the stuff."

"Saw that on the news too," Willie said.

"Georgia plates," the sheriff said, looking Willie straight in the eyes. "Small world, isn't it?"

"Georgia?" Willie asked.

"Georgia," the sheriff repeated with a little grin. "I like you, Willie. And I know you are one of us. But keep that shit out of my town."

Willie nodded and then swallowed heavily. A part of him wanted to snatch the sheriff's gun off his hip and shoot him in the face for what he had done. Another part of him, a *bigger* part, wanted to turn and run as fast as he could in the opposite direction. But he couldn't move.

He couldn't take his eyes off the white capital *E* on the black ball cap that was on the back seat of the cruiser.

The one that had belonged to Evan.

WILLIE

Two Sticks for Shanice. Show Don't Tell.

The Other Guy. Only Four Bucks.

Willie and Joseph made sure that they gave Shanice Kettle a heads-up before they made trees number four and five go bye-bye. Because of how close together they were, they decided to blast them both at the same time, which meant a couple extra sticks of dynamite would be involved along with a higher likelihood that Auntie Shanice would make chocolate surprise in her double-XL underpants.

After Willie went inside to let her know things were going to get a bit noisy, it took her about a whole minute to come back out of the house and then close to five more minutes to share what an inconvenience the whole thing was, particularly when she was rehearsing for a speech she was giving that night at the Woodruff Supper Club.

The work they were doing wasn't anything but a nuisance.

Why did they have to be there that day?

What would everyone at the supper club think if she wasn't prepared?

Would it make her look bad and didn't they know it was her turn to prepare a meal for the club on Sunday?

"What would they think if your ass got any bigger?" Willie whispered as she walked back under the tarp and into the house.

"Shhh," Joseph said, followed by a muffled laugh. "Reverend Kettle might be able to hear."

"He'd probably think it was funny," Willie said, wondering if anything would ever be funny again.

Evan died because of me.

Just because I needed pills. Fucking pills.

What am I going to do to get more?

"Speaking of hearing," Joseph said. "Don't forget about the earplugs we just bought."

Willie put the earplugs in and then shouted at Kettle, who was standing near the edge of the tarp, "You going in the house?"

"Yes!" Kettle yelled, holding up his own set of earplugs. "And making sure my better half puts these in as well."

The minister disappeared under the tarp and Willie and Joseph walked back to the side of the barn. Joseph grabbed the plunger handle on the detonator box (kick-ass-cartoon-dynamite-pusher thing) and then let go and nodded at Willie.

"You do it."

"Okay," Willie said. "Just push down?"

Joseph nodded and said, "That's it. Two stumps going at once is gonna make some noise."

"Say goodbye to the rot," Willie said, quickly imagining one stick of dynamite down Sheriff Green's throat and another up his ass. Then he leaned down on the handle.

If there was ever going to be a second World War, everyone in Woodruff would have thought it had just started. The blast was like something out of an action film and Willie would have given ten to one the blast was heard downtown. It was unreal and the remains from both stumps littered down on them and on top of the barn for a good fifteen seconds. The tarp that protected the house was covered with fresh mulch, and as the smoke cleared, they could hear fat-ass Shanice giving the reverend an earful.

"Damn," Willie said. "Listen to her. I'm thinking Reverend Kettle would pay us double to hook her up to the next stump."

Joseph laughed again, this time more high-pitched, and Kettle appeared from under the tarp.

"Safe to come out?"

"Yeah!" Willie shouted and Kettle walked toward them, fanning the dust in front of his face.

"You boys mind if we cut it short today?" Kettle asked. "Shanice needs to prepare that talk for ladies' night at the supper club and if she hears anything else, I'll be down at the divorce court first thing in the morning."

"No problem," Willie said.

"Thank you." Kettle brushed the dust off the front of his shirt. "I should have called Reggie this morning and saved you boys a trip, but I wasn't thinking."

"It's no biggie," Joseph said.

"I figure the least my tired old bones can do is help you clean up then."

"You don't have to do that, Reverend Kettle," Joseph added. "We got it."

"I want to help."

Willie was glad Kettle offered to help because he wanted to chat with the minister about some feelings he was having, mostly about what Sheriff Green did to Evan.

"All this debris goes in the back of the truck?" Kettle asked.

"Yes, please," Joseph said, as if someone had asked him if he wanted seconds of ham soup. He was probably in hog heaven, getting help from not one, but two black dudes. "But let's put it in the bags first, if you don't mind."

"Sounds good," Kettle said. "I think the Lord wanted me to spend a little time with you boys. I can feel it in my bones."

"Amen," Willie said, sort of meaning it. "The Lord puts people in our lives for a reason. One of my wisest friends once told me that."

"You must be pretty thin on friends then," Kettle said with a smile that made the big gap between his front teeth look bigger yet.

Willie thought about some of the people that had come into his life since arriving in Woodruff and how his perception of them had changed. And how all the changes weren't good, namely the one involving Sheriff Green and the way it made Willie feel. "Do you think the other guy puts people in our lives?"

"The other guy?" Kettle asked, two handing a pile of bark and dropping it into a four-foot paper bag.

"The devil," Willie said. "If there really is one."

"There is one," Kettle said. "And yes, he tempts us all the time, and many of those temptations come in the form of people."

"Even guys like you get tempted?" Willie asked. "Super believers?"

"Super believers?" Kettle said. "Either you believe or you don't. Calling yourself a Christian and being one are two different things."

"What do you mean?"

The reverend wiped away more dust, this time off the side of his face. "It's funny how so many Christians call themselves Christians without ever really taking the time to ask themselves if they really believe. And then once they believe, they don't realize the responsibility that comes with it. And that responsibility doesn't mean you jump up and down shouting that you are a believer. The responsibility comes with how you lead your life. How you show— not how you tell—people you are a believer."

"I didn't know today was Sunday," Willie said.

"You made me wanna start preaching," the minister said, smiling yet again.

"I liked what you were saying," Joseph said, chiming in.

"But you didn't answer my question," Willie said. "I consider you to be the real thing. A higher-up in the world of believers. Even you get tempted? It seems like God would protect you because you are a minister."

"Nobody is free from temptation. Even Jesus himself wasn't."

"I can't help but want swift justice on those that really deserve it," Willie said. "In fact, I've recently had thoughts of delivering that justice myself."

"I can understand that in many cases," Kettle said. "Particularly yours."

The three of them stood less than ten feet from each other and had stopped working. Kettle didn't have the faintest idea that Willie was talking about Sheriff Green, and Joseph seemed to have taken a keen interest in the conversation. Or at least he *used to did*...because he quickly walked back to the truck and grabbed another rake.

"Let the Lord handle justice," Kettle said. "And then let your behavior in the face of your adversities be a shining example of Christ's love in you so you can inspire and draw others to his kingdom."

"I'm not sure I believe," Willie said. "Just being honest. I've thought about it a lot and Joseph and I talked about karma and some other stuff. But I can't help the way I feel. I'm glad The Crown killed the guy that murdered my dad, and I hope every other murderer out there gets what he has coming to him."

"The Crown?" Kettle said. "You really don't think the man hanged himself?"

Willie shrugged. "Speaking of The Crown. Am I supposed to love them too? Are they my neighbors?"

"Yes," Kettle said. "Everyone can be saved."

"Really?" Willie whispered, pointing back toward the truck, and Joseph who stood next to the bed, still fumbling through the rakes. "That may be the nicest person I ever met. Why does God allow The Crown to do the things they do to white people just because their skin color is different? And it's not just The Crown. He was harassed just a little while ago by two losers that worked at Burger World, for crying out loud."

"I told you God doesn't see black and white," Kettle said. "It's *their* free will that allows them to do the things they do. The men in The Crown have a choice."

"Funny you say that. I was telling Joseph about something I did as a kid. I knew it was wrong, but still did it."

"Proof of God," Kettle said. "He helps us tell right from wrong."

"That's kind of what Joseph told me," Willie said. "But don't the men in The Crown have that guide? And do any of those guys go to your church?"

Kettle shook his head. "All of God's children are welcome in his house. And who are you and I to judge and turn anyone away from God's word and forgiveness?"

"So even if they know what they are doing is wrong, they can do it because they know in advance they will be forgiven?" Willie asked. He shook his head and then crossed his arms. "It seems like forgiveness should be asked for after you screw up, not expected while you are plotting the deed."

"Well put," Kettle said. "Repentance is key."

Joseph approached them and Willie figured a topic change was in order. He looked at the gaping holes in the knees of Joseph's jeans, which were a reasonable distraction from the fact that the pants were pulled halfway up his ass.

"I'm going to talk to my uncle Reggie about getting you a raise," Willie said. "In fact, we should go to the mall today and I'll buy you a new pair of jeans."

"You don't have to get me anything," Joseph said. "Mr. Reggie gives me everything I need and I'm perfectly happy with the pants I'm wearing."

Joseph headed back toward the truck and Kettle took Willie by the arm.

"Shanice will be gone to the supper club tonight. Why don't you stop by later tonight and we will continue our talk?"

"What time?"

"Seven?"

"I will be here. Better yet, let me buy you dinner."

"Deal."

"Where do you want to go?"

"The Wolfcat Diner," Kettle said. "It's right across the street from the ice cream shop."

"Seven o'clock?"

"See you there at seven."

◆◆◆

"WHY WON'T YOU LET me buy you a new pair of jeans?" Willie asked on their ride back to Uncle Reggie's. "Those things are embarrassing."

"I'll get at least another year or two out of these." Joseph ran his palms across the tops of his legs. "They ain't all that bad and they don't embarrass me."

"I wasn't talking about you," Willie said, patting Joseph on the arm. "But if we are ever near a store that sells them, I'm dragging you in and getting you a new pair."

"You can get whatever you want whenever you want, can't you?"

Willie started to answer, but then he stopped. It sure seemed like he was thinking a lot more before he talked lately.

"My father had more money than God," Willie said. "But what is funny is that I've been in Michigan a little over two weeks. And it just occurred to me that the only money I've spent was on an ice cream the day I got here and a few sodas that day I got you with the exploding can trick."

"But I got you back with the peanut butter," Joseph said.

"Seriously, Joseph. I've only spent like four bucks since I came to Michigan."

"That's more than I've spent all year."

"I never knew I didn't need money to feel good," Willie said. "And it's like I never knew what was important until I came up here."

"What's important to you now?"

Willie considered it and waited again to answer. "People like you and Reverend Kettle are what matters. And you aren't just a friend, Joseph. You are the best friend I ever had. And that is something money will never be able to buy."

"Thank you, Willie," he said. "But how could your daddy have more money than God? I don't get that part."

"It's just an expression." Willie chuckled. And then he thought about the way Demetrius Green treated people like Joseph and what he had done to Evan.

It didn't matter that he was the sheriff. It was wrong.

And he was going to pay.

WILLIE

Yikes. Darn.

Stuff. F - - k.

W illie almost ran over Maggie and Alan when he pulled into a parking space in front of the Wolfcat Diner.

Yikes.

In fairness, they agreed it was everyone's fault. Willie wasn't paying too much attention when he pulled into the spot, and Maggie and Alan probably shouldn't have been sitting on the curb between two other parked cars. The last thing he saw was them shooting up to their feet. After apologies from both sides, Alan offered an invitation for some fishing on Sunday.

"Sounds like a plan," Willie said. "Want to go to my uncle's not-so-secret spot?"

"There or I've got another spot we can go to," Alan said. "Up to you."

"I'm easy," Willie said.

There was a knock on the restaurant window. It was Reverend Kettle giving Willie a heads-up that he was there and where he was sitting.

Willie waved to him and then leaned down and whispered in Maggie's ear. "I will pick you up at the base of the road between The Row and my uncle Reggie's house at eight o'clock tomorrow night."

"That should work," Alan said, rolling his eyes. "That way no black or white people will see you. Until you try to get out of town."

"Funny guy," Willie said.

"I try," he said.

Willie nodded. "Let her know where you guys want to fish Sunday and I will plan on seeing you after church."

Willie turned and opened the door to the diner before looking back at Alan.

"I can't believe you heard me talking to her. Superhero ears?"

"Nope," he said. "Something better."

"What's that?"

"Big brother ears."

♦♦♦

DINNER AT THE WOLFCAT Diner got off to a terrible start.

It wasn't because Willie would have to go out of his way to be conscious of his swearing in the presence of Reverend Kettle.

It sure as *heck (hell)* wasn't because he was now taking less than a quarter of the pills he usually took per day and that he hadn't had a solid turd in more than a week.

It wasn't because the menu had a bunch of gross *stuff (shit)* on it ranging from rabbit to muskrat.

It *was* because one of Kettle's eight great-nieces was their *darn (damn)* waitress.

The same great-niece that worked at the ice cream shop. The smoking-hot "I didn't have the faintest idea you were a lesbian" great-niece that sent him and his courting efforts packing back on Day One in Woodruff.

He had already imagined her filling Reverend Kettle in on the whole encounter the second he got up to use the restroom. And then maybe she would see how much spit she could mix in with his entrée before bringing it out.

Fuck. (Fuck)

Fortunately, even Northern restaurants had the saving grace entrée for children and picky adults that didn't want to eat something that was climbing up a telephone pole the day before.

Willie ordered chicken strips and Reverend Kettle ordered squirrel.

"I saw you talking to your friends out there," Kettle said, buttering a roll.

"Yeah," Willie said. "That's Maggie and Alan. They are friends with Joseph."

"They are certainly hard workers," Kettle said. "Every time I come downtown they're painting addresses on curbs."

"Everybody's got to eat," Willie said. "Probably beats working at the mill."

"I suppose so."

"I went fishing with them last Sunday—with Joseph, Nancy, and my uncle Reggie. My uncle took us to his secret place."

"I've lived in Woodruff for seventy-three years," Kettle said. "There aren't any secret places to fish here."

"At least he thinks it's secret. I think we may be heading out there again this Sunday."

"How is Nancy?"

"Good," Willie said. "I haven't been here too long, but she seems all right."

"Used to see her around a lot more often, but when Joseph was born, she practically disappeared. How old is Joseph now?"

"Pretty sure he is nineteen."

"I've seen Nancy maybe a half-dozen times in nineteen years."

"Can't say I blame her for not coming out too often," Willie said. "But my uncle Reggie does his best to take care of her and Joseph. Seems like it's the least he can do."

"Why do you say that?"

"I probably shouldn't say," Willie said. "But I'm sure half the town knows."

The reverend smiled. "Willie, people come to me all the time to talk about life and I do my best to minister them. One thing you can take to the bank is that anything we ever talk about that you want to keep between us, will stay between us."

"Well, like I said, it's probably no surprise to most that my uncle is Joseph's father. He looks like a six-foot-five, half-black half-white guy with my uncle Reggie's face. I mean, why else, other than having a great cook and the best landscaper on the planet working for you, would someone have them living in the backyard?"

"Point taken," Kettle said as his great-niece returned to the table with their salads. Willie gave his a good once-over to make sure it hadn't been sprinkled with boogers.

"But I have to say that whether he is my cousin or not, getting to know Joseph has made a huge difference in my life."

"Mind if I say grace?" Kettle asked.

"Of course," Willie said, putting his fork down. "I mean, no, I don't mind."

Kettle held out his hand and so did Willie. When their hands met, the minister's fingers wrapped all the way around Willie's palm and part of his wrist. The guy seriously had the biggest hands of all time.

"Father, we thank you for this food, the opportunity to come together as friends, and for all the blessings you give us. In your son's name, we pray."

They said "amen" together and Willie waited for Kettle to pick up his fork.

"Friends," Willie said. "I like how you said that in the prayer. But what I was saying is that getting to know Joseph—*and you*—has made a huge difference in my life. Kind of like a switch went on...or off for that matter."

"That's what we are here for. To take care of each other. But why do you think we have made a difference, I mean in terms of a switch going on or off?"

"Joseph and I were just talking about this. Well, I mean, sort of. I guess that because of who my father was and what we had, I thought I could pretty much do or say whatever I wanted to whoever I wanted."

"Don't you mean the *thing* you had?"

Willie smiled. "Well, yeah. Money."

"It can do things to people," Kettle said. "Make them lose sight of what life is about."

"That's sort of what I was talking to Joseph about. What is important. And it's great how the simplest things make him happy. And seeing him happy, makes me happy. And then there is talking to you guys. The two of you listen to me and want nothing in return. And you know what? And I know this will make me sound like a total d-bag, but for the first time in my life, I want to listen back. I actually care about what you have to say."

"That's good to hear," Kettle said. "No pun intended. But what's a d-bag?"

"Slang for jerk," Willie said. "And as crazy as this sounds, by talking and listening to you guys, I've learned something about myself and how the way I've treated people has room for improvement. A *lot* of improvement and that there really is a right and a wrong, and that I have always known the difference. And now I know I will never...*ever*...let anyone like my mother, Sheriff Green, or anyone else scare me into doing the wrong thing again."

"Sheriff Green bothering you?"

"This is all between us?"

"If I said it stays, it stays."

Willie thought of telling Kettle about Evan and how he never would have been carrying a gun but decided not to for the moment.

"Sheriff Green bothers a lot of people," Willie said. "Mostly white people. In fact, in Woodruff, I'd say he bothers them all and from what I hear, he isn't afraid to make a point of the fact that he is in The Crown. That he is *brass* in The Crown."

"So I've heard."

"But he isn't going to stop me from hanging out with Alan and Maggie who, by the way, were forced to pick up his spit a couple weeks ago. Nor is he gonna mistreat Joseph anymore."

"What are you going to do about it?"

"Not sure. I just hate it though. Racism, that is."

"Racism is hate," Kettle said.

Willie nodded and shook his head. "I know I'm babbling here. But like you, a white man killed my father. I also lost my mother and sister when I was younger and I sort of blamed myself for it because of this one time I didn't do the right thing. I've got a lot of work to do on myself, but in terms of right and wrong, I won't let it happen again and I owe that to you and Joseph. Thank you."

"You are welcome," Kettle said. "Sorry to hear about your sister. Had to be tough on your father. They say a parent should never have to bury their child."

"And a child should never have to bury his whole family before he is twenty."

"I understand, Willie. But make something good come from it. You can do it. If you wallow in the past, nobody will see you now. And there is a lot of you to see. Good-looking young man. Smart. And now that you appreciate your resources, just think what a difference you can make in the world."

"I will make something good come from it," Willie said. "I know I'm not a full-fledged believer, but I'd like to talk to you more about God sometime as well."

"You seemed to have put a lot of thought into it," Kettle said. "And I'd rather talk to a well-informed atheist than an ignorant Christian any time. What I mean is a Christian that calls himself a Christian without thinking about it. Make sense?"

"I get it," Willie said.

"And when another switch goes on and you tell me you are a believer, you will be a star in helping God grow his kingdom. I'm sure of it."

Their meals showed up and the chicken strips appeared not to be tampered with. Willie reached up and grabbed the waitress's arm and she looked at him like he was cancer. He figured there was a decent chance he may screw up his newfound relationship with Kettle, but he went ahead anyway.

"I owe you an apology for what I said at the ice cream shop. What I said was stupid and I'm sorry."

She pulled her arm away and pointed at Kettle. "I'll bet you are only saying that because he is here."

"Not long ago you would have been right," Willie said. "But now, for what it's worth. I truly am sorry."

She crossed her arms and studied him. She looked at Reverend Kettle and then back at Willie. Her arms dropped to her sides and she smiled.

"I don't know exactly why, but I believe you. Apology accepted."

"Thank you," Willie said.

I did the right thing. Without fear of what anyone thought.

And it felt great.

MAGGIE

Date Night. Ice Cream.

Newspaper Clipping.

It smells brand-new," Maggie said, closing the passenger-side door of Willie's car. She'd only smelled a new car once and that was close to five years ago, when her and Alan were paid two dollars each to wash Mr. Burton's convertible only a week after he got it.

"Where we going?" Willie asked. "I'm assuming back to the Wolfcat Diner is out of the question?"

"You assumed right. I'm ducking down the second we pull off Cossit Creek. People will think we are nuts."

"I don't care what people think," Willie says. "You are with me."

"I know you don't care, tough guy," she said, deciding to change the subject before things got awkward. She glanced at his shirt and jeans. They looked expensive and his watch was beautiful, unlike anything she had ever seen. It was white faced, highlighted in gold, and was held in place by a black leather band around his right wrist. She had to compliment him. "You look very nice tonight."

He glanced back at her. "You look nice too."

Maggie gripped lightly at her pink dress. It was one of the two dresses (along with three dollars) Mrs. Owens had given her for cleaning her garage. Maggie was lucky it had dried in time for their date. She had hand-washed it just that morning and if it wasn't for the breeze that filtered through The Row the better part of the day, she wouldn't have been able to wear it.

Things were uncomfortably quiet after they passed Mr. Reggie's house and then Crazy-Lady Vee's place. When they made the left off Cossit Creek and onto Main Street, she figured it was best to duck.

"You weren't kidding, were you?" Willie said.

"Just 'til we make it through town," she said. "Believe me, it's for the best."

"I understand," Willie said, and it sounded like he did.

They drove in silence for a few minutes until Willie said, "Hey, there is Alan. He's still working on curbs at eight at night?"

"Yeah." Her face was about three inches from the stereo.

She could hear the window power down as the car slowed.

"Hey, Alan," Willie said.

"Where's Maggie?" she heard Alan say.

"She's keeping her head down."

"She what?"

"No," Willie said. "It's not what you—"

Maggie lifted her head and looked out the window. "Really, Alan?"

Alan laughed and then looked in both directions. "You guys better get out of here."

"I talked to my uncle Reggie," Willie said. "He can't make it for fishing but said we can go to his spot. Meet there around noon?"

"Sounds good," Alan said.

Maggie ducked back down, heard the window roll up, and about five minutes later, Willie said things were clear.

It took them close to half an hour to make it down to Benning. It was a quiet ride and Willie seemed nervous and what she could only describe as young.

They finally started talking and got all the small "what do you do for fun" chat out of the way while they waited in line at the Frosty King. She was the only white person in the line and ignored the stares as she ordered a hot fudge sundae before Willie got a chocolate shake. They popped back in the car and when they made it to the park, hardly anyone was there. Willie pulled to the very back of the second parking lot and stopped the car next to a row of weeping willows that bordered the shoreline of Lake Erie. They got out and sat at a bench to eat their treats and Maggie looked around. She'd never really been anywhere before and liked the elevated wooden walkways around the park.

"How long you up here for?" she asked.

"If I answered that question, I'd probably scare you off."

She laughed and admired his honesty, whatever he meant by *scare off*. "How long?"

"I was only supposed to come up for a little bit, mostly to go to my dad's funeral, but I think I'm going to stick around for probably another month. Maybe until like the end of July or beginning of August."

"What's so scary about that?"

"The extra month."

"So? Maybe you met this beautiful white girl and decided to stick around until you had the nerve to ask her to go back to Georgia with you."

"That sounds good to me," Willie said. He looked at her and his smile was sincere. He had nice teeth and she liked the shape of his lips. Regardless of his color, he was handsome.

"I don't think the real reason will scare me off," she said. "You've seen where I live so you probably know I don't scare easy."

"I'm a drug addict."

"Huh?" she said.

"You heard me."

"You? A drug addict?"

"You sound like you are about to jump in the lake and swim back up to Woodruff. Told you it was gonna freak you out."

"I'm not freaked out," she said. "Just surprised. I know lots of drug addicts. They all have bad teeth and smell. Only the Lord knows what they do to pay for their drugs. I was just thinking about how nice your teeth are and how handsome you are. You don't look like a drug addict."

"The extra month I'm here I'm going to be in rehab. In fact, me and my uncle called a place this morning, on a Saturday of all days, and got me set up at a joint up in Royal Oak in a few days. So, I guess you really won't be seeing me around all that much."

"That stinks," she said. "You still don't look like the addict type."

"One thing I've learned since being here is that what someone looks like doesn't mean jack shit," Willie said.

"To you, maybe," she said. "Try to be a white person and walk through downtown Woodruff past dark."

"I meant what they look like means nothing to me," Willie said. "Joseph and I were downtown and he pointed out how our shadows were the same color. And it occurred to me that if we were all the same color or if we couldn't see color at all, we could make our minds up about people based on how we treat each other without having our minds already made up for us by society."

"Maybe," she said.

"Let's take Woodruff for example," Willie said. "Two people with different colored *hair* could show up at the ice cream shop on Main Street in two different colored *cars*, wearing two different colored *pants*, and there won't be a problem.

But if one of them has black *skin* and the other one has white *skin*, it's somehow different. Why?"

"I don't know," Maggie said. "I'm not that smart."

"Maybe you aren't that smart," Willie said with a wink. "I mean, you don't even think I look like a drug addict. What a dummy you are."

She laughed and threw her crumpled-up napkin at him. "I'm guessing they won't let any of us pinkies visit you in rehab?"

"If I can get visitors, I will make sure you get in." He started to say something and then stopped.

"What is it?" she asked.

"Just curious," he said. "You can use the P word, but if I say it, I'm a racist."

"You aren't a racist," she said.

Willie walked over to a trash can to throw half of his shake away. He rejoined her at the bench.

"What a waste," she said. "You should have just got a small one instead."

"We own three Frosty Kings back home. I can get those whenever I want for free."

"What do you mean you own three Frosty Kings?"

"My dad bought three ice cream shops like the one we were just at. They are a franchise. You pay the company money and they help you set up the store."

"You must have all kinds of girlfriends down in Georgia."

"Never had one."

"Get out of here."

"Never even kissed one."

She couldn't believe it. But there was something about him, maybe his innocence, that made him even more attractive. "Close your eyes and pick a number between one and ten."

Willie closed his eyes. "Just pick a number?"

"Yep."

"Four."

She leaned into him and kissed him. His lips were soft and matched well with hers. He had nice breath and his skin had a natural and clean smell to it. You'd never know it was his first kiss and she pulled away. "You were wrong. The number was five."

"But you still kissed me."

"I told myself I wouldn't kiss you if you picked the right number. Want to try again?"

Willie laughed. "Of course." He closed his eyes and said, "Three and a half."

She kissed him again and this time he held on to her. It was a better kiss, longer and more experienced. In fact, it was great.

"Let's go for a walk," she said.

"I want to keep playing the game," Willie said.

"Easy, tiger," she said. "Maybe in a little bit. Guy works at three ice cream shops and he thinks he can kiss me anytime he wants."

Willie pulled her close again. "I never worked at them and neither did my father. He was a lawyer and that's sort of what got him killed. Did you know about the big case up in Detroit? The Donald Bondy case?"

"No," she said. "We don't have access to things that happen outside Woodruff."

"To make a long story short, Bondy was a white guy that killed a black guy. My dad was the lawyer that defended Bondy." Willie reached in his pocket and pulled out his wallet. He took out a folded piece of newspaper, unfolded it, and then tapped on a photo of a black man with a nice suit on. "That was my dad."

Maggie felt like someone grabbed and squeezed her stomach muscles. She was sure she recognized the man and took the clipping out of Willie's hand for a closer look.

"You all right?" Willie asked.

"This is your daddy?" she asked, studying the face. Her hands started to shake.

"Yeah, why?"

"Willie," she said, catching her breath. She spoke quickly. "I have to tell you something. I know you said you don't care what people think, but if I tell...tell you something, you have to promise you will never tell anyone I told you. *Ever.*"

"Go for it," Willie said. "You all right? You are shaking."

"I'm afraid," she said, finding it difficult to breathe. "Real afraid."

"What is it?"

She ran her hand across the side of her face.

She put the clipping back in Willie's hand and then squeezed his arm.

"Promise me you won't say anything."

"I promise. I promise."

"I saw him die. I saw it."

Park security pulled into their parking lot, but then turned around.

She just stared at Willie, not sure if she should keep talking.

"What do you mean you saw him die?" Willie asked.

She waited a few seconds. "If that's your daddy, I've seen him three times. Twice in town…"

"And where else?"

She paused again. "Come to think of it, I thought he looked a lot like Mr. Reggie, but I never said anything. Maybe just a little thinner and healthier… younger even."

"Where else did you see him? On television somewhere?"

"You promise not to say?"

"Yes!" Willie shouted, and she flinched.

"Devils' Drop," she whispered.

"What? He wouldn't go anywhere near—"

"Let me finish!" She exhaled loudly and took both of his hands in hers. "We were fishing not too far from where your uncle took us. We left real early in the morning and had no idea there was a meeting that night. It was getting dark and we had to hide in the swamp to the side of the stage. There was no other way back to The Row and Crown were everywhere. They would have heard us if we cut back through the swamp. We had to lay low and we were in the cattails no more than fifty yards from the stage, hiding in a blind that hunters use to kill ducks."

"What are you trying to say?"

"The Crown. About halfway into the meeting…" She paused yet again. "I don't know how to tell you this."

"Just tell me."

"They killed a man. A black man, and that black man was the man in that newspaper clipping."

"You have to be mistaken."

"I am positive! Alan and Joseph saw it too."

"Joseph was there?"

"Yes," Maggie said. "We were so close, and they put a torch right next to your daddy's face so everyone there could see and then they said something about 'look what we have here…a no-good pinkie lover.' Or something like that."

"Why would The Crown kill him?" Willie asked. "And why wouldn't my uncle stop—"

"I don't know why they killed him. What'd you say about your uncle?"

"Killed him for the money," Willie mumbled. "Uncle Reggie knew he was getting half…"

"What?"

"How did they do it?" Willie said. His eyes were distant, blank. "I. Have. To. Know. How. They. Did. It."

She hesitated. She could still see the man hanging upside down.

"Dipped."

Willie walked away and then stopped. He had his back to her and put his hands on top of his head.

"Sheriff Green was the one that called him a pinkie lover, wasn't he?" he said. She barely heard him.

"Yes."

"He had my father's cuff link," Willie said. "I heard him call it a 'keepsake.'"

"What?"

"And he had Evan's ball cap in the back of his cruiser," he said dreamily.

"I'm sorry," Maggie said. "Maybe I shouldn't have even said—"

"Who else knows about this?"

"Nobody," she said. "Other than Alan and Joseph."

"Okay," he said, turning and walking toward her like a man who had just discovered his purpose. "We have to go. Let's just keep everything business as usual. I won't even say anything to Joseph until we meet tomorrow. Can you and Alan still be at the fishing spot around noon?"

"I think so."

"Yes or no?"

"Yes. Yes, we will be there."

They got in the car and Willie didn't say anything the whole ride back. When they reached the bottom of the hill next to The Row, she kissed him on the cheek.

"See you at noon," she said and got out of the car.

Willie just nodded, turned the car around, and drove away.

JOSEPH

The Photo. It's in the Closet.

Witness. Spittoon.

Joseph didn't understand why Alan and Maggie didn't bring their fishing poles. It was a beautiful day, the walleye were still running, and they were at Mr. Reggie's favorite spot. He also noticed that Maggie was being extra quiet and that Alan seemed like he was mad at her.

"Why aren't we fishing?" he asked. The least they could do was tell him that.

"Where is Willie?" Alan asked. "He was supposed to be here at noon. It's almost twenty after. If the three of us get caught out here without him, we've got problems."

"You've been out here a hundred times," Maggie said.

"Shut up," Alan said. "I know you have a hard time keeping your mouth shut, so I don't know why I even tell you to shut up."

"I'm not going to apologize again," Maggie said. "Drop it."

"What's going on?" Joseph asked. "We've been out here for half an hour and you two have hardly said a word. Tell me what's wrong."

Alan nodded at the path where Willie was walking toward them. He was wearing nice clothes and it was clear he hadn't changed after church.

"Sorry I'm late," Willie said. "They had some ex-federal prisoner at church babbling his testimony. Boring as hell." His arms were crossed like he was cold.

"It's eighty degrees out here," Joseph said. "You look like you are shivering."

"Chills," Willie said, sadly. "I'm from the South. Eighty isn't that warm."

"Why is everybody in such a bad mood?" Joseph said. "We came here to fish."

Willie pulled a piece of paper out of his pocket that looked like it was from a newspaper and held it up in front of Alan's face. "He look familiar?"

Alan studied it for a good five seconds. Then he bit on his lip and turned to Maggie. "Yep."

"On a scale of one to ten, ten being positive, how positive are you?"

Alan moved Willie's hand and the paper away from his face. This time he stared at Willie for another five seconds. "Ten. It's him."

Willie walked right toward Joseph and held the newspaper article up. There was a black man wearing a suit and he looked familiar.

"This was my father," Willie said. "Did you see him get dipped?"

"That's your daddy?"

"Why didn't you tell me?"

"I didn't know it was him," Joseph said.

"We never talk about what we see down there," Alan said, turning to Maggie. "Well, at least most of us."

"It's his daddy!" Maggie said.

Willie was still looking right at Joseph. "Joseph, you knew my father was killed and that's why I was up here. You never put two and two together?"

"What's that mean?"

"It never occurred to you that the guy you saw get killed, the *black* guy you saw get killed, may have been my father?"

Joseph never talked about the man that got killed. Or the other men that got killed down there. Nobody talked about what they saw because everybody knew if you did that, the same thing would happen to you that happened to Alan and Maggie's mom and dad and the other people that talked about what they saw happen at Devil's Drop.

"I had no idea it was your daddy, Willie. Honest to goodness."

"Would you have told me if you knew it was my dad?"

"I'll answer that for you," Alan said. "Talking about what happens down there can be a death sentence. Just take it from me and Maggie. That is the truth."

Willie looked at the ground and just shook his head. "So, nobody else knows about this?"

"Just us four," Alan said. "I mean, who else would we tell...the cops?"

Willie seemed like he went from angry to focused in the blink of an eye.

"Everyone knows Sheriff Green is Trio," Willie said. "And we also know that everybody else keeps their membership under wraps, but..." He paused. "But what I'm about to say has to stay between us because *all* of our lives depend on it."

Alan nodded as did Maggie. And then they all looked at Joseph.

"I won't say anything," Joseph said. "What is it?"

"My Uncle Reggie is also Trio."

"No, he's not!" Joseph said. "There is no way Mr. Reggie would be in The Crown. Never. No."

"His black robe is in his closet," Willie said. "I can't believe you have never seen it."

"Willie, you have to be mistaken," Joseph said. "You aren't thinking right because of what happened to your daddy."

"My father was worth somewhere between thirty and fifty million dollars. I haven't seen the paperwork yet, but my uncle Reggie knew he would be getting half if something happened to my father. So, if getting fifteen to twenty-five million from an estranged and, excuse me for saying, *pinkie-loving* brother isn't motive, I don't know what is."

"Mr. Reggie doesn't care about money," Joseph said. "I can't believe it. I don't believe it."

"Listen," Willie said. "The Crown couldn't be too happy about a black lawyer defending a white guy, so there's nothing wrong with knocking him off. Then they pin it on some white homeless guy, have him 'commit suicide,' then ride off into the sunset. And take it to the bank Uncle Reggie is the mastermind behind it all and is paying some people when all the smoke clears. People like Sheriff Green. You can make a lot of promises with all that money and still have more left than you will ever know what to do with."

"Welcome to our world," Alan said. "We lost our parents like you lost your daddy. And guess what?"

"What?" Willie said.

"There ain't nothing any of us can do about it."

"Kettle will help us," Willie said. "But I need one of you to go with me."

"Forget it," Alan said. "I'm not telling any black person what I saw." Then he turned to Maggie. "And neither are you."

Willie turned and looked at Joseph. Joseph didn't know what to say except, "I want to talk to Mr. Reggie."

Willie came up and took him by the arm. "Are you crazy? The next time he leaves, I will show you The Crown outfit in the closet. What we talked about here today stays between us, remember? You need to understand that."

"Okay," Joseph said.

Behind Willie he could see someone coming down the path.

It was Sheriff Green.

Maggie and Alan bolted into the woods, but not without being seen.

"Alan and Maggie!" Sheriff Green shouted. "Get back out here now. Unless you want me to pay your house a little visit this afternoon, you best listen up."

Joseph's heart pounded at the inside walls of his chest. Sheriff Green had already seen him as well, but at least they were with Willie.

The sun glistened off the sheriff's sunglasses as he entered the opening. Maggie and Alan stepped back out of the woods with their shoulders slumped, looking at the ground.

Sheriff Green's cheek bulged with tobacco. He walked past all of them and peeked over the edge of the break wall, down into the lake. He turned around, walked directly behind Joseph, and Joseph could feel him standing there. Then the sheriff came out into the center of them and crossed his arms.

"Looks like Reggie gave you all permission to come out here," he said, spitting a healthy wad of tobacco onto the cement in front of the sea wall. He walked over and then knelt next to it. He studied it for a second and then pointed at it, his finger no more than an inch from it. "Pick that up real quick like. I'm talking to you, Maggie."

They all remained quiet, even Willie, as Maggie removed her do-rag and wiped up the sheriff's spit.

"My uncle did give us permission," Willie said.

"Good to know," the sheriff said. "You sure got out here quick after church. Next time you all go fishing, you may want to bring some fishing poles."

Joseph held up the two poles he had brought with him.

The sheriff smiled and then turned and made his way back down the path. The four of them waited until he was out of sight.

"We are toast," Alan said. "He heard everything we just said."

"No way," Willie said. "He came down the same path I did and we would have heard his fat ass coming. He didn't hear anything. Trust me."

"No offense," Alan said. "But we don't do a whole lotta trusting of black people."

"He didn't hear us," Willie said, sternly.

"So, what now?" Alan asked.

"We sit tight until I think of the best way to get Kettle's help," Willie said. "We need to go over The Crown's head and he is the only one I can think of that can get us there."

"Good luck with that," Alan said. "Come here, Joseph."

Joseph walked over next to Alan. "What?"

"Turn around." Joseph did. "Take your shirt off."

"Why?" Joseph asked.

"Just do it." Joseph did and he could see it on his T-shirt.

Sheriff Green had spit tobacco on his back.

Joseph slowly looked over at Willie. "You were right," Joseph said. "I need to stand up for myself."

Alan laughed. "Against Sheriff Green? How are you going to stand up to him?"

Joseph looked at Alan and then straight at Willie.

"Not sure, but one of these days I'm gonna do something."

WILLIE

Four Inches Low. Four Inches Left.

Bull's-eye.

I want to set Sheriff Green on fire and then stamp him out with my uncle's skull," Willie said as he and Joseph walked toward the barn. Joseph was going to teach him how to shoot Varmint Killer and as soon as Uncle Reggie left, he was going to take Joseph inside to show him The Crown robe.

"Don't say that," Joseph said. "I know you are wrong about Mr. Reggie. And I hope you aren't planning anything dumb with this gun."

"I'm not," Willie said.

"I'm sorry I didn't know that was your daddy that got killed," Joseph said. "I guess I'm not as smart as you thought I was."

"Don't worry about my father," Willie said. "And you are smart. When we finally get you out of Woodruff, the whole world will start to know it."

They went into the barn and Joseph grabbed Varmint Killer and a margarine tub full of .22 shells. Joseph tore the corner off a cardboard box and then went back to the little shack and grabbed three apples out of the bin. Joseph offered one to Willie, who declined it, and then they walked behind the barn.

"Hungry?" Willie asked. "You going to eat all three?"

"Gonna eat two," Joseph said. "We are going to shoot the other one. Or at least try."

"I don't see a gnat on one," Willie said. "How am I supposed to shoot it off if I don't see it?"

Joseph laughed. "You think you are gonna be as good of a shot as your uncle?"

"Maybe, but I don't have to be that good," Willie said. "Give me one of those apples."

Joseph handed him one and Willie bit into it.

It tasted good.

They went behind the barn and Joseph walked out to a tree stump and attached the piece of cardboard to it. He put the remaining apple above the cardboard and then stepped off fifty paces back toward Willie. He picked up Varmint Killer and pointed at the front site.

"See this single piece of metal?"

"Yeah," Willie said.

Then Joseph pointed at the rear site. "See these two pieces of metal?"

"Let me guess," Willie said. "I look between the two pieces of the rear site, line up the front site between them, and place it under my target?"

"How did you know?" Joseph asked.

"I just know," Willie said. "Actually, the sights are exactly like the sights on the plastic gun I use for *Gunrunner3*."

"What's that?"

"Nothing," Willie said.

"We are about fifty yards away," Joseph said. "I'm gonna go first to see if the sight needs adjusting. I'm going to shoot at the dead center of that piece of cardboard."

Joseph went to one knee and aimed the rifle. He cracked off three shots and then they went down and looked at the piece of cardboard. The holes in the target were close together, but were all about four inches high and four inches to the right of center.

"I need to adjust the sights," Joseph said.

"No, you don't," Willie said. "Just aim low and to the left."

"Yeah, but—"

"Give me the gun." They walked back to where they took the shots from and Willie dropped to one knee and aimed. Low left…about four inches.

He took more time in between shots than Joseph did, but fired three times.

He smiled, took yet another shot, and then raised his head in disappointment. They went and looked at the target.

"Wow!" Joseph said. "You don't need to practice anything."

His first three shots were all within two inches of the center.

"Pretty darn good," Joseph added. "What happened to your fourth shot?"

"I was aiming for the apple. I missed."

Joseph picked up the apple and studied it. "Maybe you should practice. If you can't hit the apple you ain't ever gonna hit the gnat off the apple from this far away like your uncle."

Just then, they heard Uncle Reggie and his big-ass-squinty-eyed-watermelon-fucking head come out the back door.

"Be back in a few hours!" Uncle Reggie shouted. "And Willie...don't forget about the supper club dinner tonight."

"I won't!" Willie yelled back before his uncle got in the car and backed out the driveway. He stood and put his hand on Joseph's shoulder.

"I don't need to hit a gnat," Willie said. "Or the apple."

He smiled and watched his uncle disappear down Cossit Creek Road.

"I just need to hit a watermelon."

JOSEPH

It Can't Be True. Two Tears.

Going to Talk.

Willie opened the closet door and took two steps back.

"There it is," he said. "Come take a look."

Joseph was standing in the middle of the room and still hadn't seen The Crown robe and hood. Part of him thought that Willie was messing with him and the other half knew it was in there because even Willie wouldn't mess around when his dead daddy was involved.

Joseph took a deep breath and then walked over in front of the open door.

There it was. Just like Willie said. The black Trio robe was right next to a purple one. Joseph felt like his throat was coated with sand.

"It can't be true," he said. He noticed that his voice cracked twice in those four words, making his already high voice sound like a little boy's. But he didn't care.

Willie just crossed his arms and smiled, but it didn't look like a happy smile. "We are both looking at the same thing. Who else would it belong to, your mom?"

"But Mr. Reggie has always—"

"Been on this farm and been in The Crown. But he's never had a chance to come into millions until my dad rolled back into town."

"They killed your duddy so Mr. Reggie could get a bunch of money?"

"Yes."

Joseph could feel the tear roll out the bottom of his left eye. It felt cool as it weaved its way down his cheek and on to his chin. He dabbed at it with the back of his hand and then stepped forward and closed the closet door.

"I can't trust any black people now," Joseph said, turning to Willie. "Except for you."

They stared at each other for a good thirty seconds before Joseph noticed it. Willie's eyes were watering and a tear had begun to zigzag its way across his cheek as well. Willie covered his eyes with both hands as if he were embarrassed. Then he stopped and slowly pulled his hands away from his face. Willie looked at his palms and they could both see they were tear-soaked.

Willie did another one of his not-happy smiles and it quickly faded.

"I haven't cried in over ten years," he said. And then he looked away like he was trying to hide it.

"Why you crying?" Joseph asked, stepping right up next to Willie. "Because I said I can't trust any black people but you?"

Willie didn't take long to answer. "No."

"Why then?"

Willie wiped at his eyes again. "I'm crying because you were crying."

Joseph smiled and opened his arms. Willie stepped forward and when they hugged, Willie continued to cry for a long minute before stepping backward and looking at Joseph.

"You can also trust Kettle," Willie said.

"I need to get Mama out of here," Joseph said. "I need to get her away from Mr. Reggie and that evil thing in the closet."

"Not yet," Willie said. "She's been around it this long so a little longer won't hurt. Just don't say anything to her yet and let me deal with my uncle Reggie."

"Okay," Joseph said. "And I don't care what happens to me."

"What's that supposed to mean?"

"I'm gonna talk to Reverend Kettle about what I seen."

Willie shook his head. "Don't even think about talking to him until I tell you."

"If you think that's best," Joseph said, knowing Willie had a plan.

But not telling Reverend Kettle didn't make any sense. No sense at all.

WILLIE

The Supper Club. An Invitation.

The Business Proposal.

Willie sat in the passenger's seat of Uncle Reggie's car as they sputtered down Cossit Creek toward Main Street on their way to the Woodruff Supper Club. Apparently, it was customary in Woodruff for the socialite wannabees to meet at the club and eat something prepared not by a real cook, but by some volunteer member of the club. It was the hoity-toity bullshit that Shanice Kettle (the night's honorary chef) made all the noise about the day she crapped herself in her backyard when the double dose of dynamite went off. Speaking of a double dose, Willie wouldn't have minded shoving a couple sticks up old Reggie's ass right then and there, and then when that greedy, kill-your-own-brother-murderous-fuck said hello to Sheriff Green at the supper club, Willie could say "out with the rot," then lean on the plunger and send both of them (Uncle Reggie's new asshole and all) straight to Kingdom Fuck.

"Sure are being quiet," Uncle Reggie said, snapping Willie out of his proctologist's wet dream. They were halfway down Main Street and those were the first words either of them had said since leaving the house.

"Tired," Willie said. "Getting way too low on pills and I'm kind of getting myself mentally ready for rehab. Feeling a little sick not taking the amount I normally take. Definitely detoxing a little."

"We won't stay long."

Willie took a long look at his uncle and really did feel sick. He thought about throwing up in his own mouth as he imagined his uncle Reggie and the other members of The Crown waving their torches, watching as his father was dipped... for money.

When they pulled into the club parking lot, Willie wondered what he was going to have Joseph say to Kettle when the time came and how Kettle would respond. He knew Kettle would have the balls to help them, but whether it would lead to any kind of justice for Dad was yet to be seen. At the very least, Kettle was a good place to start.

It's the only place to start...

The interior of the supper club was poorly lit and smelled musty, like empty kegs of beer, disinfecting spray, and mop water. On second glance, the place was nothing more than a low-end banquet hall. Folding chairs nestled up to folding tables that were covered with paper tablecloths. A skinny bartender with a red coat and black bow tie was mixing drinks in clear plastic cups. Next to the bar was an opening in the wall that exposed the kitchen. The opening reminded Willie of the kitchen at his school's cafeteria. It was the kind that, once everyone leaves, gets closed up by a retractable metal cover and makes a big noise when you pop the back of your fist against it when you are trying to freak out the lunch ladies. He wished it was closed, because Shanice Kettle was back there pointing at something and talking to some other woman that had that "get-me-the-fuck-away-from-Shanice" look on her face that Willie himself had undoubtedly worn more than once. To the right of the kitchen was a little dance floor in front of a small stage. All that really seemed to be missing were those sweaty-ass trays of chicken, fish, and pasta (kept warm by tiny burners) that were common amenities at these types of joints. In fact, the only other thing missing that kept it from mirroring a poor man's wedding reception was the scrum of drunk and dancing idiots on the dance floor "putting their left foot in."

Regardless, it was apparent that the club was the place to be in Woodruff when a friend was cooking. That's also if you were black and had money, or in Shanice Kettle's case, acted like you had money and drove your husband nuts until he pulled enough strings to get you to be the cook for the night.

It wasn't much of a surprise who was at their table. It was Willie, Uncle Reggie, Sheriff Green, Green's wife (a plain-looking woman that probably only spoke when spoken to), and another couple that reminded Willie of storefront mannequins—both good-looking and dressed perfectly in a country club sort of way. Willie spotted Reverend Kettle sitting at a different table and the minister gave him a friendly wave.

Seated between Sheriff Green and Uncle Reggie, Willie quickly imagined that he was The Crown Lord. The three of them would emerge from their little hut on the stage at Devil's Drop, and then they would walk to the podium where Willie would step up between them onto whatever it was The Crown Lord stood on to make him taller, exalting him over Sheriff Green and Uncle Reggie.

And then he would raise his hand, sending the mob into a frenzy. And then he would have Sheriff Green announce that there was going to be not one death, but two, both black men, men the same color as the lawyer they dipped not long ago. And as the field of purple began some deafening chant, as it became a pulse, Willie's hands would slowly emerge out from underneath his robe, each holding a pistol, and then he would fan his arms out to his sides and pull both triggers at once, dropping his uncle Reggie and Sheriff Green right there in front of them all.

Sheriff Green nudged Willie on the shoulder.

"Try not to act like you are having so much fun," he said with a grin. His breath smelled like moldy cheese and wet slivers of tobacco were crammed in between those gold teeth of his.

"I'm not feeling well," Willie said.

"That's what Reggie told me," the sheriff said. "Sorry to hear."

"Thanks," Willie said, wondering how he was going to fake his way through dinner.

A microphone turned on, followed by a bolt of high-pitched feedback that made half the room cringe. There was a tapping noise, followed by the obligatory "testing-one-two-three."

Willie guessed the rest of them cringed when they realized Shanice Kettle was the one holding the microphone. She informed everyone that what they were about to eat was from a roast beef recipe that had been in her family for hundreds of years.

Hundreds of years? What a fucking nightmare.

About thirty white women filed out of the kitchen, each two-handing servings of Auntie Shanice's roast beef. As they put plates on the tables, Shanice asked her husband to bless the food. Willie didn't really pay any attention to anything Reverend Kettle said and really couldn't think of anything to be thankful for at the moment, other than the possibility of somehow killing the two men he was sitting with, or at least watching them handed over to the authorities. The real authorities. Not The Crown.

Shanice Kettle stopped by their table and insisted that she top off Willie's roast beef with a dark brown gravy (another family recipe, though the length of time it had been passed down was not provided). As it splatted off the meat, it reminded Willie of the mess Willie's old dog, Toby, had dispatched on the living room carpet the one time he had eaten rotten fruit out of the neighbor's garbage can. He'd never forget when their housekeeper, good ol' DeeDee, came in to clean it up. She about had a stroke and was down on her hands and knees, scrubbing that wet shit out of the fabric as Toby did the doggie-drag behind her, moonwalking across the room on his ass, wiping it clean on the spotless carpet she took so much pride in.

Willie smiled and then choked on it. He took a deep breath and realized he hadn't thought about Toby in at least a year now.

He'd loved that dog.

Toby was dead too.

Everything I ever love ends up dead. Maybe that answers Cheever's question as to why I'm afraid to get too close…

"It's risky," Willie said out loud, repeating what Cheever said.

"No, it's not," Shanice Kettle said. "Try some."

He tried it, and the roast beef and gravy combo tasted like a concoction of shoe leather, shit, and roast beef. Minus the roast beef. He nodded his head, smiled, and she went away.

They ate in relative silence, and Willie was drowning in a sea of hate when Sheriff Green leaned toward him and whispered something Willie couldn't hear.

"I missed that," Willie said. He didn't miss the breath that came with it. It smelled worse than it had a few minutes earlier and was now warm and sour, like milk that had gone bad.

"How is your buddy, Joseph?"

Willie thought fast. "He's not my buddy."

The sheriff's face tilted toward his left shoulder and he squinted, as if surprised. "You two seem to be inseparable. Best of friends."

"You kidding me?" Willie felt like he sounded pretty convincing and it seemed like Green was buying it. A little. "He's a pain in my ass. He's like a pet that follows me everywhere I go."

"A pet," the sheriff echoed. "That's about all he is. A half-pink pet."

Willie nodded at his uncle, who was shoveling that roast beef shit in his mouth like it was the cure for his fucked-up eye. And then he looked back at Sheriff Green. "Only reason I tolerate Joseph is for my uncle Reggie. Don't even know why I'm still here."

Green seemed to think about it. "Why you spending time with Alan and Maggie then?"

"What do you think?" Willie said. "Maggie is hot. I don't care what color she is. I want to get some of that."

Green glanced over his shoulder at his wife and then leaned closer. "I've thought about picking Maggie up and taking her to the station for a little interrogation... if you catch my drift."

Willie smiled. Green really was a sick fuck. "Go for it. Just let me go first."

Uncle Reggie leaned forward and squinted in a fatherly sort of way before asking, "What are you two talking about?"

"About spitting on Joseph the next time we see him," Willie whispered, just loud enough for the sheriff to hear.

"Just talking about Willie's time in Woodruff," Sheriff Green said. "And how he needs to have some fun."

"He don't need any of your kind of fun, Demetrius," Uncle Reggie said. Oddly, it didn't sound like he was joking.

The sheriff waved the back of his hand at Uncle Reggie the way a Roman Emperor would dismiss one of his subjects, then turned back to Willie.

"Spitting on Joseph," Sheriff Green whispered. "You are funny. But don't get it twisted. I'd also piss on that hash brown mongrel's head. And I would do right it in front of his mama."

"I believe you," Willie said. "That was a pretty serious loogie you plopped on his back out near the fishing spot."

"That wasn't serious," Green said. "It's only serious when they know you are spitting on them. And a lot funner too."

"I see," Willie said. "I wouldn't mind spitting on every one of them after what happened to my father."

Green took a bite of his food and shrugged. "The death of a parent, it's something you never really get over. I think you just get used to it. But I certainly understand the way you are feeling."

You have no idea how I feel...

"It seems like you guys could have protected him," Willie said.

The sheriff ran his hand along the side of his face and then cocked his head toward Willie. He was big on the eye contact thing. "Law enforcement can't see everything that's happening, Willie. We do our best, but things still happen."

"I wasn't talking about law enforcement," Willie said.

His eyes were still glued to Willie's and Willie prepared for the mothership of rhetorical questions.

"Who are you talking about, then?" Sheriff Green asked.

Willie maintained eye contact and tried to listen to the other conversation happening at the table between Uncle Reggie and Mr. and Mrs. Mannequin. He was pretty sure they were talking about how bad the food sucked, but he was really just double-checking to make sure they weren't listening. Then Willie held up his fist and waggled his finger the way the sheriff did at the hospital. The way Willie had seen him do somewhere else as well. "It was you on the courthouse steps up in Detroit that day. You were the one looking at me, weren't you?"

Sheriff Green just kept staring at Willie and Willie couldn't stop the hair on the back of his neck from dancing.

"Two things," the sheriff whispered, holding up not just that waggling finger, but its next-door neighbor as well. "One. Don't ever, I mean *ever*, ask a man if he is in The Crown."

"Sheriff Green, I think the whole town knows you are in The Crown."

Green didn't respond. Those piercing brown eyes were looking right through Willie and a sharp sliver of doubt poked at Willie's gut, telling him that Green somehow knew that Willie knew The Crown had killed his father. The longer the sheriff looked at him, the deeper the sliver poked, paralyzing Willie in the sheriff's gaze.

Willie wanted to get up and leave, but then one of Green's fingers recoiled, leaving just the waggler pointing at the ceiling. It seemed as if he were waiting for Willie to ask what the second thing was, so he obliged.

"What's the second thing?"

The waggler started to waggle and then it stopped. Then a little smile started to form at the corner of Sheriff Green's mouth.

"How would you like to come to a meeting?"

"Would be awesome. When?"

"Wednesday night."

"Can't."

"Why not?"

"Have a two-hour call with a doctor down in Atlanta. Helps me with grieving. Our calls are normally at six, but this week we are doing it at eight." Pure bullshit, but believable bullshit, considering he had a quarter second to come up with it.

"Take a raincheck?" Green asked.

"Hell yes."

"And by the way," Green said. He glanced back at his wife and then over at Uncle Reggie to make sure they weren't paying attention. "I'm not just *in* The Crown."

"What do you mean?"

Green leaned closer, a matter of inches from Willie, and pulled up his shirt. "See it?"

Willie did. Just beneath the sheriff's right rib cage was the brand that had been burned into his black skin. It was a perfectly shaped crown, a little smaller than a fist, and Willie wondered what it meant.

"What is that?"

"Really?" Sheriff Green asked.

"Really," Willie repeated. He had no clue.

"Highest badge of honor a Crown could ever receive. An honor given exclusively to the big three."

"Only the Trio get those?" Willie asked.

"Can I assume your white friends already told you I'm Trio."

"Sheriff Green, I don't think talking about Crown activity is on any white person's to-do list. Particularly up on The Row."

Green tucked his shirt back in and smiled. "Looking forward to having you out to Devil's Drop sometime soon."

"Can't wait. Just let me know."

What Sheriff Green didn't know was that Willie would be there Wednesday. About fifty yards from the stage, sitting in a duck blind, hiding in the cattails where not one of those purple-hood-wearing-ass fucks could see him. But he wouldn't be concerned with them. Just two of the three guys up on stage that were wearing the black outfits.

And Willie would have his newest friend with him: Varmint Killer.

◆◆◆

"MAMA WILL KILL ME if she finds out," Joseph said. "I've never had any of that stuff before."

"It's not like we are smoking weed," Willie said, pouring a half glass of whiskey for Joseph as they sat behind the barn. He had taken the bottle out of his uncle's cupboard as soon as he fell asleep, which was about ten minutes after they had returned from the supper club, where good old Reggie had a few too many.

"I've never done drinking before or been high," Joseph said. "Plus, you shouldn't have taken that from Mr. Reggie."

"After seeing what's in the closet," Willie said, "you are worried about what my uncle thinks?"

Joseph looked up at the moon and shook his head. Then he reached down, grabbed the cup, and slugged all the whiskey down at once. He coughed and then held his hands to his throat for a moment.

"What do I do now?" Joseph gasped.

"Breathe and don't drink it so fast. Damn."

"Not about that. About me and Mama. We have to get out of here. Away from Mr. Reggie."

Mr. Reggie. My soon-to-be-dead uncle.

Uncle Reggie would be the first to go. All Willie needed was a little more practice with Varmint Killer and then he'd be off to The Crown meeting to put a bullet right in his racist uncle's good eye.

Willie guzzled down his whiskey, poured two more glasses, then put the cap back on the bottle. For some crazy-ass reason, he wanted to talk to Cheever, but he wasn't sure why. Maybe he would listen instead of just hear.

"I want to help you get out of here," Willie said.

"How you going to do that?"

"Landscapers do pretty well in my neighborhood and they don't have half the talent you have."

"Landscapers do well where you live? How?"

Willie reached over his head and tapped on the barn. "My father's bedroom is the size of this barn. With big bedrooms comes big houses comes big yards. That means big business for landscapers."

"I get it," Joseph said. "You are smart, Willie."

"Scary smart."

"What do you mean?"

Willie paused and felt a wave of sadness wash over him. Whether it was about Dad, Evan, or everything that was happening, he didn't know. But *feelings* had returned, and he didn't like the way they *felt*. He had to get more pills.

"What do mean?" Joseph repeated. "What is *scary* smart?"

"The kind of smart that scares people."

"You don't seem scary. Why are they afraid of you?"

Willie took a sip of the whiskey and it burned his throat. "I think a lot of people sense that I'm smarter than they are and that maybe I'm capable of things."

"Why would that scare them?"

The kid sure asked a lot of questions, but some of them were accidentally good ones.

Willie took a deep breath and his leg twitched. And then it twitched again. "I guess they know I don't care. And that being smart and not caring is a dangerous combination."

"What is it you don't care about?"

Willie waited and normally wouldn't answer that question, but he did.

"Me."

"Aww, man," Joseph said. "Look at all you have. You know how many people would cut a toe off to be you?"

"Ever hear that money is the root of all evil?"

"I'm thinking *lack* of money is sometimes the root of all evil," Joseph said. "Besides, it's the *love* of money that's the root of all evil."

"I'd give all my toes and all my money to have my mom and sister back," Willie said. "And my father. I was in a really good place just a few days ago. Then I found out how Dad died and now I'm a fucking mess."

"You sure curse a lot."

"I don't mean anything by it. Just sort of comes out."

"Habit?"

"I have lots of habits."

"Like drinking?" Joseph asked, pointing at the bottle. "I think Mr. Reggie has a drinking habit."

"Appreciate that revelation," Willie said. "You should be a detective."

"Really?"

"I'm just being a smartass," Willie said. He shook his head and then reached into his pocket and pulled out what was left of the pills. "These are almost gone."

"What are you going to do?"

"Probably trip out over the next few days with the withdrawals," Willie said. "But I can't think about that right now. Let's get back to you being in the landscaping business. Once we see what Kettle can do to help us with The Crown, we will pack you and your mom up and go down south and get your business started."

"You'd do that for us?"

"Count on it. It's going to happen."

Joseph smiled and took another sip of his whiskey. "I feel funny."

Willie laughed. "You are an out-of-control boozer?"

Joseph's smile went away and he took yet another sip. "Why don't we go tell Reverend Kettle right now and then leave town."

"No," Willie said. "I already told you we have to wait a little bit."

"Why?"

"Because."

Because I'm going to try and serve some justice myself…

Joseph polished off his second drink and stood. He wobbled and then braced himself against the barn. "Why do I have a feeling you are up to something no good?"

"You drunk?"

"I feel funny."

"Your mom is gonna be pissed."

"Don't say that."

"I'm kidding you," Willie said. He stood and patted Joseph on the arm. "Within a week, you won't have to put up with any of this bullshit anymore."

Joseph smiled. "You really think so?"

"I know so," Willie said, taking his turn smiling. "I promise."

JOSEPH

Headache.

How Hadn't She Seen It Before?

Mama pointed at the untouched eggs on Joseph's plate. Then she stood and put the back of her hand against his forehead.

"What's wrong with you this morning?" she asked. "You not feeling well? You haven't said a word nor touched your food."

"I'm okay, Mama."

It wasn't true. He felt like his head was splitting open.

It was a miracle that Mama was sleeping when he opened the door last night. He was also surprised she couldn't smell the whiskey on him. He could still taste it in his mouth and the more he thought about it made him even sicker.

Joseph looked across the table at Willie. Willie crossed his eyes and smiled quick like, so only the two them knew he did it. It was a little funny, but Joseph didn't feel like laughing. He felt like his brain had broken glass in it. He felt like going out behind the barn and throwing up. He wanted to go and lie down for a while.

The phone rang, and Mr. Reggie got up to answer it. Joseph wondered if it was one of his Crown friends. He still didn't want to believe the whole thing about Mr. Reggie being in The Crown, but he had to. For Mama's sake.

Mr. Reggie hung up the phone and shook his head. "That was Reverend Kettle." He sat back at the table and grabbed a piece of bacon off his plate. He put it in his mouth and spoke as he chewed.

"Nancy, would you mind going out to the Kettle place tomorrow to do a little cleaning? Mostly dusting. Shanice Kettle mentioned something last night at the supper club that our work has left a little dust on her furniture. Maybe you could shine things up while the boys take out the rest of the trees? Would greatly appreciate it."

"Will do," Mama said. Joseph wondered what Mama would think if she took a look in the closet upstairs.

And then he wondered how in the world she'd never seen it before.

WILLIE

Coyote.

There were three knocks on the bedroom door.

"Come in," Willie said.

Uncle Reggie opened the door and walked straight to the window. His ass crack was peeking out the top of his boxers again when he put his right index finger against the glass. "Why don't you and Joseph grab Varmint Killer and go put that thing down?"

Willie stood and went to the window. There was a coyote, most likely the same one they had seen before. He was out near the pond and was scurrying back and forth and sniffing at the ground. For all Willie knew, the damn thing was either getting ready to take a dump or was eating his father's ashes and preparing to wash them down with a cool sip of pond water.

"Will do," Willie said, echoing Nancy's obedience from earlier that morning.

And before long, I will put you down too...

"Good," his uncle said, still staring out the window. "Pop him when he's by himself. Go get him now before he gangs up with his buddies and starts causing real problems."

Kind of like you and your Crown friends ganging up on people, you coward fuck?

Uncle Reggie stepped back from the window and gave Willie a fatherly nod. "You sure you are up for shooting it?"

"I am," Willie said again. "I will be down in a few minutes. Just let me change and then we will go kill us a coyote."

"Roger that," Uncle Reggie said and left the room. Then he turned and looked back through the open door. "Just don't take too long. Get 'em before he leaves."

By the time Willie had taken a third of his remaining pills and gone outside, Joseph was already waiting for him with Varmint Killer in hand. He had a miserable hungover look on his face and Willie laughed for real.

"You look like you are about to barf."

"Just threw up again behind the barn," Joseph said. "I'm pretty sure Mama knows we were drinking because she asked me this morning if something smelled like whiskey."

"It was your breath," Willie said. "Now let's go get that coyote."

Joseph handed Willie the gun. "You shoot him. I've seen that coyote probably a thousand times. I've never seen him hurt nothing."

"I'll shoot him. I just need to remember to shoot four inches left and four inches low."

"This is a lot farther than fifty yards though," Joseph said. "You may have to aim even lower and more to the left from where you will be shooting."

They walked to the edge of the barn and took turns peeking around the corner. The coyote was still there, drinking from the pond, but they were a football field away from him.

"Let's get closer," Willie said, pointing at the high grass that ran all the way to the coyote. "We can stay low and he will never see us."

"Don't have to get closer," Joseph said, holding his right index finger and thumb about a quarter inch apart. "Just aim about that much more than four inches low and four inches left, and you will get him from right here."

"You sure?"

Joseph took the gun, leaned against the corner of the barn, and aimed at the pond. He pretended to pull the trigger. "Pop. Just like that."

"What do we do after I shoot him?"

Joseph shrugged and pointed at the sky. "I guess we leave him for the buzzards."

Willie took the gun and looked around the corner. The coyote was just sitting at the edge of the pond. He practically looked like someone's pet.

"He's dangerous," Willie said. "He kills. He deserves it."

Willie raised the gun and aimed it at the back of the coyote's head. Then he aimed four and a *quarter* inches low and the same amount to the left. When he clicked the safety off it was like he had gone into a world that only had two living things in it. Him and the coyote. He could hear the breeze. And even though it was so far away, he could see that same breeze moving the fur on the coyote's shoulders and the top of his head.

I've never seen him hurt nothing.

Willie felt the trigger. It was cool against the fat of his finger. The sound of the breeze was replaced by the sound of his own breathing.

"What are you waiting for?" Joseph whispered.

The coyote turned and looked back. Willie wanted to be somewhere else. Anywhere but here.

"He's dangerous," Willie repeated. "He kills. He deserves it. Doesn't he?"

Willie closed his eyes. He could see Dad's face. His mother's face. His sister's face. And then Evan's face.

They didn't deserve what happened to them.

And none of it was his fault. It wasn't.

It really wasn't...

Willie felt something move the gun and he opened his eyes. Joseph had grabbed it, just in front of the trigger. His thumb pressed the safety back on and he lifted Varmint Killer out of Willie's hand.

"I couldn't do it," Willie said.

"I tried before too," Joseph said. "Defenseless animal. Not knowing I was way far away and about to kill it. He's just out there playing his part in nature and like I said, I never seen him hurt nothing. It just didn't seem like the right thing to do."

"The right thing to do," Willie repeated dreamily, unable to stop himself from thinking about Uncle Reggie and Sheriff Green.

It will be different then.

♦♦♦

WILLIE SPENT MOST OF the afternoon thinking about Maggie and trying to remember exactly where the entrance was to the path he and Joseph had taken (the one relatively close to the ghetto and the same one black people never went down for fear of their asses) that led to Devil's Drop. He needed to scout things out and have both the perfect entrance and exit strategies for Wednesday night's Crown meeting. Not to mention the even bigger exit that would get him, Joseph, Nancy, and maybe even Maggie and Alan the hell out of Woodruff.

WILLIE

Meet Me.

Man Down. Early Exit.

Everyone was up early and after breakfast, Willie, Joseph, and Nancy left Uncle Reggie's to head downtown for cleaning supplies. As they approached the Vee place, Willie could see old Mack the dog, sitting in the same spot he was always in, chain around his neck, totally defeated, and clearly drowning in a dog's understanding that life would never get better.

Willie stopped the truck.

"Look at him," Willie said. "Poor guy. I'm serious when I say I'm going to unchain him and take him back to Georgia with me when I leave."

Nancy looked at Willie like he'd lost his marbles. "That dog belongs to Missus Vee. You can't just take him."

"That's abuse," Willie said. "He's all chained up. At least let him run around the farm. He doesn't know what he is missing. Other than breathing and eating, he has no life."

Willie started to pull away and Nancy kept looking at Mack. "What else he need?"

"I want to take both of you with me when I leave. This place sucks."

"And what are we supposed to do in Georgia?" Nancy asked

Joseph leaned forward like he was asking permission to share what he and Willie had discussed. Willie nodded and kept driving.

"Willie is going to help me get in the landscaping business down south," Joseph said. "He said there are lots of big houses like his that have lots of work done on their yards and that the work I do is as good as the people down there doing it right now."

"Your work is better," Willie said.

"I like the way that sounds," Nancy said. "What would I do then?"

They turned on to Main Street.

"You don't have to do anything," Willie said. "You can live with us and realize that there is more to life than what you have now. And I'm talking about leaving soon. Real soon."

"And just up and leave Mr. Reggie?" Nancy asked.

Joseph tilted his head toward Willie as if it were a good question.

"He is my uncle," Willie said. "He is welcome to come."

"Sounds good, doesn't it, Mama?" Joseph said as downtown came into view.

Willie thought it sounded good as well. All except the Uncle Reggie being welcome to come part. That was also assuming Willie made it out of Woodruff alive after picking off "Mr. Reggie" and Sheriff Green at Devil's Drop.

Maybe Joseph should just talk to Kettle today and we should leave.

But what if Kettle couldn't do anything? Wouldn't he already have tried to stop The Crown if he could?

And if he couldn't...that would leave Sheriff Green and Uncle Reggie with Dad's blood on their hands...still free to keep doing their thing to whoever they wanted...

Willie gripped the steering wheel tight.

They had to die. And it had to happen in front of all their followers...

Willie pulled into a parking space in front of the hardware store. To the right and about a half block down, Alan and Maggie were painting the curb.

"Go on in and get the cleaning stuff," Willie said to Nancy and Joseph. "I'm gonna go say hello to Alan and Maggie."

"I ain't going in there," Nancy said. "I ain't leaving this truck after that white man got shot down here. No way, no how."

Willie put his hand on Nancy's leg. "Joseph goes in there all the time. Besides, nobody is going to bother you with me here. I will be right back."

Nancy looked at Joseph and he nodded. "It'll be okay, Mama."

They got out and Nancy looked around like she was in another world, reminding Willie of a goldfish that had been dropped in a bigger bowl. She and Joseph went in the store and Maggie was already halfway down the sidewalk to meet Willie.

"Hey," Willie said.

"Hey back," Maggie replied.

"I need your help with something," Willie said. "Tomorrow afternoon. And it has to stay between us."

"What is it?"

"I'm going to tell my uncle I can't work tomorrow, and I want you to take me to that path behind The Row. The one black people never go on."

"Only place within a hundred miles they are afraid of," Maggie said. "Anything could happen back there."

"I know," Willie said. "There is a Crown meeting tomorrow and you guys said that whenever there is a meeting, Sheriff Green goes down to Devil's Drop the same morning."

"Every single time," Maggie said. "Everyone knows he goes there to lay out the meeting."

"I don't want to risk going out there before he does his thing," Willie said. "Nor do I want to show up too close to when the meeting begins. Regardless, I need you to take me through the trees and down near the swamp. Then I want you to show me where that spot is you guys hid the night my father was killed. The blind the hunters use?"

"Okay," Maggie said. "It's in the cattails." Then she seemed to mull things over. "But why do you want to do this? What are you going to do?"

"Don't ask me that," Willie said. "But remember when you joked about me having the nerve to ask you to go back to Georgia with me?"

"Yeah."

"If you are serious about getting out of this shithole town, I'll take you and Alan with me somewhere over the next couple days and make sure you are taken care of until you get settled in."

"Really?"

"Yes."

"I'll go with you," she blurted. Her beautiful green eyes were wide and anxious. "Just tell me what I have to do."

"We'll talk about it later," Willie said. "Can you meet me somewhere near the side of the road, down the hill, right before The Row, at exactly two o'clock tomorrow afternoon?"

"What do I tell Alan?"

"Nothing yet," Willie said. "There is no way he'll allow you to do anything that involves The Crown or Sheriff Green."

"Okay," Maggie said, looking over Willie's shoulder. "Speak of the devil."

Willie turned around just in time to see Sheriff Green walk into the hardware store.

"I better get down there," Willie said.

"What are you up to, Willie?" she asked. "Don't do anything that's going to get yourself hurt."

"I'm going to do something that should have been done a long time ago," Willie said.

"What?" she asked, those green eyes lighting up. Willie could see himself in their reflection when he started walking backward toward the hardware store.

"The right thing."

♦♦♦

THERE WERE ONLY FOUR other people in the hardware store when Willie walked in: The clerk sitting behind the counter reading *The Woodruff Gazette* (which had half its pages taken up by coverage of Evan being killed), Joseph, Nancy, and Sheriff Green.

Joseph and Nancy came out from the end of the aisle holding a can of polish, a bottle of window cleaner, and a plastic bag of what looked like used rags. They froze when they saw the sheriff.

Willie swallowed heavily and then walked over and took the supplies from them before returning to the counter. Sheriff Green was leaning back right in the center of it and didn't budge. He just kept that grin on his face, showing those tobacco-covered gold teeth. Finally, the grin disappeared and he turned his stare toward Nancy and Joseph, who hadn't moved an inch since coming around the corner of the aisle.

"Reggie Gibbons' account," Willie said.

The clerk looked up from the paper at what was on the counter and nodded. "You're all set."

The sheriff walked to the front door and then stood to the side of it. Willie nodded at Nancy and Joseph and said, "Let's go."

Willie walked past the sheriff and out the door first, followed by Joseph, who kept Nancy tucked safely behind him. They walked to the curb and Green had followed them out, only a few steps behind them. Willie made his way to the driver's side of the truck and by the time he opened the door, he heard Nancy gasp. She and Joseph were on the other side of the truck, only a foot or so from the curb. Nancy was looking at the same thing Willie was.

The huge wad of chewed up tobacco that Green had spat on Joseph's shoulder.

Without the noise Nancy had made, Joseph probably wouldn't have noticed it. He just tapped it off his shoulder to the pavement, not even looking back at Sheriff Green. The sheriff's nasty grin was bigger than ever, knowing there wasn't a thing Joseph, or anyone else for that matter, was going to do about it.

Joseph opened the passenger-side door to let Nancy in, and before she got in the truck, he took her by the arm. Joseph leaned toward her, squinted, and his cheek muscles flexed. His eyes became a pair of slits and his head began to shake like it was ready to explode.

"It's okay baby," Nancy said. "It's no worry."

Joseph turned around and glared at the sheriff.

"Best watch the way you are looking at me all tough-like," Green said. "Ain't a damn thing you are gonna do about anything."

Willie kept his eyes on the sheriff but Joseph had stepped back up on the curb.

"No worries," Willie yelled, racing back to the curb to join them. "Just like your mom said, it's okay. C'mon now. Let's just get out of here."

"That's some good advice," the sheriff said. "And you got five seconds to take it before *you* end up on the news."

Joseph took a step closer to the sheriff and Willie moved between them. Joseph's fists were balled up and the veins on the sides of his neck were bulging.

Willie took Joseph's arm and squeezed it. It was like a rock and Joseph didn't flinch.

"Let's get out of here," Willie whispered, knowing the sheriff could probably still hear him. "When I said you had to stand up for yourself, I wasn't talking about doing it with the police."

"Smart boy," Green said.

Joseph's nostrils flared as he continued staring at Sheriff Green.

"I ain't standing up for me," Joseph said, then his teeth grit together.

"Please baby," Nancy said, panic in her voice. She came up on the curb to Joseph's side, and when she turned to look up at him, that's when Willie saw it.

Though most of the evidence had been wiped away, he could still see the brown stain and wet streak of tobacco residue that was on the side of Nancy's face and neck. Green hadn't just spit on Joseph, he got them both, and the wad he unloaded on Nancy must have emptied half his mouth.

"Listen to your mother," Green said. He paused and peeked over the edge of his sunglasses. Then he unbuckled his holster.

Nancy nodded and agreed with the sheriff. "C'mon baby, let's go."

Joseph finally looked away from Green and at his mother. A wave of relief ran through Willie and then he watched Joseph's thumb dab at a tear that had started to make its way down Nancy's cheek.

"Okay, Mama," Joseph said, still facing the sheriff.

"Okay," Willie repeated. He stepped out from between the sheriff and Joseph, knowing Joseph and Nancy would follow.

"Well done, Nancy," Sheriff Green said and Willie turned around. "Nice to see you're good for something other than being a black man's whore."

Joseph's right fist shot straight out.

It reminded Willie of that old-fashioned game where the two players control plastic robots in a little boxing ring, and if an opening presented itself to one of the players, he would squeeze down on either of his thumb triggers, subsequently launching a perfectly straight jab at the other robot.

Rock 'em Sock 'em Robots.

The second Joseph's fist met Green's chest, Willie saw the air leave the sheriff's body in a moisture-filled huff that sprayed God only knew what out of his mouth.

Green buckled over, more like folded over, like a man seeing how fast he could do a toe-touch. His arms dangled like noodles, and he tilted side to side…but only twice, and on the second one he kept going, falling to the cement, banging his head, and flattening his sheriff's hat that had beat him to the sidewalk.

"No, Joseph!" Willie yelled.

He ran to him, putting both hands around Joseph's arm to pull him away. Joseph's rock-hard bicep was easily the size of a softball and by the time he had Joseph back off the curb, Green was up on his knees, holding his hand to his chest. He moaned and by the sound of it, Willie figured that maybe sheriff had a cracked sternum.

The sheriff looked over at them, and then his hand left his chest and went to his unbuckled holster.

In one swift jerk, Joseph freed himself from Willie's grip and was back up on the sidewalk, closing in on Green.

When the sheriff pulled his pistol, Joseph grabbed Green's hand and bent it backward, causing him to both drop the gun on the sidewalk and shriek like what Willie would have sworn was a woman. Green was still on his knees and Joseph's left hand gripped the collar of Green's uniform. Joseph turned his hand and twisted the shirt until a button shot off and rolled over in front of Willie and Nancy.

Joseph finally let go of Green's collar and when the sheriff looked up at him, Joseph gave him an open-hand slap to the side of his face. It was the hardest and loudest slap, make that *bitch slap*, Willie had ever heard, turning Green's face toward his shoulder and sending his sunglasses two stores down the sidewalk.

"No, Joseph!" Willie yelled again.

Joseph was taking out every frustration he ever had, that every *pinkie* in Woodruff ever had, on the sheriff, and if he didn't get Joseph out of there, he was going to kill him.

Willie went to the passenger-side door of the truck, opened it, and forced Nancy inside. He closed the door and by the time he had turned back around, Joseph had Green by the collar again. Blood was coming from Green's nose and mouth and he appeared to be only half conscious.

Joseph cocked back his fist. Willie closed his eyes and waited for the sound of Joseph's fist, propelled by his six-foot-five, two-hundred-and-thirty-pound frame, to hit and most likely destroy Green's face.

He heard nothing and Willie opened his eyes.

Joseph's fist was still pulled behind his head but it was shaking uncontrollably. He let go of the sheriff and Green went to the ground like a wet rag, banging the side of his face on the sidewalk.

Willie ran up next to Joseph who had tears running down his face.

"Joseph, listen to me."

Joseph looked at him and his bottom lip began to quiver. "He spit on Mama and called her a whore."

Willie looked around. For some reason or act of God, the only people watching what happened were Alan and Maggie, and maybe the clerk inside the hardware store.

He reached up and cradled Joseph's face in his hands. Tears were welling in his eyes.

"Let's get in the truck," Willie said. "Let's go and get in the truck…right now."

"Okay," Joseph said softly, and Willie guided him to the driver-side door and helped him get in.

"Pay attention to me," Willie said. He tried to talk slow as if speaking to a nine-year-old. "I know you are angry, scared, and have a lot going on, but you have to do exactly what I say or bad things will happen. You listening to me?"

Joseph nodded. Willie waved his hand for Nancy to pay attention as well.

"I'm going to stay here with Sheriff Green. It will buy you time. Take the truck back to my uncle Reggie's, he won't be there. He went up to Detroit scouting a rehab place for me. Go in the house and go up to my bedroom. In the nightstand drawer is my cell phone and a rubber band with a lot of money in it. Take the money and the phone. Do not get anything out of your house. Just leave and then get on the big freeway heading south until you get into Ohio. The first exits off the freeway once you make it to Ohio are for Toledo. Get off on one of them. Even counting the time to Reggie's, you should be on the freeway and down in Toledo within forty-five minutes, but I'm going to give you an hour and a half to make it there.

"I don't know where Toledo is," Joseph cried. He leaned closer to the windshield and looked over at Sheriff Green. "Never been anywhere."

"It doesn't matter," Willie said. "Just listen to what I'm saying."

"What am I gonna do?" Joseph said. "What am I—"

Willie reached in the window and covered Joseph's mouth. When he turned Joseph's head toward him their eyes immediately met. "You need to settle down and pay attention to me. Don't look over at Sheriff Green anymore. Just look at me until you leave here, and when you leave here, you are never, *ever* coming back."

"First exits in Ohio are Toledo," Nancy said, surprising Willie. "Get off one of them and we have an hour and a half to do it."

"Yes," Willie said. "And then find a bus station. If you can't find one, ask somebody."

"Find a bus station," Nancy said.

"Find a bus station," Joseph echoed.

"Get two tickets to Atlanta. It's like twelve hours driving, but I have no idea how many stops a bus makes or what route it may take."

"Find a bus station and get two tickets to Atlanta," Nancy said.

"And then I'm going to report the money, my phone, and the truck stolen."

"What?" Joseph said. "But won't we be in trouble?"

"Just trust me," Willie said. "Once you find the bus station, park the truck a few blocks away around a bunch of other cars, and then walk to the station. I will call my cell phone tonight from Uncle Reggie's between eight and nine to tell you what to do next."

"But won't we get in trouble?" Joseph repeated.

"Trouble?" Nancy said. She put her index finger under Joseph's chin and gently turned his head her way. Then she looked through the windshield at Sheriff Green, who was still out cold. "Baby...what do you call being here when he wakes up?"

"No, no, no," Joseph said, still panicked. "Why did I do that? I'm so sorry, Mama."

"We are wasting time," Willie said. "Go now."

"I'm sorry, Willie," Joseph said.

"Go," Willie repeated. "And take the long way to the freeway. The last thing we need is you coming back down Main Street. Take the route that goes out past Kettle's house. You know it, right?"

"Yes," Joseph said. "But I want to stop and tell Reverend Kettle everything. Sheriff Green is bad and I will tell him about what they did to your daddy. He will believe me. We have to stop there and tell him. He will help us. You said he could help us."

"You don't stop for anything!" Willie said through clenched teeth. He looked back at Sheriff Green. His hands were moving and he was regaining consciousness. "Go now. You guys know what to do."

"Okay," Joseph mumbled. He started the truck, wiped at his eyes, and then pulled out on to Main Street and headed toward Cossit Creek Road.

Willie opened the hardware store door and yelled, "Call an ambulance! Sheriff is hurt!"

The clerk shot up from behind the counter, startled. He grabbed the phone and dialed and Willie assumed he had apparently missed the whole thing.

Willie looked back down the street. Maggie and Alan had the smarts to disappear. Willie knelt next to the sheriff and put his hand under the back of his head, lifting it from the sidewalk. Sheriff Green's eyes opened, then closed, then slowly opened as if he were trying to regain focus.

"Stay still," Willie said. "Help is on the way."

The sheriff looked at Willie and squinted, his pupils dilated. Willie wasn't sure if the squinty look was cobweb residue from the beating Green had taken or whether the sheriff was trying to figure out whose team Willie was on.

The clerk handed Willie a wet rag and Willie dabbed at the blood around Green's nose and mouth. The sheriff had an egg-sized knot just above his temple and a two-inch cut on his cheekbone. To their left, scattered clumps of bloody spit-soaked tobacco (that had been knocked or bitch-slapped out of the sheriff's mouth) littered the sidewalk from a foot away all the way to about ten feet from where Green lay.

Willie could hear the siren in the distance and Sheriff Green heard it too.

"Help me sit up," he said, as if it hurt to talk.

"Be still, big guy," Willie said, "You hit your head pretty hard."

"I ain't going to no hospital."

"Don't move until the ambulance gets here," Willie said, realizing the ambulance was probably coming from the hospital on the other side of town. He was surprised they didn't keep one at that fancy city building two blocks away where the police station, morgue, and everything else was. Regardless, it was good news and more time for Nancy and Joseph.

"Where did the son of a bitch go?" Green whispered.

"Got in the truck with Nancy and left me here."

"Sucker-punched me."

"I couldn't believe it," Willie said. "Saw the whole thing and I will testify."

"Any other witnesses?" Green asked. It sounded less like a meaningful search for damaging testimony against Joseph and a lot more like a *please tell me nobody else just saw me get my ass drummed in broad daylight*.

"Sorry," Willie said, telling Green exactly what he wanted to hear. "I looked around and I mean *nobody* else was out here that saw it."

"Too bad," Green said and sat up, suddenly energized. He tried to stand but Willie encouraged him not to.

"Easy," Willie said, his hand on the sheriff's shoulder. "Stay put. I wasn't kidding about you taking a pretty serious shot to the head. You don't want to get up, thinking you are fine, and then fall over dead tomorrow with a brain hemorrhage or something."

"Probably not a bad idea," Green said. He looked down the sidewalk in both directions and his eyes were suddenly keen, as if his mind were back in the game. He felt around his face and stopped at the lump near his temple. Then he gave Willie that *just between us* look he used at the supper club right before he asked if he wanted to go to the next Crown meeting. "You sure you watched all this happen?"

"Positive," Willie said. "I was standing right here the whole time. Like I said, I will give my statement to whoever comes from the station."

"Nobody's coming from the station," he said. "Our shifts are one-man shows and Darnell don't come on until eight thirty tonight. I will write up what you saw and have him drop it by Reggie's for you to sign."

"Okay," Willie said as the ambulance hit its siren again. It had gone a minute or so without using it, but they hit it for a quick half-blip to let everyone know where they were.

"So, I know I was just standing near the curb talking to Nancy," Green said. He paused and portrayed the person that was on the verge of remembering everything that happened, but just needed a little push. "But I didn't see what he hit me in the chest with. Did you? I think it was something from the back of Reggie's truck. All I remember was the wind getting knocked out of me and landing on my face."

"I was too busy trying to figure out why he hit you," Willie said. "I'm sure we saw the same thing. Just write up what happened and have your deputy bring it by. I will sign it."

"Gonna noodle on it for a bit," Green said as the ambulance appeared a few blocks away down Main. "Not sure what I'm gonna do yet."

"What about my uncle Reggie?" Willie asked. "He's not gonna want anything to happen to Joseph. And to be honest, I don't want Uncle Reggie affected by this whole thing."

"I've always been lenient with Joseph because of Reggie," Green said. "For years, we've given Joseph just enough rope to hang himself, and he's stayed in line. Until today."

The ambulance stopped in the middle of the road and by the time the paramedics got out, Green was standing.

"One more thing," Green said, reeling his finger like he wanted to whisper.

"What is it?" Willie asked. He leaned over and could feel Green's stinky warm breath on his ear.

Green pulled his head back and held up his hand for the paramedics to give them some privacy. "Give us a minute, boys."

"Sir," one of the paramedics said. "We need to follow protocol until we get you to the emergency—"

"Step back for a minute or they're going to be removing both your protocol and my boot from your ass when we get to the hospital. I'm talking police business here and it involves confidential matters."

The paramedics both took a few steps back and raised the gurney. Green nodded for Willie to come closer again.

"Why are you doing all this?" Green whispered. "Helping me and all."

"Because you are hurt."

"I'm fine," Green said. "And I'm not going to pull any punches here. Just because I invited you to a meeting doesn't make us *buddy buddies.* And I also gotta tell you, again, that the way you act around pinkies makes it hard to tell whose side you are on. The black side or the other side."

"What's the other side?"

Green said it loud enough for both paramedics to hear. "Your daddy's side. The black *and* white side."

Green's pistol was about four inches from Willie's right hand. Willie could have easily grabbed it, shoved the barrel in Green's mouth, and pulled the fucking trigger. Right through those gold teeth. Right then and there. And to the applause of at least one of the paramedics.

"I'll tell you what side I'm on," Willie said, a little more reckless than he should. "I'm on the cover-my-ass-until-I-get-home side. And other than you being hurt, here is why I am helping you. When it comes to getting around Woodruff, you are the last person I want to piss off. Does that mean I'm ready to join The Crown this week? Not at all. But at the risk of getting on your shit list, I *have to* hang out with white people and am nice to them for three reasons."

"Thrill me."

"One of them I already told you," Willie said. "I do it for my uncle because of his situation with Nancy and Joseph. The second reason is to protect myself. It's risky, but for all I know, the dead guy that killed my dad has got buddies around here that know who I am. And those buddies may get drunk one night and decide that it would be a hoot to get back at Black America a little bit more for the fucking over that the black lawyer gave Donald Bondy. And what better place to start than by picking off that lawyer's kid? Kind of a father-and-son special. They obviously think my father was just some run-of-the-mill attorney that not only didn't give a shit about his white client, but made sure he played his part in the verdict. But me, on the other hand, by hanging out with a few whites, maybe those friends of the killer would get wind that I'm actually a decent dude that doesn't care about skin color and spare me."

"Not sure I agree with you on that one," Green said. "But regardless, whites killed your daddy, son. They are animals. Where is your pride and sense of vengeance?"

"Pride and sense of vengeance?" Willie said. "I'm not ready to randomly kill someone, but I'll confess right now that I fucking hate white people because of what happened to my dad. You feel better now?"

"It's a start."

"Good," Willie said. "But if you and your buddies killed every white person in town a year ago or if whites never existed, my dad would be alive. But I can't let that hate get me killed while I'm here. I'd just as soon live and take some comfort knowing your men in purple are always looking for opportunities to rid the earth of them."

"I'm ready, boys," Green blurted at the paramedics. "Appreciate your patience."

They pushed the gurney next to Green and he lay down on it. They strapped him in and loaded him in the ambulance. Mr. Boot Almost Up His Ass Paramedic jumped in and knelt beside Green. Right before the other guy closed the door, Green unstrapped himself, rolled to his side, and propped himself up.

"Willie," he said. "You said you were nice to them for three reasons. Makes sense that you do it for your uncle. Doesn't make sense to protect yourself from the Bondy nutcases, but that's your call. What's the third reason?"

"I know you will agree with me on the third one."

"What is it?"

Willie stuck his head in the back of the ambulance and smiled at Green. "I'm also nice to them so they don't kick my ass all over Main Street."

"*Pfff.*" Green batted his hand toward Willie and shook his head. "Just sit tight and watch what happens to him."

"Go for it," Willie said. "But until that happens, what do I do? What do you want me to say to Joseph when I get back to my uncle's?"

"Don't say or do anything."

"I have to say something to my uncle Reggie. I'm sure Joseph will tell him what happened."

"Wait for him to bring it up and if he does, just tell him I said don't fret and that we will deal with Joseph later."

"Who is we?" Willie asked. "The police?"

Green laughed out loud and then lay back, flat on the gurney. Then he looked at Willie and winked when he answered.

"Guess again."

WILLIE

Someone's Listening. The Cell Phone.

Kill Reggie.

After the ambulance disappeared, Willie walked up and down Main Street for close to a half an hour, wondering what move he should make next. Even if Sheriff Green made it out of the hospital that night, there were no guarantees he would be at the meeting the next day, potentially foiling Willie's plans to shoot the bastard along with Uncle Reggie (and maybe the third Trio) right in front of the entire Woodruff Crown.

Whenever Willie thought about his getaway failing (which there was a *great* chance it wouldn't), knowing that Sheriff Green and Uncle Reggie would no longer be in the hate business was an ointment that soothed his mind.

Then he thought about another getaway. Nancy and Joseph's. He could already see them sitting in the back of the bus, on the big freeway, heading south to a better life.

Where would he tell them to go when he called them tonight in Atlanta?

To his and Dad's house?

Stupid fucking idea.

Once Green finds out Joseph is gone, he will put a warrant out for his arrest and if he discovers that Joseph and Nancy are hiding at the house in Atlanta...

Fuck.

Call Dr. Cheever and tell her everything. And when you call Nancy and Joseph tonight, have them meet with Dr. Cheever. She will know what to do to keep them safe.

Scratch the plan to kill Uncle Reggie and Sheriff Green and go tell Kettle everything.

And then get the hell out of town while you still can...

Fuck. Fuck. Fuck.

Willie struggled to collect himself. It was true that The Crown killing his father would be much more believable coming from an eyewitness. But the problem now was that Alan would never talk to Kettle and for her own protection, he'd never allow Maggie to either. And with what had just happened between Sheriff Green and Joseph, the likelihood of Joseph coming back to Woodruff anytime soon (assuming he wasn't in hand cuffs) was up there with a white man winning the next presidential election.

Willie slipped into the icen cream shop and Kettle's great-niece was behind the counter. He asked her if she could close the store for a few minutes and maybe give him a quick ride somewhere.

Her boss agreed to watch the register for a few minutes and they were off to Reverend Kettle's.

On the way, Willie closed his eyes and did something he could never remember doing before. And despite the things he had done and the things he was about to do, he couldn't help an overwhelming feeling that maybe someone was going to listen.

He prayed.

♦♦♦

WILLIE THANKED KETTLE'S NIECE for the ride and said goodbye. She'd asked him twice why he was sweating so much and also what had happened to Sheriff Green. He didn't want to tell her he was going through withdrawals, but as for Sheriff Green, he played along with her assumption that maybe it had something to do with the white man that had been killed, that "drug dealer with the gun."

When Willie reached Kettle's front porch, he could see Shanice Kettle through the small window in the door. She was sitting on the couch, not wearing her wig or one of her ugly-ass hats, and she had her left index finger at least a knuckle deep into her right nostril. She took her finger out, studied her find for a few seconds, and the second Willie hit the doorbell, her head turned straight to the door.

"One minute!" she yelled, standing and then scurrying out of the room.

It was closer to five minutes, and when the door finally opened, she was wearing a hat (it was the yellow bonnet that looked like a pancake on her head) and it smelled like she had taken a quick bath in that stinky-ass perfume of hers.

"You just missed them," she said. "They left no more than ten minutes ago."

"Missed who?" Willie said.

"Joseph and his mother stopped by."

I told him not to stop, I told him not to stop, I fucking told him not to stop…

"Where did they go?" Willie asked.

"Not sure," she said. "Joseph came in and talked to Jackson for quite a while, while his poor mother waited in that old truck."

"What did they talk about?"

"Aren't we a Nosie Nelson," Mrs. Kettle said. "Jackson asked me to step away so they could have some privacy." She pointed back into the living room. "They talked right there on the couch, and when they were through, Joseph got back in the truck with Nancy and they followed Jackson, who was driving our car.

"Where did they go?"

"They went that way."

She pointed away from downtown…the long way to the freeway.

A wave of relief ran through Willie as he thought, *Kettle wanted to make sure they got out of town safely. Looks like prayers do get answered…*

"Thank you, Mrs. Kettle," Willie said, wondering how long it would take him to walk to Uncle Reggie's.

"You're welcome," she said with a nod. Then that corny smile of hers crossed that face. "Did you like the meal I cooked at the supper club?"

"It was awesome," he said. "You have to give me that recipe before I go back home so I can make it myself."

"Next time you come to remove the stumps, I will have it written out for you," she said. "I'm guessing that won't be today. When you coming back out?"

Never.

"Soon," Willie said, turning and making his way down the porch. He was halfway to the driveway when she yelled for him.

"Willie!"

He turned around and she was holding out her arm with her index finger (the same one she had picked her nose with) pointed straight up.

The door closed and in a matter of seconds, it reopened.

"This must have fallen out of Joseph's pocket!" she shouted, stepping onto the porch with something in her hand. "It was sticking out between the sofa cushions." She walked down the porch steps and was clearly out of breath. "I'm sure this isn't his. Did you let him borrow this?"

Shanice Kettle was holding Willie's cell phone.

◆◆◆

IT TOOK WILLIE AROUND an hour on foot to get back to Uncle Reggie's. Uncle Reggie hadn't returned from checking out the rehab place he thought Willie was going to check into, and between the trillion miles Willie had walked that day and the stress his body was under from needing more pills, he was exhausted.

He plopped down on the bed and continued to ponder the only thing he thought about the entire walk from Kettle's.

How do I get in touch with Joseph and Nancy? They are fucked.

He could take his car and try to catch up with them, but even with the bus making stops, that would be close to impossible.

What would Uncle Reggie say when Sheriff Green tells him what happened? How would Uncle Reggie defend Joseph…his son?

He wouldn't defend him, Willie. He keeps him out in a little piece-of-shit shack in the backyard for free help…and don't forget…he killed his brother…your father.

Willie stood and walked to the window. And then he turned around and glanced at the clock. It didn't matter what Uncle Reggie was going to do, for two reasons:

One. Assuming Nancy and Joseph left when Shanice Kettle said they did, they were most likely on the bus and gone.

Two. Willie was going to take just a few of his remaining pills, put on The Crown hood and robe (had to be the black one), grab Varmint Killer, wait downstairs (locked and loaded) for his uncle to get home, and then kill him.

Fuck waiting until The Crown meeting. He'd save that for Sheriff Green.

WILLIE

Holy Shit. HOLY Shit.

HOLY SHIT.

By the time Willie heard Uncle Reggie's car pull in the driveway, Willie had fallen asleep in the big chair in the living room. He rubbed at his eyes and glanced at the clock. It was past noon and the (*holy shit, did I sleep that long in this chair?*) nap and the few pills he had taken had done absolutely nothing to make him feel better. He sat up and watched as the car pulled past the side of the house and toward the back. He quickly slid Varmint Killer under the robe and put the Trio hood on.

Willie couldn't see the back door, but it opened, closed, and then Uncle Reggie cleared his throat a couple times before putting what sounded like a paper bag of groceries on the counter or table. A cupboard opened, a couple glasses clanked together, and then Uncle Fucking Racist was pouring what was going to be his last drink.

A chair pulled back from the kitchen table and Willie decided Uncle Reggie was going to sit in the living room instead.

"Hey, Uncle Reggie!" he shouted.

"Jeez!" his uncle cried, clearly startled. He let out a little laugh. Then he stepped out of the kitchen, glass in hand, and walked to the base of the steps and looked upstairs. "Scared the tar out of me! What you doin' home? Come on down so we can talk about the rehab place I visited. It's called Renew, and it sure is fancy. It also takes your insurance."

"I'm right here, asshole."

When Uncle Reggie turned and saw Willie, he simultaneously dropped his glass (on the spotless floor that Nancy would never polish again) and let out a high, more feminine, half-scream that sounded like it came from someone else. Looked like at least two of the three Trio sounded like women when they were afraid.

"*Jeez,*" Uncle Reggie said again, and when he caught his breath, he added the "*us-Christ.*"

"It's not nice to take the Lord's name in vain," Willie said.

"Please forgive me," Uncle Reggie said. "You frightened me."

"Forgive you?" Willie said. "Let's talk about that for a little bit."

Uncle Reggie put his hands on his knees and leaned over as if he were still having a hard time breathing. He shook his head and looked up. "Take that outfit off and help me clean this mess up."

"Sit down," Willie said, pointing at the couch. He couldn't deny that there was something about wearing the hood and robe that made him feel more…*powerful*.

"What's gotten into you?" Uncle Reggie said. "Maybe you need to check into Renew tonight. It's twenty-eight days and you'll be out by the time school starts. Let me get a cloth to wipe this spill up with and I will tell you about it."

He turned and went in the kitchen. Willie pulled Varmint Killer out from under the robe and aimed it at the television. When Uncle Reggie came back around the corner, cloth in hand, Willie fired. The shot rang through the house and was loud as hell, even frightening Willie. A small hole was now on the TV screen, surrounded by a foot-wide spiderweb of cracks that spread toward the edges of the box. Willie pointed the gun at Uncle Reggie and nodded at the couch.

"I said sit down."

Uncle Reggie's hands went in the air as if he were being held up. He shook his head again and then his open palms made little circles in the air.

"Willie," he said. "It's not having enough pills, son. You're off-kilter a bit, that's all. Put the gun down and talk to your uncle Reggie."

Willie tilted the gun to the couch and then back at his uncle.

"Sit your murdering-ass down. I know everything."

"Willie, what are you talking—"

"Sit!" Willie yelled. "Or I will fucking drop you right there for what you did to Dad!"

Uncle Reggie walked slowly over to the couch, lowered his hands, and sat. "What are you talking about?"

"You said you and my father didn't always agree on things. You told me you gave him your word that if anything happened to him, you'd do your best to see that his wishes were met."

Uncle Reggie nodded. "That's right."

"And every time I asked to see what was happening with his money, you kept saying that we will do it *in time*. Well, that time is now. You hear me?"

"Okay," Uncle Reggie said.

"You said that when I get my share, I'll have more than I know what to do with. And you also said that my father made provisions that you are involved with, or something like that. How much was he worth?"

Uncle Reggie shrugged. "Don't know exactly because some of what he has moves around in value. But the lawyers, Mr. Barnes and Mr. Kilmer, the ones your daddy appointed to help me dice things up, told me it was in the neighborhood of seventy million dollars."

"Seventy million?" Willie said. It was more than twice what he thought.

"Please put the gun down," Uncle Reggie said. "You are scaring me, son."

"And how much is my share?" Willie asked. What he was really interested in was the rest, his uncle's *provisions*.

It didn't take Uncle Reggie more than a second to answer. "Your share is half. Split two ways right down the middle."

"Joseph saw it. Maggie saw it. Alan saw it."

"Saw what?" Uncle Reggie said. "And, son…can you please put the gun down?"

Willie took the hood off because he wanted his uncle to see his face when he told him what he knew.

"They saw you kill Dad," he said. "They watched you and Sheriff Green and the rest of you sick fucks dip my father!"

"Where is Joseph?"

Willie raised the gun and aimed right at Uncle Reggie's head. "But again, you had *thirty-five million* reasons to kill him. Then it probably wasn't too tough blaming it on that white guy that you guys said hanged himself at the jail, was it?"

Uncle Reggie glanced at the ceiling and his mouth gaped open before looking back at Willie to repeat himself. "Where is Joseph?"

"Joseph is far away from here. And Nancy is with him."

"I'm sorry," Uncle Reggie said. He leaned forward and rested his elbows on his knees. He stared at the floor, shook his head, and then looked right at Willie. "I just couldn't tell you. But believe me when I say there was nothing I could do. It took them a long time, but they finally got your daddy back."

"*They?*" Willie said. "You killed him. You were there with them! And it didn't take them a long time to get him back. They killed him the night of the verdict!"

"I'm afraid there is—"

"You don't have to be afraid of anything!" Willie screamed. "Everyone in this fucking state is afraid of you! Where in the hell do you think I found this hood and robe? This *black* hood and robe?"

"I *am* afraid," Uncle Reggie whispered. He took his hands away from his face and sat up straight. "I'm afraid there is a bit more to it than what you think."

"At least you quit blaming the dude *you* hanged up at the jail."

"I never accused that man. Not once."

"Bullshit!" Willie shouted, hurting his throat.

"Not once."

Willie stood and stepped toward the couch. "You fucking liar!"

He thrust the tip of the gun barrel at Uncle Reggie's head and nailed him just above his good eye. Uncle Reggie cried out and immediately covered his eyes and forehead with his hands.

"I'm not lying," Uncle Reggie whispered.

"I'm not a fucking idiot!" Willie yelled. "Where did I get this hood and robe from? A fucking costume store? Look at me, you coward!"

Uncle Reggie peeked out between his fingers and spoke slowly. "You are not an idiot. Your daddy told me you were sharp. But I had no idea how smart you really—"

"Shut up!"

Willie couldn't yell any louder. His throat was raw and the gun had started to shake in his hands. He wanted to pull the trigger right there, to settle the score, to do the right thing…but he wasn't done talking. Uncle Reggie had to know that Willie knew everything.

Uncle Reggie lowered his hands and Willie was surprised at the amount of blood that was on them as well as how much was still pouring out of his uncle's head.

"Since you seem to remember everything," Uncle Reggie said. "You probably remember your father telling you that you had a relative that was high-ranked Crown. He told me he shared that with you."

"As high up as one could go," Willie said.

"It's true," Uncle Reggie said, studying the blood on his hands before looking back at Willie. "But that person changed. People really *can* change, Willie."

Willie wasn't buying it. He raised the gun again and pressed the barrel against the middle of his uncle's forehead.

"You haven't changed," Willie said. "You saw my father's will. You saw that you were getting half and then you and your buddies killed him."

Uncle Reggie shook his head, moving the gun with it. When he stopped, Willie lowered the barrel and centered it between his uncle's eyes. Eyes that looked like they belonged to a man that knew he was going to die. Even the fucked-up eye.

"I wasn't talking about me," Uncle Reggie said quietly. "I'm not the one who changed."

Willie's finger slid lower down the trigger, to the thin part that gets squeezed. "Lying to the very end. Say goodbye, asshole. I'll throw you in the back of the truck and go toss you in the swamp at Devil's Drop. This is for what you did to my dad."

"The robe you are wearing belonged to your father."

Nothing about Uncle Reggie changed when he said it. He never looked away. The pupils stayed the exact same size. He never blinked.

But what he said was so outrageous, Willie had to hear it one more time...just to make sure he heard it correctly. But before he asked Uncle Reggie to say it again, his uncle repeated something else he said just a few minutes earlier.

"People really can change, Willie."

Willie kept the gun aimed at Uncle Reggie but took a couple steps back and sat down in the chair. He had to sit down. Whether what Uncle Reggie said about Dad was true, the words had taken some of the strength out of Willie's mission and almost all the strength out of his legs.

And though he knew he was insulting his dead father by doing so, he still had to ask.

"Not only are you saying that my father was in The Crown, you are saying the robe I'm wearing was his? That he was Trio?"

Uncle Reggie laced his bloody fingers together and rested his hands on his lap. "I'm not just telling you he was in The Crown. I'm not just telling you he was Trio." Uncle Reggie paused and tilted his head matter-of-factly. "I'm telling you that your father, my brother, was The Crown Lord. Youngest one ever. Period."

"Crown Lord," Willie said, hating the part of himself that somehow already believed it was true. But it really was impossible, because *nobody* could change that much. "So my father just woke up some morning and decided he wanted to quit being Crown Lord and then maybe become a lawyer that would one day defend white people?"

"No," Uncle Reggie said. "Something pretty significant happened that put things in perspective for him. And when it happened, he started to change. Change is sometimes slow, but your daddy went the other way in a hurry. He said it was time to start being the man he was supposed to be by doing the right things. And then he kept saying that he was going to be the light that led people out of the darkness of hate. God is my witness, I heard him say that last thing a hundred times."

"What about the purple robe that's in the closet?" Willie asked. "Was that the one he wore before he became the leader?"

Uncle Reggie bit his lower lip and then frowned. "I'm afraid that one belongs to your uncle Reggie. And you are right. I was there the night your daddy died."

"And you just stood there and watched?"

"What was I supposed to do?" Uncle Reggie said, as if he'd asked himself the same question a thousand times.

Willie remembered the night he and Joseph watched the meeting. He could only imagine a single protester in the middle of all those purple robes.

"I'm sure it sounds easy for me to say there is nothing I could do," Uncle Reggie said, his lower lip beginning to quiver. "He and I were inducted into The Crown when I was fourteen and he was twelve. Our daddy sponsored us. And once you are in, you are in."

"Is there a black man in this town that isn't Crown?" Willie asked.

"Plenty," Uncle Reggie said. "But we wear those hoods for a purpose and other than Demetrius Green, it's just about impossible to tell who is Crown."

"Makes sense," Willie said.

"But feel free to call me a coward because I am one," Uncle Reggie said, dabbing at his eyes with his index fingers. "Not because I didn't save your daddy that night. There was no saving him."

"Why would I call you a coward then?"

"Because..." Uncle Reggie paused and then shook his head yet again before looking straight at Willie. "Because I didn't even try to save him. And that's something I will have to live with the rest of my days."

"It would have been suicide," Willie said.

"I'd be good as dead," Uncle Reggie said. "But I didn't do anything and unlike your daddy, I was unable to just get up and walk away. This house and farm are all I have, not to mention I'm the closest living black man to Devil's Drop. Still, I now live every day praying there will be something I can do that will redeem myself for the day your daddy died."

He really is telling the truth. This is fucking too much to handle...

"So, Dad just got up and walked away?" Willie said, knowing there was more to the story. *A lot* more. "You said something happened that put things in perspective for Dad. What sparked the big change?"

Uncle Reggie wiped his eyes again and then a peculiar little smile creased his lips before he answered.

"He had a son."

Willie felt his own eyes start to water and quickly closed them, causing a tear to spill out onto his left cheek. He opened his eyes back up and realized he was still pointing the gun at Uncle Reggie and lowered it.

"Sorry, Uncle Reggie. This is all too much. I don't know what to say."

"Don't say anything," Uncle Reggie said. "Just know that your father loved you very much. And that Uncle Reggie has grown quite fond of you since getting to know you and loves you very much as well."

Willie leaned back in the chair and pointed his finger at the television. "Sorry about shooting the TV. I'd buy you a new one, but with your half the money, you can probably afford it."

"I should have replaced that a long time ago," Uncle Reggie said. "But I want you to know something else."

"What's that?"

That same little smile appeared on his uncle's face.

"I'm not getting the other half of the money."

Willie put Varmint Killer on the floor and leaned forward in the chair. "I don't understand. Who gets the other half then?"

"The son I just told you about."

Willie shrugged because it made no sense. "I get the whole thing?"

"No," Uncle Reggie said.

Uncle Reggie stood and came over next to Willie. He slid Varmint Killer across the floor, knelt next to the chair, and reached up and put his hand on Willie's shoulder to give it a fatherly little squeeze. "The other half goes to the son your father had. The one I was telling you about."

"Who?" Willie asked

Uncle Reggie smiled again. "His name is Joseph."

Gooseflesh riddled the side of Willie's neck and then spread down his back. He suddenly felt lightheaded and grabbed his uncle's arm to stop from falling out of the chair.

"Can you say that again?"

Uncle Reggie squeezed Willie's shoulder one more time.

"It's Joseph," he said. "Joseph is your brother."

WILLIE

More about Dad. Uncle Reggie's Plan.

Willie and Uncle Reggie sat out on the front porch and Willie finished explaining what had happened with Joseph and Sheriff Green, and how Joseph and Nancy were supposed to get to a bus station and wait for Willie's call later that night. And how Joseph left the phone at Kettle's when he stopped by (against Willie's instructions) to tell the minister about what a bad man Sheriff Green really was, not just to white people, but sometimes to black people as well.

Willie shook his head and could practically hear Joseph berating himself in Toledo after realizing the phone was gone...

I can't believe I dropped the phone, Mama. What a dumb thing I did. I should have listened to Willie and never stopped. I'm such a dummy, Mama...I'm such a dummy.

"I guess we are lucky Joseph didn't kill Sheriff Green," Willie said.

"Amen," Uncle Reggie said. "Powerful boy."

"What now?" Willie nervously peeled a little piece of paint off the arm of the wooden rocker he sat in. "You think Reverend Kettle really knows anyone that can help us?"

"Don't know," Uncle Reggie said. His forehead was still bleeding from the knot that seemed to be growing before Willie's eyes.

"Maybe one of us should go over there," Willie said. "See what Kettle thinks of what Joseph said."

"I'll go over there tomorrow morning," Uncle Reggie said. "Reverend Kettle knows a lot of people and has an excellent reputation in Christian circles—not just in Michigan, but around the country. Still, the cold truth remains that The Crown has been killing people out at Devil's Drop for longer than I've been alive. I'm not aware of any of them ever being tried for murder. But again, I reckon lack of witnesses has been a problem."

"This is all crazy to me," Willie said. He needed more pills, and between withdrawals and everything that was happening, he couldn't stop his mind from going in a million different directions. "Now I know why I never saw my dad with his shirt off, even around the pool. He didn't want anyone to see The Crown brand near his rib cage that told the world he was Trio."

Uncle Reggie laughed. It was actually more of a scoff.

"Guess again," he said. "He had a mark there, but he had surgery to cover that up years ago, not to mention I don't remember your daddy being much of a swimmer."

More thoughts raced through Willie's mind. More questions.

"Why didn't my father set Nancy and Joseph up somewhere else? No offense, but it's not exactly a five-star resort in the backyard. Not to mention that all of Woodruff has to think you are Joseph's father."

"I reckon everyone does," Uncle Reggie said. "Your father regretted not putting Joseph and Nancy somewhere else. But it wasn't like Nancy and your daddy were in love. I'm pretty sure Joseph came from a one-nighter, and Nancy probably went in the barn with your daddy that night solely out of fear."

"She knew he was in The Crown?"

"Sure did," Uncle Reggie said. "She didn't know he was The Crown Lord, but they both grew up here on the farm and your daddy, and your granddaddy before him, was never too shy about walking out of the house in full Crown garb. That is, until your daddy ran the show."

"What does she think about you being in The Crown?"

"She knows I've got no way out," Uncle Reggie said. "More importantly, she knows what's in my heart. I've always done my best to take care of her and Joseph."

"And Joseph?" Willie said.

"He doesn't know I'm Crown and Nancy promised me she wouldn't tell him."

Willie decided not to tell Uncle Reggie that Joseph sort of knew. He took a deep breath and exhaled loudly. "Wow. My dad was The Crown Lord."

"Yes, sir," Uncle Reggie said. "Your daddy moved to the other side of Woodruff after graduating from high school. Like you, he was smart as a whip. Scholarships got him through the university and law school and there's no doubt those same smarts are what took him to the top of The Crown."

"If being the top cheese is so top secret, how did you know my dad was The Crown Lord?"

"Only Left and Right Trio know who The Crown Lord is. I had no clue your daddy was the man on top of the heap until he quit and handed me that black robe as a memento."

"So, other than the obvious, what happened with him and Nancy?"

"Your daddy hardly ever stopped by the house," Uncle Reggie said. "In fact, I didn't even know he was here the night Joseph was conceived. A few months later, I noticed Nancy's belly getting bigger and it took me at least another month to get it out of her who the father was."

"How did my dad take the news?"

"I didn't tell him until after Joseph was born," Uncle Reggie said. "If I did, I don't think Nancy would have been around for the delivery, which I performed."

"He would have killed her?"

His uncle didn't answer, as if he'd gone somewhere else for a few seconds, dreamily recalling what happened.

"Your daddy came by the house a week after I told him," Uncle Reggie said, that peculiar little smile showing up once again. "Both Nancy and I were terrified. He wanted to see the baby and we had no idea what was going to happen. But when your father saw little Joseph for the first time, I could see something in your daddy's face...something good. And then he asked to hold Joseph. Nancy looked at me like she was being asked to give her child to the Antichrist but I knew that Joseph would be all right. I nodded my approval and when she gave Joseph to your father, something happened to him. And once again, I knew it was good."

"Then what?" Willie said.

"Now don't forget that here in Woodruff, a black man messing around with a white woman means nothing. Having a child with one also means nothing. But doing *anything* that even resembles *caring* for that white woman and that half-white baby is an act that falls somewhere between socially unacceptable and sacrilegious."

"I think everyone knows that."

"With that said, how do you think The Crown would feel about their leader taking an interest in Nancy and Joseph as human beings instead of, excuse my language, a piece of ass and a by-product?"

"They probably wouldn't be big fans of the idea."

"Big fans?" Uncle Reggie said. "His Crown Lord days would be over. And then The Crown would invite him and Nancy out to Devil's Drop and make one of them drown baby Joseph in the dipping pond. And within the hour, the three of them would be united again, eating dinner with Jesus."

"So, then Dad just abandoned them?" Willie asked.

"Not quite. He offered to send them down south where things are a little more civil, but Nancy didn't want to leave."

"Why?"

"She'd been here her whole life and was adamant she wasn't going anywhere."

"And she is telling The Crown Lord this?"

"Yep," Uncle Reggie said with a quick nod. "Call it what you want, but though Nancy didn't know it, it was a showdown between a simple white woman and the most feared black man in the state, maybe the country. Your daddy could have easily just snapped his fingers and a handful of Crown would have stopped by the house within the hour to turn both Nancy and Joseph into fertilizer. Problem solved, case closed."

"So, then he just quit The Crown?"

"Just like that," Uncle Reggie said. "Quit The Crown and went south. Ended up in a place you are familiar with. It's called Atlanta."

"But poor Nancy," Willie said. "She has carried that all these years and never told anyone? Not even Joseph?"

"Joseph knows he's part black and he's been teased about me being the father. Once asked me if I was his daddy and I told him the truth that I wasn't. Probably hard for him to swallow, but I've never lied to the boy, and I think he knows it."

"But you were still left holding that socially unacceptable-slash-sacrilegious bag of caring for the white woman and her half-black child."

"True," Uncle Reggie said. "But in my case, it hasn't been that bad."

"How so?"

"Because Nancy and Joseph pretty much live like slaves. I don't mean for it to be that way, but the house is spotless, I don't cook any meals, and Joseph isn't exactly the highest-paid guy in town."

"That's exactly what I thought when I first met them. That they were basically slaves. Totally serious." Willie remembering them at the door of the pinkie hut.

"Don't blame you," Uncle Reggie said, unoffended. "But even though your daddy started another family down in Georgia, he always made sure I had enough to take care of Nancy and Joseph, and usually threw in a little extra for me. And like I said, Nancy has always made my life easier around here and once things get split up, Joseph will have enough for him and Nancy to do whatever they want."

Willie's mind wouldn't slow and he still needed answers.

"So, Dad commits political suicide by taking the Donald Bondy case as if it were his way of offsetting his time in The Crown? The old *I used to terrorize the whites, now I will defend them to make myself feel better about myself* trick?"

"It wasn't just political suicide."

Uncle Reggie was obviously right, but something still didn't make sense.

"When I was up in Detroit with him near the end of the trial, he walked right past fifteen hundred purple hoods on the courthouse steps."

"I was there," Uncle Reggie said.

"Why didn't they just nail him then?"

"For the whole world to see?" Uncle Reggie said, followed by a little laugh. "Ain't their style. Detroit ain't Woodruff. Too risky."

"What do you mean?"

"They were saving it for Devil's Drop," Uncle Reggie said. "The safest place in the world to be. That's if you are one of them."

"Fuck them," Willie said. "Sorry about the language."

"I'm the one that needs to apologize," Uncle Reggie said. And then he shrugged and smiled. "What we need to do now is think of a way to get ahold of Nancy and Joseph before they end up at the South Pole. How long of a ride is it to Atlanta?"

"Roughly twelve hours by car," Willie said. "But a bus is going to make lots of stops. Maybe Joseph or Nancy will find a pay phone or borrow a phone and call here."

"They don't know my number and wouldn't have the faintest idea how to find it," Uncle Reggie said. "We also need to stay focused on what Demetrius Green is going to do next. He and I go back forever and he has always cut me some slack with Nancy and Joseph. But Joseph laying hands on him is another thing. So be it by the law or by Crown, he is going to want to settle the score."

"Of course," Willie said. "But I still don't know what we do for now."

"You'd probably be best off to get back home," Uncle Reggie said. "Only the Lord knows what Demetrius is thinking about you right now."

"I can't leave," Willie said. "Sheriff Green will think I left with Joseph and then he'd call down and have every cop in Atlanta stopping by the house."

"I thought things are different down there."

"They are, but probably not for people that beat up fellow cops," Willie said. "I'll leave town once I convince Sheriff Green that he and I are on the same team."

"You and Demetrius Green?" Uncle Reggie said. He seemed to think about it for a whole half second and then snorted. "Good luck with that."

"Don't think I need luck. After Nancy and Joseph left, I stayed at Sheriff Green's side from the time he regained consciousness until he got in the ambulance. I could tell he was wondering why I stuck around to help him. Between that and some other things, I'm sure I'm an enigma to him, but I think he likes me."

"What's an enigma?"

"Like he can't figure me out," Willie said, knowing this part of the conversation wasn't all that important because he only needed to be buddy-buddy with Green between now and tomorrow, when Willie pulled the trigger at Devil's Drop.

"Demetrius don't like anybody," Uncle Reggie said. "Don't kid yourself. It could be dangerous."

"Not sure about that," Willie said. "I don't kiss his ass like every white *and* black person in town. I think he sees me as a challenge, but in a good way. A challenge he can win."

"He don't see anything or anyone as a challenge," Uncle Reggie said. "Not in Woodruff, anyhow."

"Maybe *challenge* is the wrong word. Better yet, instead of a *challenge*, I think he believes we have some sort of connection and maybe sees me as more of a *project*."

"That still doesn't mean he likes you."

"He invited me to a Crown meeting."

"I doubt that," Uncle Reggie said confidently. "You misunderstood him. Everyone knows he doesn't recruit anyone. Thinks it's beneath him. Somebody would have to beg him to join and he leaves it up to everyone else to bring in new guys."

"We were at the Woodruff Supper Club. There is a meeting tomorrow night and he asked me to come."

"That bastard," Uncle Reggie said. "He knows I wouldn't approve and, the Lord as my witness, you are the first I've ever heard get invited by Demetrius."

"Lucky me."

"He is still going to be very suspicious of us," Uncle Reggie said. "He's going to know I'll want to protect Joseph. And if the sheriff ever finds out that you masterminded Joseph and Nancy's exodus from Woodruff while he was unconscious on the sidewalk…"

"I know," Willie said. "Fertilizer."

"For sure."

"But I got that covered too," Willie said. "I told Joseph and Nancy they had an hour and a half to get on the bus because I was going to report the truck stolen. In fact, I should have already reported it, but I decided I was going to kill you and I didn't want a cop showing up here in the process."

"Kinda don't like the way that sounded…but I could tell by the look in your eyes you would have really done it."

"If what I believed really happened, I'd have had your body hidden by now."

"Kind of reckless, don't you think?" Uncle Reggie said. "Then what would you do?"

"I'd of thought of something."

"Reckless," Uncle Reggie repeated. "But besides that, good thinking on reporting the truck stolen...unless Nancy and Joseph are still in it when you do it."

"I think it covers my ass," Willie said. "Sheriff Green thinks the only reason I tolerate Joseph is because of you. And when Joseph steals the truck and my wallet, that's when I go ballistic and want Joseph's head."

"Ballistic sounds good, but it ain't enough. And thinking it is don't make you reckless, it makes you dumb. And you ain't no dummy."

"I don't get it."

"You really think Demetrius Green will think you losing your wallet is enough to send you, a rich kid, off the deep end?"

"Sheriff Green will have to think that—"

Uncle Reggie held his hand up for Willie to be quiet. Normally it would be ignored, but something in Willie's gut told him to zip it.

Uncle Reggie stood and leaned against the porch railing. He brought his hand to his chin and seemed to be really mulling things over.

"Joseph was there when your daddy died," he said. "Watched him get dipped by The Crown."

"Yeah," Willie said.

"I think we should tell the sheriff that Joseph told me he watched your daddy die," Uncle Reggie said. "And that I told you as well."

"Are you crazy?" Willie asked. "That's a death warrant for Joseph."

"Joseph already signed that warrant," Uncle Reggie said. "Did it himself. This morning. Upside the sheriff's head."

"You are the one being reckless," Willie said. He stood and joined his uncle at the railing. "Telling Sheriff Green that Joseph was there when The Crown killed my dad is a *huge* mistake."

"I didn't say that," Uncle Reggie said. Then he put his hand on Willie's shoulder. "I just said to tell the sheriff that Joseph watched your daddy die. For all Sheriff Green knows, you think that white fella we saw up in the jail is the one that really killed your daddy."

"The one that *hanged himself*," Willie said.

"Yep. Let me ask you something. Without knowing the truth, how would you feel if I told you Joseph was there the night that man killed your daddy? That he watched it happen?"

"I'd think he was in on it and I'd go ballistic. Like for real ballistic."

"You'd want him dead?"

"Fuck yes," Willie said. "Kind of like how I wanted you dead."

"I would too," Uncle Reggie said. "So, between your wallet getting stolen, seeing what Joseph did to me, and being made aware that Joseph was there when your daddy got killed, we could maybe do some persuading with Demetrius Green. Sort of buy us some time without him thinking we are communicating with Joseph and Nancy until we get them safely settled somewhere."

"What Joseph did to you? I don't get it."

"Are you fucking blind?" Uncle Reggie asked. He squeezed Willie's arm to drag him back into the living room. "You need to call it in! Do it now! Report your wallet stolen! The truck stolen! Report what he did to me! Do it now, you stupid-ass mother fucker! What are you waiting for?"

"What?" Willie asked, wondering if Uncle Reggie had snapped.

"What do you mean *what*?" Uncle Reggie shouted. He shoved Willie toward the kitchen. "Get your head out of your rear end, you fucking nitwit, and make the fucking call!"

Willie turned around and waited to see what was next. "Uncle Reggie... you okay?"

Uncle Reggie clenched his teeth and smacked himself across the cheek. Then he took his right pointer finger and dragged the nail across the cut on his forehead. He looked at his finger and then pressed it down on the bloody knot, causing a thin line of oily red fluid to zip out a few inches, as if it had been shot out of a squirt gun.

"I'm fucking everything but okay!" Uncle Reggie screamed, bending over to pick up Varmint Killer. He took the butt end of the gun and started pressing *it* against the bloody knot. He studied the blood on the gun and then lowered it.

"Why don't you give me the gun," Willie said, walking slowly toward his uncle.

"Why don't you wake the fuck up, numb nuts?" Uncle Reggie screamed. "Call the police and tell them what the fuck you saw when you got here! Tell them that when you came in the house, you found your uncle on the floor! He was barely conscious, bleeding from the head, and that you thought he was shot because of the bullet holes in the television and wall!" Uncle Reggie pointed the gun to his left and fired a shot *over* the television, leaving a perfect little hole in the white plaster wall. He studied the hole for a couple seconds and then fired two more right next to it. Then he tossed the gun back on the floor and continued his rant. "Then tell them that Joseph—*soon-to-be-fucking-dead Joseph*—must have struck your uncle over the head with something, because your uncle just regained consciousness. And don't fuck this part up! It's paramount…I mean, you have to make it crystal clear! Make sure you tell them that the *pinkie cocksucker* also stole all the money you brought up here with you and that they better do their fucking jobs and catch him! And when Deputy Darnell Jessup gets here to fill out his report, I'll talk about betrayal and more betrayal unlike anything anyone has ever heard. And then I will demand to be wherever it is whenever they get Joseph so I can personally make him suffer. Now don't even think about rehearsing. Pick up the phone and make the call."

Willie called the police, and when he was through, he was impressed with his own performance. When Willie hung up the phone, Uncle Reggie kicked the coffee table over, shattering the ceramic plate that was probably older than the house into about a hundred pieces.

And when Uncle Reggie sat down, it was as if a director had said "cut."

It was over.

Uncle Reggie winked, wiped at the blood that was still leaking out of his forehead, and then spoke in his normal and relaxed Uncle Reggie voice.

"Go put Varmint Killer out in the barn somewhere nobody will find it," he said. "Hide it real good. While you are doing that, I'm going to grab my thirty-eight pistol, in case something really happens."

"Okay." Willie figured all they had to do now was put on a good show for Woodruff Cop #2, Darnell Whatshisname, the one that would be coming by to make a police report. And when he and Uncle Reggie were through making their statements, Darnell would most likely relay to Sheriff Green that he may want to think about locking up Reggie and that crazy-ass nephew of his to make sure they don't go up to The Row and kill every pinkie in town.

Willie hid Varmint Killer in the barn and was halfway back to the house when he randomly thought of those words…the ones his father had told him up in Detroit…right before Dad had split that purple sea and walked in the courthouse.

It's darker than you…

"You were talking about hate, weren't you?" Willie asked the sky, half expecting his father to answer. "You told Uncle Reggie you were going to be the light that led people out of the darkness of hate. That's the light you wanted me to find."

And then Willie thought about something else Uncle Reggie had said.

Sheriff Green would never forget what happened that morning and that he was going to deal with Joseph.

That was, unless Joseph's little brother dealt with Sheriff Green first.

WILLIE

The Show Begins. Special Guest Appearance.

The Dollar Bet.

I could have bled to death by now, Tykera."

It wasn't all that important that Uncle Reggie and the police operator were on a first-name basis. They'd apparently known each other for years, and despite the two additional calls Willie and his uncle had made to the station, seven hours had passed and only two vehicles had come down Cossit Creek the entire time, both pickups. The first one had to be thirty years old and had around ten white dudes in the back, most likely mill workers being dropped off at The Row. The second one (which according to Uncle Reggie, who was still in cursing mode, was obviously driven by some "lost sonbitch") was a shiny black pickup pulling a silver moving trailer from *Speedy Trailer and Rentals*, who were apparently *Ready to Move When You Are*.

"What'd Tykera say?" Willie asked.

"Same old stuff," Uncle Reggie said. "Sheriff Green had an emergency and they can't get ahold of Darnell Jessup to come in early."

"Kind of weird an ambulance hasn't showed up either," Willie said.

"True," Uncle Reggie said.

Willie took a bite out of his peanut butter sandwich and then looked at the clock that was about a foot to the left of the three bullet holes in the wall. "Should be anytime now. I think I remember Sheriff Green telling me earlier that there are only two of them and that Darnell's shift starts at eight thirty."

Uncle Reggie nodded. "That's what she said. But we may want to plan on nobody coming out here until morning. And if that's the case, we still need to keep our minds sharp and our make-believe anger with Joseph even sharper."

"Maybe we should run you up to the hospital," Willie said. "That thing on your head looks awful and it's still leaking. While we are there, I could also run in and make a scene in the room Sheriff Green is in. You know, to sort of get his wheels turning."

"Maybe not a bad idea," Uncle Reggie said.

"And to be perfectly honest," Willie added. "I wouldn't mind having them prescribe some painkillers for you that I could tap into."

"Things getting tough?" Uncle Reggie asked.

"Been tough and I literally only have three pills left. I keep having these little spurts where my thoughts run together and then I feel like I'm going to pass out. Also, my feet and legs have been twitching without me telling them to."

"Sorry you have to go through that," Uncle Reggie said.

Willie spent the next half hour telling his uncle why a fresh supply of pills made it into Woodruff, but never made it to the house. And about the man Sheriff Green had shot and how there was no way that man would ever be carrying a gun. Uncle Reggie just sat there and listened, and as the sun went down, neither of them bothered to turn a light on, leaving them in total darkness by the time Willie was through talking about Evan.

They sat in silence for another five or ten minutes, and Willie knew they were both absorbing all that had happened.

Uncle Reggie started to say something and paused.

"What is it?" Willie asked.

"I reckon the world would be a safer place if Joseph would have just broke the sheriff's neck today."

"Safer and better," Willie said.

"Yep," Uncle Reggie said. "Crazy day. A lot to swallow. I was just thinking about how Nancy and Joseph aren't just gone, but never coming back. Life is going to be a lot different around here, and I guess that won't sink in with me for a while yet."

"I hear you," Willie said. "Half the shit that's happened since I came to Woodruff hasn't sunk in with me yet."

"If you think about it, most of our problems are because of Demetrius Green."

"Most?" Willie asked.

"*All* of our problems," Uncle Reggie added. "Every. Single. One."

"Yeah," Willie said.

Uncle Reggie sighed and covered his face with his hands, most likely wondering how he and the rest of Woodruff had let the monster known as Sheriff Green feed and grow into what he had become. And then Uncle Reggie lifted his head and glanced out the living room window. Headlights had appeared in the darkness and were coming down Cossit Creek Road.

Uncle Reggie stood and looked out the window. "I think the show is about ready to start."

"Let's leave the lights off," Willie said. "We will tell Deputy Darnell we kept it dark in here so it looks like nobody is home. And we did it just in case Joseph decided to come back."

"Good thinking," Uncle Reggie said. He walked over and grabbed his pistol off the couch. "Right before he knocks on the door, you open it and I'll be aiming the gun straight at his chest. He'll be thinking it's because we couldn't tell who was out there."

"Good idea," Willie said, surprised, blown away actually, at how quick Uncle Reggie thought under pressure.

The vehicle came to the front of the driveway and Willie could tell it wasn't a patrol car or an ambulance, but another pickup, a light-colored one.

"Deputy drive a pickup?" Willie asked.

"No," Uncle Reggie said, stepping back from the door for a better look. The pickup came all the way up to the side of the house and the headlights went off.

"Who is it?" Willie asked.

"Son of a pup," Uncle Reggie said. "It's Demetrius."

"Holy shit," Willie whispered. He could feel and *hear* his heart, which quickly began to thump at his rib cage. There wasn't going to be any relay of information from Deputy Darnell to Sheriff Green. There would be no dress rehearsal. This was it and it had to be good.

"Nothing changes," Uncle Reggie said. "When he knocks, you pull the door open and I'll be aiming at him like we thought he was Joseph."

"If Joseph was after us, he wouldn't knock," Willie said. "I'll pull it open right before he gets to the door."

"That's smart," Uncle Reggie said. "Until then, you just remember how that pinkie piece of shit watched your daddy die and almost shot me before whopping me on my head."

"Got it," Willie said as Sheriff Green walked across the lawn toward the porch steps.

"You know what?" Uncle Reggie said.

"What?" Willie asked.

"I should really shoot that son of a bitch when you open the door," Uncle Reggie whispered. He sounded serious, and something in Willie's gut knew that Uncle Reggie wasn't talking himself into shooting Green, but out of it. "I could squeeze

two off into his chest and make the world that better place we just talked about…
right here and right now. Not to mention, it ain't no patrol car out there and for all
I knew it was Joseph or one of his murderous buddies that came back to finish the
job. Then the only show we put on after that is lamenting about the unfortunate
accident that cost Demetrius his life."

Willie had no doubt the story was bulletproof and had a feeling it was maybe on.

"He's coming up on the porch," Willie said.

"I'm gonna do it," Uncle Reggie said, his arm raised with the pistol aimed at
the door.

All Willie had to do was pull the door open and it would all be over with.

He could practically see Green dead on the porch. He stepped around
Uncle Reggie, grabbed the door handle, and closed his eyes.

"Here we go," Willie whispered.

He quickly yanked the door open and waited to hear the shot.

Nothing happened.

Willie opened his eyes and all he could see was Uncle Reggie, still standing
there and aiming out the doorway. Then the gun started to shake in his hand and
he lowered it.

Call me a coward because I am one…

"What the hell are you doing, Reggie?" Sheriff Green asked.

Willie peeked around the edge of the door and the sheriff was standing there,
bandages covering half his face.

"What do you mean what is he doing?" Willie shouted. "What the fuck kind
of police department are you running?"

"Who do you think you are talking to, boy?" Green fired back.

Willie flicked the switch on the wall, lighting up half the living room.
"I'm talking to you, *Sheriff* Green. Look at my uncle's head! Look at what happened
inside here! We called the station like eight fucking hours ago and someone is just
now getting here? Great work!"

"Watch your tone, son." Sheriff Green stepped to the side of Uncle Reggie
and into the house. "I promise you, I ain't gonna say that again."

"Or what?" Willie said.

Green ignored him and looked at Uncle Reggie from the side. "Christ, Reggie.
What happened to your head?"

Uncle Reggie didn't move. He just stood there, staring out the open door,
the gun still in his hand, but now at his side. It was clear he was now playing

his part in their little show. That of the armed guy that was carefully standing guard, watching, maybe even *hoping*, for someone uninvited to come on his property.

"What happened to *your* head, Sheriff Green?" Willie asked, playing his part in yet another show.

"You didn't hear about the little problem I had downtown?" Green said.

"No," Willie said.

Sheriff Green glanced at Uncle Reggie, then gave Willie a little nod that could only have meant *Thanks for not telling anyone about me getting my ass kicked.*

"Hurt myself this morning," Sheriff Green said. "Sort of wasn't paying attention and took a little spill. Spent the better part of the day at the hospital. That's the reason for the delay in getting out here."

"Are you kidding me?" Willie said. "That's your excuse? We called the station three fucking times! The first time we told them what Joseph had done and then the other two times we wondered where the police were and what to do if Joseph came back. We thought you might be him. That's why we left the lights off. You're lucky you didn't get smoked the second you got out of the car!"

Sheriff Green's jaw flexed, chewing a little aggression in lieu of tobacco. There was no doubt he wanted to take one of the bitch slaps he'd received from Joseph and give it to Willie, but Willie knew he'd been given a free pass for not talking about what really happened to the sheriff's face.

Green turned the big lamp on next to the sofa, lighting up the rest of the room. He looked around and was clearly surprised. "Joseph did this?"

"Yeah, Joseph did it!" Willie shouted. "He also stole the truck and all my fucking money!"

Green was unfazed. He just walked over to the wall and touched the bullet holes with his right index finger. Then he went back near the door, right up beside Uncle Reggie, and crossed his arms, maybe a little suspicious. "Tell me what happened, Reggie."

Uncle Reggie didn't answer. He didn't flinch. He was in total character and now they were getting a glimpse of someone who had experienced significant trauma. Trauma that had taken most of him somewhere else, but that had left just enough of him there to be dangerous.

Sheriff Green waited a few seconds, then took the pistol out of Uncle Reggie's hand and placed it on the window sill. He returned to Uncle Reggie's side and crossed his arms again.

Uncle Reggie was amazing. He waited Green out and just when it looked like the sheriff was about to give up, Uncle Reggie slowly turned his head and looked straight at the sheriff. Then he waited *just* long enough to say only three words and those three words said more than their joint bullshit story ever could have.

"Demetrius. Get. Him."

It was perfect.

The way the words hung in the air made it feel like getting revenge on Joseph was more important than breathing and eating. For a split second, Willie even felt like grabbing the sheriff by the arm and ushering him out the door so they could get in Green's pickup to go hunt Joseph down.

Sheriff Green took a few steps back and cocked his head toward his left shoulder, almost like he needed to get a different point of view on Uncle Reggie. The sheriff's arms were still crossed and he just kept studying Uncle Reggie, waiting for something to give, maybe even using old police tricks to detect body language that would set things straight or reveal some other *tell* that would help him assess not just what Uncle Reggie said, but the way he said it, because Uncle Reggie was *that* convincing.

But Uncle Reggie didn't falter. He had truly become a different person and had been staring straight back at Green the entire time. Staring at him with eyes like those of a man that had just found out who molested his child.

"Tell him what Joseph said about being there when my dad was killed," Willie blurted.

Uncle Reggie didn't say anything. He never moved.

"Tell him," Willie repeated.

His uncle ignored him again. Uncle Reggie just turned his head back toward the open door, took a deep breath, and exhaled loudly, making it clear he'd already said all that was important.

Green looked at Willie. "What did Joseph say about your father?"

Willie shrugged as if he didn't know the entire story, just the important stuff. "Joseph said he was there the night Dad was killed. He obviously knew that guy that hanged himself in your jail. And if Joseph was there when Dad got murdered, I guarantee you there had to be others there as well."

"Not necessarily," Sheriff Green said. "But where were *you* when all this happened with Reggie and Joseph?"

"I went for a walk earlier...*downtown*," Willie said. "Don't worry, I have at least one witness."

Green rolled his eyes, picking up on the fact that he was the witness. "I'm sure of it."

"When I got back here, I noticed the truck was gone," Willie said. "And when I came inside, shit was all busted up and Uncle Reggie was lying right over there next to the television, barely conscious."

"We need to get Reggie to the hospital," Sheriff Green said. "He looks like he is in shock."

"Already tried," Willie said. "He won't go."

"He probably can't accept that it was Joseph that did this," Green said.

"You kidding?" Willie said. "That's exactly what it is."

Green gave the room another once-over. "This is unbelievable. Something must have happened to get Joseph so riled up."

Willie snorted. "Think so? You should be a fucking detective."

"Appreciate that," Sheriff Green said. Then he smiled and walked right up next to Willie. He slowly shook his head and then out of nowhere, quickly grabbed Willie by the back of his shirt collar and escorted him toward the front door. They went right past Uncle Reggie and then onto the porch. Willie tripped going down the steps and Green made sure he gave Willie's head just enough of a turn that it banged loudly off the porch railing.

Willie was off his feet and was surprised at Green's strength and how fast he was moving across the lawn while dragging him. They were headed toward Green's truck and the sheriff finally let go when they were out of Uncle Reggie's sight. Green lifted Willie to his feet, and then the sheriff turned toward the house and quickly pivoted back, driving his elbow into Willie's chest. The air fled Willie's body in an instant and before he could buckle over, Green grabbed the back of Willie's head and shoved him down on the lawn.

Willie was convinced a bone in his chest was cracked and that he'd never again catch his breath. When he finally did, he brought himself up to a knee and then looked up at Sheriff Green.

"Anything else you want to comment on?" Green asked.

Willie stood but was bent at the waist with his hands on his hips. He looked back at the porch and nobody was there. Uncle Reggie hadn't even come outside, as if he were turning a blind eye to continue to gain Green's favor so he'd buy into the story.

"Reggie ain't going to help you," Green said. "The way you are, I'm surprised he still hasn't knocked you around himself. And if he heard me take any more of your lip, he'd think I'd gone soft. Hell…*I'd* think I'd gone soft. Bottom line is you don't know anything about respect and you clearly have no idea how *nice* I've been to you."

"Why you doing it?" Willie asked. "Why have you been so *nice* to me?"

"I still ain't sure," Green said.

"Thank you for your kindness," Willie said, immediately worried how it sounded.

"You already getting smart?" Green asked. "Sounds like you want some more."

"All I want is for you to catch Joseph," Willie said, finally standing up straight. He lifted his arms over his head to make it easier to breath. Then he lowered his hands to the top of his head and pleaded to the sheriff. "Please. I don't care about the money Joseph took. I just want you to catch him and at least agree with me that if Joseph watched my father get killed, there had to be others there as well. I know you are at least that smart."

This time it was Green's fist, and he hit Willie in the exact same spot. A cold flash filled the *V* in Willie's rib cage and he went straight to his knees. As he struggled again to breathe, Green gave him a solid backhand across his left cheek, sending Willie crashing over on his side.

"Is that smart enough for you?" Green said. "And don't try to be that tough guy in the movies who keeps getting up for more. Bottom line is, you can't control your piehole and sure as shit you'll get knocked down again."

"I'm sorry," Willie sputtered. "I mean it." His right cheek was flat against the grass and as he tried to lift his head, Green stepped on the other side of his face, the side that was still burning from the slap. The sheriff wiggled his foot, as if he were wiping dog shit from his shoe on to Willie's cheek. Then he pressed his foot down just hard enough to make it hurt, reminding Willie of exactly who was in charge.

"You best be sorry," Green said.

When Green's foot came off his face, Willie waited a few long seconds before sitting up. He didn't want to risk another shot to the sternum, so he decided to ask first. "Can I talk? I won't say anything stupid, I promise."

Sheriff Green studied him, much like the way he did Uncle Reggie earlier. "Go ahead, but tread lightly."

"I swear to God that the only reasons I came up to Michigan were to find out who killed my dad, to make sure that justice was somehow going to be served, and to find out what was happening with the money I'm inheriting."

"Good reasons," Green said.

"And don't get me wrong," Willie said. "I'm thankful, I mean *really* appreciative of you catching the guy that killed my dad. But if Joseph was there, my gut tells me there had to be others as well, and I want you to get them all. I want them all dead."

"If there are others, we will round them up," Sheriff Green said.

"You have to get Joseph first," Willie said. "I reported the car stolen hours ago, and you mean to tell me not a single cop in the state saw a half-white kid and a white woman driving around in a dilapidated pickup truck?"

Sheriff Green reached out his hand and Willie flinched. Then he was surprised, realizing Green was actually trying to help him to his feet.

"Maybe you weren't paying attention to the last thing I said to you before the ambulance took me away this morning," Green said, pulling Willie up.

"I have a photographic memory," Willie said. "You were insinuating that what happened this morning with you and Joseph wasn't going to be handled by the boys in blue, but by the boys in purple."

Green's jaw flexed again, but this time Willie knew the sheriff was angered by thoughts of Joseph.

"After...what...that...*animal*...did...to...me...today," Green said. "There was never a chance any of this was going to be a police matter. And when you called in and reported your car stolen, I was contacted at the hospital and we immediately put the word out. Not to the ten or fifteen surrounding police departments and their twenty or thirty officers, but to the neighboring factions and their six thousand Crown."

"Wow," Willie said, unable to stop himself from imagining a throwback version of Joseph and Nancy, ass-deep in some swamp, running from slave catchers as the barks of hounds drew nearer.

"*Wow* is damn right," Green replied.

Despite the impressive size of the sheriff's search party, Willie knew it didn't matter because by the time he had reported the car stolen, Joseph and Nancy were safely on a bus to Atlanta.

Sheriff Green nodded at the house and Willie turned to look. They could see Uncle Reggie through the living room window. He had abandoned his near-catatonic post at the front door and was sitting on the couch. He was staring straight forward again. Willie guessed it was at the TV or the bullet holes in the wall.

"I want to be the one that does it, though," Willie said.

"Does what?"

"The one that kills Joseph."

Green laughed again. "Now Willie's mouth is writing checks that the rest of Willie can't cash. You don't have it in you, son. Hell, just this morning you told me you aren't ready to kill someone. Even if you were, you wouldn't be able to live with yourself after you did it."

"Maybe *you* weren't paying attention this morning," Willie replied, immediately regretting the way he said it. But Green didn't react, he waited to hear the rest, so Willie continued. "What I said was that I wasn't ready to *randomly* kill someone. In fact, I never will be. Killing just any white person that didn't have anything to do with my father's death would do nothing for me. Killing one that stood by and watched it happened is an entirely different story and I'd do it right now."

"Not sure why, but I believe you," Green said. "I guess when you've been in my business as long as I have, you can tell when your chain is getting yanked. It's the body's language that tells the real truth and I can tell that at least you *think* you are ready to kill."

"I am," Willie said, knowing he was as ready to kill as he'd ever be. He wouldn't have minded proving it right there, but it would have to wait just one more day. That way, the local *faction* could witness what happens to people that do the things Demetrius Green does. Willie turned back to Uncle Reggie. What a performance. He was still looking straight at the wall and Willie faced the sheriff. "And by the way, my wanting to kill Joseph has nothing to do with what he did to my uncle, even considering everything Uncle Reggie did for Joseph and Nancy."

"Don't know why I didn't ask earlier," Green said. "Where was Nancy when all this happened with Reggie?"

"No clue," Willie said. "But how could the timid little Joseph I knew, that my uncle knew, fuck...that the whole town knew, go from such a good boy to the maniac that shot up the house and then beat up my uncle? Granted, what happened with you two downtown had to get the ball rolling, but there has to be more to it than that."

"They are all unpredictable and dangerous," Green said. "But I won't deny it, I'm a little surprised at what happened with Joseph. Kind of like a good dog that got bit by a skunk and got the rabies. But at the end of the day, it's like a bad marriage. Us and pinkies just don't belong together in society. It's just not meant to be."

"And you mentioned I wouldn't be able to live with myself if I killed him," Willie said. He paused and acted like he was processing things before continuing. "The truth is that I won't be able to live with myself if I *don't* kill him, because it's personal now and I've never felt hate like this before."

"All because Joseph *said* he was there when your daddy died?" Green asked. "Just like that, a switch goes on, and that makes you hate enough to start killing pinkies?"

"Just him," Willie said. "And anyone else that was there the night my father died."

"Rest assured," Green said. "He's as good as dead but the bad news is it won't be you. Regardless of Joseph being there when your daddy was killed or what he did to Reggie, no pinkie has ever laid a hand on me and it will be *me* that pulls his life plug. But not until after I see him suffer in record ways before he goes."

"When did your switch go on?" Willie asked. It wasn't part of the show. He really wanted to know because something had to happen for Green to be the way he was. "What happened to make you hate white people?"

The sheriff ran his hand along the side of his neck and his eyes darted around like a fifth-grade bully, the one who'd just been called up by his teacher to stand at the front of the class, not to be punished or to confess his bullying sins, but to do something much worse. To read out loud in front of everyone for the first time when no one in the room knew he could barely read at all.

"Too many reasons to count," Green finally said. "If I didn't constantly keep the pinkies around town in check, what happened with Joseph and your uncle today would have happened a long time ago. Just go back in there and look at Reggie's head and the bullet holes that were fired in the wall. What else you need to see or hear?"

"They killed my father," Willie said. "I have a pretty good reason to hate whites and I was curious what your story was. What did they ever do to you?"

Green went from the eye-darting bully to a deer in the headlights and Willie realized *exactly* why.

Demetrius Green doesn't really know why he hates white people.

"Can't just bring Joseph here and let you shoot him in the head," Sheriff Green said, completely ignoring Willie's question yet again.

"Why not? Let me kill him at Devil's Drop. I'll wear a mask or you can lend me a hood."

"This conversation is over," the sheriff said. He started walking across the lawn toward the porch. "Let's get your uncle to the hospital to get him checked out."

"I will bet you a dollar I kill Joseph before you do," Willie blurted.

Green stopped in his tracks. He looked up into the night sky and shook his head, clearly a man whose patience was about to expire. *Again.* Then he turned around.

"You know what, Willie?" he said. "I think the reason I like you is because you've got balls. You speak what's on your mind and you don't give a shit whose panties get ruffled. But at least people know where you stand, and I like that. You won't get Joseph before I do. And wanting to bet me a dollar that you do leads me to believe you don't know the difference between saying something that will get you popped in the chest and doing something that gets you killed. Now, pretty please, tell me you understand that."

"I understand," Willie said.

Behind Sheriff Green there were footsteps. Uncle Reggie had come out on the porch.

"Reggie?" Sheriff Green said. "You all right?"

Uncle Reggie stared out at the yard for a few long seconds before slowly turning his head toward them. "No. I'm not all right. For Joseph to do what he did to me is beyond any betrayal or crime I could ever imagine. And he must answer for it."

"It's horrible," the sheriff said. "After all you've done, for him to lay hands on you is beyond belief. What could have happened to him to bring this about?"

"Don't care," Uncle Reggie said, still stone-faced, a man that for the only time in his life, truly wanted...*needed* revenge. "You know I'm the passive one, Demetrius. But you can take it to the bank that after all I've done for that boy, nothing will ever, *I mean fucking never*, justify what he did to me. I want you to get him. And feel free to blow the truck up at Devil's Drop when you are done. In fact, blow the damn thing up with the sumbitch in it, if you want."

"Don't think I've ever heard you curse before," Sheriff Green said. "And I agree with everything you said. But I'm surprised something like this didn't happen years earlier." Green looked at Willie and then right back at Reggie. "There is something else I talked to Willie about earlier and he didn't know because he wasn't here. Do we need to worry about Nancy? Where was she when Joseph attacked you?"

Uncle Reggie shrugged again. "Don't know. I didn't see her and she must have left town with him. If she didn't, she would have come in to make supper."

Sheriff Green took a step closer to the porch and was clearly looking at the knot on Uncle Reggie's head. "You need to go to the hospital."

"I ain't going to no hospital tonight," Uncle Reggie said. "I'm going about my life tonight and tomorrow just as if they were normal days. Except I'm going to be minus some help."

"I'm sure you can find replacements up on The Row to help you with things," Sheriff Green said.

"Hell no," Uncle Reggie said.

"Fair enough," Sheriff Green said, studying the knot on Uncle Reggie's head again. "In all seriousness, you should go get that bump on your head checked, Reggie. You don't want to think everything is okay, and then fall over dead tomorrow with a brain damage or something."

Willie recognized what Green said. What a fucking idiot. It was the aborted version of what Willie had told Green earlier in the day after Joseph kicked his ass. Besides, the only one that would be falling over dead tomorrow was going to be Green. Right in front of the other jackasses that probably never asked themselves why they don't like white people either.

"Maybe I'll have Willie take me over to the hospital in the morning," Uncle Reggie said. "Let's just see how I feel then."

Uncle Reggie turned around and went back in the house. Sheriff Green stared at the porch for a bit and then turned to Willie.

"It looks like we are all on the same page here," the sheriff said, holding out his hand for Willie to shake it.

Mission accomplished, Willie thought. He didn't shake the sheriff's hand and decided to leave him hanging until he had the answer to just one more question.

"It's been eight hours," Willie said. "Why haven't your six or seven thousand men caught Joseph yet?"

Sheriff Green laughed. "Not going to shake my hand?"

"Seriously," Willie said, staring at the sheriff's hand for an easy thirty seconds, which felt like an eternity. "Seven thousand retards would have caught him by now."

The sheriff finally pulled his hand back and when it reached his side, his other hand shot forward. It was in a fist and hit Willie in the *exact* same spot he'd been struck twice before. The strength left Willie's legs at the same time the air left his body and he fell straight over to his side, this time without going to his knees first.

Part of Willie wanted to die and another part of him wanted to laugh, knowing what the following day was *really* going to bring.

Sheriff Green put his foot back on the side of Willie's face and pressed down, this time a lot harder and a lot longer than he did before. Willie could feel the tears coming down his face before he finally cried out in pain.

"We already caught Joseph," Sheriff Green said. "He will be dipped tomorrow."

WILLIE

The Longest Day Ever.

The Last Day in Woodruff.

10:08 a.m.–3:14 p.m.

It was a little after ten in the morning and though he and Uncle Reggie knew the previous night's performance couldn't have gone any better, they also knew the only way they could save Joseph and Nancy was to have Reverend Kettle involved, who would then hopefully throw some of his weight around and get some help from his higher-up contacts not only in Michigan, but from the ones Uncle Reggie claimed the minister had throughout the country.

Willie sipped his coffee and couldn't get over how quiet the house was without Nancy shuffling through pans or the sound of Joseph's high-pitched laugh, the one that usually followed a bunch of stuff that normally wasn't all that funny.

"Now I know what you felt like when they killed Dad," Willie said.

"Not sure about that," Uncle Reggie said. The knot on his head had gotten a bit smaller, but he was going to drive himself to the hospital to "let them take a gander at it." Afterward, he was going visit Reverend Kettle, who was up in Detroit and wouldn't be back until noon. Uncle Reggie also made Willie promise to stay out of sight for the day and to be out of Woodruff by midnight.

"I promise," Willie said, knowing he could make good on both. Hiding in the cattails would definitely put him out of sight and once he picked off Sheriff Green (preferably with one bullet to the solar plexus), he'd certainly be hightailing it out of Woodruff before midnight, unless of course, he decided to run up on the stage in front of the entire Crown and step on the side of Green's face to watch him die.

"Not sure what I'll be doing after Reverend Kettle's," Uncle Reggie said. "But I will try to keep you posted."

"I've never felt more helpless in my life," Willie said. "What do we do if Kettle can't help?"

"He will help," Uncle Reggie said. "I just know it."

Willie knew deep in his gut that Kettle would do something and figured the minister had to be tired of Sheriff Green and the way he treated Kettle's "neighbors."

And Willie took comfort in knowing, at the very least, if Kettle didn't take care of Sheriff Green by the time they dipped Joseph, Varmint Killer would.

♦♦♦

WILLIE HAD TAKEN HIS last three pills and was hiding behind a tree line off Cossit Creek Road, waiting for Maggie to come down the hill from The Row.

According to his phone, it was 1:53 p.m. That gave Willie seven full minutes before Maggie arrived to finish taking inventory of all the crazy shit that had happened, bundle it together under one category, and then put it safely away in the mental storage container that he'd already labeled *Woodruff Mindfuck #1* with a thick, black imaginary marker.

Though *Woodruff Mindfuck #1* wasn't quite full, Willie had just given himself the green light to go ahead and open the container labeled *Woodruff Mindfuck #2*. And the reason he did it was that it still hadn't fully registered with him that he was out of pills. And though it was still well before dark, Mr. Painful Realization (that there *really* were no pills left...NONE...fucking ZERO) was rumored to be coming to town, and if the rumor was true, it could be worse than any physical withdrawals that were in store for him and had the potential to be a mindfuck that fell into a category all its own.

Could I have picked a worse day to run out of pills?

He shoved the thought aside and continued to wait for Maggie, who now had six full minutes to be on time.

Willie opened his black canvas duffel bag and took a tiny sip from the plastic gallon of water he had filled before leaving the house. Also in the bag were four apples, a peanut butter sandwich, a can of mosquito repellant, a pair of plastic bags (he would put those over his feet and then put his shoes back on to slow down any potential soaker he would get while walking in the swamp), a camouflage ski mask (one he had seen a few times in the barn...the bank robber kind with only eye holes and a mouth hole that Uncle Reggie probably used for hunting), a screwdriver, a box of bullets, and Varmint Killer...broken down into two easy-to-assemble parts that allowed the gun to fit perfectly in the bag.

"Look at Mr. Sneaky, hiding behind the trees," he heard.

Maggie was standing near the edge of the woods about thirty yards to his left. She had her hair pulled back into a ponytail and was wearing a gray hoodie and matching gray sweatpants, the old-school ones you'd see men wearing to the gym in fifty-year-old movies.

"Don't have to be too sneaky out here," Willie said, walking toward her. "Not a single car passed me going either way. Did Sheriff Green come by this morning?"

"Yep," she said quickly. "Has he come by the house looking for Joseph yet?"

"Nope," Willie answered.

"Alan and I were in the alley when they took Sheriff Green in the ambulance. I'm surprised he's out of the hospital."

"He must be fine," Willie said.

They walked away from the road and then onto an old grass-covered tractor trail that separated the field from the woods. Willie was dying to tell her that Joseph was his brother but held off.

"Once I'm in the swamp, you sure they won't be able to see me?" Willie asked.

"Depends what you are doing," Maggie said. "If you are really trying to hide, not a chance in the world they will see you because it will be dark. But even in broad daylight, you will be tough to see because of the cattails and the blind." She smiled for no apparent reason and took his arm. "So, what's this big plan you have?"

"Top secret," he said, as if there were any possibility he'd tell her he wanted to pick off Green. "But get your stuff ready to go to Georgia."

She stopped and looked at him like he asked her to go to the moon. "You are serious, aren't you?"

"Totally serious," he said. "As in leaving tonight. Tell Alan he is welcome to come along."

"I can't," she said and then stared at him like she *needed* him to tell her he was kidding about going to Georgia. "I mean...I like you and I dream, literally every day, about getting out of Woodruff. But...I can't just up and leave."

"Why?"

"I don't know," she said in a way that suggested she was disappointed in herself for not knowing why. "Dreaming about leaving is no big deal, but just the thought of actually doing it is...well...it's scary."

Willie dropped the duffel bag. He shook his head and waited until she looked right at him.

"Let me make sure I understand this," he said. "You are taking me into the woods to help me find a hiding spot so I can watch a black supremacist group that

routinely meets and sometimes *kills* white people right behind where you live…
and leaving *this* behind is scary?"

"Yes," she said.

Willie was surprised to see that she had taken a step back, as if he had threatened
her or was going to shove her in a van and take her to Georgia against her will.

"How is it scary?"

"Don't you understand?" she said. "I barely know you and Woodruff is the
only world I know."

"I understand that. It's a big change and change is scary and it's okay to be
afraid. But what I'm offering has no strings attached and you can always come back
if you don't like it."

"I just can't."

"But you *can*," Willie said. "Just try." He stepped closer and put his hands on
her shoulders. "Other than fear of the unknown, what's really keeping you here?"

She looked away. "I guess I really don't know."

Willie paused. "You have to trust me. I've been to both places and things are
better where I'm from."

"Things are better for you everywhere," she said without hesitation.
"You are black."

Willie took his own step back and his arms fell to his sides. Her last three
words felt like little arrows. Not like the sharp ones, the painless type that Cupid
hit him with the day he first saw Maggie, but more like arrows that had their tips
soaked in a bucket of truth and had long gone dull. But they still stuck, deep in his
head, and hurt far worse than the blows he had taken from Sheriff Green. And as
much as he wanted to, and as much as he tried to ignore the colors of their skin,
Willie knew there was something he couldn't deny.

She was right.

Blacks had it better. *Everywhere.*

But what drove Willie nuts was the need to know exactly what *it* was that was
stopping Maggie, or anyone else from The Row, from at least *trying* to leave. And
trying to have a better life. Maggie herself pretty much just said even she didn't know.

"You could always come visit one day," Willie said.

He conceded because he felt like he was supposed to. And by offering Maggie
a chance to visit, he was really giving her the opportunity to say something like *sure*
or *that sounds good*, immediately freeing them from the awkwardness of the topic,
maybe even leaving it somewhere within their reach for future consideration.

But Maggie didn't answer, which *was* an answer. Georgia would never happen and she'd probably spend the rest of her life in Woodruff.

They entered the woods and got onto the path that led behind The Row and toward Devil's Drop. Neither of them said anything until they were at the edge of the valley, right beneath the half-assed tree fort he and Joseph were in that night they spied on The Crown meeting. Willie looked down into Devil's Drop and then all the way up the open field to the front of the stage.

"I remembered you saying the blind was about fifty yards from the stage," Willie said, trying to pinpoint where he'd be hiding.

"Give or take," she said. "And up just about even with it."

"So," Willie said, studying the swamp that ran along the entire right side of the field. "If I was at a concert and wanted you to find me, I could tell you to go to the first row, make a right, and when you get to the end of the stage, keep going for fifty paces into the cattails?"

"I've never been to a concert," she said, pointing at the stage. "But assuming the stages at concerts are like that one, I think you got the idea."

"Fuck, there's a lot of cattails down there," Willie said. "I'll probably get lost coming back out."

"No, you won't," Maggie said. "Even if it's dark, you will see the cattails you knocked down to get to the hiding spot. It's just like dropping breadcrumbs. Leave the way you came in."

Maggie guided him to yet another path, one thinner and much less traveled, and then down the side of the valley until they reached the edge of the swamp and the bazillion cattails that ranged in height from three to what had to be ten feet.

Willie looked at what he'd soon be drudging through. "Any snakes in here or anything else I need to look out for?"

"Lots of snakes," she said. "Big ones too. But nothing poisonous."

"Shit," Willie said. "Why didn't you guys make a path that whittles through the cattails then?"

"Why would a white person want to be down here?" she said. "I'm thinking black people would even be afraid to come down here. That's unless they are Crown."

"Makes sense," Willie said.

Maggie pointed toward what looked like the right side of the stage.

"The back corner of the stage is your line," she said. "Once you get down in there, you won't be able to see it, so pick yourself out a tree behind it, one up on the other side of the valley that you will remember, and keep walking toward it."

"Okay," Willie said.

"Now the hunter's blind is really hard to see, even when you are close," Maggie said. "It's been there forever and it's all covered with leaves and cattails so keep your eyes peeled."

"Will do," Willie said.

"I'm gonna go back up top so I can see Cossit Creek Road and keep a lookout to see if anyone comes by like Sheriff Green. He's never come by twice before a meeting, but if today happens to be the first time he does it, I'm guessing you don't want him to see you knocking down cattails out here in broad daylight. Probably wouldn't think you are out here catching butterflies."

"Probably not," Willie said.

"Assuming we are out here alone," Maggie said. "I'll guide you when I get up there."

"I appreciate it."

"You're welcome. Now get going."

Then Maggie turned and walked back into the trees to head back up the side of the valley. There was no kiss, no hug, no nothing.

Willie entered the cattails, took three steps, and immediately had two soakers. So much for the plastic bags he forgot to put on, so he kept moving, and within five minutes, his tennis shoes were filled with swamp water and his legs were covered to his knees with oily, black mud.

And then he began to notice…that smell.

That sulfur-laden stench that reminded him before of rotting souls. The smell kept getting stronger and it seemed like it was filling him, sticking to his insides, and making him a bit nauseated.

"Go about another forty paces and then go left!" he heard, from somewhere in the trees.

Willie counted off another forty stinky steps. It took him forever.

"Okay! Now go left a little bit!"

He did, and on his third step, his right foot got stuck behind him. He lost his balance and he started to tip over, pulling his foot straight out of the shoe that stayed stuck in the mud. The cattails he clung to with his left hand were unable to hold his weight, but they slowed his fall, giving his right hand enough time to lift the duffel bag high before he found himself sitting in swamp water up to his belly button.

"Way to go, dumbass," he muttered. "Now all you need is your rubber duckie and you can finish your bath."

And then he *cocksuckered* the swamp and *motherfuckered* life before finding his shoe and putting it back on while still sitting in the water.

Then he stood and waited for Maggie's instructions. When he heard nothing, he pulled back more cattails and started moving forward.

"It's about five paces in front of you!" She had to be near the top with a bird's-eye view of the whole valley.

Willie moved through another five steps of cattails and knee-deep water, but he couldn't see the blind.

"I don't see it!"

"Just a little more!"

Willie pushed through two more steps and just like Maggie said, it was right in front of him. Had she not told him, he never would have noticed it, even being that close, as it was perfectly surrounded by the cattails that had grown and leaned against it.

"Got it!" Willie yelled.

"I'm outta here!" she shouted back.

"Thanks!"

Willie waited for Maggie's "You're welcome" to jump out of the trees and fall down the hill.

It didn't come.

But in its place came a tiny wave of sadness, one that brought with it the realization of *why* he conceded their earlier conversation about Maggie leaving Woodruff.

It wasn't either of their faults, but near the end of that conversation, things went from a Willie and Maggie talk to a black boy and white girl talk. And what sucked about it was that it felt like neither of them really had a say in it, because the world had skin-color expectations that he'd caved into without questioning them. Or without even really *trying* to question them.

Why?

Sheriff Green doesn't even know why.

Willie reached the blind, which was really nothing more than a box that had been framed out of two-by-fours. At the four corners, the blind was propped up out of the water by four thick metal rods that had been driven into solid ground, probably a few feet beneath the water and muck. Plywood that had been cracked and darkened by the elements served as three walls, a roof, and the floor. The walls were designed to only be about four feet off the floor, creating "windows" that gave the hunter ample room to lean out of the blind and shoot in any direction.

The side Willie stood at had no wall, serving as the entrance up to the floor, which looked built to last, made of three sheets of plywood stacked on top of each other.

Willie lifted the duffel to the floor. Then he leaned into the bag and shoved it next to an old chair, a few rusty cans, and a collection of what looked to be an inch or two of scattered cattail residue in the corner, suggesting nobody (other than Maggie, Alan, and Joseph) had been here for a while. Willie grabbed the chair by the leg to examine its condition, and when he pulled it toward him, a magazine fell off the seat to the floor, and despite its faded and waterlogged condition, Willie could tell it was a magazine he wouldn't have dared shown his mother. He laughed, wondering what the hunter did out here until the ducks flew in.

He pulled the chair out and placed it in the water. Then he stepped up on the chair, which barely sank, and then pulled himself up into the blind.

Willie stood and when he faced Devil's Drop, he was surprised how close he was and how much he could see. Just as Maggie said, he was even with the stage and no more than fifty yards from the front right corner and the dipping gallows.

To his left, he could see most of the open field where all The Crown members would be standing and could even see the little road that had been cut through the trees, the one those assholes would be taking to get down there from up on Cossit Creek Road.

Parked against the far side of the field, right in the middle of all the other obliterated vehicles that once belonged to the dipped, was Joseph's pickup. Willie also noticed that pylons had been placed on the ground, about six feet apart from each other, starting from the left rear corner of the pickup all the way to the lower left corner of the stage.

Fifteen feet above that, on the very corner of the platform, Willie could see a plunger handle on top of a detonator box. He could also see the ignition wire that had already been connected to it. The first fifteen feet of wire from the box had been attached to the corner of the stage and ran all the way down to the grass and the nearest pylon. Even from the blind, Willie could see the wire running from there all the way out to the rear of the pickup.

Willie sat down, leaned his head against the back wall, and closed his eyes, thinking about what the sheriff had done on his premeeting morning visit. Actually, he was thinking about what the sheriff *hadn't* done.

Demetrius Green had just hooked dynamite up to the pickup. And the ignition wire that was connected to the dynamite ran all the way up to the detonator box that was up on the front corner of the stage in *broad daylight.*

And Green just up and left. Leaving it all unprotected, where literally anyone could come by and mess with it between now and the time the meeting started.

Call it overconfident, cocky, or whatever you want. Willie thought it was pretty stupid.

But he also knew there weren't many people around, maybe not a single one, that would call it stupid.

Unless they wanted to be punched in the sternum.

Or spit on.

Or dipped.

And then Willie thought for a few seconds and realized he'd been wrong.

Sheriff Green could have just as easily left a million dollars in cash out in the center of the field with a neon sign saying: Here's a Million in Cash.

It wasn't unprotected.

It was Devil's Drop. Home of The Crown. Undisputed heavyweight champs of Woodruff.

Nobody was ever going to come down and mess with anything.

And Sheriff Green knew it.

Everyone knew it.

Willie grabbed the duffel bag and pulled out the screwdriver, the box of bullets, and the two pieces of Varmint Killer. He assembled the gun, loaded it, and stood it in the corner in the event anything crazy happened before the crazy things started happening. He looked out each side of the blind again and took comfort knowing he was perfectly hidden.

What Willie wasn't taking comfort in was his fucking jeans. They had to come off. They were soaked and glued to his legs, punishing his sack and making his ass cheeks itch. After removing his shoes and socks, it took him a full minute to peel the jeans off, and before he removed his underwear, Willie caught himself glancing only in the direction Maggie had disappeared and then he laughed out loud.

God forbid...after all that has happened to me since arriving in Woodruff, what a travesty it would be if Maggie saw my pecker.

On a similar note, only God knew what kind of swamp protozoa or parasites had been clinging to his balls since they'd drowned in swamp water. So he grabbed the water jug and flipped it upside down, giving Willie Jr. and his two neighbors a generous rinsing. When he was through, he wrung out his socks, jeans, and underwear, and put them back on. Though they were far from dry, he had no intention of sitting out there naked and pulling the trigger with his dick hanging out.

Willie emptied the duffel bag in the corner and then checked his phone to make sure the ringer was off and checked the time.

It was 3:14 p.m.

He was tired and leaned his head back against the wall, knowing he needed to catch up on some much-needed rest before the action began.

Willie yawned and closed his eyes, wishing he had a handful of pills to get him through the day. And as he dozed off, he could hear the inner voice that told him the same three things over and over again.

Get out of the swamp.

Do it now.

Before it's too late.

WILLIE

The Longest Day Ever.

The Last Day in Woodruff.

3:14 p.m.–10:18 p.m.

Willie lurched forward and his eyes shot open.

Things were blurry.

His heart was hammering at his ribs in hollow thuds.

He was outside. It was bright and sunny.

His ass was wet and itchy. He was in wooden box.

I'm in the blind. I fell asleep…

Willie checked his phone to see how long he'd been out. It was 3:18 p.m.

Four minutes. What the fuck?

His leg was twitching and he couldn't make it stop until he stood. He was restless and knew it wasn't just from waiting for the meeting to start. He could also feel the pressure building in his stomach and bowels. No doubt, Mr. Diarrhea had come knocking.

Willie took a step back and his foot landed on the waterlogged magazine. He moved his foot and studied the magazine for a few seconds and smiled. He didn't see it as the March 2013 edition of *Black Player* that featured *The Year's Ten Best Picks in Adult Films.*

He saw it as a roll of toilet paper.

Willie put the plastic bags on his feet, followed by his tennis shoes. Then he tore out and ruffled up a handful of the pages and climbed down to the chair and then into the swamp. It was clear the water had receded, making it easier to move, and Willie was careful to stick to the same areas he'd already walked, that way he wouldn't rattle any cattails and draw attention from anyone that may be in the area.

Willie pulled down his jeans and it only took him about eight seconds to cover half the cattails in the swamp with about twenty gallons of projectile ass gravy. He instantly felt better, and when he stood to wipe, his stomach did a little turn, followed by a funny gurgling noise, making him bend over yet again to deliver a second coat of spray that lasted every bit as long as the first.

Where the hell is it all coming from?

He wiped his ass, wiped his ass again, and when he finally climbed back up into the blind, he sat down and stared at Varmint Killer in the corner next to him. He was more than ready for a nap that would last longer than four minutes but was having a hard time blocking out that stupid-ass voice, the same one that had been telling him his being out in the swamp probably wasn't a good play.

Hey, Tough Guy…if you wanted to kill Sheriff Green, you would have done it by now.

Why didn't you come out here before he showed up this morning? It would have been an easy shot, with no witnesses, and no chance of getting chased. Why didn't you do it?

Willie didn't answer. He just reached over and grabbed Varmint Killer. It felt heavier than it usually did and when his index finger grazed the trigger, he quickly pulled it away and his throat went dry. He stared at the trigger for a good thirty seconds and then leaned the gun back against the corner.

You are going to pussy out, aren't you?

"Sheriff Green killed Dad in front of all of them," Willie said. "The Crown has to see it. They have to witness what happens to people that do the things Sheriff Green does. They have to."

That doesn't answer the question.

"No," he said out loud, grabbing the water jug and taking a nice swig. "I'm going to kill him. I've gone over it a million times."

Willie hadn't gone over it a million times. But enough to be ready. And it was going to happen when those one to two thousand screaming racist fucks got loud enough to drown out the sound of a bullet.

And that's where Sheriff Green came into the plan.

In addition to not knowing why he hated white people, Sheriff Green didn't have the faintest idea that Crown meetings were originally designed solely to allow cowards to come together, get brave in numbers, and then get angry.

But what Green did know was how to get them riled up.

In fact, from what Willie had seen at the meeting he and Joseph spied on, the sheriff was skilled, maybe even a *master*, in using a variety of voice inflections, carefully selected words, and a very specific rhythm of speech to take control of his followers' emotions.

And with all of them watching, Willie could already see himself taking advantage of it.

Sheriff Green would start to warm The Crown up by reminding them that they all owed something to the black world. And then he would deliver eloquent pearls of wisdom about how Jews aren't human or how gays are from outer space, or how whites had to be eradicated.

And though less than 2 percent of them would know what *eradicated* meant, it didn't really matter because Sheriff Green would continue to push them further by saying something really deep and thought-provoking (as long as it included the words *pinkie* and *brothers*) like *If our daddies tell us we should get out and hate a pinkie, we best get out and do some pinkie hating!*

And when the sheriff was ready to let them go, or when it was time to *allow* them to let off that steam, he would hit them with the mothership of all power pauses, and just when they are ready to piss themselves in anticipation of what the sheriff would say next, Green would uncork the bottle by yelling something fresh and original like *Let me hear you if you agree with me brothers!*

And then the roof would blow off Devil's Drop. Plenty loud enough to drown out the sound of a gunshot.

And then Willie would pull the trigger.

And when they settled down, and the noise began to fade, someone would mumble something, and then so would someone else, each of them trying to figure out why Sheriff Green fell down, or why he grabbed his chest before falling down.

And then Willie would aim Varmint Killer away from the stage and the Trio (now known as the Duo) and out into the crowd before firing the other seventeen bullets. They would be random potshots, ones that scattered a thousand or so purple robes just long enough for Willie to go in and save Joseph. But with so many of them in the field, there would certainly be hits. Hits that let chance decide who else paid for his father's death and hits that would prevent many survivors from ever coming to a meeting again.

Damn, Rufus. I think I might turn in my hood and quit going to those Crown meetings. That could have been you or me those bullets hit and they still haven't caught that fella with the ski mask that disappeared with that pinkie back in the swamp. What if he comes back?

It was the perfect plan, and Willie waited patiently for his inner voice to comment.

There was a long pause and just when Willie thought he had silenced that voice, it spoke just one word.

Reckless.

"That's Uncle Reggie's word," Willie whispered, followed by a short laugh. "If that's all you got, this matter is closed, and I'm going to finish my nap."

He leaned over and plopped his head down on top of the duffel, and before he closed his eyes, he noticed the message light flashing on his phone.

Maybe Uncle Reggie talked to Kettle and the cavalry is on their way to come get Sheriff Green...

He grabbed the phone and looked at it. It was a missed call, but it had nothing to do with the cavalry. It was Dr. Cheever. And for the first time in the history of Dr. Cheever, she hadn't left a message.

"That's weird," he said.

And then Willie wondered what her response would be if he called her back and was honest with her about everything.

She answered on the second ring.

"Hello, Willie," she said. "Thanks for returning my call. I just wanted to check in and see how things are with you."

"I can't talk long. Need to save my battery. I just wanted you to know I want your help when I come home. I want you to be my sponsor too."

There was a pause. Then he heard her sigh. It could have been a happy sigh, but it also could have been her *Willie's messing with me as usual* sigh. He thought they'd lost their connection when Cheever said, "Willie, that is fantastic news."

"Yeah," Willie said. "When I saw you last, I was taking around thirty pills a day. But I've cut down big time."

"I appreciate you being honest about using, Willie. It's a huge step."

"I took three pills a couple hours ago and won't have another one today." Though what he said was true, it felt like a lie because if he had twenty pills, he'd take all of them.

"Really?" she said. "Just three...down from thirty?"

"Swear to God."

There was another pause. One that most likely gave her time to double-check the battery on her *Willie Is Fucking with Me* device.

"Willie," Cheever said. "That type of reduction can be potentially dangerous. If you were to go from thirty pills to three pills a day, your body would be under considerable stress and—"

"My leg will start twitching and I will be tired and irritable?"

"Yes, but it can also be deadly, Willie. Not to mention the psychological—"

"I haven't taken a solid shit in I don't know how long and my mind is racing everywhere."

She paused, and her response surprised him. "You are telling me the truth, aren't you?"

"Yes," Willie said. "And I really want your help."

"Okay," she said. "Let's see if you mean it, then. I want you to stop whatever you are doing and get back here right now. I know a facility where you can detox under the care of qualified medical personnel. It is the best place in Georgia, maybe in the country. Are you still up north?"

"I'm still in Michigan," Willie said. He thought he heard a car door close and lowered his voice to a whisper. "But I sort of can't leave right now."

"Why are you whispering?" she asked.

Before he'd called her, he had told himself it was time to be honest with her. And to the best of his knowledge, he'd done that, so he wasn't going to stop there.

"I'm whispering because I'm sort of hiding out in the middle of a swamp."

"You are in a swamp? Hiding from whom?"

"You know about The Crown, right? Purple robes and hoods…"

"Yes," she said. "Your father told me you were quite impressed with them when he took you up to Detroit."

It was Willie's turn to pause. He *had* been impressed with them but that seemed like so long ago. And that was before he *knew* The Crown…or even more important, before he ever took the time to know *and then care about* the people The Crown oppressed.

"That's true," Willie said. "They impressed me, and I can't be more ashamed of that."

"Willie Gibbons?" she said. "What has come over you?"

"A lot of things." It was still a whisper, but it was a louder one. "But like I said, I'm out in the middle of a swamp that's near where The Crown meets. My dad used to be a leader in The Crown and they are the ones that killed him. I have a brother that lives with my uncle and he and a couple other people witnessed it. There is a meeting tonight, so I'm waiting out here and planning to do something a little crazy, but it's the right thing to do and it will end up saving a lot of other people. I'm going to shoot one of the leaders."

There was silence, but he knew she was still there.

"Help me here," Dr. Cheever said, followed by yet another pause. "Your father… who has done more for white people than probably any black man in the history of the country, was a leader in The Crown?"

"Yes," Willie said. "They are called the Trio."

"I've heard the phrase," she said. "And your brother witnessed him getting killed? How come we never knew of this brother?"

"Because he is half-white and—"

Dr. Cheever laughed out loud. "Willie, it just occurred to me that you forgot something."

"Why are you laughing?" Willie asked. "I didn't forget anything."

"You forgot the obvious," she said. "And you should be ashamed of yourself for making up such a ridiculous story about your father, who was a great man."

"I know he was a great man," Willie said. "And what I said isn't a story."

"Willie, I will never give up on you, but I've had enough for today. The only reason you returned my call was to mess with me. I'm here to help, but only if you really want it."

"Dr. Cheever...you *have* to believe me."

"Next time you tell that story, think it through a little better," she said. "After you throw in the part about you shooting the leader because they killed your father, be prepared to answer the obvious question that just about anyone with a brain in their head will ask."

"What question is that?"

"If they killed your father, why wouldn't you call the police?"

"That's easy," Willie said. "Because the sheriff is one of the leaders in The Crown, too, and he is the one I'm going to kill."

"Like I said, I'm here to help, but only if you really want it. Are we through here, Willie?"

"I guess so," Willie said.

Dr. Cheever said goodbye and the line went dead. Willie laughed a crazy little laugh and put the phone down. He knew she didn't believe a word he'd said and he also knew he pretty much deserved it.

He took a swig of water from the jug and then reached for the magazine to manufacture a little more butt wipe for when the time came, which he could tell would be soon. He opened the magazine and as he stared at the page on the left, he thought about calling Dr. Cheever back to let her know that the little rich kid she just got off the phone with was on the verge of wiping his spoiled ass with a crumpled page of a smut magazine. Then he wondered if she'd hang up on him by the time he let her know that the page he was going to use had an advertisement on it for *The Big Fella Pump* (with a money-back guarantee) that promised to *add three inches to your Johnson in less than sixty days!*

Willie snickered and then his stomach roiled, making him regret taking the sip of water. He grabbed the ruffled magazine pages off the floor and when he lifted himself to his knees, he heard a buzzing sound. It was faint, yet steady, and he closed his eyes, wondering if the noise maybe only existed between his ears, perhaps his body's way of asking in yet another language to give it some more pills.

Willie was confident the noise was real, so he glanced over the edge of the plywood window and immediately noticed his uncle's car parked right in front of the stage. And in front of the car was Uncle Reggie, who was facing the stage with his head no more than a foot away from the stone wall, swaying back and forth with the Weedwacker in his hand.

"What in the fuck are you doing here?" Willie whispered. He thought about yelling it, but had no idea what it would bring.

Uncle Reggie said last night that he was going to go about today as if it were just another day, but that he was going to be minus some help.

But wasn't he supposed to go to the hospital and then go talk to Kettle to get advice?

Willie started feeling light-headed, knowing it was withdrawals. He closed his eyes and took a deep breath, holding it until he heard the Weedwacker stop.

When he opened his eyes, he watched Uncle Reggie disappear around the far side of the stage. There was a long pause and then Willie heard the Weedwacker turn on again. The buzzing sound was muffled and Willie was pretty sure Uncle Reggie had gone under the stage and was hacking in the dark at the grass that had grown around the hundred boxes of dynamite that were there, the ones Joseph told him were going to be used to expand Devil's Drop.

But we just Weedwacked under there...

Then Willie's leg started twitching and as he became even more light-headed, his inner voice wouldn't shut up.

You are out in the middle of a swamp. You only took three pills today and you are getting your first real taste of serious withdrawals and they are a mother fucker. Why is this happening to you today...the only day in your entire life when you really need to have your shit together?

He ignored the inner voice and tried some deep breathing exercises he'd seen before on television, but all that did was make him dizzier and fill his vision with clusters of dancing black dots. He blinked and blinked until they went away. Then he closed his eyes and felt something like cool water washing over the back of his brain.

And then he could see Lucas. And then Reverend Kettle.

More black dots appeared and then there was Evan at the car wash.

And then dots appeared on Evan. And then Lucas was at the car wash with Reverend Kettle.

And it was a good thing Uncle Reggie brought the Weedwacker so his feet can stay dry in the plastic baggies of pills Cheever doesn't believe my brother who is bigger than a silver trailer so I don't need to read that magazine for toilet paper and a three-inch Johnson because I really can't shoot shoot shoot black dots bigger black dot can't shoot shoot shoot—

◆◆◆

WILLIE ROLLED OVER AND it felt like someone grabbed his wrists and pulled them over his head.

"Bring that pinkie lover all the way up here so we can have us a little fun with him!"

The words sounded like they were shot out of a cannon, but it was no cannon. It was Sheriff Green through a megaphone.

Willie opened his eyes. It was dark out and he was on his back being dragged by his arms through the swamp. Cattail stems tore into his neck and back and when he turned his head to his left, he got a mouthful of muddy sulfur water that he immediately coughed out. Part of the sky looked burnt orange and he knew it was from the torches of only God knew how many Crown. At least eight were around him. Two pulling him by the wrists, two to his left with flashlights, two to the right with torches, and another two to the rear that were each pointing shotguns at what looked like his face.

What the fuck happened?

He looked at the hand that was clasped around his left wrist. The man was wearing a digital watch and the face of it was lit in the dark.

It was 10:18 p.m.

The last thing Willie could remember was his uncle Weedwacking under the stage.

Oh shit.

Willie remembered his leg twitching.

And then getting dizzy. And then the big black dot.

What happened was you passed out and fell right out of the blind.

For six hours.

Now, you better think fast or you are going to die.

WILLIE

The Longest Day Ever.

The Last Day in Woodruff.

The Rest of It.

I t's me!" Willie yelled. "My name is Willie! Sheriff Green invited me!"

They didn't seem to care.

Think of why you would be out here…

"Ask Sheriff Green if you don't believe me," Willie yelled. The sky was getting brighter, which meant they were getting closer to all the torches and Devil's Drop. "I couldn't get ahold of him before the meeting started so I came out here before dark so I could watch without interrupting."

"Explains why you were carrying this," someone said. It was yet another Crown that came out from behind the men on Willie's left.

He was holding Varmint Killer.

"I had to walk out here behind The Row," Willie said. The man that had his right wrist was squeezing it so hard Willie's hand had fallen asleep. "I sure as hell ain't coming out here unarmed."

"Bullshit," one of them said. Willie was pretty sure it was one of the men that had a shotgun aimed at him, but he wasn't sure. "Say another word and I'll blow your fucking head off."

The second his suspicion was confirmed, Willie was filled with a bizarre sense of peace he had never felt before.

This was noticeably different than the one he experienced when his inner voice, *the dumb-ass inner voice,* somehow tricked him into believing he and Joseph were getting out of there alive. This sense of peace was clearly a by-product of the anesthetic the mind creates to numb you when it knows you are about to die.

They reached the edge of the swamp and the men brought Willie up to his feet, maybe sixty to seventy yards from the stage. Willie felt the shotgun barrel rest against his temple and the man that had the death grip on his wrist pulled both of Willie's hands behind his back. Willie felt the handcuffs go on and they walked out into the center of the crowd and turned him to face the stage.

"Light the rest of them 'em up," Sheriff Green said through the megaphone. He wasn't wearing his hood and was standing at the center of the stage, right at the front edge.

Willie was surprised how few torches had already been lit. And then, as if they all did it on the count of three, it seemed like every man there that hadn't lit his torch fired up, lighting all of Devil's Drop.

"Keep our newest guest out there until we are ready for him!" Green shouted. There were hundreds of laughs and Willie looked behind him.

Look at all the fucking torches.

They were being held by men everywhere from the base of the entry road all the way up to the front edge of the stage. It was a full house. There were easily two thousand Crown there. Way more than the meeting he and Joseph watched. Something special had to be happening.

Like a dipping.

"And I'll remind you again!" Sheriff Green yelled. "It's lower than the Jews. Even lower than the Arabs and the yellow-skinned people!"

The sheriff had moved and was about five feet from the detonator box and plunger at the front left corner of the stage. The megaphone was at his side and he raised it again, this time speaking softer and more matter-of-factly.

"Even lower than the homosexuals," he said, raising his other arm. "Let me hear you if you agree, brothers!"

They went bonkers, creating more than enough noise to drown out the sound of a gunshot, the one Willie was supposed to take. He'd have given anything to have Varmint Killer in his hands. He'd let a bullet fly into the sheriff's frank and beans, blowing his dick off so he could spend the rest of his life putting his little black stub in that pump from the dirty magazine…hoping he could regain a few inches.

As the cheers subsided and The Crown waited on the sheriff, Willie shifted his eyes to the podium, where the other two Trio stood. The Left Trio reminded Willie of a mannequin. His arms were straight down to his sides, and he just stood there, facing straight ahead, shoulders pulled back in his shiny black suit. Willie wondered what the man was like. If he had a wife. Kids. Maybe a dog. Regardless of any domesticated side he may or may not have, there was something else Willie noticed. And as much as he hated to admit it, something about the way the guy just stood there sent vibes throughout the whole valley that calmly and confidently described the man to everyone there within two combined words.

Badass.

And to his right was the Alpha *BADASS*.

The Crown Lord.

He also reminded Willie of a mannequin, but was standing on whatever that thing was called (Willie still couldn't think of the name of it) that elevated him at the podium about eight inches over the other two.

"And we owe it to each other, to our families, and God…to do our part in ridding the world of the pink cancer," Green said, the words echoing off the edges of the valley. "Brothers, I want you to take a minute right now and think about your black wife, black daughter, black sister, or black mother. Picture those faces and then I want you to place those faces in the safest parts of your minds."

Green took a few steps and stopped abruptly.

"Now, think about how much safer they are because of our work," Green said calmly through the megaphone. "Safer because of all the right things we are doing here tonight."

Willie could hear a little stir in the crowd. But Green didn't want them erupting just yet, so he paused, and while he did, Willie thought about The Crown *doing the right things*, and how much their definition probably differed from Dad's.

"Like a good pet gone bad," Green continued. "We can't always predict what a pinkie will do and that presents a constant danger."

There was another little stir, but it quickly faded.

Green held up his hand and put a pinch of urgency in his voice. "We need to remind ourselves that at any time…and at any place…if a pinkie thinks he can get away with it, he won't hesitate, not for a split-second, to violate one of our ladies… one of those same faces I just asked you to place in the safest parts of your minds. So, now I have to ask you…who is there to stop the pinkie?"

"We are!" a single Crown yelled behind Willie and maybe twenty or so echoed him.

Green waved his right hand up and down to calm them again. Then he raised the megaphone, and right before he spoke, someone yelled from close to the stage.

"Kill all them pinkie sumbitches!"

Green whispered into the megaphone, "Yes, brothers. It is we that will stop the pinkie."

There was a pause and Willie could tell they were getting restless, as if they not only wanted to stop the pinkie but stop him right away.

Green let them wait before he said anything, and the longer they waited, the more restless they became. Willie could practically feel the tension building around him as they grew louder.

"Hear! Hear!" Green shouted, and though Willie had heard Green say those words on more than one occasion, it wasn't until just then that he knew it could only mean *everyone shut the fuck up*, because silence and dead air came and came like right now.

"I'll say it again," Green said, followed by a little thread of static from the megaphone. "It is we that will stop the pinkie. Even if we have to do it one pinkie at a time. So, let us remain silent as we practice the ritual passed down from our fathers…the ritual that is not only our honor, but our obligation, and our duty in preserving the sanctity of black society."

They stayed silent and Sheriff Green turned and walked back toward the podium to take his place at the right hand of The Crown Lord. Green pulled out his hood, put it on, and then pulled back his shoulders, just like the other two, to face the entire Crown.

It was eerily quiet. The three men were perfectly still. *Mannequin* still.

Sheriff Green raised his arm for about five seconds, and when he lowered it, the entire Crown, in unison, all started that humming thing Willie recognized from both the courthouse steps up in Detroit and the other meeting he'd watched.

Hum, hum, hum…

It started out soft and Willie knew it would be a while before it grew into a pulse.

Hum, hum, hum…

A man screamed.

It was a familiar, high-pitched scream followed by a knocking sound.

He could see the knocking was the work of the Left Trio, pounding down on the podium with what had to be a gavel. When he stopped, torches started to go out. And then more and more, erasing the field before Willie's eyes. In less than a minute, the field was totally dark, leaving only the stage lit.

The man screamed again. Its high pitch was the same one Willie recognized from the man's laugh. It was Joseph.

At the back corner of the stage, Willie could see two regular Crown near the top of the ladder. They were both in purple robes, hanging on to a piece of rope and leaning back as if they were teammates in tug-of-war.

Then Willie could see something coming over the top of the ladder. They were pulling Joseph up feet first, which seemed to be bound together. When the rest of

Joseph reached the top of the ladder, it was clear his hands were tied behind his back and they had put a white pillowcase over his head.

Once on stage, Joseph started to squirm and thrash until the two Crown each delivered swift kicks to his midsection. And then they started dragging him across the floor toward the Trio.

Do something, Willie. Do something, he thought, now understanding more than ever how Uncle Reggie had to have felt the night they killed Dad.

The Crown continued to hum as they pulled Joseph past the Trio, who stayed perfectly still, facing their two thousand faithful that stood below them out in the darkness.

Unlike the way Willie had heard them do it before, the *hum, hum, hum* wasn't getting any louder, but it was steady and in perfect rhythm.

When they had Joseph within ten feet from the end of the stage, they stopped and both Crown gave him a couple more solid kicks, one to the back and one to the stomach. Joseph's knees drew up to his chest and that high-pitched scream cut through the air again.

The Left Trio banged the gavel again, and when he stopped, the torches that lit the stage began to go out until all of Devil's Drop was pitch black.

Hum, hum, hum...

"Hear, hear!" Sheriff Green blared from the darkness, startling Willie again.

The humming immediately stopped and the whole valley became quiet. Too quiet.

Then Willie could hear Joseph. It was faint, but it was clear he was crying.

Torches lit at the front right corner of the stage and Willie could see the vertical portion of the dipping gallows, the thick beam that jutted straight up from the floor of the stage.

More torches lit, ten feet higher than the previous ones, showing an outline of the upper half of the gallows.

Willie's eyes were glued to the wooden arm that hung over the dipping pond. No one could deny that it could easily serve a different purpose in hangings, but that's not how this monster was fed.

Four more torches lit. And then two more.

The dipping gallows were now the only thing in view and it reminded Willie of some lifeless wooden monster. One that had just come out of the shadows, standing tall and firm, that powerful arm held straight out to its side over the water...*waiting*.

Shadows moved in the dark part of the stage, just to the left of the torchlight that lit the gallows. Joseph was now weeping.

Joseph continued to cry and Willie was surprised how quiet The Crown remained. Other than the sounds coming from Joseph, there wasn't a single noise in the valley and it gave Willie chills as he was certain everyone else remained silent for only one reason.

To hear Joseph suffer.

The two Crown that had pulled Joseph now had him at the very edge of the stage. Joseph started to thrash wildly again on the floor, earning him a dozen more kicks, including what looked like one to the face, which may have knocked him out.

As Joseph lay still, one of The Crown attached what looked like a cable to the rope that bound Joseph's ankles.

They are going to shove him over the edge and then dip him.

"Let's get our pinkie-loving guest of honor up here for a front row seat!" Sheriff Green blared.

Torches relit the stage and a single torch was fired up in the darkness of the field, a few feet to Willie's left. He could feel the heat on the side of his face when someone grabbed the back of his neck and pushed him forward. They escorted him through the crowd and Willie felt the barrage of spit that peppered the sides of his face. Some of it got in his eyes and a fair amount of it was hanging from his right ear for a good ten seconds. When they reached the lower left corner of the stage, Willie could see the ignition wire that ran from the detonator box and plunger up on the stage all the way out to the pickup at the edge of the field. He turned and studied the truck for a few seconds, knowing they were going to blow it up later, but was spun around and pushed toward the ladder.

At the base of the ladder, one of the men pulled out the ski mask Willie had brought with him. He put it over Willie's head and then nodded for Willie to start going up the ladder. With his hands cuffed behind his back, Willie's chest was against the ladder most of the way up, making it a slow and difficult climb. When he finally made it to the top, he was greeted by one of the regular Crown who reached under the ski mask and grabbed Willie's ear to *help* him the rest of the way up.

"Let me hear you boys if you want a little more entertainment!" Sheriff Green blared, the megaphone loud as fuck from only ten feet away.

The mob erupted and Willie could feel the noise bounce off him when it reached the stage. The man that met Willie at the top of the ladder took him to where Sheriff Green was and then walked to the far edge of the stage where he joined the other Crown, who was standing over Joseph. Joseph was motionless near the far edge and the dipping gallows.

Sheriff Green stared at Willie for a second and then raised the megaphone to fire off a quick *Hear, hear!* to immediately silence The Crown. Then Green faced them and raised his other arm and held it for maybe five seconds. And then he quickly lowered it, starting the humming machine again.

"Why am I handcuffed?" Willie asked. "You invited me, didn't you?"

"That I did," the sheriff said.

"I just wanted to watch," Willie said. "But don't worry, I will just stay out of the way up here so I don't screw anything up—" He paused and faced the field. Though the humming was low, he didn't know if anyone could hear them talking.

"Nobody can hear us," Sheriff Green said, answering the question before Willie asked. "But you can bet that every single one of them is looking right at you and your silly little mask."

Hum, hum, hum . . .

"Why didn't your men just wake me up and bring me in when I first passed out?" Willie asked.

"We didn't know you were out there until right before the meeting started."

The sheriff turned toward the two men that were standing over Joseph and then reeled his right index finger. One of the men quickly came and Sheriff Green said something to him, sending the man behind the Trio hut. He was back there for a few seconds before returning with a white rag that looked like something someone had used to wipe their ass with.

Sheriff Green said to Willie. "This rag is to prevent any more bullshit from coming out of your piehole until it's your turn."

"My turn at what?"

The sheriff laughed and pointed at the dipping gallows. "Willie, I'm surprised you haven't asked how I knew you were hiding in the swamp."

Maggie was the only person that knew, and no way would she say anything.

"I have no idea," he said. "And I wasn't hiding. I was just trying to stay out of the way while having a good view."

"Thank goodness I returned her call," Sheriff Green said. "She called the station a little before suppertime and I didn't call her back until a few hours later."

"Call who back?" Willie asked, puzzled. Maggie didn't have a phone and even if she did, there was no way she would say anything.

"Your doctor was worried about you," the sheriff said. "Cheever, is it?"

No.

Sheriff Green grabbed Willie by the throat and squeezed. Willie felt his Adam's apple press in and thought his trachea was going to collapse.

"Open your mouth," the sheriff said.

Willie did and Sheriff Green pulled up the mask just far enough to stuff the rag deep into Willie's mouth with his other hand. It tasted like gasoline and when the material touched way back in the soft part of his throat, Willie gagged and coughed, causing his nose to run and making it hard to breathe.

"Now, I hated to do that," Sheriff Green said. "But Dr. Cheever said you were talking crazy stuff about The Crown killing your father and how you were plotting to kill one of the Trio, namely one who was involved in local law enforcement."

Then he turned and pulled Willie by the arm, taking him toward Joseph and the gallows.

Hum, hum, hum...

When they went behind The Crown Lord and the Left Trio, Willie noticed The Crown Lord wasn't standing on that thing that exalted him high above the other two. In fact, The Crown Lord wasn't standing on anything at all. He didn't need it. He was tall already. Easily six-four or six-five.

"At the very least, you better be thankful," Sheriff Green said. "After that bullshit festival you laid on me last night, I'm still going to give you the best seat in the house to watch the mongrel die. And when we are through with him, we are going to do the same thing to you...or would you prefer I say *like father like son?*"

When they reached the side of the stage, one of the two regular Crown started turning the wheel that was connected to the gallows, slowly winding in the cable that was connected to the rope around Joseph's ankles.

Hum, hum, hum...

When the slack in the cable disappeared, Joseph's legs began to lift off the floor and the other Crown quickly removed the pillowcase from Joseph's head before pushing him over the edge, causing Joseph to unleash another high-pitched scream that tore into Willie. Joseph fell about six feet and his body was parallel with the water until the cable caught, causing Joseph's ankles to absorb the brunt of his weight before flipping him upside down over the center of the pond.

The man that controlled the wheel began to turn it even more, pulling Joseph back up and away from the pond until his head was even with the stage floor.

Sheriff Green gave Willie's neck a firm squeeze and then had him sit at the edge of the stage, his legs dangling over the pond, right in front of Joseph.

"Enjoy the show," Sheriff Green said.

Sheriff Green stepped back. The pounding of the gavel immediately filled the air, killing the torches on the stage and leaving Devil's Drop in the dark.

All except the torches still burning at the edge of the stage, the ones that gave everyone in attendance the perfect view of the gallows and Joseph.

"Hear, hear!" Green yelled and when the humming stopped, they started to lower Joseph toward the pond.

Less than two seconds after Joseph's head hit the water, he started to thrash. They lowered him farther, dipping his entire head. Then they lowered him farther yet, past his shoulders. As Joseph squirmed, the cable attached to his legs twisted and swayed only a few inches. There was nothing Joseph could do to really move, let alone get his head out of the water.

When they pulled Joseph back up, he was facing Willie. Joseph coughed for a good twenty seconds. His face was shiny and his white T-shirt was stuck to him from his chest down to his neck. When he could finally take a breath, he was trying to free his hands from behind his back, a total waste of energy.

"No!" Joseph cried. "Please...please stop it!"

Willie tried to turn back around to get Sheriff Green's attention and lost his balance, almost falling off the edge of the stage and into the pond. He looked back at Joseph and when their eyes met, Willie's filled with tears and he would have given everything he had to tell Joseph he loved him and that they were brothers.

The man started turning the wheel again and Joseph headed slowly back down toward the pond. Willie's throat felt like it was coated with gas fumes from the rag. He blinked until the tears were gone and tried to yell for Sheriff Green, but hardly anything came out, the rag too far down in his mouth.

Joseph entered the water again and kept going until he was under just past his waist. When they stopped lowering him, he started to squirm again, his movements creating thick ripples in the water that ran away from his hips and toward the edges of the pond.

Joseph soon became still and Willie hoped it was because he realized the squirming was another waste of energy.

Air bubbles finally surfaced around Joseph's waist. He'd been underwater for close to two minutes and the guy controlling the wheel waited another fifteen to twenty seconds after the last air bubble before pulling Joseph back out of the pond.

Joseph's entire T-shirt was glued to him and the water had darkened the top part of his jeans up to the pockets. Willie could see Joseph's sides expanding and contracting, clearly doing whatever he could to make the most of his chance to breathe.

Then they lowered him quicker, and before he hit the water, Joseph opened his eyes and looked right at Willie again, not having any idea who was behind the mask.

"Please mister," he said, barely audible. "Please help me. Please make them stop."

There is nothing I can do...

Joseph went under again and Willie watched the surface of the pond, hoping the bubbles would come, but not too soon.

Willie tried again to turn around and get the sheriff's attention, but this time he did it slower, maintaining his balance until he could see the Trio. Green had his hood back on and the three men had stepped back from the podium and were standing at the edge of torchlight, facing the gallows. Willie could see their eyes behind the masks as they watched Joseph struggle.

Willie tried again to say something that Sheriff Green could hear, something that would let the sheriff know he had something to say that was important. But all that came out was something that sounded like a caveman grunting, and Green never even moved. Then Willie moved his head back and forth to get the sheriff's attention and was still ignored, so he turned back to face the pond.

Joseph was under for well over two minutes when the air bubbles finally came. This time the man at the wheel waited close to thirty seconds after the bubbles ended to pull Joseph back up.

Joseph's back was now to the stage and Willie could see his hands slowly wriggle behind his back. There was a delay before Joseph's coughs came, coughs that were intermittent with too much time between them. Willie knew Joseph had taken some water into his lungs and even though his chest was still contracting, they were short, shallow breaths.

They lowered Joseph again, this time until all you could see above the water were Joseph's calves and bare feet, which weren't moving at all. Joseph didn't have anywhere near enough time to recover and Willie knew he would be drowning.

"Let me hear your appreciation, brothers!" Green shouted, and The Crown went ballistic, their *appreciation* probably heard all the way out to Main Street.

Joseph had now been under for too long.

"Hear, hear!" Green shouted, muting the crowd.

Willie studied the surface of the pond, waiting for bubbles.

"Ain't going to be that easy for him!" Sheriff Green said, and the man at the wheel started pulling Joseph back out.

Joseph was completely soaked. His back was to Willie but the cable was turning, bringing Joseph around with it.

Joseph's hands were still. His chest was no longer contracting. He just hung there, motionless and shiny, oddly making Willie think of a freshly delivered stillborn—one that was wet from birth and being held upside down from the feet by some twisted doctor that was getting off examining it.

Willie closed his eyes and tried to make it just another weird dream like the one he had when he fainted into the cattails. He tried to make it all go away… because he was also drowning…not in a stinky pond, but in a sea of helplessness.

"No," Willie heard and opened his eyes.

It was barely audible. But he knew it was Joseph, who had rotated with the cable and was now facing the stage again.

"Please," Joseph said.

Willie couldn't see his chest contracting, but if Joseph was talking, he was breathing.

"Please," Joseph repeated, this time louder. "I'm sorry, Sheriff Green."

"Oh, that's a no-no," Sheriff Green barked into the megaphone. "Someone doesn't seem to know the rules around here about using names, and he just mentioned yours truly. How unfortunate."

And then the sheriff stepped out of the darkness right up next to Willie's left side. He pulled his pistol out from under his robe and fired a quick shot at Joseph, who only seemed to flinch, not as if he were shot, but only frightened.

Willie could see that Joseph's flinch had forced the cable to turn once again, taking Joseph with it until his back was to the stage.

Willie waited for the cable to rotate Joseph back and he couldn't stand the impossible silence.

How in the world can two thousand people and a dying man be that quiet out here in the middle of fucking nowhere?

Joseph screamed.

Willie turned his head to shield himself, but the high-pitched sound raced straight onto the stage, cutting through Willie like a shard of broken glass.

When Willie opened his eyes, Joseph's head was jerking from shoulder to shoulder, twisting the cable again until Joseph turned and faced the stage.

And when the scream turned into a hollow moan, Willie could see why.

Sheriff Green wasn't trying to scare Joseph with the gunshot.

There was a dark spot that had appeared over Joseph's soaked jeans. Green had fired a shot into Joseph's left thigh, causing Joseph to immediately pass out only to wake right back up to this new pain.

Willie's fists bunched behind his back and he couldn't take it anymore. There had to be something he could do, something he could try. He tried to think but all he could hear were the sounds of Joseph's suffering.

Joseph screamed again, echoing around the sides of the valley and then fading into another moan that sounded like an animal caught in the sharp teeth of a beartrap, its leg snapped, slowly freezing to death, *knowing* that nobody was coming to rescue it.

"Brothers!" Green shouted. "Let me hear you if that's sweet music to your ears!"

They went berserk, every bit as loud as Willie had ever heard them and Green silenced them after about fifteen seconds.

Willie glanced up at the sheriff, who was still standing next to him with his pistol in his hand, and Willie couldn't stop himself from thinking about the time he was going to kill the coyote in Uncle Reggie's backyard…and what he told himself to justify it.

He's dangerous. He kills. He deserves it…

Then Willie looked at Joseph and thought about why he hadn't killed the coyote. And what Joseph had said to make Willie change his mind.

I've never seen him hurt nothing…

Joseph's wailing went away. His eyes opened wide, his mouth starting to quiver.

"Having fun?" Sheriff Green asked, kneeling next to Willie. "I'm guessing you are a little bothered. Are you okay?"

Willie shook his head and Green didn't seem to care whether or not it meant *yes* or *no*, because he just kept talking.

"I know how smart you are and I'm sure you remember me telling you last night that wanting to kill someone and actually doing it are two different things," Green said. "But shucks…here you are just *watching* it, not *doing* it, and the look in the eyeholes of that ski mask tells me you are about ready to lose your cookies."

Willie tried to speak again and it was clear Sheriff Green wasn't even entertaining the idea of removing the rag.

"But don't feel bad," the sheriff said. "It'll be over before you know it because you are going to die the same way."

Sheriff Green grabbed Willie by his arms and pulled him up to his feet. The man that controlled the wheel started turning it, lowering Joseph toward the water once again. Sheriff Green quickly made a hand signal, one that ended with his index finger going in little circles, and whatever it meant, it included an order to stop lowering Joseph and to pull him back up.

"I have to tell you something," Sheriff Green said, squeezing Willie's arm above the elbow until it felt like it was on fire. He was taking Willie to the back right corner of the stage, to the side of the Trio hut where the man that controlled the wheel waited. "I've been around the block more than my fair share and my experience has given me a pretty reliable bullshit meter that has never malfunctioned like it did last night. But with that said, I've got to stay honest and I want you to know that you really had me going with that story of yours. I mean, I bought into everything you told me...lock, stock, and barrel. Still not sure about the extent of Reggie's involvement, but despite some extra security measures or what I guess we could call some *persuasive interrogation*... your uncle is sticking to his guns in saying that until today, he was unaware that when Joseph said he saw your daddy die, that he was talking about *watching us kill him*. Which, by the way, we did."

They stood right next to The Crown that controlled the wheel and Willie thought about kicking Sheriff Green square in the balls and jumping off the back of the stage. But if there was any chance of somehow getting him and Joseph out of this mess, that would put an end to things.

"Please...please stop," they heard.

It was Joseph.

His face now looked shiny and smooth as if it were made of wax. His eyes were about halfway open but mostly rolled back in his head.

"Suffer, you betraying sonbitch!" the wheel operator yelled.

Joseph's eyes opened all the way and Willie's widened as well.

They both recognized the voice.

It was Uncle Reggie.

"No, Mr. Regg—" Joseph said, shaking his head and stopping himself from saying someone's name. He rattled off a series of quick coughs that were clearly producing water, and as he struggled to catch his breath, Willie could see the tears rolling down his already soaked cheeks. "Please, don't let them hurt me no more. Please let me go home so Mama can fix my leg."

"He wants his Mama!" Uncle Reggie yelled.

The only thing Willie could hear was Joseph trying to breathe until Uncle Reggie walked to the edge of the stage. He went past Joseph and turned his back to the crowd. And then he lifted his mask so only the sheriff, Willie, and Joseph could see his face. On second glance, Willie was sure The Crown Lord and the Left Trio could see Uncle Reggie's face as well, but they never flinched.

Uncle Reggie had been beaten good, most likely explaining what Sheriff Green meant by *persuasive interrogation.*

Uncle Reggie's good eye was swollen closed beneath the bloody knot that drew all the attention the night before. He was bruising around both cheekbones and his lower lip was swollen and split. In addition, his nose was clearly broken, the bridge dented awkwardly to the left and both of his nostrils were caked with half dry blood, reminding Willie a little of the beating Stanley Collins had taken at the jail. *Innocent* Stanley Collins.

Dead Stanley Collins.

Regardless, Uncle Reggie had apparently passed whatever tests they'd put him through and Willie guessed that when you coupled that with him not making a fuss over Dad's murder, they had to think he was about as tried-and-true purple as someone could get.

"Mama can fix me," Joseph cried.

"Your mama ain't going to be fixing anything anymore!" Uncle Reggie yelled. "Other than the six guys that fucked her out on the boat a few hours ago, myself included."

"Hear, hear," Sheriff Green said, without the megaphone. He said it just loud enough for Willie and Uncle Reggie to hear. It was meant to chastise Uncle Reggie and get him back in line after he obviously broke some sort of rule by talking when he wasn't supposed to. Either way, Uncle Reggie's words were filled with hate, *real* hate. Not like the show they put on the night before, because if Uncle Reggie was still acting, the script was awful because it was absolutely no benefit to Willie, Joseph, and Nancy's immediate cause of getting out of Woodruff.

"Let's enjoy this precious site just a little longer," Sheriff Green said, using the megaphone once again as he pointed at Joseph. And then he turned and faced The Crown to kick on the humming machine yet again.

Willie just stared at Uncle Reggie. What a pathetic mouse.

There was no doubt that Uncle Reggie wasn't kidding about raping Nancy and it couldn't be clearer that the fucking coward was doing whatever it took to cover his ass, including obliterating the closest thing he would ever have to a family.

Willie thought about the jab he gave his uncle's head with Varmint Killer. If he could do it all over, he'd bury the tip of the barrel about four inches deep into that loser's soft watermelon skull.

Hum, hum, hum…

Willie could only imagine what was going through Joseph's mind when Sheriff Green sidled up next to Uncle Reggie and began whispering.

"I didn't notice you taking a turn with Nancy," the sheriff said. "But if you did, good for you. But again, I can't imagine you not getting liquored up every once in a while and calling her into the house to give her a little bonus."

"Bet your ass on that," Uncle Reggie said, staring straight at Joseph.

"You hear him, mongrel?" Sheriff Green said, sticking his neck out toward Joseph. "There were six of us your whore mother serviced today and if I didn't know any better, it sounded like she enjoyed the first three or four." Then the sheriff pointed past Joseph at the cattails and then out toward the factory and the lake. "And as far as your leg goes, your mama won't be fixing anything for some time. She's somewhere out between here and Canada. When we were through with her, we tossed her just about smack-dab in the middle of Lake Erie. Unfortunately, all them stereotypes about pinkies being such good swimmers ain't quite true. So, just to be safe, we decided to help her out a little and gave her a couple cinder blocks to hang on to."

They. Fucking. Killed. Her.

Willie wanted to die. And then he wanted to make yet another trip back in time to the previous night where he had just killed Uncle Reggie with the tip of Varmint Killer's barrel. He would wait the seven or eight hours it took for Sheriff Green to show up in his pickup and this time when he came to the door, Willie would be the one both opening the door and holding the gun.

He'd shoot Green in *both* thighs. And then in the collar bone. And then in the arm. And just before he unloaded the rest of the gun in the sheriff's chest, he'd step on the side of his face with both feet. One for Willie, and one for Dad.

Willie could sense the mob getting restless, but that's the way Sheriff Green liked them. Willie tried yet again to shout, but his effort only made him choke more on the stinky rag, sending him into his own painful fit of coughs.

Sheriff Green grabbed Willie by the back of the neck and then peeled the mask off him. Then he yanked the rag out of Willie's mouth.

"You've been trying to run that piehole for the last fifteen minutes," the sheriff said. "But now that you can see the predicament you are in, I can't wait any longer to hear what your smartass has to say."

Hum, hum, hum...

Willie took a couple deep breaths and looked at Uncle Reggie.

"Please, Uncle Reggie," Willie said. "Now is your chance to right some wrongs. Joseph loves you. I love you. Please get us out of here. I know you can do it."

Uncle Reggie just stared at Willie for a good ten seconds.

"Fuck you, boy."

Willie coughed twice and the second one was productive, filling half his throat with phlegm that tasted like the rag. He looked to appeal to Sheriff Green but decided to say a few more things to Uncle Reggie first.

"I have a proposal," Willie said, making sure The Crown Lord and the Left Trio couldn't hear him. "And if that proposal doesn't work, I can't see any other way that Joseph and I are going to make it out of here."

"Smart boy," Uncle Reggie said.

"But first I have a question for you, Uncle Reggie," Willie replied. "And then I have something I'd like to give you."

"Make it quick," Sheriff Green said.

"I will," Willie said, staring down his uncle. "Yesterday, you said all of our problems are because of Demetrius Green. And then, when he came to the door last night, you said you should just squeeze a couple rounds off in his chest and make the world a better place. But you pussied out on that like the coward you really are. Like the one you have been your whole life."

"What's your question?" Uncle Reggie said. "Are you going to get to it or are you going to keep lying and trying to set me up like you did yesterday?"

"Right *after* I jabbed you in the head with the gun and gave you that nasty knot...but *before* you shot the wall and decided to blame it all on Joseph, you said so many nice things about people that truly cared about you. People that loved you. After today, they will all be gone and my question isn't how you are going to be able to live with yourself, my question is whether or not you think you will be lonely? And regardless of your answer, I have a gift for you. Something that will remind you of me and make those lonely days a little less lonely."

"I'll be just fine without my pinkie-loving brother, my pinkie-loving nephew, and the two pinkies that kept me glued to the farm and robbed me of what should have been my best years."

"I'm sure your best years are ahead of you," Willie said.

Hum, hum, hum...

Sheriff Green picked a stone up off the edge of the stage and chucked it at Joseph. It struck him in the midsection and Joseph barely winced.

"You have a gift for me?" Uncle Reggie said with a little laugh. "Other than the millions you are leaving me?"

"It's right here," Willie said, smiling. And then he let the loogie he coughed up slide from between his cheek and gum to the front of his mouth.

"Where?" Uncle Reggie said.

"Right here," Willie said and spit it straight at his uncle. It nailed Uncle Reggie right on that knot that was caused by Varmint Killer. The phlegm was thick and just sticky enough to stay attached to the knot for at least five seconds before most of it melted down into Uncle Reggie's eye.

His good eye.

Uncle Reggie wiped it away and then stepped forward and smacked Willie hard across his left cheek.

"You are doing all this lying and trying to put things on me because you are afraid," Uncle Reggie said. "Good Lord knows who is telling the truth here. And it's me. The one that knows the difference between black and white."

"God doesn't see black and white," Willie said. "And I hope he deals with you for the things you've done today."

Hum, hum, hum...

"What's your proposal?" Sheriff Green asked. "I'm thinking that people with less than a half an hour to live normally don't have their pockets lined with bargaining chips, so I'm sure this will be entertaining. But before you start yapping, let's make sure we are clear on something. If you try to spit on me, I'll start you on fire and let you hang upside down for a few minutes before your uncle lowers you in the pond to put you out."

Willie stepped right in front of the sheriff and looked him straight in the eyes.

"You and I will never agree on most things," Willie said. "And right now, it really doesn't matter who is wrong and who is right. But you have something I want. And if you give it to me, I will make you a rich man."

"Let me guess," Sheriff Green said, tilting his head toward the pond. "You want the mongrel?"

"Yes," Willie said. "Pull Joseph in and escort us out of here. If you do that, I will see to it that a million dollars is wired into your account tomorrow. And once we get Joseph to a hospital, you can keep me up in your jail until your money shows up. After that, you will never hear nor see from either of us ever again."

Sheriff Green laughed and looked at Uncle Reggie. And then he glanced over at The Crown Lord and the Left Trio who hadn't moved an inch in twenty minutes. And when the sheriff spoke, it was clear he didn't want them hearing what he said.

"Million sure seems to be a popular number," Sheriff Green muttered. "Want to take a wild guess what Reggie offered me today to be the one that dips Joseph? We made a phone call today from my office down to those fancy lawyers that worked with your daddy. They didn't seem overly enthused about the idea, but Reggie controls your father's money, not you, and a million will be coming my way shortly."

As the two thousand Crown continued to hum, Willie let the sheriff's words sink in for a whole half a second before laughing out loud. He knew when he'd woken up being dragged through the cattails that he was a dead man, but he could never be deader than he would have been spending the last minutes of his life knowing he never even tried to save himself and Joseph. But unlike his coward uncle, Willie had tried the only thing that he thought may work, but now that nothing really mattered, he wasn't going to die without letting the sheriff know how he felt.

"You are a clown," Willie said, right before spitting on the floor in front of Sheriff Green, missing his boot by maybe three inches. "I asked you last night why you hate whites and you choked on the answer. You are on this fucked-up mission and you don't even know why. You are nothing but a pathetic coward like my uncle and the rest of these jackasses that follow you. But we found out yesterday what happens when things are one-on-one, didn't we? Joseph had his way with you like a drunk fucking date."

Sheriff Green smiled and the light from one of the torches glistened off his gold teeth. Then he pointed at Joseph and nodded. "Looks like having your way with drunk dates has its consequences."

Willie turned and faced the entire Crown before nodding over his shoulder at Joseph.

"That man kicked Sheriff Green's ass! Sheriff Green, your Right Trio, got his fucking ass beat by that hash brown pinkie mongrel just yesterday!"

"They can't hear you," Sheriff Green said.

"Sheriff Green is a fuckup when it comes to keeping a pinkie in its place! He sucks big dick when it comes to protecting the women in your life from pinkies!"

"That's enough," Sheriff Green said. "Like I said, they can't hear you."

"It doesn't matter if they hear me or not," Willie said. "It doesn't matter because *you* know the truth. And by the way, I lied to you *before* last night. It was when you asked me if anyone saw what happened with you and Joseph downtown and I said *no*. The truth is, when you were down on your knees like a little bitch and Joseph was slapping you, *a lot* of people came out to watch it happen. And when you *fainted*, they all disappeared before you woke up because they were afraid. Not of you, because when you are by yourself you like to get your ass beat. What they are afraid of is your two thousand friends and the lopsided fights they pick."

Sheriff Green pressed his pistol firmly against Willie's stomach. Willie looked down at the barrel and then straight at Green, speaking just loud enough that only Green could hear.

"Fucking do it," Willie said. "Shoot me right now, that way you don't have to listen to the truth anymore. All you'll have to do is live with it."

Joseph groaned, just loud enough to be heard over the humming.

And when Joseph somehow found the energy to scream one more time, it had to be heard by everyone up on The Row. It came out of nowhere and drowned out the humming before it echoed against the sides of the valley.

And once the terror and misery bled out of Joseph's scream, it also turned into a moan.

But this moan was different, and Willie knew what it was. It was life that was begging to leave Joseph's body. But before it left, it had decided to tell whoever would listen about the unfathomable pain, misery, and injustices people can sometimes inflict on each other.

"Not sure how much more of that mongrel's howling I can handle," Sheriff Green said. "I think I may just put an end to all of this right here and now."

And then he raised his pistol and aimed it at Joseph.

Uncle Reggie walked up next to Sheriff Green and leaned in to say something only the sheriff could hear. Willie wouldn't be surprised if the only nerve his coward-ass uncle had left was to offer the sheriff another million dollars of Willie's money to be the one that shoots Joseph.

Sheriff Green just stared at Uncle Reggie for a few seconds before nodding and then lowering the pistol. And then the sheriff turned and walked over to where The Crown Lord and the Left Trio were. As Sheriff Green spoke, the other two remained perfectly still until The Crown Lord nodded, apparently in approval of what Sheriff Green had said.

Sheriff Green turned around and walked over to Willie.

"Thank you," the sheriff said.

"For what?"

"I just made another million and I owe it all to you."

"To let Uncle Reggie shoot Joseph?" Willie couldn't believe it. "Fuck that. I'll give you twenty million to let me shoot Uncle Reggie. In fact, you can have it all."

"Nobody is shooting nobody," Sheriff Green said, giddier than Willie had ever seen him. "We are going to make us some Crown history today."

The sheriff pointed at the wheel and then waved to the other Crown that had helped Uncle Reggie pull Joseph up the ladder before taking turns kicking him. The man had been standing patiently at the front corner of the stage and immediately rushed over to join Uncle Reggie at the wheel.

"Hear, hear!" Sheriff Green said, silencing the hums. Then he put the pistol back in his holster, grabbed Willie by the arm, and led him to the front center of the stage where the sheriff raised the megaphone.

"Ain't too often we get to host both a mongrel pinkie and a pinkie lover on the same evening," the sheriff said, followed by a quick thread of static from the megaphone.

"Push him off!" someone yelled from the middle of the field. "Let us take care of him!"

Sheriff Green shook his head and pointed out toward the edge of the field to where all the torched cars were. "And it ain't every night we get to have us a fireworks show." And then he paused, the way he normally did right before he'd rile them up. "Are you boys in the mood for some fireworks tonight?"

Willie turned his head to shelter himself from the noise. Sheriff Green was a rock star and Willie was the plague, but there was a quick *Hear, hear!* and Devil's Drop was silent on the spot.

"You boys are going to be part of history," Sheriff Green said calmly. "Part of a first…part of something that has never been done here before. Part of something that will be talked about not just in our circles, but everywhere for years to come."

Joseph moaned, and Willie turned around. They had unhooked him from the dipping post and he was lying in the fetal position on the stage. His hands were still tied behind his back but his feet were untied.

"We are going to have us a little two-for-one special," the sheriff said. "We've decided that we are going to rid the black world of both the mongrel…and this pinkie lover…*at the exact same time.*"

There were some cheers, but Sheriff Green patted at the air with his open hand to quiet them.

"But that's not the two-for-one special I'm talking about," Sheriff Green said. He left Willie standing there and started to walk slowly across the stage, the showman working his crowd. "The two-for-one special I'm talking about involves two other things. Fireworks and a barbecue."

Willie already knew where the sheriff was going. How he and Joseph were going to die.

"Fireworks and a barbecue," Sheriff Green repeated. "Now let me hear you boys if you want to be part of history tonight. The night where we blow up an old pickup truck with a hash brown mongrel and his pinkie-loving friend inside of it!"

Willie couldn't imagine them being any louder.

Sheriff Green dropped the megaphone to the floor of the stage like some half-assed rapper. And then he picked it back up and walked straight toward Willie. He took Willie by the arm, and as he led him toward the podium, the sheriff motioned to the back right corner of the stage to Uncle Reggie and the other Crown. Joseph was now standing, which was a miracle considering the bullet in his thigh, and he limped horribly as they escorted him toward the podium as well.

They positioned Willie and Joseph side by side in front of the podium, their backs to the crowd, facing the Left Trio and The Crown Lord.

Sheriff Green took his place at the podium, and Willie could hear him talk over the crowd as he spoke to The Crown Lord.

"This is for black society! God's society!"

The Crown Lord nodded and then Willie looked at Joseph. He was barely conscious, but he turned his head and looked right back at Willie.

"God doesn't see black and white!" Willie shouted, right in the faces of the Trio. "The three of you are cowards! Show your faces!"

The sheriff waved the back of his hand and Uncle Reggie and the other Crown took Willie and Joseph to lead them toward the ladder.

"Feel good, Uncle Reggie?" Willie shouted, as the crowd continued to roar.

Uncle Reggie didn't answer. They kept walking slowly toward the edge of the stage.

"You are a real big man!" Willie yelled. "I hope you are happy."

"Hear, hear!" Sheriff Green shouted through the megaphone, and the place went silent.

Willie looked over his shoulder and Sheriff Green had come out from behind the podium and was standing front and center, megaphone in hand. He did that other hand thing that restarted the humming and then just stared at Willie until they made it to the ladder.

"God doesn't see black and white!" Willie yelled again, knowing at least some of them had to hear it over the humming. "You are all cowards! You are all fucking cowards!"

Four more Crown were already at the bottom of the ladder. Uncle Reggie untied Joseph's hands and Joseph was the first to go down. Willie was surprised he didn't fall, and when he reached the bottom, he looked up at Willie, as if to make sure he was coming.

Willie was pushed toward the ladder. Uncle Reggie unlocked Willie's handcuffs and as he knelt to get on the ladder, Uncle Reggie took him by the shoulder.

"Out with the rot," Uncle Reggie said.

"Fuck you!" Willie replied.

"You boys take care of each other now," his uncle whispered.

"Go fuck yourself, coward," Willie added, and started down the ladder.

When Willie reached the bottom, he glanced up at his uncle Reggie. Willie mouthed another *fuck you* and when Uncle Reggie lifted his mask, Willie could see tears in his eyes.

"Why don't you all show your faces?" Willie shouted. "You are all cowards!"

The four Crown walked Willie and Joseph along the pylons and toward the pickup. Willie couldn't help but notice that as they walked, not a single Crown from the field had turned and faced them. They all just continued to hum and hum, their eyes fixed on their leaders.

"Hear, hear!" Sheriff Green yelled, and for the umpteenth time, it muted the crowd.

They kept walking slowly toward the pickup, getting closer and closer to dying.

"I love you, Joseph," Willie said. Joseph hadn't said a word since being unhooked from the dipping gallows and just kept limping without even turning his head.

"Salute!" Sheriff Green yelled. The second the word left the megaphone, every Crown member, in unison, all raised their right arms and leaned them toward the stage.

Even the men that were escorting Willie and Joseph to the truck stopped and turned around, doing the same with their right arms as well.

Willie and Joseph both faced the stage. All three Trio were now behind the podium and Sheriff Green had his hood back on. The Left Trio's right arm was extended up above his head, and between that and the *Salute* Sheriff Green belted off, Willie remembered the combination as a cue that The Crown Lord was getting ready to do something.

The Trio walked out from behind the podium. The Left Trio had been handed the megaphone and went up to the far front corner of the stage. The Crown Lord walked to the front edge of the stage as well, but right in the middle. Sheriff Green went to the near front corner, right next to the detonator box and plunger.

Next to Sheriff Green was Uncle Reggie, the only Crown there that wasn't holding his right arm out in front of him.

The Left Trio raised the megaphone to his mouth and everyone waited and listened.

"There are no cowards here, Willie Gibbons," he said. The Left Trio had a high and harmless voice and it surprised Willie, sounding everything but *badass*.

Willie glanced back at Uncle Reggie, whose arms were still at his side, totally out of formation.

"My brothers," the Left Trio said, followed by a little pause. "I command you to do as I do in demonstrating your fearless commitment to our cause."

And then, with his other hand, the Left Trio reached up and pulled off his hood. It was Mr. Bellows. The fifth-grade teacher Willie had met at the ice cream shop his first day in Woodruff. *The one all the kids loved.*

Willie glanced out in the field and as their right arms still leaned toward the stage, Crown were removing their hoods in the hundreds, revealing smart-looking faces, dumb-looking faces, old men, middle-aged men, and countless teenage boys that were The Crown.

Sheriff Green removed his hood and within minutes, the only man in Devil's Drop that was still wearing his hood was The Crown Lord.

"And it is true what Willie Gibbons said!" Mr. Bellows shouted, followed by yet another pause. "God does not see black and white!"

And then he lowered the megaphone to his side and both he and Sheriff Green walked to the center of the stage and took their places next to The Crown Lord.

The Crown Lord held out his hand and the Left Trio passed the megaphone to him.

And then The Crown Lord slowly raised it to his mouth.

"God does not see black and white!" he shouted in a familiar voice that was filled with both confidence and authority. And then with his other hand, he reached up and pulled off his hood.

Willie's heart almost leaped out of his chest and whatever strength he still had in his legs immediately left, sending him straight to his knees.

The Crown Lord was Reverend Kettle.

Willie struggled to catch his breath, now knowing that Joseph and Nancy never made it out of Woodruff before being caught. They never even made it out of Kettle's driveway.

"And there is only one reason that God doesn't see black and white!" Kettle shouted.

Every Crown there waited patiently for Kettle to tell them the reason.

Kettle raised his right arm and then shouted into the megaphone.

"It's because God only sees black!"

Then Kettle lowered his right arm, and when he quickly raised it back up and pointed it at the mob, the noise was immediately unbearable. The volume didn't rise as if someone turned a dial, it came out of nowhere, zero to ten, like the volume was already up all the way and Kettle plugged in the speakers. Willie wondered if Kettle had maybe pissed off God because it felt and sounded like an earthquake was coming through the valley. And it wasn't stopping.

The four men turned Willie and Joseph around and they started toward the truck again.

Willie thought about Kettle's God and then prayed to the real God. The one that really didn't care about skin color. When they neared the truck, one of the men walked Willie straight to the driver-side door and told him to get in.

Willie did and the man closed the door and stood right next to it.

The other Crown walked Joseph around to the passenger's side, let Joseph get in, and then stood right outside his door.

"This is really happening, isn't it?" Willie said, shaking his head.

Joseph didn't answer. He just looked straight ahead.

The man near Joseph's window stepped away from the truck and he and the guy next to Willie's window went to the other side of the pylons. They grabbed a couple other guys and they started backing men up, away from the pylons, cramming them together near the center of the field.

Willie glanced in the rearview mirror and could see Uncle Reggie standing over the detonator box. His uncle had clearly paid to be the one to blow them up.

"Coward," Willie said, closing his eyes. When he opened them, he noticed the keys were in the ignition.

He looked in the mirror again and his heart began to hammer at his rib cage.

Start the truck and try to get out of here...you've got nothing to lose.

His palms were lined with a film of sweat and when he grabbed the steering wheel, his right hand slid right off it. He grabbed the key and turned it, and for the first time in only God knew how long, the truck started on the first try.

But it was too late.

He glanced in the mirror and right as Uncle Reggie leaned down on the plunger, Willie threw the truck in drive and hit the gas.

A brilliant light flashed over the entire stage and then rushed toward them and then briefly over the back of the truck. Willie heard the initial explosion, but the sound immediately went away, replaced by the sound of Willie's breathing. He knew the truck was moving and it looked like they were driving into a cave, nothing but darkness and dust.

Another hand appeared on the wheel and Willie looked to his right. It was Joseph, who was helping him steer the car.

Willie felt a bump under the truck, and then another. Whatever the things were that the truck was running over, they were big.

He felt a couple more bumps and looked in the rearview mirror and realized the back window of the truck was gone. He could see men scrambling in the fire and darkness behind him.

His hearing returned.

Rocks and what sounded like pieces of wood were littering the roof of the truck. The dust was disappearing, making it easier to see, and before he could do anything, a man appeared out of the darkness in front of them and then disappeared, recreating one of the bumps that Willie felt earlier.

Joseph pulled on the wheel, turning the car to the right, and Willie knew they were at the base of the trail that led out of the valley and up to Cossit Creek Road. Willie looked out Joseph's window at what was left of Devil's Drop. It was practically all lit, but now by one giant torch that seemed to stretch from what was once the stage all the way out to the middle of the field. At least half the men had to be dead and those between Willie and the fire were screaming and running all over the place through debris that continued to fall from the sky. To the far right side of the field, near the cattails, a man emerged from the light completely engulfed in flames before diving into the swamp.

Willie drove to the top of the hill and noticed the unlicensed pickup trucks parked to his right. Then Willie made a left on to Cossit Creek Road and drove slowly, remembering that the trucks were driven by leaders that drove Crown members to meetings and that those leaders stood near the front of the stage.

"Toast," Willie said, glancing down at the speedometer. They were only going ten miles an hour. "Nobody is going to follow us out anytime soon."

They were still a hundred yards from The Row and Willie couldn't stop himself from saying something out loud.

"How did we not get blown up?" And then he thought about that little prayer he said before getting in the truck. "It's a miracle."

And then Willie remembered something else.

He remembered what happened before he passed out and fell out of the blind.

"Uncle Reggie," he said. "He didn't come out here to Weedwack. He came out to hook the ignition wire to the dynamite under the stage."

You boys take care of each other now.

Willie looked in the mirror yet again and even from up on the road, could see flames spilling out of the valley.

A hundred boxes of dynamite had just eaten Devil's Drop.

Out with the rot.

"Thank you, Uncle Reggie," Willie whispered, still seeing the tears in his uncle's eyes at the top of the ladder.

Just like his lawyer brother, Uncle Reggie knew he was going to die.

They entered The Row and both sides of the road were lined with people, most barefoot and likely brought out of sleep by the explosion.

"What do we say to them?" Willie asked.

Joseph didn't answer. He was barely conscious.

"Their lives should be a little easier now, don't you think?" Willie said, spotting Alan and Maggie up on his left.

Willie slowed down and stopped next to them.

"What happened?" Maggie asked.

"Don't answer that," Alan said.

Not answering was protecting both Willie and Maggie, and Willie appreciated it.

"Thanks, Alan," Willie said.

Alan glanced back at the light over Devil's Drop. "Maybe we should be thanking you."

Willie wanted to ask Maggie again. Ask her to come with him, but nothing would have changed since that afternoon. And whatever that invisible force was that would keep her and most of the people at The Row from at least *trying* to have a better life, Willie didn't have the strength to try to identify it. He was too busy drowning in the realization that he was still alive, and that alive was *good*.

"Come to Georgia any time you guys want," Willie said. "Invitation is always open."

Even that made Maggie take a step back. Alan looked at her and then back at Willie. It was clear that even Alan knew it was never going to happen.

"We will keep that in mind," Alan said. "Have a safe trip."

"Take care," Willie said, knowing that was the last time he'd see them.

He drove away slowly, keeping Maggie in his rearview mirror until he went down the hill that led out of The Row. Willie didn't say a word as they neared Uncle Reggie's house, and as they drove by, Willie looked out the window and noticed the moon had cast a peaceful glow over his car, the side of the barn, and the little place where Joseph and Nancy lived. Willie looked again at the speedometer. Though they were still only going ten miles an hour, they weren't stopping for anything, and every foot they went past Uncle Reggie's, more reality set in, and as it did, the adrenaline that came with survival faded into feelings of loss.

The speedometer finally blurred, and Willie felt the tears that had begun to stream down his face. One fell off his chin and it made an odd tapping sound as it landed on the side of his seat.

By the time they passed Old Lady Vee's place, Willie was weeping and had to pull the car over.

Joseph reached over and put the truck in reverse and Willie put his hand on top of Joseph's.

"We can't go back for anything," Willie said. "Not my car, not your stuff, nothing. We have to get you to a hospital."

"We are getting that dog," Joseph said. He sounded like someone else.

Willie's foot started to do the tapping thing, but now he didn't mind. "We don't have time."

"Get the dog," Joseph said. "He is going with us."

Willie backed the truck up.

They both stared at the Vee house for an easy minute, making sure no lights were on. He could see Mack's silhouette, just sitting out in that field as he always did.

"He doesn't deserve to live like that," Joseph said. "Nothing does."

Willie got out of the truck and walked into the field. Mack just sat there as Willie approached, and when he came within ten feet, he slowed down to see what Mack would do.

"Hey, Mack," Willie whispered, stepping closer.

Mack whimpered as if he couldn't believe someone actually wanted to spend time with him.

Willie moved closer still and could smell the mounds of dog shit that surrounded them and he figured that even if he got bit over the next few minutes, he was still taking Mack to Georgia.

"It's okay," Willie said, and Mack moaned louder.

Willie could see the dog's tail fanning back and forth in the dirt.

Willie held his hand out to see what would happen, no more than a foot from Mack's face. Mack whined, the dog was begging to be touched, so he put his hand on the side of Mack's face and began to pet him.

Willie knelt and started to pet Mack's side. The dog smelled like shit and piss and then licked Willie's face with the worst dog breath of all time, but Willie couldn't stop loving on the dog.

Willie rubbed again at the sides of Mack's face and then felt the metal collar around the dog's neck. It was solid steel and had a lock on it. The crazy bitch had an old slave collar on the dog that was so heavy it hurt Willie's neck just touching it. And then Willie felt the chain the collar was attached to, which was thicker yet. Even if Willie had a hacksaw, Mack wasn't going anywhere. Most likely ever.

"You all right?" Joseph shouted from the car.

"Coming," Willie said, standing.

Mack began to whine as Willie backed away and it broke the rest of Willie's heart. It felt all too familiar, and Willie started to cry again.

"I know this is the only world you know," he said. "But it's better where I'm from and I wish you could have come with me."

He looked back at the chain.

Willie ran his palms across his cheeks, wiping away the tears. And then he turned and walked quickly back to the truck, covering his ears to block out the sound of Mack's whining.

He opened the driver-side door, got in, and closed the door.

"We are outta here," he said.

"Gotta let him in," Joseph said.

"Can't," Willie said. "Collar is attached to this big-ass chain and the collar has a lock on it. Sucks because he is a nice dog and he has no idea how shitty his life is here."

"He don't know any better," Joseph said. "This place is all he knows."

"Yeah," Willie said. "I've heard that before."

"But I still think we should take him," Joseph said, looking out the passenger-side window. "I'm going to let him in and we will cut it off with something tomorrow."

Willie leaned over Joseph and looked as well.

Mack was sitting right next to the truck, looking up at them, tongue sticking out and tail wagging.

Willie opened the door and went around the truck to kneel next to the dog.

The collar was still attached to the chain, but the chain wasn't attached to anything.

"What do you think, Mack?" Willie said. "You want to come with us and try to have a better life?"

Mack just looked at him, tail still wagging steady.

"What's keeping you from giving it a try?" Willie asked. "Looks to me like *nothing* is stopping you."

Mack cried and pawed at the dirt like he was ready.

"Let's go, boy," Willie said, patting Mack on the head. Willie led him around to the open driver-side door and tapped on the seat.

Mack piled in, as did Willie, and they continued up Cossit Creek Road in silence until Joseph broke it.

"Why did you do it?" he asked.

"Do what?"

"Try to save me."

It wasn't the time to explain that they were brothers, but Willie knew that even if they weren't, he still would have tried to save Joseph.

"Because you are my best friend."

"You mean it, don't you?"

"Yeah, I mean it."

"What made *you* change?" Joseph asked. He could barely keep his eyes open. "When you first came up here you didn't care about anybody but you, let alone any *pinkie*."

Willie didn't have to think about it at all.

"Brother, it was you that started it," Willie said. His leg was twitching uncontrollably and his head was starting to hurt. "Getting to know you made a huge difference in my life. But at the end of the day, I guess I want to believe that if the shoe was on the other foot, or if things were the other way around and whites had the upper hand, that there is no way they would mistreat blacks as bad as we mistreated them."

"Answer couldn't get any better than that," Joseph said, running his finger across the bullet hole in his jeans.

A few minutes later, they neared Main Street.

"What do you think?" Willie said. "Take Main Street or stay low-key and go out Kettle's way?"

"Up to you," Joseph said, nodding off.

"Right down Main Street," Willie said.

Even though Sheriff Green was gone, Main Street was where his replacement would always be.

And it didn't scare Willie in the least.

Willie reached over and petted Mack, who cried in appreciation.

Then he thought about Dad, Nancy, and Uncle Reggie and felt his own tears again.

And though he would always miss them, he also knew they would always be a part of him.

His leg kept twitching and he ignored it.

And then he smiled, taking comfort in knowing tomorrow would be a different day.

And that he'd be part of the *light* that came with it.

Author's Note

We are all stuck here for a while, let's try to work it out...

THE FIRST TIME I heard those words was roughly fifteen years before I spent my first night in federal prison, and though Rodney King will always be more remembered for a very important question he asked that same day, being *stuck* and having a need to *work it out* played much larger roles in the lives of this privileged white boy white-collar criminal and the black inner-city drug dealer I was bunked with.

"Eric" and I knew we had nothing in common. He was black and I was white and society had already taught us all we really needed to know and that we were at the *only* place two guys like us would ever meet or spend any meaningful time together.

Fortunately, we had no choice.

Within a week, Eric had caught on to my Jolly Rancher addiction and I had caught on to the fact that he was selling slices of what was rumored to be the best homemade pizza in the history of pizzas out of our space. One day he was making one and I asked him how much he charged and he said, "free," before dropping a piece in the little plastic bowl on top of my locker. I plopped down from my bunk and we each had a piece of pizza. Hell's bells. We each liked pizza.

Within a month, Eric had *also* developed a Jolly Rancher addiction, (particularly the apple flavored) and I was eating pizza three or four nights a week in lieu of the mystery meat in the prison cafeteria.

The more we talked and the better we came to know each other, the less color we saw. We told each other jokes and talked about our lives before prison. We talked about how much we each missed our kids and our families. We were just two guys that had made mistakes that couldn't wait to get home to the people they loved. We were two people that had *learned* to ignore their differences, those same differences that had previously prevented them from seeing the things they have in common.

I can remember this conversation like it happened ten seconds ago. One night, Eric returned from the TV room and was telling me about something he had watched on BET. I had jokingly asked him why white people don't have their own entertainment channel, and he looked me straight in the eye and said, "You do… all the ones except BET." I laughed, but within a matter of seconds, I realized there was a great deal of truth to what he said and it bothered me. That night, I told him the impact his words had on me, and promised him that if I ever made it as a writer I'd try to do a story that put the racial shoe on the other foot. Eric and I were both released from prison and I was blessed to have considerable success with my first two books, *The Reason* and *The Sinners' Garden*. While on probation, former bad guys are prohibited from making contact with each other so Eric and I fell out of touch. One day I decided to look him up, knowing the day was coming where we could hang out and talk about the second chances we had been given to start our lives over. The very first thing that popped up under his name was a brief clip about a man that had been shot and killed during a home invasion. I remembered a promise I had made that man, and that night I started the outline for what ultimately became *The Crown Lord*. Though it is impossible for a white man to fully understand the oppression black people have experienced, I did my best and I hope you enjoyed the story.

Writing a book is a team effort and I have a lot of people to thank.

Thank you, Eric.

Thanks to my family, and a special thanks to my brother, Ken. I appreciate all you do and love you very much.

I'm so grateful to the early readers and for their amazing feedback. Thanks to Norm Fenton, Kaci Willis, Sonya Miller, Kristi Smith, Tom Murrah, Karla Dorman, Michele Hangen, Robert Conder, Sandy Bridges-Overton, Jada Love, Mike Mallet, Hope Thursdale, Jewel Landrum, Billie Higgs, David Fickes, Tara Low, Susan Vermiere, Juliette Ford, Hyacinth Palmer, Lisa Richmond, Cyrus Webb, Paulette Pedigo, Richard Finn, Sandy Dickson, Bob Deragisch, Nile Bloom, and Fred Bisaro. You were all incredible and made this story better, thank you.

Thanks to my friend and editor, Natalie Hanemann. I always tell you that you are the best. You really are.

Pat Walsh. I'm glad I met you. You know the book business, and I know we will continue to do big things together. Thank you.

Thanks to Tyson Cornell and his crew at Rare Bird. Publishers that love books are a joy to do business with, and the second I stepped into your office I knew I was home. Thanks for your belief in the story and I hope what we have done makes a difference in the world.

On a final note, I don't know how many times I've said it, but prison is something I wouldn't wish on anyone. At the same time, there are few things I would trade for the experience because it was a much-needed "time out" that gave me the opportunity to slow down and figure out who I really was and what was important in life.

It also taught me the answer to that very important question Rodney King asked back on May 1, 1992: *Can we all get along?*

Yes, Mr. King. We can.

But we all have to try.

William Sirls
Los Angeles, California
November 19, 2017